What's being said about NANKING?

"Once the story exploded into action, Nanking becomes a page turner in the truest sense, a novel that I had a hard time setting down. I felt like I was witnessing and living history rather than reading about it."

– ELLIOT RICHMOND

"As I read this book, it played on the screen of my mind like a feature film. Powerful, technicolor images... a gorgeous land, filled with fascinating people... events that stagger the mind... involving people whose love, caring and passion I'll never forget. Nanking – Its story should NOT be forgotten. Thanks to Kevin Kent... perhaps it never will."

– KAREN L. HUTTON

"I couldn't put this book down. Kevin Kent has written a tribute to an American herione who saved 10,000 lives during the siege of Nanking. He intertwines fiction with fact beautifully. I highly recommend this as a satisfyingly good read."

– KAREN ADLER

"As I turned the pages, I couldn't help but feel panic rush in waves about my body, with heart pounding and head sweating. I could see vividly the petit American missionary, Minnie Vautrin, running the risk of her own life, attempted to rescue thousands of innocent women and girls from the savage attacks.

– DR. ZHONG LIU

The complete reader reviews above available on Amazon.com and Nankingthebook.com

All too often in the literary world, the horrors of war are made even more grotesque by bad writing about war, from poorly plotted action-adventure tales to cloying melodramas. In contrast, author Kevin A. Kent's WWII epic, *Nanking*, is a highly informed, crisply written novel that, though set in a period of intense conflict, does not rely upon the setting alone to drive the tautly paced narrative.

Nanking is the story of the eponymous city in China that was the target of invading Japanese forces in the late 1930s. More than a historic account of a siege, it is the heart wrenching drama of the everyday heroes–mostly foreign–who stayed through the city's occupation in order to help save its beleaguered residents.

Kent's hero is diminutive Minnie Vautrin, an idealistic American missionary who chooses to remain in the doomed city to safeguard the students of the all-girls school she administers. Yet, this is no overblown melodrama; Minnie's journey is tragic, and Kent knows better than to romanticize even the most inconsequential detail. Yes, the reality is stark, but the tone is never maudlin, while Kent's carefully executed series of flashbacks, along with deliberate and tautly stylized pacing, allow readers to empathize with the characters and the situation—one that, thankfully, falls outside the bounds of common experience.

Nanking is vivid and cinematic, a tale that is evocative of a place and time that, played out on so many ferocious fronts, forever changed the world. Readers will no doubt look forward to future works by this author—although writing a novel as compelling as *Nanking* would be a feat, indeed.

Dear Carole ♡
Merry Christmas !
Love you ♡ Gail

NANKING

KEVIN A. KENT

*A novel inspired by the true story of Minnie Vautrin,
An American hero in China.*

All Rights Reserved.

愛 *Carole*
Thanks s- much fo
your kind help.
[signature]
Dec. '06

For orders other than by individual consumers, discounts on the purchase of 10 or more copies of this titles for special markets or premium use, contact special markets sales at info@NankingTheBook.com or go to: www.NankingTheBook.com

For individual sales, please go to our web site at www.NankingTheBook.com We provide links to Booksurge.com and Amazon.com

For complete customer reviews go to Amazon.com

For Book retailers, please go to our web site and link you to Baker & Taylor

Author's Note:
Though based on historical events, many characters are fiction and created to enhance the story.

Published by Booksurge, LLC, an Amazon.com company

Library of Congress Cataloging-in-Publication Data applied for November – 2005

Cover Design – Inspired Arts & Media, LLC
Photo: Peter Lawler

BOOKSURGE and AMAZON are registered trademarks.

We must accept finite disappointment,
but never lose infinite hope.

– Martin Luther King, Jr.

FOREWORD

The written history of China spans 5,000 years and dwarfs that of Europe and certainly America. A relatively short time ago, in the 1920s, with the rise to power of Sun Yat-sen and his son-in-law, Generalissimo Chiang Kai-shek, China was unified. This unification helped to bring China into the modern world. In keeping with this trend toward modernization, Chiang Kai-shek's able-minded wife, Madame Chiang Kai-shek, was one of the first of a generation of Chinese women educated by Americans. She graduated from Wellesley College in 1917. She saw the importance of the west and sought to bring its influence into her husband's government as he rose to power. During this time, American missionaries living in China educated thousands of Chinese women. The missionaries were well received by Chiang Kai-shek's Nationalists. In fact, the good Madame was a Christian and her husband was baptized in 1929.

Growth, education, and prosperity seemed to finally be in China's destiny. The missionaries and their schools were well respected and it became a privilege to have one's children educated there. Like all of the important cities, Nanking boasted its own valued school, the Ginling Girls' College. During the 1930s, an American missionary named Minnie Vautrin ran the college. It was there that she devoted her life to her students and to China. She was a woman of unusual strength, heart and soul. Our story begins and ends with this most unusual hero.

ONE

Minnie Vautrin stood in her little house, the air still and heavy, the curtains drawn against a muggy afternoon on the Midwestern plains. She caressed the solid oak of the front door and then unlocked its three brass locks. Now, if she could only gather enough resolve to open it, to step into the bright, late sun, the fresh air, and the pleasant breeze stirring on the front porch.

Minnie was fifty-five, but felt seventy. She knew she looked it, too, having lost her youthful enthusiasm—having had it wrenched from her. Even her spirit was gone, as were those days when she was courageous and alive. Now, when she looked in the mirror, the eyes staring back were unfamiliar. They had once sparkled with excitement, with possibilities. No more.

Minnie touched her hair. She still wore it long, but it was gray-streaked and lifeless, tied back and tight, severe, like her. When was the last time anyone had commented on her rosy cheeks set against milky skin? She was pale now, and weighted down by her own history.

She gripped the doorknob and pulled open the door a few inches. Peering onto the porch and beyond, to where wildflowers dotted the countryside, she marveled at their backdrop, a glorious Midwestern sunset. Opening the door a bit more, she slipped out of the house, where a breeze transforming into a strong gust of air caught her by surprise. Minnie savored the loamy smell of the earth, the sweet scent of flowers, and the promise of rain. She looked eastward, toward the place she considered home. Not here, not here in America, certainly not at the edge of some small town in Illinois. Despite her having been reared nearby, she was not at all comforted to be back. How could she be, after having inhaled the spices of Chinese cooking, wandered in the magnificent gardens of her Ginling Girls' College—after having dedicated her heart and soul to her Nanking family.

Minnie stood on the weathered porch, as if waiting for something to happen. The house's white paint, dry and cracked, revealed neglect. Across the small lawn, past the struggling sunflowers and the sagging picket fence; past the old country mailbox perched at the edge of a deeply rutted county road, was emptiness. She longed to find that mailbox full, but not much mail came down the country road these days. It was wartime, and the only news she received was when another farmer's son died in Africa, Europe, or Asia.

Minnie walked tentatively, embarrassed by her faltering gait. She made her way down the porch steps and glanced toward the darkening horizon heralding a day gone by. Although unable to see across the sky and around the globe to the Asia she loved, she knew it was there, and that knowledge caused her distress. So much distress that she had slipped into a debilitating depression. It made her wonder how a country boasting the latest technology and the brightest doctors could come up with nothing better than this atrocious treatment to which she was being regularly subjected?

"How many more times?" she had asked her doctors. "How many more volts? I'm a very small woman!" And they always smiled patiently, patronizingly. They explained that electroshock therapy was the preferred treatment for emotional ailments, that it was certain to calm her nerves and put an end to her hallucinations. She could not argue that she yearned for peace, but was this barbaric treatment her only recourse?

She shook off the sensation of voltage running through her body and tried to focus on the magnificent scene.

Above the setting sun, the sky was painted with red and orange clouds; startling beams of light reached down from the heavens. Minnie's gaze traced an arc across the horizon, into the clouds, toward the darkening zenith and beyond. The moon was aglow and nudging its way upward.

Minnie recalled standing at the top of the stairs at the college and experiencing the spiritual pull of those magnificent Purple Mountains just beyond Nanking. They were sacred, the legend being that the first people of Nanking descended from them in order to dwell on the shores of the mighty Yangtze river.

Standing in front of her Midwest home, Minnie was able to feel the Purple Mountains smiling upon her and she was warmed by the knowledge that they were just beyond those clouds. She looked up to where heaven awaited her and God kept a loving watch. With an unsteady gait, she passed the neglected garden, where scrawny sunflowers stretched their faces westward, as if they, too, were unable to watch all that had become of Minnie Vautrin.

Minnie steadied the old mailbox while opening the flapping door. Inside was an envelope of heavy bond. She removed it and tried opening it, her fingers fumbling as they forced the seal. She was breathing heavily as she finally managed to make a jagged opening across the top. Removing the paper, she unfolded it and turned her back to the last rays of the sun. Holding the paper up to the light, she squinted to read the sparse handwriting.

Dearest Minnie,

Let me know if I need to send someone to pick you up. We can meet after the screening. I heard you have been out of the hospital for some time. God's speed—

Most sincerely yours,
Rev. John Magee

Minnie read the note a second time. "I heard you were feeling better," she mumbled, and then her voice became stronger as she announced, "Oh, yes, dear John, much better." She walked inside, closed the door, and decisively turned all three locks.

Minnie carried the letter into the dining room, where she pulled a chair away from the table and sat. Candles of many colors were casting their flickering glow across the darkening room. They were part of an ersatz shrine that Minnie had created on the sideboard. Under a bit of tattered lace sat the candles and, in no coherent arrangement, a Buddha, a crucifix, a jade cross and a Bible. The candles were dutifully playing out their last threads of wick, wisps of paraffin-scented smoke rising toward the ceiling.

Minnie placed the invitation on the dining room table and turned on the old chandelier that hung cockeyed by three of its four cords over the table. She blew out the candles, causing dust particles to stir around her. The antique table was fully extended and ready to seat eight. Across its cherry wood surface rested her timeless mementos of Nanking. Photographs and newspapers covered all but the center of the table; some pictures had not been moved for weeks, while others showed signs of having been touched often.

Minnie picked up the invitation from the Reverend John Magee, read it again, and then placed it on the center of the table. It sat there, inanimate, yet she felt it staring back at her. She would have to make a decision about this, she knew, but it was so much easier to focus on the mementos stacked about and devote her energies to focusing on the past.

Hero Returns Home proclaimed a headline from a Peoria newspaper. A Chicago Tribune article declared *Nanking Invasion—Atrocities Rampant*. From the New York Times, she read *Nanking Safety Zone Saves 250,000* and there was another headline from a local paper: *Local Hero Saves 10,000 Innocent Girls*.

Minnie gripped the arms of the chair and settled into its sagging seat. To her right were black and white photographs of a beautiful Chinese city, images slightly obscured by a thin patina of dust. She had only to think of Nanking in the spring, the scent of flowers and blooming cherry trees, for those images to become suddenly sharp and colorful. There was no need to close her eyes to see trees nestled among the many ponds and lakes scattered around Nanking. She picked up a photograph and saw a peaceful pond, a small bridge nestled in the middle of the pond. The photo had been taken by her dear friend, Yen Hsu and evoked stirring memories of walking with him. In all its placid and gentle beauty, Nanking had been magnificent. If ever there existed a heaven on earth, it was there, in Nanking.

She smiled and returned the photograph to its place. Next to it was a larger one, edges worn from handling. It bore the caption *Nanking, Ginling Girl's College -Class of 1937*. The image was of several hundred fresh young faces, girls beaming at the camera, everyone dressed in crisp school uniforms. Teachers and friends of the school stood with them to the sides, poised and pristine.

A sudden jolt of memory caused a tremor to run through Minnie, a wave of longing that washed over her and brought tears to her eyes. She stared intently, then wiped the dampness from her cheeks.

Had it really been twenty-five years since she had packed her life into a little valise and left for China? Her mission had been to educate illiterate Chinese girls, to reach out to them and bring God into their lives, allowing no soul to be untouched by His loving hand. She recalled so clearly the impact upon first seeing her girls, many of them with feet bound, most of them Godless and illiterate. She had been touched by her mission and knew that she would do her part. She was, after all, an educated, hardworking and God-loving woman of twenty-five, a trusting soul whose entire life lay before her, a *tabula rasa* onto which she would etch her future.

That was then, thirty years ago. Minnie picked up another stack of photos and leafed through images of the people whose lives had so profoundly touched hers. Tears fell onto the news clippings and disappeared into the newsprint.

Minnie stood and crossed to the little shrine, where she lit the last of the unburned candles. The room felt so empty, as did the entire house. "Music…ah, Bach." she whispered, moving to the Victrola. She checked that the record was firmly in place and then lowered the needle onto the platter. Within seconds, the haunting notes of Bach's *Suscepit* were filling her heart, a man's full, rich alto touching her senses, one lone melodious voice serving as counterpoint to the heavy organ melody welling up and penetrating her bones. Minnie sighed, as if hearing this were tantamount to hearing the voice of God. Bach did that to her, made her think that his compositions came directly from God and then rose to the heavens.

They had played Bach at her mother's funeral. She was a child, yet the music was the one thing that spoke to her that day, the one thing that rose above the blur of babbling condolences and reminded her that she was not alone. Later, even now, she sometimes wondered what kind of merciful God would snatch away a loving mother from a little girl; would take the lives of so many innocent people in her beloved Nanking.

Minnie absorbed the Bach, allowed it to penetrate through her sadness and fatigue. At her mother's funeral, she had heard a voice calling for her to leave her gruff old father to his miserable self and be free. At that very moment, Minnie had changed from the docile child to the confident young lady. Now, nearly forty years later, her heart and soul questioned who she was, questioned what her place was on this earth, among its survivors. The hand that she placed on the photographs trembled.

Minnie knew that it was unhealthy, yet she often sat for hours staring into these photographs of mass graves, of row upon row of innocents; of peasants forced to stand, pinned to poles, bodies pierced by bayonets. Every time she looked, she asked herself the same heartrending question: Could she have done more to save them? Such savagery befell her friends, her girls and their families. What had she had done—what had she failed to do—that these people would deserve such a fate?

When Minnie had volunteered to go to China, she was a girl, innocent and inspired, a teacher of souls, a young missionary of faith, with a heart larger than China itself. She had risen to the occasion through her own tenacity, urged along by her love of God, education, and Yen Hsu, the man who was never hers to love, only to admire.

Minnie held the last class picture taken at the college and studied the faces of each student posed on the steps. Standing with them were her teachers who had become like family, stalwart and dedicated souls who had chosen to stay when asked to leave. She looked at the faces of each member of her Chinese staff and smiled.

Despite most of her students arriving illiterate, they had come from privilege and were sent by their families to learn English, math, science and, at the insistence of Madame Chiang Kai-shek, the Christian way of life. When she arrived it was only twenty years past the days of the Boxer rebellion, when the Chinese peasantry rose up and cast out the notion of foreigners, especially Christian missionaries, out of China. Most of the parents who were sending their girls off to the Ginling remembered the rebellion, but they were looking toward a bright future for their children and for China. This is something that resonated with Minnie; it was in her heart. She was loved by those Chinese families. What a difference those twenty years since the Boxer rebellion had made.

Minnie was lost in the memory of those years and those families, her nostalgia interrupted by the sound of a passing car. The noise annoyed her, caused her to shift her focus away from the loving, smiling faces and back to those other images, the ones that offended her sense of civility and caused too many sleepless nights.

One photo revealed a Japanese soldier standing next to a Chinese man tied to a stake, a bayonet shoved into his belly, an eviscerating wound exposing flesh and muscle in his throat. The soldier appeared smug, proud of his work. Another photograph revealed a woman in the street, her peasant's mouth opened wide to what Minnie knew had to have been a heart-wrenching cry of desperation because, at the woman's feet, lay her children, blood oozing from distended bellies. Had they been shot, or was this the result of a bayonet? Nearby, propped against a telephone pole, was a man's body, perhaps their father. His head, lopped off, rested at his feet, eyes open, startled, as if wondering how they had all come to this.

There was yet another photo of a woman tied to a chair, hands bound behind her, neck slashed. Her lower half was naked, legs spread, as if the soldiers who had raped her were no longer interested.

Minnie squared the photos into a neat stack and pushed them toward the back of the table. How could she be expected to cleanse her mind of these memories? To date, the electro-shock therapy had in no way diminished the unrelenting nightmares or the fearful days.

Her glance drifted to the modest shrine and the fat little Buddha staring at her, reaching out as if to embrace her. It took an effort to stand again and fully straighten her back. She walked into the kitchen and took an ornate Chinese teapot from the cupboard. Setting matching cup and saucer next to it, she checked that there was sufficient water in the kettle and then turned on the stove, the burner hissed at her as she walked away.

She returned to the dining room and studied the image of an elegant Chinese house. Homesickness engulfed her and she longed for her life in Nanking before the war. Standing before the house was a handsome Chinese family, the nearby cherry tree in full and glorious bloom, the ground around it blanketed with a carpet of fallen blossoms. Two small boys peered out from behind their father; two beautiful girls, age sixteen and twenty-one, stood proudly next to their elegant mother. One girl appeared happy and good-natured, the other was lost in thought.

Minnie's tears blurred the image, but the memory was sharp and defined. She felt the crispness of those cherry blossoms, heard the laughter of the boys and was warmed by the indulgent love of Yen Hsu, their father. He and his wife, Jade, loved their children without reservation. In Minnie's mind, he was the father against whom all other fathers should be measured.

What Yen Hsu shared with his children was so unlike her relationship with her own father, a narrow-minded man who preferred that his daughter remain silent and unseen. Whereas Yen Hsu indulged his children with love and pride, Minnie had known no such parental gifts. She looked at the photo one more time and shivered at the recollection of that day, when there was a fall chill in the air and everyone shared the expectation of a life of joy and continuity.

How had she survived this long without Nanking? Without the surge of hope and promise she had once felt with Yen Hsu and his family—her family—always there, close by, loving one another, embracing Minnie as one of their own.

Behind her, the stove continued to hiss.

TWO

Yen Hsu stood in front of his impressive residence, back straight and chin high with the pride of family and accomplishments. He had gathered everyone—family and friends—for a photograph. Yen Hsu was happiest when he had guests in his home and his friends responded with equal joy and affection.

Minnie watched Yen with admiration. She considered him one of the finest men in China, the kind of man who helped secure the future of her beloved country in a changing world. She was happy to be there, privileged to stand with this family, and she felt part of it.

Within Yen Hsu's front courtyard was an elegant gurgling fountain. In the chilly water a flotilla of cherry blossoms had drifted down from the large cherry tree shading the pond. This tree always made Minnie think of tiny umbrellas, the falling blossoms like pink snow.

In the circular drive, adjacent to where they all stood, sat Yen Hsu's enormous black sedan, befitting his diplomatic status.

Minnie appreciated that Yen Hsu had climbed his way up from the position of clerk in his father's dockside store to become a high-level official with Chiang Kai-shek's Nationalist Government. At the age of fifty, he was successful, he had power, and he was loved.

Minnie had known Yen Hsu for twenty-five years and clearly remembered the day they met. It was late on a sunny September afternoon in 1916, near the Ginling's new gardens and Minnie's first year as the school's educational director. Yen Hsu had been working in his father's business at the waterfront for several years and had become quite muscular. On this day, he was delivering a basket of fish to the head mistress. As he arrived, he saw Minnie walking from the vegetable garden. She was wearing a sun hat, carrying an armful of onions, and humming a tune he would later learn was Baroque. In the back of the garden were the largest sunflowers he had ever seen. Yen Hsu stared at this funny little woman and, as she came closer, the odor of onions converged with the stink of fish. Anyone nearby would have found it difficult to determine who smelled worse, the fish or Minnie.

Minnie Vautrin possessed a rare brand of faith and trust, as well as an abiding hope in everyone. She was part of a group of American missionaries, a faithful lot who believed that destiny was at hand. Minnie loved being a teacher and, at twenty-eight, was imbued with a zeal for God and all things godly. Like so many missionaries in China, she heard her calling and acted on it, and she was perfectly suited to the profession. In her heart, Nanking was meant to be her home.

Minnie had grown up knowing hard work. She had put herself through school by working relentlessly; she had never asked for anything. Not even at the age of six, when her mother died, did she request comforting. Instead, she did what she could to make things better for everyone around her. "She carries the glow of God's good graces," said her father's friends. When Minnie was given the opportunity to build a girls' college in Nanking, no one doubted she would succeed. Like so many missionaries of her time, Minnie was out to change the world, but her success was more than this. It was also based on her intellect, her tenacity, and her big heart. Perhaps even more, it was that Minnie's faith in herself and in her God was unflappable.

When Minnie met Yen Hsu, she realized that he had spent little time with western women and knew almost nothing about their spirit and determination. Shortly after their meeting, she took it upon herself to help the very inquisitive Yen Hsu learn English. At the same time, she was able to polish her Chinese dialect with him and was attentive to the depths of his knowledge of Chinese culture and religion. Whenever Yen Hsu delivered supplies from the harbor, he would not leave until Minnie taught him a new phrase in English.

Over the years, Minnie realized that Yen Hsu was one of the quickest studies she had ever known. He hungered to understand Western habits in the same way that she had a fierce appetite for his culture. They passed many hours drinking tea and devouring art, music and religion.

Yen was often shocked at how little the Westerners knew about the religion of his people. He enjoyed quoting Confucius to Minnie and she retaliated with words from the Bible. They were an odd sight, these two, and it was unclear who was the more stubborn.

In 1925, when Yen Hsu was hired to run the diplomatic mission for the new government in Nanking, he was one of the few Chinese who spoke flawless English. Minnie was proud of his achievements and understood that this marked the beginning of a life of prestige for her dear friend. Yen and Minnie were best friends, but their emotions occasionally confused and overwhelmed them, especially when they reached their early thirties and were still single.

Yen had been blessed with alarming good looks, a perfect symmetry between his wide eyes and a broad smile that could disarm anyone. When he informed Minnie that Nanking was being considered as the new seat of the Nationalist government, his excitement was palpable and his handsome face shone with anticipation. "This is great news for us, for you and me," he told her. "As Nanking grows in importance, so, too, will your school. Just think, you will teach the most important daughters of our distinguished government officials."

"So I chose wisely to stay here," said Minnie. When Yen seemed confused, she explained that she had been thinking of taking a furlough and returning to the States. "Not for long," she added. "But I do want to enhance my studies."

Yen Hsu suggested that she wait until there was a firm relationship between the very powerful Madame Chiang Kai-shek and the Ginling Girls' College. "There is a proverb," he told her. "A jade stone is useless before it is processed; a man is good for nothing until he is educated."

"And is this a proverb that you have made up for the occasion?" she asked, her eyes searching for truth.

"No, it is true, I promise," he avowed, his expression sincere. "However, in your case, it should say that a woman is good for nothing until she is educated." Yen Hsu turned his gaze away, across the park and toward the new Japanese embassy. "Minnie, China needs you now, needs what you can teach our women. Please stay."

Minnie was happy to help Yen Hsu establish a solid relationship with the American Embassy. Several years later, she would help him with the British Embassy as well. She even introduced Yen Hsu to John Rabe, the Nazi who headed the Siemens organization in Nanking. Minnie was not alone in her belief that Yen was a man on the move in Nanking. Even as a young diplomat, he would come by after work and catch up on the progress in her school. He had often expressed his respect at how well the Americans had educated his boss, Chiang Kai-shek, and his leader's illustrious wife. The brilliant Madame loved having long conversations with Yen Hsu and frequently commented that it was as if he, too, had been educated at an American University. She was very proud of her degree from Wesleyan College in Georgia. Her pronounced southern drawl over her native Chinese accent brought smiles to his face on many occasions. Yen Hsu thought so highly of this woman that he told her that he would name his first-born daughter after her Chinese name, Mei Ling.

Another pastime Yen particularly enjoyed was listening to Western music. Initially, he listened on Minnie's old hand-cranked Victrola; later, he listened on his own Victrola, a gift from Chiang Kai-shek. Sometimes, though, Minnie would find her friend in the back of her little campus church listening intently to the girls' choir as they rehearsed. He loved most the counterpoint of Bach. Like his American mentor, he was fascinated by how one simple melody could be woven into such a glorious harmony. It was through this music that Yen first felt the rapture of Minnie's God. By 1927, he had become a Christian, further supporting the mission of both the great Madame Chiang Kai-shek and the five-foot-one Minnie Vautrin.

One night, Minnie invited Yen Hsu to her quarters to hear a new recording of Bach that she had just received from a friend in the States. She had insisted on having Mrs. Twynam chaperon them, although the woman's presence did nothing to diminish Minnie's pleasure at educating her only male pupil, or of sharing with him her love of Bach. She loved dearly listening to Bach and how he married one brilliant motif with another until, arriving at the third and then the fourth melody, pulled in the recurring melody that started it all, until all parts recapitulated into a divine and perfect harmony.

"Until Bach," she explained, "there had never been true harmony. He invented it, a rare gift passed down from God to man." Her voice was impassioned, as if she knew something no one else did.

Later that year, Yen Hsu arrived before dinner to introduce his new girlfriend, Jade Teng. After the introductions were made, Jade produced a new record from America and suggested they listen to it. "Yen Hsu has told me about your love of music," she explained.

Minnie could see that Jade wanted to impress her sweetheart's best American friend. As soon as the music began, Minnie thought the loud drums and jazzy downbeat strident and dissonant. Nevertheless, she stood in her parlor watching Yen's eyes and saw that he was truly enjoying this noise She forced a smile as Jade danced around the room and noted that Yen could not take his eyes off of this young woman's graceful moves. As the brass and pulse of the drums filled the room, Minnie's heart pounded in her chest and the sensation confused her. What was this surge of blood rushing through her body? Was it the unfettered beat of the syncopated drums, or something else, something more personal, more intimate? She turned away from Yen to hide her flushed face. At the same time, she surreptitiously studied this lovely young woman from Shanghai.

Jade was vivacious and extremely attractive, with skin so perfect that Minnie instinctively knew that she could never compete with this beauty, especially for the affections of Yen. The thought startled her, forced her to admit that perhaps she wanted from Yen something more than a wonderful friendship.

There were other comparisons evident even to this inexperienced young missionary. Minnie knew that she was austere and often stoic, whereas Jade carried herself with a sensuality that was both audacious and marginally offensive. When Jade showed Minnie the way "flappers" danced in Shanghai, Minnie was shocked. At the same time, she recognized in Jade a woman of intelligence, keen wit and beguiling charm. It was some comfort to remind herself that women like Jade could never teach school, nor could they manage the well-being of hundreds of impressionable girls. What Jade could handle, however, was one very smitten Yen Hsu.

While the Roaring Twenties music played, Minnie tried to listen with best intentions. It was not easy, because her emotions felt as strident to her as did the music.

By the end of the evening, Minnie surrendered to Jade's charms and had to admit to herself that she liked the woman. Jade was one of those women others strive to be, and that most men would do anything to possess. It pained Minnie to see Yen so attentive to this radiant woman, but what could she do?

Shortly before it came time for her guests to leave, they tried to engage Minnie in a discussion about jazz and the kind of people playing it in America. "I'm sure it's composed with the best intentions," she told them. "But I have to be honest: I find jazz very primal and un-Christian."

The moment Yen Hsu and Jade departed, Minnie turned to Mary Twynam and confided, "It's not music, in my book. That would take some real getting used to," she explained, as if having the need to be heard.

It wasn't until later that night that Minnie forced herself to analyze her feelings. Yes, the music grated on her, but was that the honest explanation? The answer came back with a boldness that formed a knot in her stomach: "Perhaps I love this man," she told herself, and then pushed the thought away. She could not love him; she would not.

Six months later, surrounded by everyone of importance in Nanking, Yen Hsu and Jade married in a formal Chinese wedding. The clothing and food were from another era. Jade chose every entrée, every noodle and appetizer, of which there were more than twenty. While making their social rounds during the reception, they approached Minnie. She was gracious and congratulatory, blessing them as she would two dear and trusted friends. In truth, she was pleased to see Yen Hsu so happy, and how could she fault him for marrying the woman whom all the western men declared the loveliest woman in all of China?

Minnie's wedding present to Yen and Jade was a winter-blooming cherry tree. "It will grow strong and beautiful through the years," she said. "And this tree will bring God's shade to your life and a scent of heaven to your new garden." She reminded them that, according to Chinese custom, it needed to be planted in a home within one year's time. Otherwise, there would be no good luck. "So get that man of yours to buy you a nice house!" she told Jade.

And buy it Yen Hsu did. The house was located in one of the nicer areas of the new Nanking and he had designed most of the house himself. It was very large and stately, with an enormous kitchen for Jade to exercise her culinary skills and an extra-large dining room for dinner parties. The high walls and elaborate gates in the front of the house made it appear very prestigious. Upon entering the gates, there was a broad semi–circular driveway. At the top of the drive and through an ornate little gate was a courtyard. In its center was a lovely fountain and meditation pond. In the middle of this pond was a tiny island on which Jade had planted Minnie's little cherry tree. It was expected that, over the years, this gift would grow as large as any cherry tree ever seen in Nanking and that, when it bloomed, its fragrance would waft throughout the house.

It was not long before Jade, like the tree, established herself in the Nanking community as a constant and beautiful presence.

Now, many years later, Jade was still the most beautiful woman in the region and her devoted husband, Yen Hsu, had matured into a well respected citizen and government statesmen. Between Yen and Jade, their dashing good looks and agreeable demeanor made them loved by all.

At nearly six feet, which was quite tall for a Chinese man, Yen possessed a commanding presence both in business and in his position as a diplomat. His eager smile and quick wit made him a welcome sight among his friends, colleagues, and the Nanking social set. Yen Hsu preferred to wear western suits, but he always added a splash of Chinese silk peeking from a breast pocket, or a matching silk scarf slung over his shoulder.

It was a surprise to no one that Jade matured into a graceful mother with a serene, calming smile, and with eyes attentive to her family and the world around her. Jade had given Yen Hsu two lovely daughters, Mei Ling and Su Lin. As little girls, they were always dressed like matching dolls. When Jade first brought them to visit Minnie at the college, they sat demurely, hands clasped in their laps, eyes always watching, assessing. Now, as lovely young women, they donned the most popular fashions, outfits worn by the well-to-do and bought at the expensive shops in Shanghai and Nanking.

Mei Ling, twenty-one, and Su Lin, sixteen, were stunning young women. They wore their hair long, the jet black a startling contrast against their alabaster skin. Their hands were like their mother's as well, long and graceful, with elegant fingers intended to play the flute or piano.

Mei Ling was taller than her sister and much shapelier. She had developed a way to walk that made men pause. The younger Su Lin had her father's high cheekbones and eyes, but she was still gangly. Whenever she walked with her older sister she liked to hold hands, as they did when they were little girls.

Because Mei Ling was the oldest of Yen's children, she had been taught skills typically reserved for boys. She enjoyed the game of chess and often played with her father for hours. In stark contrast, Su Lin admired her mother's prowess in the kitchen and was always anxious to be taught her secrets. Everyone admired Jade's cooking and Yen Hsu often teased that he had fallen in love with her cooking first...and then with her. He loved having new friends to dinner for the first time, knowing that his wife could tantalize the taste buds of even the most difficult and finicky guests. In fact, Jade's reputation was so well established in Nanking that chefs typically shuddered when she entered their restaurant, or when she was a guest at a state dinner. At the same time, these chefs also knew that she would impart some little tidbit of magic. "If you add a squeeze of tangerine juice to this sauce..." or "Why not try taking the meat out just before it's done roasting and braise it with a plum sauce?"

Mei Ling lacked the patience to work in the kitchen, whereas Su Lin spent countless hours watching her mother prepare her special dishes. As she worked, the two of them chatted about which spices to use, and should they be fresh or dried; which fruits to add and how certain meats and vegetables were best cut. The kitchen was their place to share and bring them closer together. If Mei Ling was Daddy's girl, then Su Lin was attached to her mother at the kitchen sink.

Yen was always the official taster of the household, followed by Mei Ling and then Jade's mother, who lived with them.

No one questioned that Mei Ling was her father's favorite. Yen and Mei Ling found great pleasure in facing off in debate, be it political, social, or historical. Mei Ling became impassioned when she and her father discussed the political ramifications of nationalism verses communism in a populated country. Her father was a staunch nationalist, a proud supporter of Chiang Kai-shek. When he argued against his daughter's opinion, she counterattacked, reminding him of the obvious fallacies of fascism and monarchies. She had a knack for taking the opposite side of any argument and knew her material well enough to intimidate and outwit even the best-educated among them, whether professors or politicians.

Unlike her older sister, Su Lin disliked being anywhere near a conflict, no matter how friendly it was. She was gentler than her sister, a characteristic she believed would serve her well in the future. The fact that Mei Ling had the young men in their neighborhood clamoring after her hardly fazed Su Lin. Besides, did Mei Ling not ignore them, focusing her attention instead toward something more important, like her family or her education?

So much had happened by 1937, so much had changed, that Minnie reached her late forties and wondered where the years had gone. Today, however, was a day she would not soon forget. There was to be a family photograph taken in front of Yen and Jade's home. In preparation, Minnie had slipped on a more formal dress and a stylish little hat favored by the Chinese women. A small jade crucifix hung at her throat, dangling from a thin silver necklace.

Minnie watched her fellow missionary, the Reverend John Magee, prepare to take what was always an overly-posed photograph. Her gentle, yet always alert eyes, kept watch on the activity around her.

Were a friend to step back and study her face, they might see that her chin was too strong for a woman barely five feet tall; that when she was determined or angry, that same strong chin would thrust forward, as if to give warning. But they would also know that few felt afraid or nervous, because Minnie Vautrin was of such warm heart and caring disposition that anyone in her presence swore that she was without guile, incapable of even the most subtle cruelty. This is what made her students, teachers and community love her; it is also what made her an exceptional teacher and missionary.

By the age of fifty, Minnie had developed laugh lines around her eyes. She loved to laugh and often laughed at herself, at the girls and their adolescent ways; she even laughed at her way of life in China and how happy she was. Twenty-five years after she negotiated the purchase of the forty acres now inhabited by the Ginling Girls' College, she sometimes forgot that her roots were in the Midwest. How was it that she had been able to leave behind that lonely, unloved life and rise to such a place of love and honor in Nanking? The wonder of this often slipped over her and brought a serene smile to her face.

The good Reverend John Magee stood and surveyed Yen Hsu's large family, their sturdy house and the fountain in the middle of the yard. Could he squeeze it all in one shot? He studied the cherry tree, grown so large that its canopy now covered one-third of the yard. "Let's see what this does for us," he said, peering through the lens of the camera. Magee wanted very much to take the perfect picture of the perfect family, on the perfect December day in Nanking, China.

John Magee was a slim man, middle-aged and with a preference for fedoras, which he often wore perched on his head. The jaunty hat appeared as an unusual juxtaposition to the starched white collar of the Lord. Minnie had told him on several occasions that the fedora was a bit much for a missionary, but she could not deny that he wore it well. Today, he also wore his newest fashion statement: the Red Cross armband. With trouble stirring up everywhere in China, all Americans in Nanking were instructed by their government to sport this symbol of neutrality and humanitarianism.

Minnie could not believe how obsessed Magee had become about photography and watched his set-up process with fond amusement. He loved everything about it, from opening up the cases to cleaning the lenses, loading the film to mounting the 35-millimeter camera perfectly on the tripod. It was more than a ritual, it was his source of joy. How many times had he told Minnie that looking through the lens at an image that was about to become frozen in time never failed to stir within him a sense of wonder. He was convinced that he was a better photographer—particularly of Nature—than he was a minister. Since the role of resident American photographer had fallen to him, he was the one called when there was a big event. What lay before him certainly qualified as an event.

Magee clicked off a shot to test his shutter and f-stop settings. Had Yen Hsu known there were any questions about these settings, he would have rushed over to give counsel. A strong link in the bond of friendship between John Magee and Yen Hsu was their shared love of photography. Minnie thought it was silly, but she respected both men and enjoyed the repartee that existed between them. On one side was Yen, the successful diplomat who viewed everything, including photography, as an art form, something to challenge his creativity. Magee, however, approached each shot as a science, with settings to learn and framing concepts to test.

Reverend Magee backed away from the camera, brow furrowed, as he absent-mindedly rubbed his cheek. Facing the lens was Ernest Forster, a handsome, blonde, blue-eyed man in his mid-thirties. Next to him stood Su Lin. Forster took the girl by the shoulders and turned her until her back was to the camera. "How about this, John?" he asked, his gentle southern lilt bringing a melody to his voice. "Is that better, or would you rather she stood on her head?"

They all understood the serious nature of this gathering, yet Forster's comment gave them a reason to relax, even allowed them to laugh.

In the middle of the mirth, Yen Hsu's driver, Xiang, inched his way down the stairs. He was carrying too many suitcases and bags and several seemed about to topple from his grasp. Xiang was a loyal and dedicated member of Yen Hsu's extended family, a strong and hard-working man whose lithe step belied his seven decades of life. Xiang's expression was always hurried but merry, his mouth twitching as if he knew something that no one else could know. He had worked for Yen Hsu's father and then, when the patriarch died, had moved his life to Yen's house. Unlike so many of his age, Xiang had crossed the threshold from the old China to the new. As a teenager, he had worn the traditional ponytail of the working coulee class and was reminded often to expect little from his plight in life. As he grew to be a gracious and honorable man, his life became bigger, his world more enriched. Xiang truly loved the family of Yen Hsu and considered them the focus of his life. The girls were loved like daughters, and he was the old tiger who guarded the safety of his cubs. Yen and Jade's two young boys were like grandsons to Xiang and he was often found playing with them, or merely sitting under the tree and telling them some fantastic story about growing up in the provinces.

Xiang loved Jade, too, but she was so beautiful that he averted his eye when speaking to her. She made him feel like a nervous school boy, yet he was old enough to be her father. Whenever she walked around the house wearing only her silk robe, Xiang averted his eyes and left the room. "Your beauty is too great for this old man's heart," teased Xiang, but everyone in the family knew his reaction was born out of respect for Jade and for the great Hsu family that employed him.

Minnie and the others watched Xiang struggle to negotiate the stairs. There were only nine steps, but he was a small man and his load was burdensome. She silently counted off each step of his descent, knowing that Yen considered nine his lucky number. Nine front stairs faced east, which made his home even more fortuitous.

Minnie touched the cross that always hung from her neck and recalled Yen's conversion to Christianity. His decision had been reluctant, based as much on political expediency as a spiritual need, and yet Yen Hsu was one of the most spiritual men she knew. He trusted in God as a presence that imbued all things. She found it interesting that he never spoke of God as an entity, which was common among Christians. It was as if he had pulled enough out of Taoism to keep his light shining, yet by becoming a Christian was born anew. It certainly helped that he lived in a country run by two converts, the Chiang Kai-sheks. Like so many of his compatriots, Yen held his Chinese ways close to his heart, but was careful to keep them off his sleeve. He was a true Nationalist in that he loved his country and its people, and he believed strongly in the progress being made among the middle class. Even more, he believed with all his might in a unified Chinese people.

Minnie watched Xiang make his way past the family to the car, muttering his apologies as he bumped past the photography session. He dropped one small box but kept moving and smiling. Yen's long sedan bore the Nationalist flags, which were mounted firmly over the front wheel wells and flapped proudly whenever the car moved through the street. For some, those flags were a badge of courage and defiance; for others, they symbolized treason. In the climate of the day, those flags could make a nice target for a Japanese bomber.

Xiang placed the baggage into the trunk and then worked to force everything to fit. With a satisfied grin, he closed the trunk, the car doors, and then saluted Yen Hsu. Xiang had never served in the military, but his boss was an important government diplomat and therefore deserved the honor of being saluted. He had once witnessed Yen saluting Chiang Kai-shek and decided that his boss deserved no less. From then on, Xiang saluted Yen's comings and goings. Before long, Yen's young sons were saluting Xiang, so that it became somewhat of a comedy. Yen would leave to buy a newspaper or take a walk with his wife and Xiang would salute him at the door. The boys would then salute Xiang, who would salute the boys, who would again salute their father. Jade, not wanting to be left behind in this farce, would salute the boys, which meant that Xiang would have to salute Jade. If, for whatever reason, Xiang saluted Yen again, the entire routine would start anew.

Yen smiled at Xiang, who was still grinning at his success at squeezing the last bags into the car. Xiang saluted, Yen smiled and winked at his daughters, then glanced at Jade. "I told you to pack lightly, sweetheart," he told her. "Now there's no room in the trunk for your mother." He nudged Jade, who was sensitive to comments about the old woman.

Jade's mother appeared at the top of the stairs. "The boys want to sit next to me," she said. "Perhaps the three of us should sit on the roof of the car." The stately woman was wearing the traditional Chinese clothing, and of the highest quality, with embroidery befitting an empress. Her movements were slow and deliberate. Had she attempted to descend the stairs without assistance, each step would have been difficult and painful. She was from that last generation of Chinese women, when it was the practice to bind the feet of little girls. In the social class of Jade's mother, small feet had been considered not only attractive, but mandatory. Sadly, girls whose feet were bound at an early age lived out their lives in unrelenting pain.

Jade's mother remained at the top of the stairs until Xiang scampered across the yard and up to assist her. Just as he reached her side, Yen's two boys—Ping, who was six, and Chiang, now eight—shuffled out the front door. Without breaking stride, the older boy hoisted himself onto on the railing and slid down, much to the horror of everyone but his sisters, who covered their mouths and giggled.

"Sorry, Ma," he yelled, as he flew off the handrail, able to plant his heels just before his bottom hit the ground.

Ping cackled with glee as he raced down the steps and stopped beside his mother. He grasped her hand and held it tightly. With a mischievous smile, he looked back and forth, between his mother and father, in order to determine the punishment to be meted out to his unruly older brother. Today, however, would be different because the family was leaving, the boys accompanying their grandmother on the boat. There was added excitement and anticipation because the boys had never been away without their parents.

"I've told you not to do that, Chiang," Jade said sternly, although there was more disappointment in her voice than anger.

The look on Chiang's face was triumphant. "Ping dared me to do it one more time before we left!"

"All right, then!" barked their father. "We don't need any problems and we certainly can't have you looking like common refugees on the ship. Come here," he ordered, gesturing toward Chiang.

The boy crossed the walkway to his father, twisting awkwardly to see if the seat of his pants had been dirtied. Yen Hsu swatted the child harder than was required, brushing off an accumulation of dust.

"Hey!" announced the boy. "That was a spank."

"Almost," said Yen. "And if you disobey your mother again, you'll feel a real one."

Chiang looked up affectionately, yet cautiously, at his father's broad smile, laughing when the man gave his dusted pants a few more gentle swats.

"You boys must mind your grandmother," said Jade. "It is not as safe outside as it is here, so remember what we told you: you can't go running off and acting like little tigers."

"Oh, they won't get too far from me," said Jade's mother. "The woman reached out and grabbed each child by the ear, pulling them to her. "Will you boys?"

"No, Grandma, not my ears!" said Chiang. "We are the best tigers in all of Nanking and we should not have our ears pulled. Grandmother, you disgrace us."

The woman stared down at the brash child. "Then stand up and act like your father's boys."

" I am the biggest," Ping shouted, as his grandmother relaxed her hold. His older brother rolled his eyes.

"Well, you may be someday," said Yen Hsu, bending down to hug his sons. He glanced up at his daughters and smiled, but there was sadness in his eyes. "With children like these, I am the proudest father in Nanking." He looked at Jade. "No, the proudest in China."

Jade put a hand on her husband's shoulder and gave it a gentle squeeze.

"Time is short," said Xiang.

Yen Hsu bowed his head and shook Xiang's hand. "To divide our family for a day or a week is unpleasant; to separate us possibly for months is not right." He looked to Jade, as if searching her face for the answer to some riddle not yet announced. Jade cocked her head, her mouth hardening into a tight line. "Mother will keep a close eye on the boys and we will meet up in Hangkow, as planned. But they must go," she added, a new urgency to her voice. "If they are to seek the safety of the American ship, it must be now." Jade looked at Minnie and some of the tension left her face. "Is your luggage already at the dock?"

Minnie braced herself for what she feared would follow. "I've decided to stay."

"You what!" declared Yen Hsu, his eyes wide and jaw clenched. He took a step closer to Minnie and demanded, "You must not stay. Even *my* orders to remain have been changed. Everyone is leaving." He gestured toward his entire household. "Do you see? Our army is all but gone, there may be scarce protection." When next he spoke, his voice was softer, pleading. "You have been told to leave by your government, Minnie. All the embassies issued the same orders. You need to leave."

Minnie stood straighter, hands clenched into tiny fists. "And what of the girls who have no place to go? Am I to leave them to fend for themselves? No, it is God's will that I stay to protect my campus and my girls. And very soon, we will have refugees; I will be here to welcome them."

Yen dug into the inside pocket of his jacket. "But you are scheduled to leave with my family on the *Panay*," he argued, withdrawing a handful of tickets and fanning them for effect. "Do you see? Here is one for you." Yen turned to the others. "Magee, Forster please help me convince her. Everyone needs to leave now. We have perhaps forty-eight hours, Minnie, so you need to leave at once!"

John Magee stepped toward Yen and crossed his arms, the Red Cross armband prominent against the dark jacket. Before he could speak, Ernest Forster came and stood beside him, slipping an arm around Magee's shoulder. "Yen, there will be around twenty of us staying behind."

Yen shook his head and looked away, kicking at the ground, then staring up at his cherry tree.

Minnie saw the distress in her friend's face and placed one arm around the petite Jade and another around the waist of Yen Hsu. "You must go, Jade, to protect your family. Yen, you know my life is my school; I must stay and protect the girls who have no place to go. So many parents were not able to return for them. People from Shanghai, parents from farms outside of town, they have no way to come for their children. Who will look after these girls if I leave?" She shook her head, fatigue evident in her eyes. "The girls of Ginling are my responsibility; God will provide."

Tears appeared in Jade's eyes, but it was clear that her dear Minnie was impervious to begging or cajoling.

"I've been through troubles in China, remember?" continued Minnie. "Twenty years ago, our beloved Nanking was not much more than a fishing village on the banks of the Yangtze. I met a young man there who sold fish to. Do you remember? Do you think I would let a few Japanese soldiers make me abandon my duties, my college, or Nanking itself?"

Yen recoiled at the harshness of her words. "Then I am abandoning my city?"

Minnie understood Yen's concern, both for his reputation and his own standing among his family and peers, but the reality was that diplomats were often the only ones left to make sense of things when a government fell. "Not at all," she said. "You're a government man and you are required to follow your leader to the new capital. That's where you can fulfill your responsibilities. Mine will be fulfilled right here." When Yen began to speak, Minnie held up a hand. "Yen, I'm a missionary and *my* leader says to stay put. We both have families to protect. I respect what you must do; never imagine that I do not."

Yen shifted his weight, doing his best to appear calm, but anxiety pulled at the corners of his mouth. Jade stepped forward and said, "Minnie, everyone is leaving because no place here is safe, especially for a government family like ours. How can you possibly think you'll be safe? This is a war against decency, against our culture. I've heard what the good Madame has to say, that we are to be made slaves by the Japanese. You can't believe for a moment that you'll be safe inside the walls of the Ginling."

Minnie reached out, but stopped short of touching Jade's shoulder. "There will be perhaps as many as twenty of us keeping an eye on things. And remember, it's not America that's at war, thank God!" She saw the skepticism on her friend's face and smiled. "We should be fine, truly. I read that Shanghai is settling into its occupation and that the international zone they established there was not attacked." She looked to the others for agreement. "We internationals will do the same and we will be safe."

Jade shook her head vigorously. "They showed no mercy in Shanghai and bombed everything. What makes you think Nanking will be any better! Minnie, please, we will make room for you."

Minnie did not want to argue with Jade, nor did she want them to linger and miss their ship. How could she persuade these loving friends that she could not be convinced? "What you forget is that I'm not at war with anyone, except perhaps my own shortcomings as they regard my faith. Nothing will convince me to leave my school or my life in Nanking, and you of all people should understand that. Do you think I would abandon your daughters, were you not able to come for them?" When Jade did not respond, Minnie added, "Do you see what I mean? Do you?" She placed a hand on the woman's arm. "Truly, Jade, I'm not being stubborn, as you suggest. What I'm being is fair-minded and practical."

Jade gave Minnie a puzzled look, as if wondering why was making no headway. Perhaps Minnie would follow Yen's advice, as she had always done. Everyone knew that a special bond existed between them. And since Yen had become a Christian, Minnie listened even more intently.

Magee raised his hand. "Listen, I'm staying for the Red Cross and I promise you that we'll be fine." He nodded toward the camera. "But this picture will not happen if you don't all gather together at least once. So come on, hide your tears and let's take the shot." He resumed his place behind the camera and waited for everyone to get into position.

Forster hurried to the car to help Xiang extract the old woman. They carefully led her to Jade, who slipped an arm under the woman's elbow.

Yen positioned himself for the picture. "Magee," he said, a scowl on his face. "Do you realize the toll the battle in Shanghai took on the Nationalist army? Come on, come with us tonight. What can you do here, really?"

"Not sure yet, ol' boy, but I do know that you can pose for this picture, so stand still." Magee bent down and looked through the viewfinder. "Come on, everyone, crack a smile. One, two, three!" The big magnesium flash went off and he stepped back, squinting and waving smoke from his face.

Minnie looked down the line at each member of the family, faces solemn again after forced smiles. She wanted to hold this picture in her mind, as Magee would preserve it on film. She wanted always to see herself standing with this family, the warmth of their hearts permanently etched in her own.

As Xiang and Forster helped Jade's fragile mother into the car, Jade moved closer to Mei Ling. "Did you know that Minnie intended to stay?" she asked her daughter.

Mei Ling looked away, glancing toward Minnie, eyes imploring. "Actually, Mother, I intend to stay, too. Minnie will need help."

Minnie watched Jade's jaw tighten and her neck contract into her shoulders.

Yen Hsu stepped forward. "Mother and the boys will leave today on the *Panay* and the rest of the family will depart tomorrow at noon. I will not hear of such nonsense." He moved closer to Minnie and beckoned Magee and Forster to join them. "Forgive me for being so honest, but it is foolhardy to stay and face the onslaught of a brutal army. It is proven what they can do. Now please." He raised his eyebrows, as if asking for agreement. "You are my closest friends and allies," he continued, fighting to control his emotions. "You are the very fabric of China's future. You represent education and health care and the growth and opportunities for our schools, doctors, hospitals and universities. You must not put yourselves in harm's way." Yen looked away, as if able to see the terrible scenes yet to come. "Your government and mine have ordered all foreigners to leave, so there is nothing more to say. It's done!" This last declaration was emphasized with a slicing movement of his hand. Magee shrugged and shook his head. "I'm afraid it's just not that simple, my friend." Minnie and Forster nodded in agreement, but said nothing. They had learned long ago that arguing with Yen was tantamount to speaking into the wind.

"You must listen," insisted Yen Hsu. "I have a family to protect, but I would not leave any of you behind any more than I would my family." He turned to John Magee. "Do you know that Minnie was my first American friend? Why don't we all convoy together?" He gestured toward Minnie, his expression increasingly agitated. "John Magee, you baptized my wife and me. I cannot bear the thought of injury coming to you. Taking a picture of war will not save you. Please John, at least think about how you will leave." When his friends remained silent, Yen Hsu threw up his arms. "Don't you see? All of you could be sailing down the Yangtze on the *Panay* in less than an hour!" One by one, he looked into the faces of his friends, the expression on his face pleading, desperate. "Can't you understand that you will be safe in Hangkow? That's where I'm going, so I know it will be safe. Would I go there if it were not safe for my family?"

Minnie sighed and touched Yen's arm. "I do understand, Yen Hsu, but you must also understand my resolve.

God does not look kindly upon those of us who exhibit a lack of faith."

Mei Ling, who had been standing nearby and hanging on every word, said "I have a higher calling, too."

Yen Hsu whipped around and faced his daughter. "No! Don't even–"

Minnie took a step closer to the young woman. "You need to be with your family, wherever they are."

Mei Ling stood taller, chin up and shoulders back. Everything about her spoke of defiance. When she crossed her arms, Minnie felt Yen's frustration about to explode.

"God is patient," said Minnie. "He will wait for you to fulfill your calling at a more appropriate time." Having spoken, she glanced toward Yen. Standing up to him on her own behalf was one thing, but deciding what was best for his family needed to come from him.

"Perhaps I should have told you sooner," said Mei Ling, holding her father's gaze. "But if I had, you would have had me removed from Nanking altogether. I know my faith, Father. I also know that I must stay and protect my school." She turned to Minnie and smiled. "And to help Minnie."

Jade listened to this exchange and then stepped forward, eyes flashing with maternal rage. "Mei Ling is not staying under any circumstances!" she announced. With that, she shot Minnie a stern look, one that demanded her support. When Minnie nodded in agreement, Jade exhaled loudly.

Mei Ling did a slow burn, shifting her stance until she was facing Minnie. "If you agree with my parents," she asked, teeth clenched in anger, "then why did you deceive me into believing otherwise?"

Minnie looked to the others for support, but everyone seemed genuinely surprised by Mei Ling's accusation. Had she been deceived? Minnie felt the weight of the girl's resentment and it was heavy against her heart. "Mei Ling, please, this is not like you. Your father offered to help the refugees. All of us, including you, must respect his leadership."

"If I couldn't trust you, then—"

"It's not about trust," interrupted Minnie. "It's about family and faith, both of which you have in abundance, so please do not say something you will regret."

Mei Ling threw up her arms and declared, "I had faith, Minnie! Faith that you'd want me to stay with you, faith that I could help you. And especially now, with most of the staff gone. I was ready to stay by your side, Minnie, me and my faith." Tears welled in her eyes and she wiped them away with an angry gesture. "Thank you for your excellent lesson." Defiance settled into her face. Suddenly, like a bolt of lightning, she announced "I'm sure that Kenji-san would let me stay with him, if I asked."

"Is that what this is about?" said Minnie. "Is this really about Kenji Nezumi?"

"Over my dead body," declared Jade, her normally quiet voice nearly a roar. "Never in my lifetime will you be with a Japanese man, a foreign devil! Look at what he's done to Shanghai! Look at China in the north, look at our people forced to be slaves and concubines. These foreign devils are disgusting, that's what they are!"

"How provincial, Mother," retorted Mei Ling, staring hard at her mother, eyes smoldering with indignation. "You cannot stop me."

Jade reached out and slapped her daughter's cheek quite hard. The sound of hand against face startled the little group into silence.

Mei Ling touched her cheek. Her hair was slightly disheveled, her eyes narrowed with emotion. Turning, she ran up the stairs and disappeared into the house.

Yen Hsu turned to his wife. "We cannot treat her as though she were a child." With a heavy sigh, he motioned to Xiang to prepare the car.

Jade would not be deterred. "Does she not realize what happened to my father and brothers at the hands of these devils just four years ago? I thought she was the smart one! It was not so far away, not so long ago and not so easy to forget."

Yen took another deep breath and then turned to his sons. He may have never been so frustrated in his entire life. "Come on, boys, we have to get you and Ma to the *Panay*. Right, Xiang? Turning to his mother-in-law, he asked, "Mother, will you be comfortable in the back seat?"

"It is not comfortable," said the elderly woman. "It is not good for boys to be away from their father for too long, Yen Hsu. We should all leave together. I, too, do not want to leave."

Yen closed his eyes for a moment. "Please, not you, too. Can you get into the car and put one boy on each side?" He held up the tickets. "Do you see that I got the last tickets available?" The old woman said nothing. "Mother, you are frail and the boys are young. They should not ride with us in a car, all the way to Hangkow. It is simply too treacherous. The *Panay* will be safe and my brother will meet you when you arrive in the Hangkow port." Yen Hsu then turned back to Minnie. "Please," he begged. "I have a ticket here. Take it, go."

"I cannot," she replied flatly.

Xiang stepped up to Yen. "Sir, I am so sorry, but we must go now, we are running late." He bowed several times to his master and trusted friend and then turned and bowed to Jade. "Mei Ling will be fine, Madame. She is in love like a kitten in the garden. And although she is still a kitten, we know that she stands like a tiger." He smiled reassuringly and bowed again.

Jade tried to return the smile, but could not muster the heart. Instead, she quickly kissed Xiang on the cheek.

Such a display was uncommon, and the sight of it touched Minnie. She had observed the family's love for Xiang and his unwavering devotion to them. He was the grandfather they never knew.

The little man winked at Yen Hsu and turned toward Jade. "Madame Jade, do not tell your husband you have kissed me, or he might send me back to the provinces."

The comment seemed to relax Jade. With a genuine smile, she said, "After so many years, you silly man, I do not think that you will live in the provinces again. Now go on, get mother and the boys to the *Panay* and we'll see you back here in about an hour. Remember, we still have the rest of our packing to finish."

"Yes, Madame," replied Xiang, bowing yet again. He slipped in behind the wheel of the car and closed the door. Removing a hanky from his pocket, he polished the rear view mirror.

Ping and Chiang leaned out the window just as Mei Ling came running to the car. Mei Ling's eyes were puffy and her nose red. She leaned through the windows and kissed her brothers and grandmother as the car slowly crept away. When she finished, she turned back toward the house, making a point not to look at her mother or Minnie.

Yen Hsu ran ahead and opened the gate. As the car slowed, Jade approached it, her eyes wet with the pain of separation. She leaned in and hugged her sons, kissing them repeatedly on their foreheads.

It took Xiang forever to creep around the driveway, with the family running to the car windows for yet another quick good–bye. Jade jumped on the running board and hung on until the car reached the gate where Yen Hsu stood. He caught her and held her tightly as Xiang pulled out onto the crowded street. Yen caught a last glimpse of Jade's mother trying to calm the boys as they peered out the little oval window at the back of the car. They waved excitedly, as though believing this just one more adventure in their young lives. They didn't seem to notice the worried and fearful faces of not only their family, but all those in the street, men and women and children who were also leaving their homes behind, frenzied to get out of Nanking alive.

The assembly of family and friends fell silent. Minnie turned away from a cold gust of wind that blew across her face and propelled a cluster of fading leaves from the cherry tree into the nearly frozen fountain. Leaves were driven across the driveway as well, as if rushing to catch up with the sedan and its precious occupants. Minnie hugged her coat tightly around her and watched Jade and Yen Hsu. They were tearful with pride for their sons, yet devastated by the sadness of their departure during this time of war.

THREE

A gust of wind whispered around the little house and a branch skittered across the roof. Another touched the window with a scraping sound. It was as if all the elements on this blustery Illinois day were conspiring to come inside.

Minnie made no effort to compose herself. She felt vulnerable and alone. Pulling the old Chinese robe tightly around her, she crossed to the high table that held her little shrine. Only one candle remained lit and she blew it out. Picking up the necklace beside it, she rubbed a finger across the dangling kanji symbol made of gold.

So much of her life was strewn across the dining table. It had been her father's and she could still hear him saying, "I'm glad you're taking it, Minnie. It can seat eight during the holidays." But eight people never came and now it seated only one…and held the reminders of two hundred and fifty-thousand hearts that spoke to her soul every day.

Minnie lowered herself into the chair and leaned back, eyeing the collection of photographs, newspaper articles, her tattered Bible and her diary. At the moment, nothing held any meaning for her. Nothing, that is, except the picture in her hand. She looked at it again and shuddered. She picked up a pen and wrote: "Dear God, how can they call me a hero? I have failed you. I have failed my China, and the people I loved. I have failed them all. I beseech you to speed the day when war is no more."

The curtains hanging over the dining room windows suddenly glowed at the edges with flashes of lightning. Was there anything more violent in the Midwest than a springtime thunderstorm? Minnie counted the seconds for the thunder to arrive, as she had done as a little girl living on these same prairies. That was before she was a teacher and a missionary, before Nanking.

At the count of five, the thunder caused the windows to vibrate. It was during an evening like this that her mother died. Thunder reminded her of two things: her mother's death and the bombing of Nanking.

The photographs around her only served to illuminate the stark reality of her life in Nanking during the invasion. The images stretched out across this table churned up emotions of intense love and unparalleled hatred, neither of which she was prepared to handle.

Another tear fell, this one onto the photograph of the Yangtze River whose current carried so many of the innocent dead.

What she wanted now was a cup of tea, something to calm her nerves and her memories. As she thought about it, questioned whether she had the strength to rise and walk into the kitchen to prepare it, her deliberations were interrupted by someone knocking on the front door.

FOUR

Sergeant Nomo, exhausted and hungry, stood with his men and awaited General Yatsui's orders. The air was cold and filled with the odor of dampness and the cloying scent of decay. A fog-like mist hung over the Yangtze and objects drifted past the banks, their forms obscured by weather and mutilation. The surrounding fields were in ruin, low vegetation trampled and trees so blown apart by shelling that the inner pulp was exposed and hanging off the bark, like the entrails of a bayoneted giant.

On the orders of General Yatsui, the sergeant and his men rounded up the last of the area's peasant farmers and positioned them along the bank, their backs to the river. They had been stripped of their meager belongings, which were now strewn about and being picked over by Japanese soldiers.

Nomo assumed that the general intended to address the villagers, but he was not certain why. For one thing, the man spoke little, if any, Chinese, and it was doubtful that these peasants understood anything but their native tongue. Even if they did understand Japanese, what could these people possibly glean from anything the general might say? General Yatsui was a short man of Napoleonic stature and needed to stand on a small ammunitions box to increase both his size and his importance. Whatever nonsense the general intended to share with his captives, Sergeant Nomo wanted him to do so quickly. Despite Yatsui's dry clothing and extended belly, Nomo's men were cold, tired, and had not eaten for nearly twenty-four hours. When Yatsui nodded with satisfaction and cleared his throat, Nomo took these as positive signs.

General Yatsui drew his sword, waved it at the peasants, and then he raised the sword high in the air. "Sergeant Nomo!" he ordered.

"Yes, sir, General!"

"Fire!"

Nomo looked at the general, at his men, and then glanced toward the peasants. "General, fire at what?"

Yatsui threw his second-in-command a stern look and used his sword yet again to indicate the families huddled on the river's banks. Leaning forward, he hollered into the sergeant's face, "These are spies and Nationalist soldiers and they are to be executed at once!"

Nomo wanted desperately to wipe the sputum from his face, but he dared not. Instead, he turned his gaze toward the terrified children clinging to parents who were eying the soldiers in horror. There was no need to speak Japanese to know that these words, spoken in rage and contempt, signaled their doom.

Sergeant Nomo gestured toward the villagers. "But these are peasants, General, not soldiers or spies."

"Army deserters," accused Yatsui, his sword cutting through the air in threatening arcs. "Spies, spies and soldiers." He hopped down from the box and took a few steps toward the peasants. In the blade of his sword were reflected faces paralyzed with terror. "Fire!" he yelled.

"But how can we kill them, General?"

The general took several menacing steps toward Nomo. "Sergeant, surely you know how to kill Chinese soldiers." He stormed back and forth, between the stricken villagers and his men. "It is your job, but if you are not capable of shooting them, you might try—" Without another word, he raised his sword above the head of one of his own soldiers and brought the blade down and across the man's neck, decapitating him.

The head rolled down the bank and into the water. Children screamed and one teenage boy began to run. The general pulled his pistol from its holster and shot the boy in the back, causing him to fall to the ground as if having tripped on a log while running full speed. Several peasants turned toward the frigid waters and tried to jump in. Others huddled closer together, the smallest children in the middle, as if this show of community might save them.

Nomo felt his last meal rise in his throat. Swallowing hard, he shouted "Fire!" In a storm of lightening and thunder, guns blasted and peasants fell. Within seconds, flesh and bone were everywhere and the red of war stained the earth once again. There were bodies on the banks, bodies rolling and sliding into the river. Most were dead, a few more were dying. Soon, a scarlet stain swirled in little eddies on the dull, gray water.

With his ears still ringing, Nomo watched the general stroll among the carnage. The man nodded proudly as he surveyed the remains of old men, women, and children, all defined by him as dangerous and powerful adversaries. Nomo ordered his men to do as they had done upriver: toss carcasses into the water like sacks of rotten rice. Two soldiers were about to grab one of the victims, but General Yatsui stopped them. The woman was clutching weakly at the muddy bank. "This one is not dead," he said, and he drew his sidearm. Taking aim, he shot her through the head. "Proceed," he told his soldiers, and holstered his weapon.

One of the soldiers attempted to grab the woman's arm, but it was slippery with blood and he could not hold on. She slid on her face into the river, one arm extended, as if reaching for the two dead children floating nearby.

General Yatsui walked up the hill, out of the smoke and the fog. "Sergeant Nomo," he said, sword raised and bloody. He used the tip to point at a road sign. "Nanking, forty-nine kilometers," he said with a grunt. "Not much farther to the capital, yes? And I can promise that there, victory will be swift and proud."

FIVE

John Magee moved quickly as he maneuvered the hand truck along the tidy pathways of his American Church Mission in Nanking. He had just returned from the American Red Cross headquarters with two large crates and he was on the verge of giddiness, palms sweating even in this brisk December air. He opened the door to his office and carefully backed the hand truck over the threshold. Easing it down, he blew on his hands and rubbed them together.

When he was a child, his father would give him one nice present for Christmas. As a missionary's son, that was as much as he could hope for and he was grateful to receive it. Now he felt as if he were back at home on Christmas morning. The Red Cross crates always contained many goodies, but there was only one item that qualified as a Christmas present to John Magee and he had requested it over and over. He had even prayed for it.

Magee opened his pocketknife and realized that he was still wearing his fedora. A bit old fashioned, he thought it rude to wear a hat indoors and had grown up thinking it unlucky as well. Tossing the hat on the desk, he used the blade to snap the ropes on the first crate, anxious to see the contents of this last crate off the *U.S.S. Panay*.

Now that Nanking was virtually cut off from the rest of the world, Magee knew that there would be nothing going in or out for some time. That was unsettling, but he had been in tight spots before and understood that these inconveniences came with the job. He smiled, a voice in his head reminding him that this was not a job, it was a mission, and faith in the Lord had always seen him through. Faith, and his own resourcefulness.

Few men were as suited to a career as John Magee. The man possessed not only an agile and spiritual mind, but a body of fortitude and resilience. His best friend, Forster, and the others could rib him all they wanted about his appearance and mannerisms, but he was very comfortable with the man he had become. And while he might look like a prim and proper clergyman, he had a grip so powerful that it could crack two walnuts with one fast squeeze. As a college student, his swiftness and dexterity were legend. He could outrun every student, climb ropes faster than his gym teachers, and wrestle well enough to earn a varsity letter when he was a freshman. It was during his senior year that he took up the camera and the cross, and his life changed forever.

Magee lifted the lid off the first crate and saw that it was filled with medical supplies. "Thank God," he murmured, relieved that these vital goods weren't "deflected" while en route to Hangkow As long as his crates were bundled with American Red Cross supplies and loaded onto British trucks, he was safe. "God and the Red Cross work in mysterious ways," he thought, while pushing the crate into a sequestered space under his desk. He cut through the ropes binding the second crate and removed the well-traveled lid. First, he took out several layers of protective packing material and then another layer of wadded papers. His heart raced as he lifted out a custom designed metal travel case. He placed it almost tenderly on the desk and just stood there, desperate to open the box, yet afraid it might be something other than the big prize he had been waiting for. "Get on with it, old man!" he declared. He pried off the top and looked inside like a schoolboy. There it was, the Bell and Howell 16-millimeter movie camera. Packed with it was a smaller leather case and many reels of film, including a bunch of short ends. He held the camera in both hands, felt its heft, how well it fit in his eager hands. He had requested this camera nearly two years ago. Whether it had taken this long to accumulate the donations needed to buy it, or that such a fine apparatus was difficult to locate, it made no difference. Someone had made this happen, despite the dreadful Depression in the States, and he was so very grateful. He loaded the camera and then walked to the window, opened it, and pointed the camera at the street. There was a commotion going on. It seemed to be about someone's well-hidden basket of rice. As he filmed the hubbub, he heard three knocks at the door and decided to ignore them. The knocking became louder, more insistent, causing him to shake his head and call out for the person to enter. When he saw that it was Forster, he resumed shooting.

Forster crossed the room and approached Magee, his attention drawn to the camera. "New toy from the States?"

Magee continued looking through the viewfinder. "It's a shame we're shooting stills today. This is the most amazing piece of mechanical wizardry I've ever seen! Truly, it's better technology than a car...and its modern!" He lowered the camera and shook his head. "A motion picture camera, Forster. Can you believe it? I have a motion picture camera!"

Forster scowled. "Nothing's better than a car, especially in China." When Magee did not respond, he laughed. "You know, I might believe it's a motion picture camera if I could get my hands on it. Let me take a look."

Magee held the camera in the same position, pointed out the window.

Forster reached out for it, but Magee would not release his grip. "Can't I even hold it?"

"Not just yet."

"Why not?"

"You know."

"No, I don't know. "

"No one has ever touched it, but me."

"So you're saying this camera is a holy relic?"

"No, but she might be, well, you know—"

Forster smiled and lowered his voice. "A virgin?"

Magee nearly gasped with laughter. "For God's sake, Forster, I am a minister of God, mind what you say!"

Forster shook his head. "John, you are such an odd man, and now this. Perhaps you believe that you were ordained for this sort of work, too?"

"No, I'm quite clear that I was ordained for _this_," and he wrestled a finger under his white collar.

Forster rolled his eyes. "Come on, Minnie will be waiting. She's been so adamant about this photo shoot, you would think it was a graduation ceremony. I'm thinking she must have heard something from that Kenji fellow." He moved closer, as if conspiratorial, his voice more serious. "Or do you think Yen leaked something new to her?"

Magee snapped the protective cover over the lens. "Yen Hsu said the Chinese consulate is clearing out, but they don't expect the Japanese to really enter the city for a number of days. On some cable he intercepted, there was the mention of restocking supply lines."

"What about this dinner with Yen Hsu? Shouldn't he be long gone? I feel obligated, of course, but really now– is it smart?"

Magee slipped the camera into its carry case and turned to face his friend. "Of course it is. Yen's been the best friend imaginable, here or stateside. He taught me most of what I know about China, including its culture, its sense of art and balance. And it's interesting to some of us," he added. "Most of what he knows—well, he just _knows_. He's a damn genius, truly a blessed man. I've not met many with such a great mind, an artful eye, and a heart as big as all of Asia."

Magee pulled out his desk chair. Before sitting, he gestured for Forster to sit in the other one. When the men were settled, he leaned back and thought for a moment, absent-mindedly scratching at an ink stain on the arm of the old wood chair. For a moment, it seemed as if a sadness had passed over him. "Yen has a real cautious side, as you know. Jade's mother and the two boys are already gone, on the *Panay* and headed for Hangkow. To be honest, I think Yen and Jade's presence has more to do with Mei Ling and Su Lin than any embassy responsibilities. For one thing, he promised them he'd let them join the photo shoot, and that should have been a week ago. But really, I think he just needs to make sure that everyone gets out safely. You know he must be the last official of the government still here, but that's just him."

Magee gestured toward the opened crate "They sent me all this film so I could shoot what I love about China. At least, that's how my proposal was spelled out. But soon there may be little left of the China I love."

Forster's eyes opened wide. "You mean, other than the twenty of us and those thousands of refugees crowded inside the walls."

The two friends sat in silence, each one lost in his own interpretation of what was happening outside.

Finally, Forster broke the silence. "Look old boy, there will be hell to pay if I can't get you to the photo shoot on time. It's half past now. Do you have your still camera packed up?"

"It's all in the car," responded Magee. "Do you think I should bring the movie camera as well? I could show it to Yen before we eat."

"Are you kidding?" Magee grabbed the leather case and retrieved his hat from the floor. He stopped long enough to take a good look in the mirror. "Stunning strong jaw, don't you think?"

"You're one of a kind," laughed Forster. "One of a kind!"

The two men left Magee's office, climbed into his car and drove the short distance to the Ginling Girls' College.

SIX

The Ginling Girls' College in Nanking was the manifestation of everything Minnie Vautrin lived and breathed: faith, hope, vision, learning, growth, and God. She managed the school from top to bottom, knew what everyone was doing and where. She also understood the hopes, dreams, and ambitions of every student. Minnie spoke fluently the Nanking variety of the Mandarin dialect, which she began to study immediately upon arriving. With the language came knowledge of customs, foods, horticulture, and architecture. Over the years, she had taken a few furloughs to visit the States, but that was primarily for course work that she could bring back to the college.

Minnie was known among her staff as demanding, yet fair. She expected excellent performance in the classrooms and the administration offices. Her students rarely let her down, rising to their beloved headmistress's highest standards. As a devout Christian, her belief in God and the goodness he represented never wavered, nor did her faith in what she and her staff were doing for Him at the college.

The average enrollment at the college was around three hundred students. Many more wanted admission, but there simply was not enough room. That was fine with Minnie, because crowds made her quite uncomfortable. At this number, and with the girls spread around the large campus, she rarely felt closed in. The open spaces of the campus also appealed to her. The perfect day was when she caught sight of an ibis flying high toward the marshes at the foot of the Purple Mountains. She loved these gracious birds, how they were gangly and awkward on land, but elegant and lofty as hope itself when in the sky. When a pair of these birds landed and nested in one of the ponds on her campus, it was as if God were rewarding her personally.

Minnie stood in the entry of the main building, a magnificent two-story structure shown in the school's brochures. In the crisp December air, she appreciated the architecture of this edifice, so western in some ways and yet Chinese in others. There was the grand swooping roof, its large clay tiles turning up at the ends. The pillars framing the entrance were also Chinese and gave the building an ancient and noble look. In many ways, the building represented what she was trying to do at the college, which was to teach her girls about the whole world, but within the context of their Chinese heritage and culture. Such depth of thought, design, and purpose was simply a part of who Minnie was.

On this particular morning, Minnie looked across her campus and saw harmony everywhere. The architecture was organic and contextual; the lawns were neatly manicured; the gardens held the promise of a beautiful spring. Had it already been twenty years since she had set out to make her school a reflection of the city? One of the ways she had achieved this was to cultivate beautiful gardens throughout the campus. She used native flora, especially the flowering varieties, and by late spring her gardens rivaled the very best in all of Asia. Two decades of commitment and tenderness had transformed this place into a harmony of strength and color, like Minnie herself.

Minnie watched two girls run about, trying to get their Chinese box kites up and over the eastern garden. She smiled as their long pigtails danced, noted how the long skirts of their uniforms impeded their movements. The trees and the high walls of the campus might be blocking the wind, but these girls were having fun trying. Minnie's dogs, two medium-sized mutts acquired on one of her stateside visits chased the girls back and forth across the lawn, barking and prancing, getting tangled in the girls' feet. Watching this scene, Minnie felt like a proud parent. In the adjacent archway, a small flock of finches landed on an ornate bird feeder, their beaks causing little rainbows of color as they pecked at the seed. Minnie found the larger birds more interesting, not nervous and lazy like these little finches.

Minnie's smile faded as the blast of a distant cannon rolled across the city. The shock caused the finches to dart away, only to return shortly after the rumbling subsided. She noticed the white egrets in the pond nearest the kitchen and how, when the cannon sounded, they didn't fly off. Instead, they lifted their large heads, looked around, and then went right back to sifting through the mud beneath the cold water. As much as Minnie loved the egrets, she far preferred her pair of wild-crested ibis that had shared her pond for almost ten years. There was now one lone ibis standing on the grass, so still it could have been a statue.

Another rumbling sound filled the air, as if a bomb had exploded far away. She was surprised by how much louder this second blast was and how the birds remained, as if unwilling to be intimidated by something as banal as a bomb.

Minnie watched the ibis for almost a minute, fascinated as always by the band of red plumage sprouting from its elegant head. "It's as if God had circled them with a brush full of red paint," she had once told Yen. "After that, He attached a black, curved beak for added drama and then those long, white feathers."

Her two ibis stood like statues and there was not even a ripple where their long legs entered the water. One of the birds suddenly struck the surface and snatched up a little water bug in its beak. Cocking its head back, it swallowed its catch and settled back into its statuesque pose.

Most of this species had been killed for its plumage. It appalled Minnie that something so regal could be slaughtered for a bit of plumage. Milliners paid top dollar for those feathers and women paid a fortune for those milliners' creations. It made Minnie dislike women's hats and strengthened her resolve never again to wear a hat with feathers.

Without warning, a huge explosion sounded in the industrial part of town. Both of the birds snapped to attention and then catapulted themselves— with their long legs, webbed feet and powerful graceful wings—into the air and across the pond, over the Ginling walls and away from Nanking. "There they go," she thought. "And soon it begins."

Minnie wrapped the scarf around her neck and tugged the coat tighter around her. She walked through the gardens toward the chapel, the pure voices of her choir singing Bach's *Suscepit* beckoning her closer. The music's spirit resonated in the air with the pure purpose of Bach at his best.

She continued toward the chapel, which sent echoing sounds into the air. It was perhaps the most innocent sound on earth: the soprano voices of young girls. Even the powerful organ was dwarfed by the purity and innocence of the melody as it wafted out of the chapel and between the campus buildings. Minnie continued on, making her way past the classrooms toward the sound. It was as if God were speaking to her through Bach and it made her feel warmer inside, made her head feel clearer. She listened for more bombs, but they seemed to have stopped. Relaxing her shoulders, she felt like a spiritual moth drawn to the warm light of Bach and God.

As she neared the chapel, Minnie glanced into the windows of several buildings and saw clusters of girls. She wanted them to be moved by this music as well, to be spirited out of their warm habitats and into the chapel. Was this asking too much?

The sky had been gray for weeks, but never quite so foreboding as today. Perhaps the essence of the music would cast off the gloom for her students, as it did for her. She paused before the chapel, wanting so much to linger, but there was so much to do. With a resigned sigh, she forged ahead to one of the classroom buildings.

Mei Ling Hsu was among the newer teachers at the college, but she had been around for years. She had been a student there, Minnie's favorite when she taught, and Minnie considered her a remarkable young woman who embodied everything the Ginling meant to Minnie and to the future of women in China.

Minnie gave her new teacher a classroom of average size, filled with the brightest young stars in her school. Who better to teach them than Mei Ling, herself a former luminary? Minnie had assigned Mei Ling to teach English and soon discovered that her exceptional pupil had matured into a talented and passionate teacher. It was obvious that she loved her work and her students, as Minnie had when she was a young teacher.

Minnie approached Mei Ling's classroom and saw Mr. Wong watching the young teacher through the classroom door's window. Wong was a reliable man, stout and strong, who had the inexplicable habit of lying about his age. Though he was obviously in his late sixties, perhaps beyond seventy, he told everyone that he was forty-nine. He had grown up on a farm in the north. In 1931, the Communists burned his farm to the ground. After that, the Japanese destroyed his crops and forced him to stand and watch as his wife, children, and grandchildren were murdered.

Minnie had found Wong wandering the streets near the campus. A lost soul, he was looking for work, sustenance, and some indication of humanity. She offered him food in exchange for labor and he never left. Looking back, it was unclear if she had adopted him, or he had adopted her. In either case, the relationship worked very well. He watched over Minnie like a father and she trusted his wisdom, strength, and integrity.

Minnie was fascinated by the way Wong loved to watch Mei Ling teach. He would stand there sometimes for hours, looking like he was repairing something in the room or fixing a window. Minnie often wondered if Mei Ling was, in some way, replacing his lost family. Perhaps he saw in her his granddaughter, who would have been Mei Ling's age. She saw the pride in his eyes as he watched the young teacher. On occasion, she saw the tears in his eye as well.

Minnie had once overheard a conversation that Wong was having with Mei Ling. "You must hold your head high," he said. "With the dignity of a noble woman. You are the best of the best of China, the most beautiful girl in all of Nanking, and you must walk as if you know this." He went on to tell the young woman that she was of noble blood—he knew it in his heart. What he did not say—yet it was clear to Minnie—was that Wong invested in Mei Ling all the hopes and dreams he had once held for his own family.

At the time, Minnie thought, "We call a woman who loses her husband a widow, and a man who loses his wife a widower, but what do we call a man who loses his children?" Even now, she could not answer that question.

Minnie sidled up to Wong and peered through the window with him. "What are you doing, Old Man?"

He glanced at her, smiled, then pointed through the window. "Watch."

Mei Ling's long dark hair cascaded down her back as she wrote on the chalkboard. Some of the teachers teased her about her hair, but she was not ready to cut it. She was, after all, still single. She took her time writing the English words and phrases on the blackboard. The young women seated behind her appeared attentive, yet Minnie knew that several were struggling to keep focused on their studies. War was coming, there was no denying that now, and concentration was becoming more difficult.

Most of the girls were scheduled to leave with their parents later in the day. Some, who had families on the outskirts of Nanking or in neighboring towns and villages to the north, had not heard from their parents at all. Everyone was anxious. Still, they did their best to give their attention to Mei Ling.

Minnie watched the girls, each one well trained in the art of study. She understood that they had plenty to worry about and had promised them through word and deed that she would keep them safe.

Mei Ling stepped back from the board and pointed to the words she had just written in Chinese and in English. "Let's start at the top," she said. "Slow cart," she read, saying the words slowly, enunciating clearly.

The class parroted not just her pronunciation, but her eyebrow movements and hand gestures as well. Mei Ling tried to hide her embarrassment, seeing her gestures in the hands and faces of her girls.

At the window, Minnie and Wong suppressed their laughter.

"Fine, now let's try the next one," said Mei Ling. "Big boat." This time, she kept her hands at her sides and tried not to move her eyebrows.

The class repeated dutifully and Wong's laughter started to get away from him. "Shhh," said Minnie, trying to contain herself.

"Fast plane," said Mei Ling.

The class repeated her words.

"No, no!" she said. "PLLL--ane." She leaned forward and exaggerated the shape of her mouth for the correct pronunciation. The girls, too, leaned forward, dramatically mirroring their teacher's efforts. Minnie led Wong several feet away and they broke into giggles.

Within minutes a composed Minnie returned to Mei Ling's classroom and was promptly spotted by two of the most attentive students. They waved, but then quickly tucked their hands back in their laps, in order to be polite to their favorite teacher.

Mei Ling followed the girls' gaze and, looking through the window, a broad smile broke across her face. She took a few quick steps toward the door, opened it and gestured for Minnie to enter. "Good morning, Miss Vautrin. Won't you come in?"

"Thank you, Mei Ling." Minnie stepped into the room.

There was a minor flurry of activity as the girls stood for their headmistress. "I am so sorry to interrupt this great session," said Minnie. "But may I say a few words to these bright young ladies? "

"We'd be quite pleased if you did."

Minnie looked out at all the eager faces. "Good morning, ladies."

"Good morning, Miss Minnie," said the class in unison.

"Many of you are leaving with your families today, after the class photo. I just want to say that I love you all and wish you all the best of luck and, of course, God's speed on your journey."

Minnie continued to smile at the girls, but she recognized confusion in their faces. Their world had reached an impasse and no matter how much luck and assistance from God she wished for them, they all sensed that troubled times were ahead. Most of the girls were the daughters of well-to-do Chinese elite businessmen and landholders. No one doubted that the Japanese invasion would level the field for all Chinese. Rich or poor, everyone was in danger. These students were also good Christians. Some of their families questioned Minnie's approach when it came to saving souls, but she was indifferent to their opinions. Her approach would give them an advantage that their social class could not. If they put their faith in God, he would protect them. Of this, she had no doubt.

"The world will be a safer place when all this fighting stops," Minnie said. "I look forward to your safe return to the Ginling. The embrace of your school and your head mistress will always be here for you. Please, never forget this. Until we're together again, God bless you all."

"God bless you, Miss Minnie," the girls declared in one strong voice.

Minnie looked into the innocent faces and tried to tell herself that this was simply another day, yet tears formed in her eyes. The standards she set for herself were such that she believed it most improper to let her girls see her cry. "Thank you," she responded, struggling to conceal her emotions. "You know that I love you all so much, I will see you soon." She then turned to Mei Ling. "Please stop by my office when you've concluded this class. You and I should go together and Mr. Wong will direct your class to the photo shoot. Remember that it is scheduled for noon."

"Of course, Miss Vautrin." Mei Ling could see the tears welling up so uncharacteristically in Minnie's eyes and her own expression revealed surprise at seeing this.

Minnie left the room as fast as she could and still remain calm. It struck her that her exit might have seemed rude, but better to risk that judgment than to let her girls see her true emotions. If for no other reason, she needed to be strong because the girls would follow her example.

Minnie walked across the campus to her own quarters, lost in thought. There was so much here that she loved, so much she feared of losing. Just before she reached the Practice School Building, where she lived, she turned and looked back across the campus, past the library and into the quadrangle. John Magee had just arrived and was setting up his camera. Ernest Forster stood by, ready to assist with the arrangement of everyone in the photograph.

Minnie arrived at the door and slipped her key into the lock. Suddenly, there was a roar of engines and a plane flew low, just above the buildings. The drone of its powerful engine shook the door and the whole campus. Minnie looked up and recognized the markings of a Japanese plane. A gust of biting wind struck her and she shivered. Around her, girls were halted in their tracks, none of them smiling. They were staring at the sky with an awe reserved for fear, not reverence.

Inside, Minnie calmed herself, assured herself that they were safe, everyone would be fine. She looked around her quarters and was reassured by her little nest. It was orderly and spotless, with nothing out of place. There were three pieces of furniture that she particularly loved: a large roll-top desk, an old rocking chair and a Victrola that she had had shipped from the States during her last visit. Her room was filled with well-worn Chinese rugs and a large cross was hung between two quaint windows that looked out onto a patch of garden near the east wall. In one window stood a statue of an ibis and in the other, a second fat little Buddha that was turned toward the window. It was not considered Christian to have two Buddhas in her room, but she thought of them as representing the China of old.

A few yards beyond the east campus wall, and visible through her window, was the wall marking surrounding the city wall. It was more than twenty feet high in some places and was now considered the demarcation for the newly formed International Safety Zone. There were another eight buildings and a few dormitories near the college and many of them backed up to the wall as well.

Over the past two-weeks, the college staff had removed most of the furnishings from the living spaces of these college buildings. Attics and basements were literally packed to the rafters, in order to make room for the onslaught of refugees. In the days before the invasion, Minnie had managed to tuck just over two thousand refugees into these back buildings and she intended to account for every individual by name. Most of them came from the provinces, some from as far away as Shanghai. She was also concerned for the school's valuables. In the event that soldiers overran the campus and engaged in looting, she had sequestered most of the items in the safe to hiding spots around the campus. As another precaution, the meticulous head mistress also transferred nearly half of her school's fortune to the United States Embassy which, in turn, put the funds on the U.S.S. *Panay* for safe transport back to the States.

Minnie glanced at her watch and saw that she still had a few minutes before the photo shoot. With John Magee behind the lens, the picture would be perfectly planned. For once, she wanted to take some time and look her best. Seated before the small vanity, she studied her reflection in the mirror. Not a strand of hair was out of place and her cheeks were full of color. Even her eyes were bright, which surprised her, considering the uncertainty around her. She adjusted her starched collar so that it was perfectly positioned and touched a tiny drop of perfume to her wrist. A knock at the door caused her to turn away from the mirror. She recognized Mei Ling's special knock, a rhythm she had used since she was a little girl. She opened the door to Mei Ling and the two women shared a brief hug. Minnie quickly resumed her place in front of the mirror and applied a little make-up. "You look perfect," said Mei Ling.

"Wonderful of you to say, though we both know better," replied Minnie, smiling at her favorite teacher.

"Perfection is your biggest fault," said Mei Ling, returning the smile. "Perhaps your only fault. But you, your room, your school—everything must be perfect, right?" And then she winked.

"The world is becoming an evil place," said Mei Ling. "I hate that I'm forced to leave Nanking with my parents, just when you need me most. I'm an adult now, Minnie, and I should stay here with you and—"

Minnie rose from the vanity and faced Mei Ling. She held up a hand, as if hoping to extinguish a spark before it became another inferno. "You are not married; you have a career to concern yourself with, and you're one of the first Chinese women of the new generation to have a proper education. Just like Madame Chiang Kai-shek, Mei Ling, you can change things with your knowledge and your wit. That is why you must put these thoughts of staying out of your head. It's vital that you go with your parents to Hangkow. Your father will need you and I know in my heart that you'll be able to come back when it's over." Before Mei Ling could respond, Minnie quickly added, "You have become a fine young woman, and I am so proud of you. Please don't sour this last day, all right?"

Mei Ling cocked her head in frustration. "Thank you, Minnie, but—"

"Your father has agreed that I can take you to America next June, but only if you go with him to the South now. He knows more about what is going on than either of us, so you must trust him. Remember, he's both a competent statesman and a concerned father."

Mei Ling looked away, the muscles around her jaw clenched. "But when do I have a say in how my life is lived?"

Minnie felt her anger rise and worked to suppress it. "Mei Ling, you simply must trust me on this." "I have put my trust in you, but when will you finally trust me?"

Minnie put her arm around the young woman and led her out the door. "I do trust you, and I also trust your father. Even more, I trust in God that everything will turn out well for all of us." She stopped walking and faced her friend. "And do you know what else I trust? That you will look beautiful in the class picture and I will look like the old spinster!" Minnie laughed. The contrast between the two was obvious: Minnie's calm reserve of a middle-aged woman and Mei Ling's sparkling smile and pure Asian beauty.

Minnie and Mei Ling walked arm in arm, like two school chums. In the distance, there was a low reverberation caused by another bomb. Minnie looked toward the Purple Mountains and the roar of the violence. Before them was the normally peaceful garden, which sat beside the quad where the photo shoot was being assembled with a bustle of activity. "Look at Reverend Magee," Mei Ling said, laughing. Magee was oblivious to everyone moving around him, his focus directed toward cleaning his big camera. He did so as if it were an act of pure devotion or childhood fascination. Nearby, Forster and several other Americans were engaged in conversation.

Before they arrived at the center of activity, Mei Ling had one last plea to make on behalf of her father. "Minnie, please, it's going to be dangerous here. If I'm being forced to go to Hangkow, you should come with us."

Minnie sighed, having failed to distract Mei Ling from this ongoing argument. "It's been discussed, I'm staying." As if this explanation were not enough for her young friend, she added "Mei Ling, my dear, I was your age when I arrived in China. I was young and so full of promise, just like you. But much of that promise is fulfilled right here, with my girls and my college. Certainly, you can see that I must stay and protect what I have built. Also, many of the girls don't know if their parents can make it back, so I must protect them like a mother." She felt Mei Ling's arm tighten against hers and again concealed her frustration. "My dear, you really must learn to trust those who have garnered wisdom, and you must also have trust and faith in God. After all, what handsome man wants a miserable wife with no faith and a lack of trust?"

"Only one man has ever wanted me," Mei Ling murmured.

"Yes, and I suggest putting him out of your my mind at once. You know how far off-limits Kenji is with your parents." Minnie knew that love was a mysterious thing that didn't always yield to reason. However, this situation with Kenji-san of the Japanese Consul made such little sense that she strongly supported Yen Hsu and Jade's stand.

"Kenji is a diplomat, just like my father," said Mei Ling. "What's so wrong with a man who's following the same path as my father? Isn't that honorable?"

"Perhaps it's the government he works for?"

"My father works for the government."

"China is not invading Japan and never has," Minnie snapped back

"It makes no sense!" Kenji is not invading Nanking, he's lived here for almost five years. We can't even stand and face them, let alone invade them. Maybe we will do better under Japanese rule."

A flush rose in Minnie's cheeks. "And we wouldn't invade them," she said, impatience creeping into her voice. "China has not invaded another country in the last five thousand years. Don't you think that speaks volumes about who is in the wrong?"

Mei Ling's eyes opened wide. "My God, you sound just like my mother! Go ahead and say it."

"Say what?" asked Minnie.

Mei Ling crossed her arms. "That Kenji is a foreign devil!"

Minnie's posture slumped and she released a sighing moan. "Don't be ridiculous! What I am saying has nothing to do with Kenji. Do you think I don't know that Kenji and the Japanese Embassy have been friends to the college? For the love of God, Mei Ling, I taught him English, and I know when and where you met. And yes, I'm as much at fault as anyone for allowing this friendship to be nurtured when you started teaching him, so it will certainly be my undoing if I fail your family. I will not fail your father."

Another rumble of bombs washed over the campus and two more planes marked with the rising sun of Japan flew over the streets of Nanking. The planes were just outside the International Safety Zone, and the old city walls, but not by much.

Mei Ling put her hand on Minnie's shoulder. "I'm sorry. I know you don't think ill of Kenji, but of the invaders. I could help the Ginling because of my relationship with Kenji, not in spite of it. Please, Minnie, I want stay here with you. Then, if it really is bad, we can leave together for America whenever you are ready. You know you will need my help."

"Your loyalty should be to your father and your family, my dear, not to me or the school."

Mei Ling was tenacious. "I've thought about this a great deal and I realize that there are more reasons for me to stay than there are to go. You are the one who taught me how to think through issues, to use logic. I'm just doing what you taught me!"

A reconnaissance plane suddenly appeared and flew directly across the campus, so low that Minnie and Mei Ling instinctively ducked into an archway.

Minnie's heart was pounding. She looked onto the busy quad at the center of her campus and saw that the students were like nervous little birds, fluttering in and out of formation. Even the calm and cool John Magee was visibly rattled, struggling not to drop his film. Minnie looked at Mei Ling and saw courage sweep across her lovely face. She grabbed the young teacher by the shoulders and insisted, "Look, my lovely, I made promises, commitments, so now, it's a matter of trust. The faith people put in us should be sacred."

"People other than me, you mean?" Mei Ling backed away a few steps, turned and walked purposefully toward the quad and her students.

Minnie watched her go, this former student and now close friend and teacher. Seeing Mei Ling's frustration caused Minnie's stomach to become unsettled. She felt a tightening inside her chest, like a fist squeezing her heart.

SEVEN

Nanking's streets—normally broad, orderly, and orna-
mented with stately trees— were now overflowing with
humanity in chaos. Soldiers were running away, refugees
were running everywhere, and there was a general sense of
pandemonium. For the last ten years, this capital city had
been the place to live; now, it was the place to leave, and by
any means possible.

Yen Hsu looked out the window of the Government
Headquarters building and marveled at the scene. Class dis-
tinction had disappeared and, for the first time, peasants,
shopkeepers, farmers, businessmen, families—what was left
of any of them—shared one purpose: escape. Thousands
upon thousands of frightened Chinese flooded the streets,
nearly all of them toting boxes, suitcases, baskets and bags
until they resembled human rivers about to burst the dam of
the city limits and flow unabated to the southeast, a fast-
moving current of terror. In the haste of this massive exo-
dus, personal belongings all sizes were dislodged from the
arms of one fleeing group and promptly picked up another.
Some of the items were crushed under rushing feet and left
there, adding to the growing debris on the streets.

Yen Hsu spotted Chinese soldiers in the mob and saw
that they were trying to make themselves less obvious. He
watched a few run into a shop and come out moments later,
stripped of their military garb and buttoning civilian coats
either purchased or stolen. On the opposite corner, and in
clear view of many, soldiers were ransacking a refugee's

cart, pushing aside their culture's modesty and removing their uniforms in plain sight, changing into whatever they could find. Yen Hsu knew what fate awaited them if they were in military uniforms when the Japanese entered the city: they would be singled out and killed without hesitation.

The headquarters of Nanking's Chinese government and Chiang Kai-shek was located near the garden district. It was a proud and distinct building, modern yet formidable in its architecture, official and well built. Yen Hsu had always liked the building and thought it a perfect symbol for the future of the unified Chinese government. Nanking became the capital of China in 1928, but now, less than ten years later, Chiang Kai-shek had already left, along with all his top ministers and generals. It was unclear who was in charge. From Yen's vantage point on the third floor, looking across the city, no one was. Yen Hsu was relieved to be inside, safe from the mob in the streets. It wouldn't be safe for long, but at the moment he would be just fine.

It was close to noon and Yen Hsu had to leave soon to pick up his girls at the Ginling. His oldest daughter was a respected new teacher and his youngest was one of the best math students the school had ever seen. The school wasn't far and he still had time to take care of some *last minute business*, his euphemism for destroying documents.

Yen Hsu was a well-respected diplomat who loved his job and particularly relished being at the forefront of Nanking's transformation into the new capital. He was a talented bureaucrat who had won favor with Chiang Kai-shek by proving able and dedicated. Now, what the generalissimo needed most was destroying government documents, many of which Yen had labored over for weeks, months and some even years.

Yen's junior diplomat, Hu Xipong, helped, but half-heartedly. "I don't know how you can do this," said the man. "All of your plans for new gardens, roads, and schools..." His voice trailed off and then he whispered,

"Into the ashes." Having said this, he tossed another stack of papers into the metal barrel near the window. It had been fired up for most of the morning. The container was so hot that it glowed deep red, reminding Yen of the dried blood that was appearing more frequently on the sidewalks of Nanking. Smoke rose from the fire and escaped out the open window, swirling in the wind and disappearing into the gray sky.

Yen Hsu wiped damp soot from his face and then doused it with water before wiping it clean. "We should be getting out of here, like everyone else. I think we got everything," he told his faithful friend, as if he had just written a report and it was time for a cup of tea.

Suddenly, a thunderous blast rocked the building, shaking its foundation, and rattling chandeliers, ornate ceremonial Chinese lanterns, and Yen Hsu's nerves. He watched the light fixtures swing as he made sure he still had his footing. "You all right?" he asked Hu Xipong.

"At the moment, yes, but one more of those and we might not be. Has your family left yet?"

"I put Ma and the boys on the *U.S.S. Panay*."

Hu Xipong smiled. " Ah yes, the ever cautious Yen Hsu. And the girls and your lovely wife?"

Yen Hsu looked at the wall clock. "I must go and collect them now."

"We've given our government more loyalty than it has given us," said the man. "My wife and son are already in Hangkow. Chiang Kai-shek should be there now, too, but the lines still aren't back up for a communiqué. I suggest you don't waste any time getting out of Nanking, Yen. It's crumbling around us. With the defense lines down now, we should have left two days ago."

"You could have," replied Yen. "I could not."

"All these plans for this great city of ours, up in smoke in a matter of hours. Ten years of hoping and planning. It's more than unfair to you, I'm sure," said Hu. "After all, I'm just a communications guy."

Yen Hsu had trouble accepting it. He was born in Nanking and had never lived anywhere else. He had watched a sleepy little trading town on the shores of the Yangtze become the capital of all of China and here he was, the chief of the diplomatic corps for the country. In so many ways, he was Nanking.

Yen dropped more papers onto the flames. "It's all I know, really. Other than my father's old store at the wharf, that is. I'm a diplomat, so I can only hope there's a place for me in Hangkow. Don't you think somehow, with my city under siege, that I have failed it?"

"There's always a place for you," said Hu, brushing away Yen's attempt at self-blame. "Besides, you have the most beautiful wife in Nanking and she will be the most beautiful wife in Hangkow." Hu Xipong picked up an arm-load of documents and fed the flames one last time. "You'll do well there," he said, wiping soot from his forehead. "Just make sure you leave Nanking before the Japanese find you."

It was unlike Hu Xipong to be sentimental and Yen felt a sadness wash over him. Hu was right, all their dreams about a future Nanking were smoke. In Hangkow, he and Jade would have to start over. He was almost fifty now, so this would not be easy. How long would they be safe there? The Japanese had been relentless since 1931, starting in Manchuria, so why would they stop at Nanking? He wondered if he would ever see Hu Xipong again. After tonight, would he ever again see his beloved Nanking?

"We'll be fine," Yen said, grabbing his briefcase. "We'll leave tonight under the cover of darkness, well ahead of the invasion. I figure the streets will be clear by nightfall. It's too damned cold, if nothing else." He was counting on the Japanese waiting until daybreak, which would give him time to get his family out safely. As he was using a second container to snuff the fire, another blast shook the building, causing dust from the ceiling to drift through the room until both men began to cough and were forced to cover their mouths.

"Good luck and God's graces to you, now let's go!" gasped Yen.

"And to you, my old friend," said Hu Xipong, brushing debris from his hair and shoulders. As he turned, he pointed and said, "You don't want to leave that behind."

Yen Hsu turned and saw the beautifully framed photograph of his family. Jade, his daughters, two sons, and his mother-in-law were standing in front of their large home. Nearby, a great fountain spouted water and a plum tree was in full bloom. He removed the photo and tucked it under his arm, grabbing the small Nationalist flag as well.

Yen and Hu rushed through the hallways of a government no longer there, a government in flight. Emerging from the front entrance, they nearly ran to the gate, where Xiang waited in the sedan. As Yen climbed into the back, Hu Xipong said, "Remember to keep your diplomatic pouch near you. People like us are always useful to a government, whatever it is."

Yen Hsu gave his friend a little salute and the man rushed off to open the gate. Yen Hsu took one last look at his office window on the third floor and then at the garden he had designed. He inhaled, trying to find a scent by which to remember this place, but he got only car fumes and the pungent smell of spent gunpowder that drifted in the cold air Yen couldn't help but wonder what he had left behind for looters or the Japanese command. The thought roiled in his stomach at they drove away.

Yen's official sedan still flew its Nationalist flags, but he questioned if it was a good idea, especially with the Japanese arriving. If nothing else, the flags might help with the crowds. Xiang maneuvered the car, creating a small trough through the teeming streets. The mass of people were forced aside by the bulk of the car. The space this created was immediately filled as the car passed, like mud being hoed in a hard rain.

Everyone was going somewhere with purpose, except for those few lost souls who had become separated from their families. Some wandered without purpose, as if completely disoriented in the commotion; others appeared emotionally or physically exhausted, stopping on the edge of the street and weeping, hoping that someone, anyone, would help them.

"Look at them all, Xiang," said Yen Hsu. "I wish to God there was something we could do for them."

"That's a good wish," replied Xiang, "but what? Where would we take them? It's like taking a cup of water from one side of the lake and pouring it back on the other side. The lake is still the lake." Xiang turned the wheel quickly to avoid a small child. Right behind came the mother, bedraggled and pale, barely able to lift her child. "Besides, your family is most important now; you must think of them first."

Yen knew that Xiang was right. He wanted desperately to help, but what choice did he have? The sad truth was that no one had a choice and they needed to do whatever they could to escape.

The car inched forward. Occasionally, someone would place a hand on Yen's window and beg to be let inside. He was ashamed when he checked to be sure the doors were locked. So many people, so many displaced. Yen prayed that they were moving in the right directions. In this case, that meant south, away from the Japanese invasion. He was heading north, back toward the old city walls, inside which was Minnie's college.

EIGHT

Kenji Nezumi sat quietly. His boss, Mr. Tanaka, gazed out the office window into the open space in front of the building, where the flag of the rising sun flapped boldly in the cold wind. Kenji loved the Japanese flag, its symbol reminding him of all the challenging and wonderful days ahead. He watched Tanaka tuck in his shirt, straighten his tie, and smooth his hair. The man had a reputation for worrying about what others thought of his appearance. Despite this insecurity, he made it very clear that no one was to second-guess his opinions or decisions. Kenji was careful not to smile. How would Tanaka respond if he were told the truth, that he was a puppet of the army generals who were about to invade his domain, his little kingdom of Nanking?

As well-suited as Tanaka was for his position as an Imperialist, Kenji and the others on staff knew that decisions claimed by Tanaka actually came from the generals. Tanaka was a facilitator, a man who had spent months planning this day, as well as countless hours transferring information to the Imperial commanders. It was he who laid the groundwork so that, once inside the city, the army's movements would be swift and forceful. Tanaka was Japanese, Nanking was Chinese. Nevertheless, he considered Nanking his city. In his opinion, there was no excuse for a battle. He was certain that he could have a new government up and running in a month. "The last thing I want to see in my lovely city is destruction," muttered Tanaka, not acknowledging Kenji's presence. "These bombings and barrages—why?" He shook his head. "The city will fall in a day; the soldiers will do some looting. This is expected. But overall, Nanking will be preserved, and then we will make her even better."

Finally, he turned and looked at Kenji. "I expect to be placed in the position of civil leadership, once our army has control. After all, this is *my* plan, and it's going very smoothly. My instructions have been clear and concise. Isn't that so, Kenji?"

"Yes, sir," responded the young Japanese diplomat.

"You have observed that yourself, isn't that so? My family is well respected in Tokyo." He nodded thoughtfully. "You'll want to stick quite close to me now, Kenji. I have one last, very important piece of work for you to do before the plan comes together."

"Of course, sir."

Tanaka handed Kenji a small stack of leaflets. "You'll need to give a copy of this edict to all of the embassies and buildings in the safety zone, and the two outside our area as well. Make certain that you give copies to those pompous fools at the British and American embassies, the ones who seem too proud to leave." Tanaka paused a moment, his brow furrowed. "We told them to leave for their own safety; their own governments have asked them as well. Why are the Americans so interested in China to begin with? It will be our colony, not theirs. Do they believe they could manage from so far away? We are the natural leaders in this part of the world. Just look at how nice things are in Manchuria!" Kenji felt Tanaka's eyes on him and realized that his own had glazed over. Before he could reply, Tanaka made an abrupt gesture with his hand. "I see that I'm losing my touch with you, Kenji. Go on, get out and deliver these. But leave me the car, you can take a rickshaw."

"Yes, sir, I will go right away," Kenji said, and turned to leave the office with the papers.

"See that Miss Minnie Vautrin gets a copy as well," said Tanaka. "She's got the best of intentions, but she's so damned righteous."

Kenji took a step toward his boss. "She won't be a problem, sir, and she has always been forthright with the embassy."

"Forthright, yes, but running a school and tolerating our invasion..." He ended the thought with a shrug. "She has many Chinese allies. After you deliver the edict, I want to hear about her reaction."

"Yes, sir, I'll stop there on the way back. I'd like to look around a bit, if you don't mind."

"You mean look around at the young ladies! Just remember that Chinese girls are good for only one thing."

Kenji pulled himself to full height, bristling. "Sir, I'm from a good and honorable family."

A smirk crossed Tanaka's face. "Aren't we all. Now go on, get out of here."

Kenji left the office and headed down the hall, at the same time glancing at the papers. Each page was stamped with the official seal of Imperial Japan. Under the seal, in English, German, and Chinese, was *Official Edict—Imperial Japanese Embassy.*

Kenji's rickshaw stalled at the entrance marked by a sign declaring *International Safety Zone.* The crowds pressed in, guards struggling to stem the flood of people, while trying to keep out deserting soldiers. When they saw Kenji, they pushed back on the crowd, shouting over the din and urging people aside so the rickshaw could pass inside.

There had been perhaps a few thousand congregating near the gates that morning; now, their numbers exceeded ten thousand. The majority of these people were peasants and farmers who had little to cling to but survival. Some of the exhausted and frantic refugees had made their way from the fallen city of Shanghai and its extensive environs.

The old city wall around the safety zone had been constructed centuries earlier as a protection against invaders.

The structure was no defense against modern warfare such as Japanese bombs, warplanes, and soldiers with massive machinery. Like an aging movie star sporting a toupee and a new facelift, the cluster of foreign flags flying over the various buildings inside the zone suggested similar naiveté. The actor could no more hold back old age than the Chinese could the power of the Japanese invaders.

Kenji made his way through the gates and thought about the twenty or so individuals who had chosen to remain, missionaries, doctors, and Red Cross workers who had volunteered to stay and keep order, making whatever peace they could. How could so few well-meaning individuals hold back ten thousand desperate souls? And what would happen when that desperate crowd reached thirty thousand, fifty thousand, or even a quarter million? Would those stalwart men and women still be there, protecting and feeding everyone inside the safety zone?

Kenji was aware that it was sheer luck that within the safety zone were located numerous embassies, foreign-controlled buildings, and the Japanese and German consulates. Another site protected from strafing and bombs was the Ginling Girls' College, located across a little park from his consulate. Not that he was concerned about the college, but he cared very much for someone who worked inside.

The rickshaw driver maneuvered through the congested gate and Kenji saw that his situation had not improved. In fact, they were now in the center of a pushing sea of evacuees; movement in any direction was nearly impossible. The blast of an air raid siren only added to the sense of mayhem

"Come on, faster!" Kenji yelled at the poor driver, relieved that the British Embassy was nearby. The thought of being caught in a bombing raid by his own government's planes sent a frisson up his spine. The driver pushed ahead, calling out his warning to the frantic children and the old women whose backs were bent under bundles of their possessions. Merchants wanting to escape before disaster struck closed and shuttered their stores. Kenji caught sight of an opium smoker perched beside the street and his nostrils flared with emotion. Perhaps it was easier to sit by and opiate oneself to death, rather than wait to be blown to bits? Tanaka's plan to control it all—opium, the trains, all agriculture and exports to Japan—added up to unlimited power. Soon, much of that power would fall into Kenji's hands. That is, when the Japanese occupied Nanking and Tanaka became general consul for this new district in the Japanese empire.

The rickshaw made minor headway, with sounds and smells becoming more intense. There were small fires set to keep poor souls warm on the side streets, their odors mixed with those of decaying fruit and vegetables. And, of course, human waste. A Chinese soldier suddenly ran in front of the rickshaw. The man was tearing off his army jacket and preparing to abandon his duty. Turning, he caught sight of the rising sun insignia on Kenji's coat and, after spitting an invective against the Japanese, he ran in the opposite direction. "No wonder there's no resistance," murmured Kenji. As they inched forward, he Kenji took time to read the edict.

To all Chinese Government Members and Foreign Nationals:

The Japanese Army will be assuming control of Nanking. Please cooperate with Japanese soldiers and you will be treated with all courtesies and consideration.

S. Tanaka, Consul General
The Imperial Japanese Consulate

They neared the British Embassy and he leaned forward, calling out "Over there, by the flag!" The driver angled his rickshaw and ran through oncoming traffic. When they arrived at the entrance, Kenji shouted "Wait here, do not move!" and ran up the steps to the front door. He flashed his credentials to the guard and was promptly given entry.

The offices of Consular Secretary Jeffrey Hayden were stodgy, but comfortable. Hayden was chatting with his assistant over afternoon tea accompanied by cake and biscuits. Two Chinese servants attended them. Kenji walked up to Hayden and handed him the memo.

"What's all this?" He frowned, read the memo, and then handed it without reaction to his assistant. Turning to Kenji, he said "May I offer you some tea, my good man?"

Kenji stood ramrod straight. "No thank you, sir." With an equally no-nonsense tone, he added, "I assume you are moving into the International Safety Zone."

Hayden took a slow sip of tea and then smiled. " Actually, we're quite comfortable here. In any case," he added, locking eyes with this uninvited Japanese visitor, "the British are not at war with Japan." He glanced at his assistant and then back at Kenji. "I should think we would be quite safe in our own embassy, don't you agree?"

"You were asked to leave thirty days ago."

Hayden gazed out the window, as if enjoying a lovely view, rather than the threatening formation of Japanese planes filling the sky. He turned back to Kenji. "Have you objections to our being here?"

"Nanking will fall in a day or two; it would be best if you left the city." Just then, a deafening roar rattled the windows, followed by the sight of a Japanese plane buzzing the embassy. It flew so close that both pilot and gunner were identifiable. Kenji watched Hayden place cup and saucer on the desk and noted how the man's hand trembled. Turning to leave, he suppressed a smile.

The rickshaw was waiting as ordered and Kenji was soon heading toward the German Embassy. He knew that a fortune had recently been spent on improvements, both inside and out. Nothing that was done, however, could mask that this building was German. It was solid and most likely impenetrable. Staff had recently added extra flags to the exterior, giving the boxy structure a rather ornate appearance. There were flags around the building, extending from every possible crevice, even flying from every corner of the roof.

Kenji was ushered into the office of Consular General Rosen by his assistant. He liked the quiet resolve of the Germans and respected the way they did what they said they would do. What he did not like was their proclivity for pointing out the shortcomings of others.

As Kenji expected, John Rabe was with Rosen. Rabe was a small, bespectacled businessman who ran the Siemens office in Nanking. Like Rosen, Rabe was a member of the Nazi party. The man's primary business concern was to assure the most efficient administration of the Siemens Electrical Power Plant, which sat just outside Nanking.

Kenji stared at both men as a short wave radio playing the background. It was Wagner, with intermittent static and an occasional burst of Japanese military speak.

"Excuse me, Herr Rosen, Herr Rabe," he said. "I bring you this message from our consulate." He bowed politely and handed over the note. As was customary for a man of his status, he took two steps back and bowed again.

Rosen read the memo and handed it to Rabe, who leaned toward the lamp, adjusted his glasses and began to read. The lights, fans, and radio stuttered for a moment and then died completely.

"Kenji-san," said Rosen, "we are now without power. May I ask the location of your army?"

Rabe crumpled the memo and scowled at the emissary. "Perhaps they're at my power plant? Perhaps this is why the power has gone out?"

Kenji stood for a long moment, as if at a loss for words. "I cannot say for certain, Herr Rabe, but we are ready to conquer Nanking. The Imperial Japanese Army has rooted out Chinese soldiers everywhere. Perhaps some of these soldiers sabotaged your power plant, before they left."

When Rabe looked suspiciously over his spectacles, Kenji added, "You can be assured that our army will be at your service to restart your generators, as soon as we have conquered the city."

Rosen glanced outside, where signs of chaos could not be ignored. "I think Nanking is conquering itself," he murmured.

A brief smirk of superiority crossed Rabe's face. "Your army must be forbidden to harm any of my valuable workers. Inform your generals that electricity will be supplied by the Siemens Company of Germany when we can safely operate our plant. All of my men must be safe, even if they are Chinese."

"I will inform Tanaka," acknowledged Kenji. "He will pass your statement to General Matsui. We take your comments very seriously."

Rabe turned to Rosen. "Do you have candles and lanterns?"

Rosen nodded brusquely. "Yes, and we also have these." He opened a large envelope and pulled out Nazi armbands, each one emblazoned with a blood red and black swastika. He handed one to Rabe and both men wrapped them around their left bicep.

Kenji nodded approvingly. "We also have armbands for the Americans to wear," he told them, and then thanked both men. "We look forward to working with you on the power plant," he told Rabe, and then bowed as he prepared to leave.

"One more thing, Kenji-san," said Rabe. "In order not to surprise you later, I want you to know that I've been elected by the remaining internationals to be chairman of their International Safety Zone Committee. Of course, we will do whatever we can to provide safety and solace to the displaced." The German's voice was firm, his gaze unwavering.

Kenji understood Rabe's position, as well as that of the committee, but he could not leave with Rabe thinking he and his friends would be given carte blanche. "We have heard of this committee and we look forward to your help in managing the peasant class and refugees. We are also certain that you understand our position about deserting soldiers that are moving among the masses. We may need help rooting them out—for the safety of everyone, of course."

Rabe nodded. "No soldiers will be permitted to enter the safety zone. We are setting up check points at the gates in the old city walls."

Kenji appeared to be satisfied by this response. If the Germans understood that their cooperation meant less interference by the Imperial Army, that meant fewer problems during the invasion. "I must be going," said Kenji. "Thank you for your time." He bowed low and departed with a click of his heels, German style.

The rickshaw driver jumped up when Kenji approached and Kenji directed the man through the streets and toward the American Embassy. As they approached the building, he remembered the miscommunication in front of the British Embassy. "The flag!" he yelled to the driver. "Stop at the building with the red, white and blue flag."

The driver smiled, nodded and said "American, yes."

Kenji grimaced. Did even illiterate rickshaw drivers know that damned flag? "Wait here," he said.

There was considerable commotion in front of the big white building. The last people leaving were gathered and waiting to be picked up by one of the few remaining cars. Several American sailors were loading a large truck with steamer trunks, cases, and courier packages bound for the river port. Had Kenji been able, he would have looked inside those packages. He rushed into the building and down the hall, where he was hindered by an oversized wardrobe blocking a large door. The man attempting to move it held up a index finger and Kenji seem confused. Was he indicating one minute, an hour? He looked at his watch and shifted his feet. After a moment, he reminded himself who was in charge and stepped closer to the wardrobe to hear what was being said in the nearby office. A thin gap separated the container and the doorway; allowing Kenji to see and hear the occupants.

John Allison was a balding, paunchy man with a goatee trimmed so short it was barely visible. He had been the head Consul at the U.S. Embassy for several years. He was seated, one hand cradling a saucer, the other holding a delicate teacup. With him was a distinguished looking visitor seated at a large Chinese desk. Kenji recognized the man as Lewis Smythe, a university professor whom everyone called Smitty. The professor was in his mid-thirties, sported a broad moustache, and wore his hair somewhat longer than was the fashion of the day. He always had a pipe with him and sometimes smoked it. When he wasn't smoking, he was fidgeting with it. Smitty was a jovial man who usually was seen with a grin, but he was not grinning today.

"I understand, Allison," he said. "But trying to keep the safety zone secure from marauding Jap soldiers is going to be nearly impossible."

Allison chewed on that for a moment before responding. "You may be right, but I'm trusting that they'll honor their pacts with everyone: the Red Cross, the U.S. Government, even the International Safety Zone Committee." His expression changed. "With the little Nazi leading that group, that makes the Germans our allies now, doesn't it?"

Kenji smiled to himself. It was always good to get an earful of these private conversations.

The large wardrobe container was suddenly shifted away from the door and Kenji casually stepped onto to the threshold.

"It's about time," Allison called after the movers, ignoring the Japanese visitor. "I was beginning to think we'd be trapped in here like rats." On the last word, his gaze shifted to Kenji. "And speaking of rodents, Smitty, look what we have here." Smitty shifted, nodded to Kenji and resumed his position. In a low voice, he said, "Hand in the proverbial cookie jar of espionage, what?"

Allison cleared his throat and looked past his friend to the doorway. "I wasn't serious about the rodent thing, Kenji-san. Come in, come in. How are you?"

Kenji stepped into the office and said, "The year of the rat was last year, Mr. Allison, a year to achieve one's goals and to attract the opposite sex." He slowly took in the office, as if he might soon own the place.

Allison laughed uncomfortably. "Of course you would know this, Kenji-san. But then, you know most things, isn't that right?"

Kenji forced a smile. "I know that this is the year of the ox and that oxen are known to have a fierce temper." He got on fine with most Americans, but Allison was a sly person. A lot like himself, he supposed.

Allison was known to support the Chiang Kai-shek government in Nanking, while another American contingent supported Mao Tse Tung, who was still hiding in the western provinces. Nevertheless, the Americans were supplying Japan with the raw materials needed for ships and guns and Kenji had been instructed more than once not to rile the Americans. He did his best, but John Allison annoyed him and got on his nerves.

"Rats, dragons, tigers, monkeys," said Allison with a shrug. "And what about you, Kenji-san: were you born in the year of the snake?"

Kenji lifted his head proudly and locked eyes with the insubordinate man. "I am twenty-three, sir, meaning that I was born in 1914, the year of the tiger."

"What kind of man does that make you?" asked Smitty, leaning forward as if to catch every word.

"Tigers are generally suspicious, courageous, and stubborn."

"Hell, Allison," laughed Smitty. "That sounds like you, too!"

Kenji chuckled, remembering to cover his mouth. In his culture, it was improper to be seen laughing at someone else's expense, especially a fellow diplomat.

"Other than this wonderful lesson of the Chinese zodiac," said Allison, with no hint of humor, "just why are you here? Already looking for new offices?"

"It is imperative that this edict be posted on your premises for all to see." Kenji took a few steps forward and delivered the memo.

Allison took it tossed it dismissively onto his desk. "We shall post it, thank you. I trust it is of great importance to all concerned."

Kenji removed from his pocket several armbands emblazoned with the rising sun. "I have also brought you these to further insure your safety. Please wear them."

Smitty took them and held one out like a smelly sock.

Allison took his as well, with no more enthusiasm than his friend. "Are these to become the latest fashion?"

" I suggest you keep them handy," instructed Kenji. "You may find them useful in occupied Nanking. Good day, gentlemen," he added, and then turned and left the room. Japanese men like Kenji found the Americans confusing. They made only the most meager attempts at diplomatic protocol and their informality bordered on rude. Aside from their formal Japanese, everything they did and said smacked of disrespect, both for others and for their own positions.

Kenji left the building, scorn marring his handsome young face. He was an important man and, along with his government, deserved to be shown respect. These embassy men were nothing like the American missionaries he knew. Those Americans showed respect, especially Minnie Vautrin.

Kenji climbed into the rickshaw for the last leg of this journey, turned to the building and muttered "Good riddance."

NINE

Fall semester at the University Hospital of Nanking began with anticipation, but most of the students who had shown up had vacated the dorms and the city. A number of Chinese health workers volunteered to stay, believing that refugees would die without their assistance. The American-sponsored hospital was located just south of the Ginling and, like the school, sat on a large campus of nearly ten acres. The stately, multi-story buildings were of a modern architecture that coincided with the budding new capital. While distinctly western in design, there were also traditional gardens, with indigenous trees and shrubs, a reminder that one was still China. Since 1888, the school had served as an educational respite, a place of learning nestled within the old city walls, yet in the middle of a modern city. Gifted students from throughout the provinces learned modern medicine and healthcare under the guidance of an adept and dedicated faculty. Now, however, between constant warnings, edicts, terrible news coming from Shanghai, and now these evacuations, the once stately university offered little more than a skeleton crew of workers. At the same time, it was poised to be central to the survival of the wounded pouring in from all parts surrounding Nanking.

The early arrivals were from the outlying farming districts and they told stories of unbelievable atrocities. Most of the staff thought the peasants were mostly in shock and exaggerating to a large degree, although many of the wounds made no sense and seemed to be the result of torture. Evacuation casualties were beginning to mount. The hospital had been inundated for several weeks with sick and wounded, including a few who had made their way from Shanghai. Only through strength of spirit and a desire to survive did so many manage that trip. Many died within hours of their arrival.

George Fitch, the director of the YMCA in Nanking, stood in the halls of the hospital and observed a commotion between a Chinese businessman and hospital staff. American by heritage, Fitch was the son of missionaries and was born in China the same year the hospital was constructed. Although he knew the Chinese ways better than most non-Chinese, he was nevertheless the consummate Christian missionary.

Fitch considered himself dapper and was rarely seen without suit and tie, no matter what the conditions or temperature. He was also known to sport garish silk ties and far too much French cologne. There was a time when he was the first to smile and the last to condemn, but that had changed since the Japanese began their onslaught on his beloved city of birth.

As he watched the altercation, Miner Bates, one of the professors, arrived at his side.

"What's this all about?" asked Bates.

"An interesting dilemma," responded Fitch, pointing to the businessman. "This fellow is in pain and apparently has a great deal of money. The man in the bed," he added, gesturing toward the group, "is a peasant and is dying. It seems the businessman would like to buy the bed right out from under the peasant, and he wants to do so right now, before the man dies. What did they teach you about this quandary in medical school?"

Both men knew that this was a Christian Hospital. While it was dedicated to higher education, the concept of Christian harmony and the word of God prevailed.

"One might think that money has suddenly trumped kindness," observed Fitch. "What is the price of buying a bed from a dying man?" mused Bates, shaking his head at the unpleasantly of it all.

In truth, Bates was far more worried about his family surviving this invasion than he was the goings-on at the hospital. As a precaution, he had sent his wife and children to Japan, but all communication was lost when the fighting started. Bates was a Rhodes scholar who had studied at Oxford and Harvard, as well as a Rockefeller Foundation fellow. Now he was a select member of the newly formed International Safety Zone Committee. Standing in that hallway, viewing the early stages of what would become untold misery, his face reflected deep concern. Turning to Fitch, he asked, "What are the chances this level of anxiety will diminish when the Japanese army shows up?"

As they stood there in shared apprehension of what lay ahead, Kenji approached with a document in hand. He explained that it was an edict from the Japanese Embassy. "Mr. Tanaka would like you to read this at your earliest convenience and post it in a prominent place for all to see." Having said this, Kenji waited, hands fidgeting as if he were intimidated by this strong-jawed doctor and the missionary.

Bates gave Kenji a little nod. "Thank you, young man. Am I to assume that we'll be seeing more of you, what with this imminent occupation?"

Kenji studied Bates' face, as if trying to discern some hidden meaning to this friendly question. "Could be, sir. But as you know, I am merely the assistant to the Consul of the Imperialist Embassy." Having appropriately humbled himself, Kenji kowtowed.

"Kenji-san," replied Dr. Bates. "We view you as an important man in Nanking. We also hope that you understand our plan to help civilians in any way God provides. We need your help to make sure this happens without obstruction."

Kenji stood a little straighter. "Yes, sir, and we understand that your service is honorable and loyal. We hope that after you see the benevolence of our Imperial leadership, you will have the same feelings of honor and loyalty toward our great country."

Fitch began to speak and then fell silent, his eyes never leaving the face of this very clever and diplomatic young Japanese.

"I appreciate your position," said the doctor. "Now, I wonder if you can get a message to my wife and two boys who are residing in Tokyo. Could you wire them on my behalf?"

Kenji pondered over this for a moment and then nodded. "Very soon, this should not be a problem. Over the next few days we must limit use of those lines to the business at hand. When they become available, I will do this for you."

Fitch smiled and shook Kenji's hand. "You're a good man, Kenji-san."

Kenji kowtowed repeatedly, a gesture of respect and submission. "Thank you, sir. If there's nothing more, I must get to the Ginling." He turned to leave and stopped when he saw that Bates was about to speak.

"There is one more thing, Kenji-san."

"Yes, sir?"

"When?"

"It will not be long before you see the honorable way in which the Japanese assume control of our great city. Soon, sir. But that is just my thought. Nothing official, of course." He gave a reassuring, but politically nebulous glance toward Fitch.

Fitch nodded and then all three men bowed several times.

Kenji ran down the steps and climbed into the rickshaw, which headed north to the college. It was his last stop. It might also be his last chance to see Mei-Ling.

Ernest Forster ascended the steps to the hospital and passed Kenji, who was on his way out. The American had arrived the previous month and had immediately begun to help with the wounded. It was particularly pressing at the train station, where people needed bedding and rations. Forster and Reverend Magee had been working tirelessly together, but the pressure was often overwhelming. He saw Bates and Fitch standing near a bustling ward and approached them. "I see you've received the edict," said Forster, gesturing toward the document.

"Looks like we'll be fine, if we don't start misbehaving," Fitch countered.

Bates looked at the two men, a tightness around his mouth. "But we'll be alright here, in the safety zone, don't you agree?" He looked at Forster for reassurance.

"I certainly hope so," Forster replied, his smile forced. "Magee sent me over to tell you that the Safety Zone Committee is meeting tonight."

The others nodded and murmured their intentions to attend.

"Right you are, then, nine o'clock," said Forster. "Magee thinks we should go over the top with flags, to make sure the bombers and the army don't mistake us for Chinese. Have you started putting up all the patriotic plumage?" After Bates agreed to see to that, Forster informed them that they had already hung out every American flag they could find. "Even a few nasty old ones," he added, "including one with only forty-six stars. I hope Arizona and New Mexico don't mind being left out!" Bates nodded, while trying to keep watch over the patients moving through the hallway. "We have no problem with the Japanese. American sovereignty will be respected here, no matter how many stars on the flag." He glanced toward Minnie's college. There was someone on a nearby roof, placing weights on the corners of a large American flag.

Fitch followed the doctor's gaze and saw that large flags were flying all over the college, and in plain sight. "Looks like the Fourth of July over there," he observed with a quick laugh. "As always, hats off to Minnie."

Forster pulled their attention away from the college when he announced, "Magee told me that they just got some supplies over at the Red Cross, so if you need anything at the hospital, let me know." He explained that many of the supplies were being used to help those wounded soldiers at the train station, but that even those poor souls would be sent away as the Japanese approached.

Bates tipped his head toward Forster in thanks. "Please express my appreciation to Magee. As for the supplies, I'll give you a list before tonight's meeting. "

Fitch informed the others that a Chinese colonel had given the Red Cross $35,000 to feed his abandoned troops. "But we don't know where to put those troops," complained Fitch. "We certainly cannot allow them inside the safety zone."

"I hope you informed him that we would have no part in hiding his troops in the zone," insisted Forster.

The exchanged looks confirmed that all of them understood the dangers. Let the Japanese into the safety zone, no matter how much they paid, and everyone would soon be in jeopardy.

Down the hall, Dr. C. S. Trimmer, a surgeon and teacher at the hospital, walked briskly toward the exit. At nearly six feet, he was significantly taller than his patients. Trimmer was in his late forties, happily married, and known as an incessant, but innocent, flirt. At the moment, he was on his way to Minnie's campus. Turning a corner, he nearly collided with Grace Bauer. Bauer was one of the more attractive nurses in the hospital, a capable, no-nonsense woman in her early thirties, blonde hair pulled back to reveal striking cheek bones and large blue eyes. The tall doctor and lovely blonde nurse often left their Chinese patients in silent awe.

Forster, Grace Bauer and Trimmer ran into each other as they all walked toward the Ginling. "Hey, there," hollered Grace from across the lawn, her pristine white uniform a stark contrast to the gray weather.

"Are you headed for the Ginling too?" Fitch asked, falling into step.

"For the photo shoot," explained Trimmer.

Forster glanced at the beautiful nurse. "I can't believe you were able to get away." "

Grace made her way across the lawn. "We've got good interns and Chinese nurses holding down the fort, so it'll be fine for an hour or so. But honestly, it's becoming a godforsaken mess. How're things at the Red Cross?"

Forster shook his head, while sidestepping a fallen branch. "We're trying our best to manage. I think we got the last shipment yesterday, which included medical supplies and Magee's new camera. Oh Lordy," he added. "Just wait until you see him with it," and they all smiled.

"I've never understood that," she laughed. "He's a real nutter for cameras isn't he?"

"This time," acknowledged Forster, "I share his excitement. It's a motion picture camera and the poor man is upset that there's nothing good to shoot. He wants it to be spring in the purple mountains, with fair maidens frolicking in the ferns. I fear he's dreaming of miracles."

"Tell him to come to the hospital anytime and witness some real miracles," said the doctor.

Grace nodded enthusiastically. "This very morning, the good doctor here saved two women from stab wounds and, well, women problems and the worst of it…." Her voice trailed off and it was clear that she was embarrassed. As much as they hated to discuss it, saving women from botched abortions was a common occurrence at the hospital.

"I'm serious," said Trimmer, as if Grace had never spoken. "Magee should document everything on film. No one else will, and you never know—" The unsaid caused the others to sigh loudly. "Send him over to the hospital."

The three chatted quietly as they approached the gates of the Ginling. The appointed guardian, Mr. Tsen, stood watch. When he recognized Forster and the two medics, he stepped aside. Grace acknowledged this and turned to Forster. "We're working 'round the clock. What else can we do?"

She went on to explain that they were running low on suture thread, but not on patients who required stitching. Forster promised to talk to Magee about releasing more supplies from the Red Cross store and offered to deliver them later in the day. The three visitors turned the corner and came upon Magee, who clapped Forster on the back.

"Glad you could make it," he declared. "And I see that you've met the lovely Grace Bauer. Now," he added, "would you mind helping me herd all the little kitties into some order, when they start filing out?"

Forster turned to Grace. "The artist calls. I'll see you later with the supplies."

"You're a dear," she said, blowing a little kiss his way.

"He's a married man, my dear," murmured the doctor.

"How come all the good ones are taken?" Her voice was tinged with both humor and pleading. With a little shrug, she walked into the quadrangle and prepared for the picture.

TEN

Magee was done setting up. His equipment in place, his fedora on top of his camera bag, he glanced around and tried to determine the best location for the optimum shot. He was excited about this opportunity to take a very important photograph and understood its relevance to Minnie. He walked around, toting camera and tripod, peering through the lens and checking for shadows. When the perfect spot was determined, Magee anchored the tripod, peered through the camera lens and caught sight of several friends as they began to gather in the quad.

The car carrying Yen Hsu came to a stop near the open space. When the photo shoot was completed, there would be no time to waste before they took off for the docks. The Chinese Nationalist flags flying from the shiny black sedan, along with the heavy dark curtains covering the back windows, made it clear that this vehicle belonged to a diplomat.

Yen's driver, Xiang, helped the family out of the car and then stood beside it his eyes following the planes in the distance. He leaned into the car and turned the knob on the radio, scanning for any station that revealed how far the Japanese army was from Nanking. He heard another plane in the distance and frowned. Was it necessary to take time for a photograph, when the enemy was at the gate? Xiang polished the windshield and continued listening for news on the radio.

Yen Hsu had also been watching the skies. When the second plane disappeared, he approached Magee. "Do you need any help?" he asked. "Light meter, framing?"

Magee smiled and shook his head. "I've got it, thanks. Too bad you weren't here ten minutes ago," he admitted.

Forster turned back, eyebrows drawn together. "You mean I'm not as much a photographer's assistant as Yen Hsu?"

Magee laughed and said, "Not an assistant, Forster, an artist! This man has the eye of an artist. He taught me everything I know about shadows and light. Right, Yen?"

Yen smiled rather awkwardly. "Well, we talk about it."

"Talk? You taught it like a scholar!"

It was evident that Yen was both enjoying the accolades and trying to be appropriately humble. "The Chinese eye for art is more subtle than the Western," he explained.

"Always the diplomat," said Forster, smiling broadly.

"I could use that keen Chinese eye," said Magee, gesturing for Yen to look into the viewfinder. "So what would you do if it were your shot?"

Yen studied the area, checked the settings, and then stood straight. "Since my daughters will be in this shot, I have a vested interest." He put his hand on the camera and asked, "May I?" When Magee gestured for him to do as he pleased, Yen changed the speed and lens settings. Having done this, he turned back to his friend. "If you frame it here, while focusing on the group in the foreground, you pick up a little of this tree," he explained, gesturing toward the perimeter of the shot. "That will indicate that it is winter, as there are so few leaves, but it will also act as a softening frame around the group. I would put more of the faculty on the left, to balance the stark foreground on the right."

One hour later, with nearly every student, faculty member, and school administrator assembled, it was time for the historic photograph. While no one mentioned that it could also be the last, there was a sense of tension among the participants. Magee and Yen had discussed every possible angle and Magee eventually chose Yen's preference, one that promised the best light and the most interesting composition. "You harness everyone's energy and get them into place," suggested Magee, bending forward to gaze through the lens. With that, Yen waved his arms, motioning the group to move this way and that. As if by magic, everyone shifted and turned, responding to the hand of the master.

Magee stared at the gathering, placed his eye against the lens, and declared "My good God in Heaven, Yen, you *are* a genius. This shot has real depth; it shall stand the test of time!"

"If that is the goal," smiled Yen, "then I pray you are right and that all of us stand the test of time as well." He turned to join the others and then stopped. "John, speaking of time, I have something for you and the others at my house. Because we're leaving at dusk, please come this afternoon for a little going away meal."

"Certainly," answered Magee, but the energy had left his voice. This was perhaps the beginning of the end. "But why wait until dusk?" As he spoke, Forster approached them.

"I think it will be safer then," said Yen. "And the roads will be less crowded. I've arranged to caravan with a few of the embassy people."

"We'll miss you more than you know," said Forster.

The three men stood there, lost in their thoughts, and were soon joined by George Fitch. Normally a reserved man, Fitch appeared harried and unkempt. He sported his signature plaid golf cap and was dressed in his usual attire—a suit with suspenders, a snappy bow tie, and a large Red Cross armband—but nothing hung comfortably on him.

Planes continued making passes over the campus and everyone seemed skittish. They knew that this photo was important to Minnie, perhaps the last that would ever be taken on the campus. The fact that it was being shot months before the scheduled graduation spoke to the uncertainty of their lives and made it even more important that they capture a slice of Ginling life before it disappeared. Minnie chatted with the many friends of the college as they waited for any latecomers to arrive.

John Truman, from the Chicago Tribune, was among the guests. The only western newsman left, he didn't want to miss this final gathering. "All the news that's fit to print," he announced, holding up a dated copy of the paper. "And perhaps some that's not. Anyone want it?"

Truman had been in the provinces working on a piece about the extensive and devastating opium trade. He had found evidence of the Japanese military not only introducing opium to its occupied territories, but also using it as a weapon to weaken the resistance before the invasion. The trail of the story had led him from occupied Korea, where the opium was grown and processed, to Nanking, in October of 1937. He refused to leave until he was done with his story which maintained that, as of this year, the Japanese were the largest drug traffickers in the world and were routinely using heroin as payments to anyone who would accept it. As it happened, this addictive drug was the invader's favorite currency. For months prior to the invasion, the rate of new addicts in Nanking was staggering. If only Truman could get his story out to the world.

Dr. Trimmer reached for the newspaper and glanced at the headline. "Japanese bomb Shanghai civilians, strafe the streets," he read aloud. "Imperialists bombing civilians," he exclaimed. "My God, what are they thinking?"

Truman calmly surveyed the group. "It's murder, no doubt. Best we all plan to get out while we can, don't you think?"

Fitch scowled at this lack of faith. "We're staying right here; that's why we've got an International Safety Zone Committee. Why not write about *that* when you get home!"

"I'm stuck, just like the rest of you, unless I want to chance it by car," Truman retorted. "But hey, there might be a great story here." With exaggerated speech, he intoned, "Small band of westerners fend for small piece of dirt in the heart of China's capital!"

Fitch never liked reporters. "I'll bet you could get on a fishing junk down at the water's edge. Then you'd have a big fish story as well, ol' boy."

"I've got a much bigger story about corruption and addiction," Truman responded. "But honestly, if I can't get to a place to send it, what's the point? The Japs cut all the wires running between here and Shanghai or Hangkow. But hey, I'm not ready to blow this pop stand just yet!"

Everyone around them recognized that, despite Magee's edginess, his goal of getting a great photo would not be deterred.

Yen Hsu had been listening to Truman's every word. He had read his stories in the newspapers and, like Truman, one of his biggest concerns was the rampant increase of Nanking's opium use.

"It'll all be over in days, trust me," Truman went on. "The Chinese Nationalist Army is all but gone. Isn't that right, Yen Hsu?"

Before Yen could respond, Magee jumped in with "Yen can't say anything, not even to his dearest friends: his job is with the Nationalists."

No men were more loyal to China and its people than Yen Hsu. At the same time, he loved being with these American friends who had come to teach, build hospitals, learn about and discuss Asian art, photography and gardens. He felt so close to these people that he even tolerated their incessant obsession with, and conversations about, God. Yen was a Christian now, but he preferred to keep his deepest beliefs to himself.

Truman turned to Yen. "If you leave, Magee will win that Pulitzer for photography.   Yen smiled and glanced toward Xiang, who stood patiently next to the sedan.

"Truman, are you really staying?" asked Magee.

"I'm covering the war...and my ass. Hell, even that German—what's his name, Rabe?—tried to leave yesterday. Isn't he the head of your safety committee?"

Fitch tugged on Forster's sleeve. "You mean our Nazi friend made a break for it?"

"Tried, but didn't make it," Truman said bluntly. "And here he comes now."

All eyes turned and watched John Rabe approach. With him were Rosen, also from the German Embassy. Both men wore Nazi armbands and greeted the others with a friendly nod.

Minnie walked up to the cluster and smiled. "Everyone ready for the class picture?"

Rabe, in his light German accent, demanded, "Why are these students still here? They should be going home or secured in their dormitories." Before Minnie could respond, he added, "And why this photo today? Minnie, please, it is too late for such foolishness."

Magee overheard the German's comments and tapped his camera. "One for the history books, Rabe. You'll go down in posterity."

Truman jumped in with "Did your boys at the embassy get the news about the protocol, Rabe? It was signed two weeks ago. Seems that you're now on the team with the Japanese and those fascists in Italy. Care to comment?"

A buzz of activity silenced the crowd. The last group of girls was filing out of the building, led by their respective teachers. Most of the remaining classes only had about a third of normal attendance. The richest families had left weeks earlier, while most of the daughters of the dignitaries and merchants had left in the past days.

Magee raised a hand in greeting, but most of the girls were too cold to respond. Despite the cold wind kicking up across the quad, the students exhibited unwavering stillness, their faces resembling a collection of fine porcelain. .

Gesturing toward the group of adults, Magee asked Forster and Yen to join the students and teachers who were now forming neat rows along the stairs in front of the library.

Nearly one hundred girls lined up along the steps, with another twenty members of the staff and assorted friends flanking the students. Forster, on Magee's advice, arranged the girls by height, until they were arranged into a symmetrical formation.

Minnie noted how her Chinese staff attempted to hide behind the girls. It was in their nature to be reluctant, even embarrassed by the attention. With Mei Ling's help, everyone was finally in position and ready for the shot. Magee looked through the viewfinder at perhaps two hundred and thirty faces trying their best to smile and not think about the bombers humming overhead and the chill. As for that distant sound of shelling that had been going on for weeks, it was considered normal background noise.

Two girls scampered in late and rushed up to the group. As Minnie directed them into their places, she caught sight of Kenji hovering near the side of the building. "Join us!" she insisted, urging him to step forward. He walked toward the group, saying his hellos and bowing slightly. When Minnie placed him next to Mei Ling, his face transformed from politeness to absolute delight. Mei Ling had her little sister, Su Lin, on one side and her secret love, Kenji, on the other. She, too, displayed a broad smile. Minnie took her place among her staff. To her right was Mary Twynam, who was Minnie's age and her closest advisor for years. Mary served as administrator, nurse, social worker, and history buff, and she could always be counted on as the first in line to offer a hand. She was an Irish redhead, self-confident, with a face both open and gentle. Despite her years in Nanking, she had lost neither her Irish lilt nor her Irish sense of humor. Hanging proudly from her neck was a Catholic crucifix, a gift from her parents. On the other side of Mary was Mrs. Tsen, an older woman who took care of the dormitories. Next to her was Mr. Wong, the aging handyman and part-time English teacher who learned the King's English during his stint in Hong Kong. Lined up behind this group were Rabe, Rosen, Fitch, Yen, Magee and Forster.

Magee stooped to take the picture and was interrupted by yet another low-flying bomber, its thunderous engines frightening most of the girls and causing them to huddle closer together. A few of them began to cry, while others appeared frantic as they looked for safety. Forster jumped to the task of calming them, while several of the women wiped their tears. It was nearly five minutes before the group was quieted. With calm reinstated, Magee looked into the lens, held up a hand and called out "Hold still, everyone! One, two, three, smile!" The flash burst into light and the picture was finally taken.

Amid cheers and applause, the group scattered. Students ran off to their dorms to finish packing, to prepare for guests, or to hide from the threatening aircraft, while the adults headed toward their cars and rickshaws waiting near the gates. After Magee informed Minnie that he would transport her to Yen Hsu's house, he rushed off to the Red Cross sedan and stored the camera safely in the trunk. Pausing, he looked back, his face pensive. Had he spoken, he might have expressed sadness that this was perhaps the last photograph ever to be taken of Minnie and her Ginling Girls' College.

Across the quad, Minnie was watching her girls running into the buildings. There was no need to speak to know that she suffered the same thoughts as her friend, Magee. A hand suddenly touched her shoulder and she turned to find Yen Hsu. As much as she wanted to place her hand upon his, she did not. "It's a sad moment," he murmured.

Minnie sighed more loudly than intended. "You are a dear, Yen. It hurts me so that you and your family—" Her voice drifted off and then she did something she swore to herself she would never do: she reached up and touched his face.

Yen Hsu quickly cleared his throat, the flush in his cheeks belying his suddenly professional demeanor. "As a government man, I may be on the wrong side of history," he admitted. "However, we have no choice, we must leave. Chiang Kai-shek has ordered the army to retreat." He looked into the distance, beyond the quad and his waiting car, beyond the city and the mountains. "I fear the worst, Minnie, and I would be most happy if you came to Hang-kow with us."

"I've been in Nanking for over twenty years," she responded. "I will not leave; I will not abandon my school."

Yen Hsu clenched his fists. This was a stubborn woman; convincing her would not be easy. "Leave your school to the caretakers and come with us. We've made room for you. Remaining here is dangerous and foolhardy."

Minnie admired Yen for his perseverance, although both knew what her response would be. "Need I tell you that I would never leave my girls, even if only a few remain? I'm certain that the Red Cross will need my help with the refugees as well. Don't be afraid, Yen, God will take care of me."

He nodded and remained quiet. Having done all he could, he must now turn his energies on his family. He saw Mei Ling talking to someone and realized it was Kenji. When Mei Ling felt her father's stare, she looked at him without emotion. Turning away from Kenji, she bowed to Minnie, smiled at her father, and announced, "I will clear out my desk now, and collect a few personal things. Father," she added, "I'll be back in five minutes."

"Five minutes, no more," he insisted. "We must get across town and we have yet to pack." Mei Ling briskly walked toward her classroom, while Kenji slipped away from the group.

Kenji and Mei Ling had been meeting secretly since she was only seventeen. Both students, bright and with great promise, she allowed him to hold her hand for a year. After one year, he was permitted to kiss her hand and, upon departing, her cheek. The time came when she permitted a kiss on both cheeks when they greeted, but only if no one was watching. Kenji looked forward to those hours they spent together studying English, because Mei Ling allowed the shy student to hold her had.

Kenji had watched a beautiful girl blossom into a more beautiful woman. Now, at twenty-one, Mei Ling was, in his eyes, perfect and Kenji could hardly contain himself. Simply standing next to her made him nervous with passion, anxious to reach out and touch her soft skin. When he saw Mei Ling excuse herself from the others and leave, he knew where she was going. As he walked toward their favored rendezvous location, he remembered the day he met her, when she walked tall and stood for everything proud and honorable about being Chinese. Not only was she beautiful, she was to be admired. Mei Ling was confident, what some people called being "full of herself", but Kenji found this charming and seductive. She was a woman who knew her capabilities and intended to use them. Kenji was often told that Chinese women were dogs or chickens. How wrong! Mei Ling was a Chinese woman and she was sacred, perfect in every way.

He rounded a corner and remembered how his young mind had explored her body, how it did so even today. From her glistening black hair, so bright as the sun danced on the top of her head, to her wide shoulders and perfect body. He could not allow himself to think about how she appeared like a peach or a nectarine in her silken outfits, or how the fabric clung to her breasts in a way that was almost indecent. How could the school permit Mei Ling to wear something so lovely, when all the other girls were limited to uniforms? It was shocking! At the same time, it made her stand out even more; it made her glow.

When Kenji discovered that Mei Ling was a diplomat's daughter, he knew at once that he wanted her forever. She was noble and intelligent, sensuous and funny, and with all the misgivings that came with a wealthy upbringing. Just like himself, he thought, which made the match perfect. Kenji strode through the halls toward their meeting place. He daydreamed about her constantly: her softness, her touch, those sharp eyes looking into his. Together, they would create what would be great about Asia. It mattered not at all that she was Chinese. That she cared for him was a gift and he must protect her at all costs. He had the power and he could use it. If he did nothing else during the invasion but to protect her, he will have succeeded.

On the quad, Su Lin ran up to Minnie and Yen Hsu. The car was ready and Yen Hsu was about to gather his family. "Father, Minnie told me she was staying. Tell her she must go with us, that she won't be safe here all alone."

Yen Hsu touched his younger daughter's cheek. "Miss Minnie has many hearts and souls to watch over at the Ginling, my dear."

"But Father, Mei Ling says that she's staying with Minnie to help the Ginling and China. You know, like you do. Is it true? Is Mei Ling staying with her?"

"No, of course not. Now stop worrying and get into the car. Mei Ling will be back in a few minutes and we'll leave." When the girl stayed put, he gave her a loving nudge. "Go on, Su Lin. You'll see Minnie in an hour or so." He turned back to the head mistress. "Isn't that so?"

"I'll be there," she agreed, smiling warmly at the concerned girl. "Don't you worry, Su Lin. Your sister is going with you, I'll make sure of that."

A bomber flew low, this time circling the lively campus in one large formation. Everyone ducked and scrambled for cover, the younger girls screaming in fear. Minnie wanted desperately for their families to arrive soon and take their children out of Nanking. She said a quick prayer that it was not too late.

As the plane crossed over, Grace Bauer allowed Dr. Trimmer to guide her into a shelter. "You alright?" he asked.

The nurse took a few moments to compose herself. "I guess so, but that was really scary. Are they trying to scare the hell out of us?" She shuddered as if cold, but the response was to fear.

Trimmer reluctantly placed his arm around her, being as cautious as a gentleman could be under the circumstances. "Fortunately," he said reassuringly, "we are inside the safety zone. Also, we're close to the Japanese embassy and it's unlikely they'll bomb their own."

Grace moved even closer, until she was pressed against the doctor. "Are they trying to scare us?"

Trimmer paused a long beat before answering. "I think this is the real thing, that they're preparing for the full offensive to take the city. As it happens, there are more important targets than a girl's college, a university, even a Red Cross hospital. It'll be a mess, I'm sure, but we'll be fine." With every word, it was difficult to determine which of them the doctor was trying to calm.

Another plane flew so low that Grace and Trimmer could actually see the pilot's face. Nearby, everyone again scrambled for shelter. Grace cowered against Trimmer and shook. "You're sure they won't bomb their own embassy?"

"Not on purpose," he told her, leading her out of the shelter. "Let's get back to the hospital and prepare what's left of our Chinese staff."

They ran past the large archways and saw that Kenji had Mei Ling cornered in a classroom door well. Trimmer and Bauer continued toward the hospital, as if seeing nothing.

Standing in that door well, Kenji tried to pull Mei Ling closer, her box of personal items clutched between them. He took the box from her hands and placed it on the floor. Standing, he put his arms around her and held her tight. Mei Ling glanced left and right, checking to be certain that no one saw. It was one thing if people knew they liked each other; it was another if they were found in an embrace. Kenji's grip tightened around her and, caught up in the moment, she allowed him to kiss her mouth. It became a passionate kiss, intensifying as he pushed her against the wall. Finally pulling away, breathing heavily, he pleaded, "Stay with me, Mei Ling, please."

"You know I want to," she said, her heart beating wildly, tears forming in her eyes. "I can protect you," he promised. "I have power!" He placed her hand on his chest. "Can't you feel how my heart needs you?"

He placed a hand on her breast and kissed her again. She nearly melted, but instead stood straight, as if awakened from a dream. "Not like this, not here and not now. Father is waiting in the car and I must go to him. Let me think–"

"I've got to have you with me!" Kenji declared. "You are everything in the world to me. I would not stay here, except to protect you."

Mei Ling thought fast. "Come to the house in an hour," she said, the plan unfolding before her eyes. "Bring some-thing official, perhaps those papers we discussed. In the meantime, I'll work on a plan. Now go on, you lovely man, go." She pushed him away, picked up the box and the satchel, kissed him once more, then turned and ran down the hall and toward her father's waiting car.

With Mei Ling, Su Lin, and Yen safely in the vehicle, Xiang closed the doors, which also shut out the distant thunder of machine guns and bomber planes. As the car sped off, dust and gravel flew, a single piece traveling nearly thirty feet before landing near Minnie's foot. She watched the family she loved most pass through the gates of her school and disappear into the teeming throng of Nank-ing. All that was left was this pebble on the ground. She was thankful that she would see them one last time for tea, although she had no idea what Yen Hsu's surprise might be.

Kenji emerged from behind the building and watched the sedan drive away. He, too, was thankful to be seeing his love one more time, perhaps forever.

Yen Hsu watched Xiang fiddle with car radio, trying to pick up Chinese programs. He found the static annoying, but understood the man's need to know his fate. Yen turned so that he faced Mei Ling. "What did Kenji want?"

"He has some papers for you, Father. He said he'll bring them to the house."

"Why couldn't he have given them to me now?" Yen Hsu raised an eyebrow and cocked his head, as if he were on to his daughter's secretive meeting.

"I don't know about political things, Father. You diplomats are all so cunning and I'm just a school teacher."

Xiang, as if sensing tension, adjusted the radio yet again, but this time found only static and Japanese broadcasts. "What's that say, Mei Ling? What are they saying?"

She leaned forward in her seat. "They're asking us to please accept the Imperialist Commander's orders, and we will be safe."

"Lies, all lies!" Yen Hsu huffed.

"Your Japanese is getting very good, Miss Mei Ling," Xiang chimed in, nodding and smiling at the girl he loved like a daughter.

"Maybe too good," said Yen Hsu.

Mei Ling shifted until she was very close to her little sister. "Is all your stuff packed, Su Lin?"

The girl ignored the question. She scooted to the edge of her seat and hung onto the backrest of the front seat, where her father sat. "Will they let us escape, like they did Grandma and the boys?"

Yen Hsu reached back and pressed his hand over Su Lin's. "I am a diplomat, my dear, not a soldier. We'll have immunity and will be free to leave." What more could he say to a frightened child whose life was about to be changed forever?

ELEVEN

High in the hills, flanking three sides of the city, stood rows of Japanese cannons and a battalion of troops ready to attack the heart of Nanking.

Far below, Fitch drove the Red Cross sedan, with Magee seated in front and Forster in the back. They passed the Japanese Embassy and saw guards who standing at the ready near the stairs, with four other soldiers standing by the flagpole. The Americans drove by confidently, with Red Cross flags waving in quiet defiance.

A hundred yards further, they entered the gates of the college. Men were working on a thicker gate, adding locks to increase security. Fitch honked the car's horn and the workers stood aside. The car pulled up to Minnie's quarters. Magee got out, walked to her door and knocked once, lightly. When nothing happened, he knocked again, this time rapidly and louder. He leaned against the doorframe and crossed his legs at the ankles. Where could she be? Knowing Minnie, she was either praying or was lost in thought. It was not unusual for him to have to wait before she appeared, smiling and ready to go. The door finally opened and Magee found himself facing a woman bundled in two coats and several scarves, one over her head and another around her neck. From his vantage, she looked a fright. Minnie never liked the cold damp winters in Nanking. She was prone to a chill and today the temperature had plummeted.

Magee escorted Minnie to the car and opened the back door. "Everything alright?" he asked, " giving her a hand.

"Yes, thank you," she replied, sliding onto the seat. "But I'm so sad to see so many people I love now leaving; I worry about the future for my lovely children and our school." She settled into the seat and looked up at Magee. "I keep thinking about those poor refugees in the cold, there must be thousands now. I know that God will provide us safekeeping, but it would help if we knew his ultimate plan."

"Perhaps we need to step up our prayers?" Forster said from the front seat.

Magee nodded solemnly as they sped out the gate, and under the English sign that read *Ginling Girls' College*. Adjacent to that were the Chinese characters that spelled out *Abundant Life*.

The small band of Yen Hsu's loyal American friends drove down the center of the International Safety Zone. This zone had been carved out inside of a large portion of the old Nanking City walls. Chung Shan Street traversed the area, with the British Embassy, the Metropolitan Hotel, and the International Club, Further down was the enclave of larger buildings that included the Ginling, the Nanking University, the American and German embassies. Everything was near this important thoroughfare that bordered the edge of the zone. Chung Yang Street, the first road at the westernmost edge of the zone, was where the Japanese Embassy and the Ginling Girls' College sat.

As the Americans drove across the safety zone, they noticed that lean-tos and tents were set up wherever space allowed. The inhabitants were not merchants, soldiers or members of the government class. These were the poor working, individuals and families who had no place to go while the Japanese swept across the countryside and the outskirts of Nanking. They huddled and waited. For what, they had no idea.

Minnie stared out at the chaos. Her nature was to like things organized, with everything in its place. This characteristic, which made her such a great leader of a girls' school, was making her a bundle of nerves today.

The car reached the outermost Ho Ping Men Gate and Minnie saw the extra fortifications. They were meant not only to stem the Japanese invasion, but to thwart, or at least quell, the onslaught of refugees. There was already a long line of those refugees waiting to be admitted. Because no soldiers were permitted inside the safety zone under any conditions, each male entering was checked carefully. Every time a distant bomb echoed across the Nanking delta, all heads turned to the source of the sound and then, en masse, bodies squeezed tighter toward the gates, with children being trapped in the crush. By the time someone made it to the front of the lines, there was not even enough space for parents to pick up their children and hold them.

The car drove away from the ancient stone gates, the way just wide enough for a truck, just narrow enough to stop a stampede or a military tank. "It feels like we're a cork being popped from a bottle," observed Minnie, anxious to break free from the crowds. No matter where she looked, however, it was the same in every direction: thousands upon thousands of people were amassed outside the gates of the International Safety Zone. The sedan passed the road that led out from Nanking and its occupants witnessed yet another ten thousand milling about the streets. "Are they trying to leave," murmured Minnie, "or just hoping to find a safe place to stay?"

Rickshaws were running helter-skelter, as if trying to get through a rat's maze, and the streets were cobwebs of humanity strung together, sharing a common fear for survival and a desperate need to flee. Babies were strapped cocoon-like on the backs of their mothers and nearly all of the women ran toward the south, in the direction of Wubu, Hofei or Hangkow. Simply put, anywhere away from the Japanese.

Shops were boarded up, suggesting that the entire business district had fled. With the rumble of distant bombs increasing, the shuffling of feet on the dirty streets was also creating a hazard to those with respiratory problems. Old people gasped and coughed for clean air. The poor huddled together, many of them wearing everything they owned, in an attempt to stay warm.

Minnie released a bleat of alarm when a peasant jumped onto the running board and tried to hang on. The car was going against the flood of humanity and the poor woman was scraped off the side like an insect. Minnie was deeply moved by the chaos around her and stared into her lap and prayed. When she looked up, she saw four children near the car, holding hands and walking behind their parents. They were being pushed and prodded by the grandparents behind them, the old people nearly bent in half by the weight on their back. She could not imagine that those old eyes could see more than a few steps in front of them.

The car paused in front of an orphanage where a dozen wretched children huddled together. They wore rags and their faces were beseeching. The oldest child appeared to be no more than perhaps ten and he led the others, hands extended, eyes imploring for someone, anyone, to take them away from this madness. Minnie wanted to stop. Instead, she continued to pray.

Ahead of the car, four soldiers ran out from an alleyway and smashed a storefront window. They grabbed jackets and pants off the tailor's display, stripped off their own uniforms and changed right in the street.

"I've never seen anything like this," vowed John Magee. "Not in all my years. It is dreadful, simply dreadful."

"Do you think Chang's army has completely abandoned Nanking?" Forster wondered aloud.

When Minnie spoke, it was barely above a whisper. "Maybe we should head back to the safety zone; Yen would understand."

Magee seemed about to agree and then said, "Yen Hsu came to us and has supported us for years. My faith in him is resolute. If he asks, I think we should go to him. Besides, we could never get word to him and he might stay longer than he should, in hopes of our arrival. It's still early and it's only another few blocks, so let's press on, share some thoughts and wish the good man on his way." The others remained silent and the car continued on.

"It is only another minute or so," conceded Forster, as if they were on a Sunday drive.

Magee bent down and began fiddling with something on the floor that rested between his feet. "I should capture this," he said, lowering the window by six inches. He steadied his arm against the door and aimed the loaded camera outside. "Yen said something about the test of time; perhaps this is what he meant."

The car picked up speed as Fitch drove down the middle of one of Nanking's broadest streets. His passengers prayed that the cable cars had stopped running, since he was driving on their tracks. They sped along until they approached an intersection. Only then did they learn the true definition of *pandemonium*. Thousands of people were running in all directions, some weeping, others mute with fear. Magee hoisted the camera onto his shoulder. "I know it's cold, folks, but I need to crack the window just a bit further." When no one responded, he cranked down the window, hung out of it and began filming. The silence in the car was stark contrast to the din outside. It was as if everyone knew that John Magee was capturing a moment in time. One that, hopefully, would never be repeated.

Minnie peered out at the scene before her. "The inhumanity of it all," she whispered. "Where will these people go and when will this misery stop?"

Fitch maneuvered around a stalled car and nearly hit a rickshaw. "I wonder if this'll be occupied territory by tomorrow night?" he murmured, eyes never leaving the road.

Magee leaned back, away from the camera, and looked at Fitch. "With no army to defend the city, I pray they just walk in and take over."

"Maybe there won't be any fighting at all," suggested Minnie.

Magee resumed his filming. His vision was blocked when a couple and their child attempted to jump on the running board. The little girl fell off and her parents jumped onto the road to collect her.

Minnie squeezed her crucifix and inhaled slowly.

"I've never seen such a nightmare," mumbled Magee. "I need one of those wide-angle lenses."

Forster turned the corner and approached Yen's house. "Do you think Yen will be proud of you, taking movies that show his government's loss? And besides," he added. "Do you have any idea how dangerous this film could be?"

"It's a testimonial," Magee defended.

"It might make Yen Hsu look bad," responded Minnie. "But then again, if John doesn't get those images, who would believe this?"

Minnie was afraid for Yen. He had supported her and the school since 1916, almost half her life. What if something happened to him? The man was loyal to a fault and honored their friendship above all others. Had he not entrusted his daughter's education and spiritual enlightenment to Minnie? After all these years, she felt as much of a mother to these children as any she had ever known, but she had no idea what to think now. Her world was coming apart, yet here was her dear American colleague, Magee, insisting on a good story to tell. It occurred to her that filming this misery was his way of dealing with the atrocities around them. How tragic that the Nanking they all knew, loved and nurtured was dissolving in front of his lens.

Fitch slammed on his brakes to avoid an overturned cart filled with baskets and supplies, carpets and clothes and then kept driving. An old woman was on the street, having tumbled off the top of the cart. Minnie called out for Fitch to stop, but he refused.

"But we must help her!" she begged. Fitch shook his head. "If we stop, we'll be mobbed. Look," he added, pointing ahead. "We're two hundred feet from Yen Hsu's gate."

Magee lowered the camera and began packing it into its case. Fitch honked the horn, three short beeps, and Xiang appeared at the gate. When he opened it, beggars, peasants, and refugees surrounded him and held out their hands, faces pleading and soiled. Minnie opened her window and handed them a few coins, causing them to surge forward in a near panic. Xiang held the gate open wide enough for the car to pass through. As it did, he brushed away the filthy beggars like flies on a scrap of bread.

TWELVE

Fitch pulled the sedan into the circular drive and past the cherry tree that towered above the elegant Chinese fountain in the center of the courtyard. A man of quiet discretion, he parked the missionary-issue Plymouth behind the newer Ford that Chiang Kai-shek and the generous treasury of the Nationalists Party had provided for Yen's use. Yen was always looking forward to the newest car; in his position he had to impress. Fitch, on the other hand, took whatever the Red Cross sent him.

Minnie got out of the car and stopped to appreciate how well the grounds were kept, even now. The garden was sparse, everything trimmed, pruned and shaped, even on such a dreary winter's day, when the family was preparing to leave their home for the first time in their lives. Jade had designed the garden many years before and had paid attention to the sun and the cycle of flowers. Prominent among her treasures was the winter- blooming cherry tree, a gift from Minnie so many years ago.

During the winter, the Purple Mountains to the northwest gave the December sun the appearance of setting even earlier. Minnie studied the sky, nearly dark, and shivered. The chill was setting in fast as the sun was disappearing behind the mountains. She knew the progression of darkness. First, the valleys, followed by the many ponds and lakes and, finally, the city and its inhabitants. As lovely as it was, she could have done without the cold.

Minnie glanced toward Yen Hsu and saw that he, too, was feeling the effects. He was rubbing his hands together and giving off dramatic shivers. When he reached into the pocket of his coat and pulled out warm gloves, she smiled to herself. Even the greatest among men can fall victim to the weather.

Yen motioned everyone to hurry into the house, while Xiang carried the last boxes out to the well-polished sedan. Yen had just received this Ford in the spring and often teased Xiang that the shining automobile did not necessarily belong to the driver. Nevertheless, the old man loved that car and maintained it to perfection.

The rest of Yen's household staff had been sent off to their families two days before. Jade thought this a prudent move, since they were without cars and could not easily escape the city. Yen did not know the exact day the invasion was planned, but he sensed it was very soon. He knew from the Chinese officers that the Japanese Army was advancing from the north and northeast, that they were poised to enter, but that they would probably wait until daytime to move their troops into Nanking. The Japanese had no idea that the Nationalist Army had all but deserted the city. Yen was patient enough to wait until the roads were clear, which would be in the dead of night. Only then would he take his wife and daughters, driving south as fast as possible. They had perhaps another three to four more hours to enjoy their home, family and friends before it was time to flee. Only then would Yen Hsu allow the splintered effects of war take another home and force another family away.

Yen watched his friends arrive. How strange that now, in the Year of the Ox, the ox's fate seemed to be the hauling away of Nanking. His eyes shifted from his friends to the gates and back to his friends. Outside that locked gate was the never-ending river of bodies, poor souls running for their lives, most of them with nowhere to go.

Chiang Kai-shek had ordered Yen to clear out of the embassy and take his family to Hangkow, but that was two days ago. Nevertheless, Yen calculated that they could reach the city by morning if the roads were reasonably clear. They had a fast car, plenty of fuel, and Xiang had already filled the hidden second tank.

Candles burned in ceremonial lanterns, Jade's elegant touch for lighting up the large house. It looked like any other party at the Hsu household, except for the extravagant works of art stacked in the hallway. No decisions had been made regarding which pieces would be packed in the car. As it was, the car was already packed to bursting. In addition to art, there was luxurious furniture, clothing made from the finest fabrics, but nearly all would have to remain. It saddened the family that so many precious objects would be left behind for the looters.

Yen Hsu welcomed each of his American friends with a hug and then rushed them into the house. "We have much to do in such little time," he explained. "First we will eat and celebrate, then we will pray, hope, and say goodbye. I have some gifts for my dearest friends, but that is for later."

Magee clapped Yen on the back. "Wait until you see what I have to show you, my friend." Speaking almost reverently, he added "Something special…from America."

"Well, let's see it," declared Yen, herding everyone into the parlor, his favorite room of the house.

Magee clutched the camera case and laughed. "In good time!"

Yen Hsu was a born host and his friends always felt welcomed in his home. For some, this place was like a second home, where they could congregate for tea, dinners, Sunday lunches, baptisms and birthdays. As much as the Americans felt at home here, the Hsu family was equally integrated into the lives and accomplishments of these dedicated Americans.

Jade's love for these friends was evident in so many ways. In the kitchen, she prepared the most complicated and creative dishes, always with the aim to please. Her sense of culinary adventure was rare for a woman of a fine family—most elite Chinese used cooks, with the mistress of the house rarely entering the kitchen. The spices she used in her cooking were so exotic that Minnie lovingly accused her of mixing potions.

Jade had not been born to wealth and comfort. She had learned her cooking skills in the rural areas of the north, then earned her keep as a cook when she lived in Shanghai. There, she refined her skills first at the elbow of a French chef, and then a chef from Thailand. By the time she became a head chef, her prowess was known throughout Shanghai.

Jade entered the room to greet her guests, intoxicating scents wafting in behind her from the kitchen. "I admit it," she laughed. "I've been cooking instead of packing." She removed her apron and ran a hand through perfect hair. "To be honest, I didn't have the heart to pack. Besides, there's little room left. I really can't believe I have to leave my home, it's so unjust."

"It's overwhelming," acknowledged Minnie, glancing around at the extensive collection of art, furniture and books. "I wouldn't know where to begin."

The tension around Jade's eyes suddenly relaxed, as if she were grateful that someone understood her plight. "How does one decide what to leave behind?" she asked. "When I left home in my teens, I had the clothes on my back and my bible, nothing more. But this—" She gestured broadly and sighed.

"Magee has trouble picking his hat!" announced Fitch, his comment quickly lightening the mood.

Magee stepped forward. "Jade, what can we do?" He looked at all the bowls and pots spread across the large table and saw that there was barely room for plates. "Looks like you've outdone yourself again. I guess we'll just have to suffer through another perfect meal!"

"I'll say," declared Fitch. "Your table is fit for kings and princes, certainly not Red Cross workers!"

Jade laughed, the lilting sound rising above the others. "I thought about all the different dishes I wanted to make and couldn't decide– so I decided to prepare them all! You should have seen me, like a woman possessed, pulling everything out of the pantry, slicing and chopping and marinating. Not only was it fun, but it helped me forget about those foreign devils."

Yen walked over to his wife and took her hand. "If you must know the truth," he said, trying to look appropriately serious, "she just didn't want to leave any food for the looters."

Jade turned and removed a cloth that had been draped over a second table. Under it sat plate after plate of delicacies.

Fitch stared wide-eyed and made a dramatic show of inhaling deeply. He walked from one end of the table to the other, commenting on the aromas emanating from each sauce and curry. "Jade, there's enough food to feed an army!" he declared, and then blushed at what could have been a serious faux pas.

"A very rich army!" responded Yen, as if rushing in to save his friend from embarrassment.

Jade walked over to the table and unceremoniously popped a morsel of egg roll in her mouth. "It's bad enough to leave our home and belongings," she said. "But, my food? No, I could not bear that."

Yen stepped to the front of the group and said, "Which brings me to—"

"Dear, please," interrupted his wife. "Wait until after we eat." Jade reached out and took his arm, eyes begging for his cooperation.

At that moment, Mei Ling and Su Lin bounded down the stairwell and rushed to their mother's side. "Ma, I'm hungry," Su Lin declared.

"I'm with you, my dear," chimed in Fitch, his enthusiasm causing the child to blush.

Su Lin was always the shy one. She was sweet where Mei Ling was smart, a dancer where Mei Ling loved music. She adored her older sister and was in heaven when dancing around the room, accompanied by Mei Ling on either the Chinese guzheng or the piano. Su Lin was the willowy and slender daughter. Standing next to her sister, one could see that she had not yet entered womanhood like Mei Ling, who was curvaceous and attracted male attention.

When Mei Ling stood beside her mother, the two women seemed to be the same age. Not because Jade looked so young or because Mei Ling carried an air of sophistication beguiling her youth. It was more that they were both elegant and almost timeless beauties. Mei Ling had inherited her mother's grace, but from her father came a cunning wit, too often ill-perceived among Chinese women. "Mei Ling is too smart for her own good," her mother often observed, but Mei Ling did not understand. She was who she was. That she happened to be a near perfect student in school, a girl who could easily beat most men in chess, checkers, go, or nearly any game devised by man—including the odd game of poker—was not something she planned. On this particular evening, she exhibited none of these talents. Instead, she had the appearance of a concerned young woman. Her hands fidgeted with the silk of her dress and her eyes moved about, from face to face, as if searching for someone not yet arrived.

Jade was not focused on her elder daughter, but on welcoming her guests. "You may start with these appetizers," she announced. "Minnie," she added, turning to her dear friend. "Could you lend me a hand with the duck?"

"Love to," she replied, and then added "Girls?" Draping an arm over the shoulders of Mei Ling and Su Lin, she guided them toward the kitchen.

Jade was already handling the pan. Inside sat a large cooked duck, beak, feet and all. She moved the extremities aside and added another few cups of steaming, pungent plum sauce. "Minnie," she said, her back to her friend.

"How was the drive over? Are you still driving around? Because if you are, I'd feel less worried about doing the same." She rotated the large pan on the stove and added another cupful of sauce. "Just how bad is it out there?"

Minnie reached for a special tea basket and studied the elegant workmanship. Then she glanced at the girls, as if weighing her response. "It's not good, but Yen said the roads should empty by nightfall. It is so very cold, too." When there was no response, she added, "From what I'm hearing, there may still be a few days before the full invasion."

"Have you seen the crowd in the streets?" declared Mei Ling. "Even in the front of the house. How is anyone supposed to get across town with that throng?"

"In my life, I've never seen this. But we managed," Minnie responded.

"Were there a lot of cars out, too?" asked Mei Ling, as if digging for something.

Minnie studied the young woman's face. "Mostly rickshaws and carts, but it's dreadful. Those poor souls, where are they all going?"

"I'll trust in my husband, as I always have," sighed Jade, as if wishing to abandon responsibility for such a untenable situation.

"Ma," asked Mei Ling. "Exactly what time did Pa say he wanted to leave?"

"I'm not sure, it's up to him, I'm just the chef. Why don't you grab some of the dishes and bring them into the dining room."

Minnie and Mei Ling grabbed large platters. Before they could start toward the dining room, Jade said, "We talked about leaving next week. And then it was three days from now, and then tomorrow. Now, Yen says we must leave tonight, under the cover of darkness. That's when I decided to just go with the flow or I may go mad." The corners of her mouth turned down and then trembled. "Thank God we have an official car."

Minnie nodded, while not really understanding what that meant. "We saw Chinese soldiers changing into civilian clothes and running. I'll be damned before I let any soldiers into the Ginling!"

Mei Ling's opened wide. "Minnie Vautrin, I've never heard you swear!"

Jade turned away from her daughter and leaned close to Minnie's ear. "Yen has two pistols under the front seat, just in case." As if not having shared this information, she put on a large smile and announced, "Let's get this food out there! Come on, no one can function on an empty stomach!"

The women headed toward the door. Just then, a thumping sound and laughter came from the other room. Minnie smiled. "Just what could that lot be up to now?"

Jade kicked open the swinging door, entered the dining room and set down her tray. The others followed suit. "We'd better see," she said with a laugh. "Knowing my husband—"

The noises increased, only this time laughter was accompanied by the sound of chairs being scooted across the wood floor. Jade and Minnie entered the parlor and found Forster, Fitch, Magee and Yen. Minnie approached Magee. " Jade has gone all out for us, so let's not have you men dawdle."

Jade was right behind Minnie and heard the warning. She smiled and shook her head. "Dinner can wait," she said, acknowledging that if Yen had led everyone into his parlor, it must be something important. And who knew? This could be the last time.

Yen's parlor was more a gallery for his photographic art. There was a Victrola against the wall, and next to it a large collection of records. A sofa covered with muted brocade and several matching chairs filled the space. This was a room designed for the enjoyment of life. Today, partially packed boxes rested along the walls and between the furniture. Antique Chinese rugs were now rolled and ready to be moved.

"Magee, come on," Forster blurted out. "Hurry up and show Yen your surprise, before you burst!"

Yen's face brightened, eyes dancing. "By all means, show me what you have!"

Magee grinned and winked at Forster. At the same time, he lovingly removed his new camera from its protective case. Holding it up for all to see, he announced like a proud new father "This is a 16-millimeter camera that shoots moving pictures!" He handed it reluctantly to his friend.

Yen examined the camera with great care and then looked up, his face reminiscent of a boy in love with a new wagon. "Oh, she's beautiful, John, simply beautiful."

Forster stared at the two men and shook his head. For one thing, Magee wouldn't allow him to even touch the darn thing. But now it was suddenly a treasure to be shared with Yen Hsu. Like a petulant child, he announced, "It's used, y'know. Probably a donation from a rich old widow." The moment the words left his mouth, his face turned hot red. With a shrug, he quickly added, "Sour grapes, sorry!"

Magee took back the prized camera. "It gives me a new purpose in life, isn't that odd? As if God has entrusted me with this to do something great."

"Don't let his spiritual comments fool you," teased Forster. "It's also his new best friend. Good luck any of us non-movie folks getting the time of day!"

Magee smiled, but it was more muted, pensive, as if his pride had been showing. As a man of God, he knew to contain—in truth, to cast out—all that smacked of self-importance.

Fitch strolled around the parlor, leaning in to view the many photographs remaining on the walls. Gone were the pictures of Chiang Kai-shek with the good Madame, including the one taken the year before with all the local diplomats and consulates. Fitch stopped in front of one image and declared, "Yen, what a great eye you have. You're an artist, not a diplomat. That's it, isn't it?"

Yen crossed the room and stood at Forster's side. "Maybe I should have been an artist," he said. "This diplomatic work seems to be a failed endeavor."

Both men studied a particular photograph hanging on the wall. It was the Yangtze, the shot taken on a bright fall day, when leaves were sweeping across a rolling embankment leading down to the massive river, with thousands of more leaves floating on the river's edge. The photograph was so vivid, yet it seemed to be painted with little dabs of color, as if Monet had set up his easel and had used tiny brushstrokes to create each leaf, each ripple on the water. Every conceivable shade of blue comprised the sky; every gray known was reflected in the animated water.

"That was one of the first Kodachrome shots developed in China," said Yen. "I had the film developed the last time I was in Shanghai. They had just had the technology installed." His voice was proud, without being boastful. "I never thought it would be the last time I'd see the place." He released a heavy sigh and then reached out to straighten the frame. "Don't worry," assured Magee. "The road will open again. After all, that's where the commerce is and I'm guessing that the Japanese want to make money on this invasion. Isn't that what war's usually all about, greed and power?"

Yen Hsu turned to face the minister. "I'm not sure anymore," he admitted, his voice suddenly controlled. "I read a memo the other day that America was supplying Japan with raw materials, most of which are being used for the Japanese war effort against us. The Americans did nothing when Japan started it all in Manchuria. And here we are now, with our capital under attack. It must be hard," he said, his voice now that of the diplomat.

"To be allies with everyone in the world. One day, isolationism could come back to haunt you, mark my words."

He glanced at Magee. "Did you think the Japanese would stop at Manchuria, at Shanghai, and now at Nanking?"

Magee raised an eyebrow. "From what I understand, the United States is not at war with anyone and we are supplying your Chiang Kai-shek with military help. Isn't that right? At least, that's what I thought."

"Yes," responded Yen, "and it is appreciated. But your country is also aiding Mao Tse Tung, our Communist enemy. A country cannot support all sides of a conflict. And look how we in the middle suffer! Chiang has the best plan for the Chinese people and he understands how industry and open commerce is our future. He could have united this country—I still believe he can—in commerce, but Japan has other ideas. America should have learned about imperialism in the last century. History is a fine teacher, but we have to pay attention to the lessons. Too often, sadly, the lesson taught is not the lesson that should be learned."

Forster waved away the comment. "I'm not a political guy like you, Yen, and I certainly respect that this is an Asian issue and America should not be involved except as humanitarians and Christians. But I can tell you one thing: Japan would never attack America. I mean, what good would that do? We're across the great divide of the Pacific, much too far away for Japan's interests."

Yen glanced toward his wife, whose face was darkened with displeasure. "Don't say I never warned you," he said, his voice softer. "I've heard about a master plan, a very imperialist master plan. Think of it: Japan is an imperialist nation at war against exactly the kind of world we want to live in. Do you think what happened in Shanghai cannot happen in San Francisco?"

"Now you're just being an alarmist," pointed out Forster. "And don't forget that you're talking to the Red Cross and some missionaries here, *not* members of the U.S. government. We're not really important in our country. We're in that humanitarian Bible- thumping class of folk." He smiled half-heartedly and added, "We're honored to be your friend and we're honored to be in your home as a guest of Nanking's most respected diplomat. And we're lucky to have ever met someone was astute as you."

Yen was not to be so easily appeased. "But don't you see? You have this incredible camera built in the United States. You come here and build universities, colleges, even hospitals, everything that my government has had trouble doing for its people. Our people consider you missionaries as the best of what America has to offer, so why wouldn't we think of you as being America? That's what Minnie's students think, that's what the merchants think, that you represent America. That every American does."

Forster and Magee stood quietly, as if recognizing that they were on a precipice and needed to proceed with care. It was Magee who finally said, "Yen, we might represent America, but we are not America. Who knows what that really is? Not me, for certain, I've lived in China since 1912."

"You are my friends, my hope for my children," said Yen. "Without you, there would be no proper education for our girls."

Magee took Yen by the shoulders. Looking directly into his eyes, he said, "We missionaries never wanted to possess China; we never wanted anything but the hearts of the Chinese people to be opened up to the love of God. Faith is what gets us by and sometimes faith is all have."

Fitch interjected. "Yes, but—"

"I have faith," interrupted Yen. "But if you believe a benevolent God will protect us all and that he doesn't want us to be afraid, why is so much of the world living in fear?"

Forster plucked another photograph from the wall. This image was a close-up of a cherry blossom, the background blurry, with one little cluster of flowers dominating the foreground. Forster knew this to be a simple long-lens trick; he had been there when Magee instructed Yen. How typical of this man to perfect it and then fashion it with his own artistic view of the world. "It was a glorious spring, Yen Hsu, with the plum blossoms at peak. Just look at this composition! It's one of my favorites."

Yen Hsu turned to Forster and urged "Please, it is my gift, take it."

" I don't know what to say, Fitch" responded Yen. "And I have nothing for you." He suddenly smiled. "Photographs are windows to the soul, each a story to tell. Think of this one as the story of Yen Hsu, the man as an artist." As if suddenly realizing his purpose for being in this room, he turned to his friends and announced, "Please, each of you, take one. Take as many as you like, as you can." His voice suddenly turning sad, tinged with uncharacteristic bitterness. "Something by which to remember the failed diplomat."

The comment silenced the room. All those energetic souls and not a sound could be heard. Finally, Fitch said what the others could only think: "I would be insulted to take one of these photographs on that premise, my friend. However, I will accept one in honor of a man I deeply respect."

Yen looked at Forster for a moment and then his face softened. "Think of these as a gift from my heart and my soul. They are how I want you to remember me. Now," he added, his face brightening once again. "Let me see this camera once more!"

Magee laughed and handed it over. In no time, they were playing with the focus, testing the various dials. Forster made a selection of three photos from Yen's collection. Yen smiled at his choices, acknowledging with a nod that Forster had good taste.

Yen played with the settings and pointed the lens out the parlor door. "This is really amazing; a portable moving picture camera."

"Best of its kind," Maggie boasted.

"I think it truly is," Yen Hsu agreed. He toyed with the focus and looked through the lens, where he caught sight of Jade, Mei Ling, Su Lin, and Minnie. "Why does this lens make everyone look so thin?" he teased.

Jade, hands on hips, declared, "You must put that machine down before it gets you into trouble, old man!" When the laughter subsided, she announced that their last dinner in this home was being served.

Jade and Minnie followed Mei Ling, who checked to be sure that the men were close behind. They passed a long, exquisite table made from cherry wood. Underneath was a little decorative rug that Minnie had never seen. On the table sat ten packages, each one wrapped with the best hand-made gift paper and silk ribbons available and each package bearing the name of friends. "What's all this?" Fitch asked, eyeing the boxes.

"After we eat, I'll tell you," said Jade, entering the dining room. "Look, my duck isn't even steaming anymore! We must eat now, really." With that, she started affectionately nudging her guests down the hall and into their seats. The men loved it.

Jade began to prepare the plates, passing them along as they were filled. From the other side of the table, Yen Hsu poured the special tea. "You know," he told his guests. "My family was not always of the gentle diplomatic disposition of Yen Hsu. My ancestors were fighters. One was Sergeant of Arms during the early Ming Dynasty. My family tree is as long as the Yangtze. We protect our family tree and our valuable heritage with determination. It is all we can pass along at the end of our days."

"Don't be so gloomy over my food, please," Jade admonished. "Let's enjoy. A toast Yen, please?"

Yen was happy to shift gears. "To friendships, to God and country and to a safe passage for us all. God bless China. Ganbei!"

"Ganbei! Here, here!" they all toasted.

Mei Ling waited for her father to finish and then held her hands out, until everyone at the table joined hands. "Lord, we give thanks for your harvest, and for the love and support of all of our friends and family during this time of great uncertainty. God, speed the day when there will be war no more. Amen."

"Amen," came the choral response. "Lovely, Mei Ling, as always," said Minnie.

"Mei Ling, dinner music?" suggested her father. Yen Hsu and Mei Ling loved classical music the way Jade loved American jazz. "We have very different tastes in music," explained Yen, "But Minnie, I guess you know that, with Jade's influence, Mei Ling is leaning towards the jazzy stuff, especially that American, Gershwin.

"True, that's a fact," laughed Mei Ling. "And the Victrola gets plenty of use." She jumped up, a piece of fresh water shrimp still in her mouth, and announced, "I know just the thing, Father." Within moments, the house filled with Gershwin's *An American in Paris*.

When Mei Ling resumed her place at the table, Magee raised his glass. "A toast to the most beautiful and hospitable women of China. Bless their hearts, each and every one."

Su Lin, irresistible as ever, said "And the girls? What about us girls?"

"God bless them all, too!" declared Fitch.

"And to our most lovely and honorable friends!" added Jade. "A toast to life and love. God knows, life can never have enough love!"

"Here, here, ganbei!" proclaimed Yen Hsu.

As quickly as the energetic toasts were made, the room fell silent, each person lost for a moment in private thoughts. Yen Hsu sat at the head of the table. To his left were Jade, Mei Ling, Su Lin, and Minnie; to his right were Magee, Forster, and Fitch. It was a bittersweet moment for this extended family, all of them sharing hope, faith, friendship and love.

The meal was lavish and piled high on the table. The tablecloth and napkins were silk and the glassware reflected extravagant designs in jeweled colors. The aroma of the food wafted with every movement of air. It seemed that merely waving a hand would cause a new scent to drift softly across the palate.

Jade studied everyone around her and felt blessed. Having been the child of humble peasants and suffering the neglect experienced by so many unwanted girls, she had once felt herself a terrible burden. At twelve, her father forced her to leave. A premier chef by eighteen, she was now living a story-book life. She had survived impossible times as a child. Now, as an adult, she was certain that they would all persevere.

As the meal progressed, Minnie's cheeks ached from laughter. Looking around at her friends, she thought what she always did while seated in this room. "If I never eat again or live another day, I will have known the very best of China."

There was love in this extended family and it served to soften the fear in their hearts. A rumble of distant guns continued in the hills, low waves of concussion making Gershwin's string movement seem out of tune when the thunderous aftermath rolled across the river city's valley. The dissonance was ignored by all, as if turning an ear away from the neighbor's annoying dog.

Unbeknownst to Yen Hsu and Jade, a large Mercedes pulled up outside the walls of their home, its flag bearing the insignia of the rising sun. The car was hidden behind the brick wall that separated the house from the road and surrounded the property. The driver exited the car and walked to the gates. Finding them locked, he returned to the vehicle. Seated in the back seat was Kenji Nezumi.

Kenji jumped out of the car and climbed onto the spare tire, then grabbed a low-lying branch and hoisted himself onto the fence. Working his way across tangled vines, he jumped into the front yard. Xiang, who was coming around from the rear, was surprised to see Kenji. Knowing him, he let the young man proceed toward the front door. At the same time, Xiang reminded himself that a revolver was waiting in the glove compartment of the sedan. Kenji checked his inside coat pocket for the documents and then felt for his leg holster. Slipped inside was the small caliber pistol issued to all junior diplomats.

Xiang saw the weapon and rushed to Yen's car. He removed the revolver and slipped it into his pocket, while eying the man's movements.

After one deep breath, Kenji rang the doorbell.

Yen motioned everyone to remain seated, but Mei Ling bounced from her chair and followed her father into the foyer. "Father, Kenji said he was going to help our family, so that must be him!"

Yen studied his daughter's face for a moment, "Mei, please go to the parlor and turn off the music," he instructed. "I will call for you." He waited for her to go into the next room and then approached the front door. Peering through the glass, he saw Xiang nodding, as if all were under control. Only then did Yen open the door. "Good evening, Kenji-san," he stated politely.

"Good evening, Honorable Yen Hsu. I apologize for interrupting your party. "

Yen's eyes narrowed and he examined his adversary. "What can I do for you, Kenji-san?"

Kenji removed the documents from his pocket. "I have transit papers, sir, to make it safer for you and your family in case you are stopped. I am proud to extend this courtesy, as a token of respect from our embassy." He bowed.

Yen Hsu nodded his appreciation, distrust still evident in his eyes. "This is a most honorable and appreciated gesture," he intoned. "It is also a gesture that surprises me, since your government severed negotiations with my government two days ago." He opened the documents and scanned them. "Who signed these?" The tall Yen Hsu was a commanding figure opposite this smaller man.

"I did," declared Kenji, pulling his shoulders back to attain full stature. "I have this power now and I thought I must help you. You have been a friend and you were an honorable negotiator, I am sorry things turned out as they did for you." Again, Kenji bowed his submission.

"I cannot say the same for your government," Yen shot back. The response was a silence made even more poignant by the cold evening. Yen Hsu finally stepped aside and motioned Kenji to enter.

"You *are* leaving tonight, right, sir?" Kenji nodded toward the suitcases and boxes stacked in the hall.

"Should we?"

"It is time, I think."

The men locked eyes, neither moving, until Mei Ling flung open the parlor door. She passed her father, placed herself next to the Japanese visitor and took his hand. "Kenji, how are you?"

Yen Hsu kept a watch on the visitor, this Japanese man with his rising sun, a man who was smiling too intimately at his daughter. "Transit papers," explained Yen. "In case we get stopped by his army."

"For all of us?" asked Mei Ling.

"As I promised," Kenji replied.

Yen looked at the man. "Promised?"

If the question had been intended to cause Nezumi discomfort, he showed no signs. "Sir, your daughter has been my English tutor for almost two years."

Yen studied them both suspiciously. If he weren't so Japanese, they might make an attractive couple.

"And your daughter is an excellent teacher, Honorable Consulate Hsu."

Jade walked in on this awkward moment and appeared confused. Kenji took one step backward and kowtowed, showing respect for the mother of the woman he loved, the wife of an important man, and a woman reputed to be a close friend of Madame Chiang Kai-shek, wife of his enemy. That Jade made no secret of hating the Japanese might have added to his obsequious behavior.

"What's going on here?" Jade asked, fuming at this interruption. She turned to her husband, one eyebrow raised, as if to say, What does this Japanese devil want now? It must be something, or why venture across town?

As if sensing her mother's anger, Mei Ling explained, "Kenji brought us transit papers, Mother, so we won't be detained. It's a gesture of honor for our family and—"

"Thank you," interrupted Jade, turning to the interloper. "That was most respectful of you; perhaps there is hope." Each word arrived as if squeezed from her throat. "Now, if you please, you must leave, we have guests." She bowed deeply, as did Kenji.

Mei Ling bowed as well, motioning to Kenji with her eyes toward the back of the house.

Kenji exited the house and saw that Xiang was no longer there. He slipped around to the side of the house, holding close to the fence that protected the garden. At the same time, Mei Ling was putting on another jazz record before sneaking down the hallway, toward the back of the house.

Suddenly, the electricity shuddered off, all the lights blinked and then went dark. The hand-cranked Victrola kept playing and the jazz riffs could be heard in all the rooms. The only light came from the Chinese lanterns. It was 4:15 in the afternoon. Not quite light, not yet dark. Neither heaven nor hell, at least not yet.

"Here are your shadows and light, Yen," said Magee. Everyone laughed nervously, but no one noticed Mei Ling slip out of the house and close the back door with precise silence.

"We have enough light to present our gifts, I guess this is a sign to pack it in," announced Jade.

As if on command, Yen Hsu fetched the packages and carried them to the table. The first package was handed to

John Magee, who opened it and found an antique bowl. "This bowl dates back to the most ancient times of the Chinese people," explained Yen. "By rights, it should be in a museum. John, I know that you will never allow that museum to be in Japan. Therefore, I leave it under your care."

Magee held the bowl tenderly, turning it around to marvel at its design. "You have my word, Yen, it will always be safe."

"It has been handed down in my husband's family for many generations," explained Jade. "We believe it to be more than five thousand years old."

Magee raised his eyebrows. "But I cannot take such a thing from you. This is your history."

"Which is why you must take it," said Yen. "And there is something more for you." He reached over and took a satchel from the corner. "Please, take this for the Chinese who seek help from the Red Cross." He handed the large bag to Magee and explained, "This is from my vault, plus an additional $50,000 US dollars was added by my government so the Red Cross can buy rice for the poor and the refugees. We are hoping that even the Japanese would not dare to rob the American Red Cross."

"God Bless you, Yen Hsu," whispered Magee, accepting the satchel.

Yen Hsu next turned to Fitch and picked up the second box. "Inside is a vessel from the Shang Dynasty, which ruled three thousand years ago. Do not worry, it is not from my family. However, I give it to you for safekeeping. It is invaluable, one of the finest examples of this art and among only a few existing in all of China. Please hide it well from the invaders."

Fitch took the box, his hands shaking. "Yen Hsu, you speak as if we will never see you again, but we will, I'm certain of it. Governments need men like you to run things, you know that."

Yen nodded to Fitch, emotion and gratitude evident in his eyes, and then turned toward Forster. "You always speak so highly of your European roots, so I naturally thought of you when deciding what to do with this." Yen Hsu carefully unrolled a beautiful pen and ink drawing done on parchment, a classic Chinese scene of a mountain setting. In the picture was a large Ibis and two people afloat in a small boat on a still pond. "This was done by Tang, from the Ming Dynasty, probably in mid-twelfth century. You know, Forster, when Europe was still in the dark ages." Yen smiled broadly, clearing enjoying the opportunity to boast his culture's long and illustrious history. He rolled up the parchment, slipped it into a bamboo tube and handed it to his friend. With that, he picked up the next box and smiled at Minnie. "These, dear friend, are for you." He removed the lid and everyone saw that there were two items inside. Yen took out a vase and placed it on the table. Next, he removed a scroll and opened it.

"Yen," breathed Minnie, a hand pressed against her chest.

"Minnie, this vase holds untold value. As for the calligraphy, it is known throughout China and is from the Ming Dynasty. It speaks to the meanings of the heart from a famous poet, Confucius. I think you will understand and appreciate the meaning. I feel as though I owe this to you for all the pranks I played on you in our youth."

Minnie took the scroll and opened it with great care. She studied the Chinese characters for nearly a minute, as if wanting to be certain to translate them to perfection. Finally, she read:

"A white house perching on yonder sunny hill,
Sons and daughters working with fun
Fetching water from the bamboo hut
Baking tea leaves in the oven
Pa grinds tea on the mill
Ma packs tea into cakes
After all the work is done
Time to keep the bamboo gates shut

Light aroma filled the moonlit mountain

Minnie looked at her friends, tears welling in her eyes.

Yen Hsu, holding Jade's hand, took Minnie's hand as well. The three smiled at each other, unable to speak. In the silence, Su Lin crossed to her mother and hugged her.

A cold breeze entered the room, causing Jade to glance toward the door. She caught sight of Mei Ling entering the room. Several lanterns flickered before being extinguished by the wind. "Where have you been?" asked Jade. "Your father has given out the gifts."

"Sorry," replied Mei Ling. "I thought I heard something outside."

Jade looked suspiciously at her daughter, but said nothing. The group launched into lively conversation. Magee was talking to Minnie about the thoughtfulness of these gifts and how sad he felt that he had nothing to give but his gold watch. "And for what?" he added. "The one on Yen Hsu's wrist is far nicer."

Fitch and Forster discussed the days to come and wondered aloud just when the invasion would take place. "According to Kenji," said Forster, "it will be any day."

Fitch pondered over that and nodded. "My last reports indicated that the Japanese are undersupplied, so perhaps this will give us a few more days. Either way, we're out of here tonight."

"I know, I know," acknowledged Forster. "But it will never be the same, will it?" Having admitted his concerns, he fell into a melancholy silence.

After an uncomfortable moment of guessing and hoping, Yen stood before his friends and family and held up a hand. The room became quiet. "It is time to gather things and to say our goodbyes. Forgive me, but it is getting dark and we must prepare." Yen was not someone to show much emotion; he was proud of that in his line of work. But tonight, looking into the questioning eyes of his dear friends, he could not help himself. Jade tried to comfort him, but it only made it worse.

Everyone nodded and murmured their hopes to see each other soon, but they knew better than to hope too high. They took their precious packages, photos and some food that Jade insisted they take and then walked to the front foyer, where Mei Ling and Su Lin fetched their coats from the hall tree and from the fainting couch in the parlor. Yen and Jade helped everyone secure their priceless heirlooms and artifacts and then stood at the door, not really wanting to open it. Fitch, Forster, Magee and Minnie made no move to leave, as if stalling for time; as if knowing that what was about to happen was anathema to them all. They looked at Yen, then at Jade, but no words could be found. Instead, they allowed their tears to speak for them.

Yen opened the thick front door and a cold blast of night air was sent through the broad hallway. There were prolonged hugs, each one a reminder of how much they had cherished being friends. When there was nothing more to be done, the little troupe of tearful missionaries retreated down the stairs to their old car. Xiang, also in tears, opened everyone's door, kowtowing to each one as they arrived at the car door. No one needed to tell him that he might never see these wonderful people again.

"You cleaned the windows," said Magee, placing his hand on Xiang's arm, understanding that this little gesture was replete with love and respect.

Xiang rushed to the gate, opened it, and then stood there at attention while the missionary car half-circled the drive and headed onto the road. Magee stuck his head out the window and yelled, "Safe journey!" As the car moved into the main road, Minnie put her face in her hands and wept.

The roads were much less cluttered than earlier. It was almost dark, so perhaps Yen was right. As the car rounded the curve, Fitch saw the Japanese consul's car and the silhouette of a man smoking in the front seat. "Kenji never smoked," he thought, but he said nothing.

"I can hardly wait for the day when we all meet up with Yen and Jade again," said Forster. "I guess maybe in Hangkow?"

The sedan picked up speed, its occupants holding tight to their gifts. Each of them understood the weight of the gesture, which far exceeded the value of each piece. As much as he tried to push the thought aside, Magee could not stop thinking of the enormous sum of cash now sequestered under the front seat. He had never held fifty thousand dollars before. The sooner he returned to the safety of the Red Cross building, inside the old city walls, the sooner he could relax.

The early night sky changed hues as the four friends continued toward the old city walls and the Xuan Wu Gate. As they passed through intersections, they caught glimpses of the Purple Mountains. It took a moment to realize that the lovely glow and flashes across the sky were caused by distant explosions of canon fire.

As soon as Yen and Jade were upstairs, Mei Ling ran out the rear door. There, hidden in the shrubs between the front and back yard, waited her love. Mei Ling took one glance behind her and then turned and threw herself into Kenji Nezumi's silent arms. He held her firmly against him and then kissed her passionately. When she tried to pull away, he held her and kissed her again.

"Kenji, don't," she protested, glancing up to where she knew her parents were packing. "Father could see us."

"It doesn't matter," Kenji responded. "You're coming with me." He looked around. "Where are your things, Mei Ling? We must go now!"

Mei Ling pushed back and looked directly in his eyes. "Not yet. I must say goodbye in my own way. I can't just disappear in the night air."

Kenji's expression darkened slightly. "I'll send a messenger."

Mei Ling shook her head. "My father will come for me and then what would you do?"

"My car is just outside your gate." He took her by the elbow and made as if to leave. When Mei Ling pulled away, he exhaled loudly.

Mei Ling touched Kenji's face. "I love you, but this is not the way. Where would we live? How could we–"

Kenji waved away her questions. "We will live in my quarters, as if we were man and wife!"

"As if we were—"

"Mei Ling, you must realize that I cannot marry you in a time of war. "

"But, this is not right and my family would never allow it."

His expression of frustration quickly shifted to scorn. As if he knew he were about to say something that would anger her, he took a slow deep breath. "The truth is, your parents will never stand for us being together, whether in time of war or peace. This you must accept sooner or later."

"I don't know, Kenji," said Mei Ling, doubt crossing her lovely face. "To me, my family is everything, they have always been very understanding."

Kenji removed something from his pocket and held it out to her. "Mei Ling, a woman wears this so that her man will have luck and good fortune during challenging times. I want you to wear it for me." He took the chain and placed it around her neck. Hanging from it was a large gold ingot emblazoned with a Kanji symbol. "This stands for love and faith," he said.

Mei Ling held the ingot and turned it until it caught the faint light. "It is very nice and very…heavy."

"My mother gave it to me before she died," said Kenji. "She would want the woman I love to have it."

Mei Ling gazed at Kenji with the eyes of a young woman in love for the first time. That she was the daughter of a Chinese diplomat, that he was now the enemy, weighed heavily on her. Mei Ling nearly wept at the hopeless situation they were facing.

The quiet between them was shattered by Jade's voice. "Mei Ling!" she called out. "Mei Ling!"

Mei Ling slipped the chain off and handed the necklace to Kenji. "Hold on to it, I'll be back soon," she promised. "I'm already packed."

Kenji pressed the necklace into her hand. "You must keep it close, wear it always." When she resisted, he begged, "You can't leave with them. You won't leave, right? Mei Ling, please, stay with me!"

Mei Ling kissed him with fervor. "Give me five minutes, wait for me in your car." Her heart pounded over the distant rumble of canons as she rushed into the house. She stopped by the door and slipped on the necklace, making sure to tuck the ingot under her bodice. As she bounded up the steps, she was unaware that the necklace was now visible.

Jade was waiting at the top of the stairs. When Mei Ling entered, Jade closed the door behind them. The electricity flickered on, illuminating the ingot. Jade stepped forward and touched it, then stared hard at her defiant daughter. "This will never be, it cannot!"

Mei Ling raised her chin and returned the hard stare. "I am packed, but I am staying. If Minnie won't have me, I'll be with Kenji."

"Yen!" shouted Jade. "Yen!" She tried to speak, to reason with this insolent child, but no words would come. All she could do was stare, eyes wide with fury and fear.

The city was about to fall to ruins and here were two beautiful women, mother and daughter, facing off in shared defiance. Jade was enraged, she also realized that, in some ways, she had created this by allowing Mei Ling such latitude. What she was seeing was the same willfulness so evident in Yen Hsu. The difference was that he was an adult and a man. But hadn't he repeatedly told Mei Ling how smart she was, how far she could go? But why a Japanese, why the enemy? Jade wanted to rant, to accuse her daughter of foolishness, but something was stopping her. Jade knew in her heart that she would have left her family for the man she loved. In truth, she had done just that, and so had her mother. Chinese girls were taught to act with submission, but this was not a trait passed on to Jade, nor to her daughters. Now, she recognized this as less a blessing than a curse.

Jade was anxious for Yen Hsu to appear. Surely he could use his diplomatic finesse to convince Mei Ling that this choice might result in her never seeing her family again.

The women continued to stare at each other. They might have remained like that for hours had Yen not suddenly arrived. When Jade spilled out her fears about their daughter, he was clearly agitated. He, too, fell silent. The void was suddenly filled by a loud explosion. Yen embraced his wife and daughter, struggling with his own fears and anger. "Daughter, you are me," he told her. "You are my life. You will leave with us and we will leave in five minutes, that is final." With that, he turned and left them, joining Xiang who was struggling with yet another load of boxes.

Mei Ling reached out to her mother in tears. "You have lived with no regrets," she said, her voice pleading, nearly a whisper. "Please, you must let me do the same."

Jade turned away and cried out "Yen! Please, don't leave us here trying to—" But he was out of earshot and of no help to her.

Outside, Kenji darted behind the bushes and climbed over the fence, getting leverage from the branches of trees surrounding the courtyard. He reached his car and began to pace, blowing into his hands for warmth. His driver waved him inside, but instead he climbed onto the car and peered over the fence. He saw Yen Hsu sitting on the trunk of his car and attempting to close it. He saw Xiang replace his master, bouncing hard in hopes of securing the trunk. He watched Yen enter the house and heard Jade's cries. Kenji tried to hear, but the voices were too far away.

There was a sudden ripping sound, the crackle and explosion of large cannon fire probably two blocks away. A building exploded. This was the first cannon attack inside the inner city.

Xiang yelled, "We must go now! It is time to go" Seconds later, there was a piercing whistle high in the sky, which became louder and more menacing as it neared the house. As if having been delivered from hell, a canon shell exploded in the courtyard exactly where Xiang was waiting, having landed precisely in the middle of that shiny black sedan that was Yen's. The explosion was trebled by the detonating of the car's gas tank. A millisecond later, the backup tank exploded and shock waves blasted out all the windows in the front of the house, sending shards of glass everywhere. When the air cleared, there was nothing left. No Xiang, no car, only a charred hole where they had once stood. The front of the house was a mass of charcoal, blood and tissue. The lovely plum tree was splintered down the middle, a section of the car's bumper wedged into its woody foundation.

Kenji had been standing on the car, on the other side of the wall. The blast knocked him to the street and reverberated through his body, ears clanging and pain flashing behind his eyes. He stumbled, nearly knocking over a peasant who was reeling. There was blood on this stranger's tattered clothing and a jagged piece of glass projecting from his shoulder. Kenji started for the gate, but his driver grabbed him and pulled him back.

"We need to return to the embassy," insisted the driver.

Kenji shook him off and tried to run for the gate, which now hung by one tenacious hinge. He got close enough to see that the front of Mei Ling's home was nearly destroyed. There were smoldering flames and puddles of molten steel where the car had once been. He felt a strong clutch on his arm and he allowed his driver to lead him back to the car. In seconds, they were in the car and driving away.

Before the chauffeur could get clear of the disaster, however, another shell landed. It was perhaps two hundred yards behind them and smaller than the first. Kenji huddled down in the back seat, his body trembling from the shock. Had the entire house been destroyed, or only the front? And if it was the house, had anyone survived?

The car advanced slowly, debris still hanging in the air like black snow. Kenji stared out of the little oval window, looking more like a lonely child peering through the back of a bus. Tears traced a path down his cheeks, yet his fists were balled in frustration. He could have protected her! Why was she so stubborn? The thought of a life without Mei Ling was impossible to comprehend, unbearable.

Inside the house, Yen was crumpled on the floor, cut and bleeding from dozens of glass fragments piercing his skin. He released a moan, which reminded him that he was alive. What only minutes earlier were the most deafening sounds he had ever experienced was now utter silence. Nothing but dust, blood and silence.

Yen groaned again and managed to roll onto his side. He caught sight of Jade and Mei Ling, the impact pushing them against the wall at the far end of the hallway. They lay in two heaps, rag dolls thrown into the corner. Su Lin was nearby, propped against a chair, head hanging forward.

It took some time for the family to stir. Jade made it to her knees and crawled toward Mei Ling, who was just beginning to look around in shock. Jade tried to stand, but found it difficult, so she dragged herself to Su Lin and satisfied herself that the child was unharmed. Finally, Jade stood and returned to her oldest child, using all of her strength to help the young woman to her feet. Everyone made an effort to speak. Only then did they realize that they could not hear a word. They could move their mouths, but nothing seemed to cross their eardrums. Yen got to his feet and hobbled toward his family. Su Lin went to him, arms out, clothing tattered. Mei Ling and Jade joined them and followed Yen through the debris and toward the front of the house. As they neared the door, Su Lin stopped. She opened her mouth, but no sound came out as she pointed at the abyss that had once been their front yard, where their car had once sat.

It took several moments for them to realize that Xiang was gone, vaporized by a direct hit of a shell launched by the Japanese. Small sections of the car smoldered around the deep pit. Su Lin ran into the open space and screamed "Xiang! Xiang!" Her mother rushed up behind her and held her close. Yen barked at his family to come inside. Guiding them along what remained of the hallway, he pushed aside a charred rug under the table and revealed a trap door. Motioning them into total silence, he opened the door and revealed a staircase leading down into total darkness. One by one, he helped Jade and the girls crawl down the stairs into the bomb shelter.

When everyone was safely below, Yen reached up, pulled the carpet over the trap door, and then lowered it. Jade lit a single lantern in the basement, where they huddled, shivered and cried. Very soon, another bomb exploded just outside the house, causing everything stored on the shelves to rattle.

It was nearly a half hour before their hearing began to return. They heard Su Lin cry, silently at first, and then her sobs increased. Jade held her, shushing the girl and rocking her. "Father," asked the girl. "Are we going to die, too?"

Yen Hsu looked at his younger child and pulled her onto his lap. He glanced toward his wife, eyes beseeching as he worked to comfort Su Lin.

"We'll be fine," whispered Jade. "We have supplies, we'll be fine."

Su Lin cocked her head as if hearing something overhead. Fear was apparent in her face. Jade reacted by blowing out the candle and holding a finger to her lips.

Kenji's driver wove through the streets, driving over anything in his way. Kenji sat in the back, hands clenching and unclenching, sweat pouring from his face, leaning forward to get some blood to his head so he wouldn't throw up. "Mei Ling!" he shouted. "Mei Ling! Oh God, what have they done? What have I done?" The car suddenly collided with a young peasant, who bounced off the fender, face gushing with blood as he slid past Kenji's window. Kenji buried his head in his hands, a broken man. If his Emperor were truly a man-God, how could he allow this to happen? How could he deprive his faithful servant of the only woman he had ever loved?

The bomb had devastated a house and a family, but it had also destroyed one of the greatest supporters of the invasion. Kenji had believed with ferocity never before experienced that greatness was in his future and that his life would glow under the rising sun. Now, he was nothing.

His driver leaned on the horn to clear the road of the victimized. Bombs exploded everywhere, buildings disintegrated and bodies were cremated on the spot. The invasion had begun early and it was hell on earth. It had been ordered so.

Kenji's hell had just begun.

THIRTEEN

There was anarchy in the streets. The Japanese army advanced rapidly into Nanking, gunshots and screaming emanating from every corner. Fires raged in stores, with flames jumping from building to building in minutes. Food and provisions that could have sustained a population were destroyed. Japanese soldiers swarmed into the city and found peasants huddled everywhere: in alleyways, churches, shops and schools. The bedraggled homeless offered no resistance. When discovered, they emerged from hiding with hands raised. After a quick inspection, men of army age were shot on sight, while the women were dragged into side streets. Brutality was the order of the day and soldiers readily slit the throats or abdomens of the women after they were done with them. They were instructed to demoralize the Chinese. After all, this was the capital of China, so let the Chinese people see how futile it was to resist the mighty Imperialist.

Minnie, Fitch, Forster and Magee rode in silence near the safety zone, only one mile ahead of the oncoming soldiers. The lines of refugees became more compressed as they reached the entrance to the safety zone, primarily because there was no place for them to go. Magee filmed whatever he could, desperately hoping to capture in perpetuity this entire nightmare, but it was too dark outside. As for his companions, the scenes were being etched in their minds, images that would remain forever.

Minnie pressed her face against the window and prayed for these people being victimized by the brutal Japanese. She asked God why such suffering and destruction were taking place, but no answers came. The violence seemed even more brutal because the Chinese army was not fighting back, nor were the citizens. Nanking had been abandoned and was there for the Japanese to seize quickly and peacefully, but this was not happening.

As the car pulled up in front of the gates leading to the college, Minnie gasped. In a few short hours, the magnitude of the crowd had grown substantially. How many there were, she had no idea, but they were pressing against the gates, desperate for food and shelter. Minnie climbed out of the car and, as she made her way through the gate, a bomb exploded somewhere outside the safety zone, perhaps a half-mile away. The noise caused her to stumble, but she regained her footing and rushed into a building. She hoped to find Mary Twynam, who would help her move the students belowground to safety.

Within a few minutes, the women had shifted everyone into the basement. Outside, the night sky above Nanking was on fire with exploding shells, the work of the Japanese army entering the city from the west.

"Are we going to get bombed, Miss Minnie?" asked a twelve year-old girl.

"We'll be fine," soothed her headmistress. "Remember, we're in the safety zone, so no harm will befall us. Besides," she added, giving the girl a reassuring hug. "We're luckier than most because it's not so noisy down here! Have faith girls," she announced. "It will stop, once they advance on the city,"

More girls filed in, many of them sitting on the floor on little blankets, but the supply was short. Mary left the basement in search of blankets and water.

The girls huddled together, a single lantern illuminating their sanctuary. The walls around them were lined with shelves filled with items from their classrooms and the library. Minnie noted some of the more valuable items and then looked at her girls. Was this the last place they would ever be? Was this where all of them would meet their end? She noted how the girls fidgeted, some of them shivering from fear or cold.

Just as Mary returned, another explosion caused objects to vibrate throughout the basement. Several of the girls screamed and the youngest girls, not yet teenagers, hugged one another and trembled with fear. Soon, the bombs were detonating every ten to twenty seconds. Minnie began to hum "What a Friend We Have in Jesus" and, after the first few bars, Mary declared "My goodness, with music in our hearts, we fear not. Let's sing, girls!" Soon, the basement was filled with soprano voices, joined together to create a unified sense of security and hope. With Minnie leading the choir, they sang:

What a Friend we have in Jesus, all our sins and griefs to bear!

What a privilege to carry everything to God in prayer!

O what peace we often forfeit, O what needless pain we bear,

All because we do not carry everything to God in prayer.

Have we trials and temptations? Is there trouble any-where?

As they sang, much of the fear evident in their faces only minutes earlier began to ease away, and then, as if by a miracle, the echo of the bombs diminished as well. For the younger girls, this was seen as a good sign. The older ones, however, were not so easily convinced.

Jun, a nineteen year-old sophomore, whispered to Minnie, "Does this mean the Japanese army is in Nanking?"

Minnie bent closer until only Jun could hear. "I think so, and we must thank God that we are deep in the safety zone, tucked away in the Ginling College."

"But I have heard terrible things, Miss Minnie. I heard that in Shanghai, the women and children—" She could not go on and leaned into Minnie for comforting.

Minnie stroked Jun's arm. "We're next to the Japanese and German embassies, remember? Japanese planes won't bomb their own people. Also, what do have that soldiers could possibly need? We're no threat, just a school filled with hungry peasants and students. Remember," she added, "God is in your heart and you must keep Him close.

Suddenly, the world outside became eerily quiet. Minnie stood and straightened her skirt. "So you see?" she announced. "The shelling has stopped and the worst might now be over!" Turning, she walked up the stairs very slowly, feeling at her back the eyes of Mary and the girls. When she was high enough to see through a window, she peeked through and nearly cried out. Nanking was in flames. As if driven by an unseen force, she looked down into her children's faces. Their world was on fire and it was her responsibility to be strong and show that she still had faith, that she still carried the strength of the Lord in her heart.

She descended the steps and stood before the girls. "Let us all kneel and pray. In so doing, we will be closer to God." Together, they knelt and murmured the Lord's Prayer. The words were Chinese, but the rhythm was that of the English version. When they finished reciting this prayer, Minnie began anew. Soon, they were chanting it repeatedly, until the sound rose as a song and filled every space of this dark, fusty space. After a verse and a chorus, Minnie nodded and, in English, the congregation intoned "Amen".

The group remained quiet, the only sounds being another distant blast, followed by an illumination that filled the night sky. One explosion followed another, each one causing quiet panic among the children. Minnie's face appeared pallid, almost ghostlike, whenever a flash lit up the basement. She could never admit this—at least, not then—but she struggled to control her breathing, made faster by fear, and she had to fight the urge to clutch her chest. In her head came the pounding of her heart, as if every fourth beat was synchronized with the thunder of bombs exploding nearby.

FOURTEEN

General Matsui Iwane was the leader of the invasion force, a veteran who had led the attack on Shanghai the previous month. Nanking was presenting unexpected problems; he never expected getting to this port city to take so long, but they were having constant problems keeping the supply lines open. Continental Decree Number Seven had been issued a week earlier and it was very clear: The Central China Theater Commander was to cooperate with the Navy regarding the attack of Nanking, the capital of the enemy nation. This put into motion the advancement of Japanese soldiers from all sides but one, which was the 6th Division, headed west from Huzhou. When the 6th caught up with a second division, they proceeded from the left flank. A third division joined in for the maritime assault and would later cross the Yangtze into Nanking.

High in the Zijan Mountains, four fighting units stared down at their prey, Nanking. The city shone with early morning life, but after a night of bombing, it was the glow of smoldering sadness and a forlorn destiny.

The Japanese army was certain the city could be theirs even before it marched in earnest. They skulked through the thick morning mist surrounding the gelid city, carrying the flag of the Rising Sun proudly before them. They intended to demoralize the Chinese government and its people, to break the back of every resistor. The Japanese military was fraught with hubris and sincerely believed that they could conquer all of China. One way to maximize the possibility was to paralyze the major cities and Nanking was the capital of Chiang Kai-shek's new government. Taking Nanking also meant bringing to their knees Chiang and his arrogant wife. The army's orders were to be relentless, to move through Nanking and leave the mark of Japan on every building. The Japanese soldiers had undergone a rigorous and lengthy training and they looked forward to the day when China became a Japanese colony. A concise and brutal victory over the people of Nanking was what they needed. That was the order; the time had finally arrived.

General Matsui was furious when told that pockets of strong resistance continued to surround the city. The Chinese would not quit! He knew that members of the noble class—government workers, businessmen, the wealthy— had long since fled; he also knew that the opium lords had stayed. They had already been contacted and were awaiting further instructions. The opium lords were Chinese, but business was business.

From the air, planes dropped their bombs and shelled the small boats on the river. As the bombs landed, people and belongings became confetti. The lucky ones perished quickly, but many others were less fortunate and suffered blood loss, while many drowned fighting to escape the river's clutches. On land, Japanese soldiers invaded the Siemens power plant and then inspected each worker's hands for signs of calluses, which would indicate military service. They hauled most of the men out of the buildings, lined them up against walls and shot them.

The larger cannons fired on the city center, destroying power poles, buildings, homes, vehicles and the roads that had been like veins pumping life out of the city as the populace fled. Men, women, and children ran for their lives, but many did not make it. Everywhere one looked there were scattered pockets of lagging Chinese Nationalist soldiers, many of them feverishly ripping off their uniforms and running for their lives. From a Japanese truck's loudspeaker came "Lay down your weapons and your life will be spared!" Propaganda trucks rolled up and down the streets blaring the same mantra.

On a hillside above Nanking, General Yatsui was ordering another bombing attack. "We will have the city by lunch, if this is our Emperor's desire," he announced. "This will not be a repeat of Shanghai. It is time to show these people the high cost of resistance."

Sergeant Nomo turned to his superior. "General, sir, our cannons can't reach the middle of the city."

"Then use bigger shells!" demanded the general.

"We have exhausted our supply, sir, and only a few large shells remain."

Yatsui snorted his frustration. He looked toward the city, the target awaiting his attack, and hardly flinched when the radio suddenly barked Japanese orders to halt the shelling.

"This is General Yatsui," he responded. "Why must we stop shelling?" When he learned that his shells were landing on his own troops, he was aghast. "Sergeant Nomo!" he bellowed, stepping away from the radio.

Nomo rushed toward him. "Yes, sir!"

The General pointed his sword high in the air. "One more for the Emperor, Nomo, so aim high. This one's for my family's honor!" He gestured skyward, a vein running along his temple pulsing with force. "Aim as Hirohito would have it!" He pointed to his artillerymen. In seconds, the cannon was in place and aimed high.

Fire!" Nomo screamed, and the cannon discharged one last shot that blasted into the air, flying high across the dark sky, its arc wide as it descended past some of the finest homes and the widest streets and traveled toward Yen Hsu's neighborhood.

FIFTEEN

Yen Hsu took two of the family photos from his coat pocket and looked at Jade. His family would be fine, as long as the rug still covered the trapdoor. When it was safe. they would sneak out in the early morning and run to the safety zone. Hoping to calm everyone, he smiled and hugged Jade, the girls clinging to their mother's side.

Jade took one of the photos from her husband and could not help but look long at Xiang's face, he had been part of their family and was taken so suddenly. She was deeply grateful that her girls had not witnessed the death of a man they dearly loved.

Jade whispered a silent thanks that Yen had not been outside and wondered how she could ever live without him. She also thanked God for the insight to get her mother and the two young boys out the day before.

Yen Hsu and his family huddled together, wrapped in multiple blankets, Yen rubbing his ears and working his jaw, as if this would help his hearing to return. The girls were frightened and tired, and everyone was trying to cling to sanity. Yen looked into their faces and could not help but think how beautiful they were.

In truth, Mei Ling was one of the most beautiful young women Nanking had ever seen. Members of the Hsu family had always possessed a noble look, but Mei Ling was unusually stunning. That she was also smart and determined added to her uniqueness. At this moment, however, Yen saw her only as his little girl, the one who asked the most difficult questions and who had always shown a fierce determination to protect her family. He recalled that even as a child of ten, Mei Ling's fiery eyes could make the family elders stand back with wonder. Chinese girls were not supposed to act with such spirit. Perhaps she would grow to be like her heroine, Madame Chiang Kai-shek.

Yen heard the girls whisper and was relieved that his hearing had returned. He was about to say something when, with no warning, an enormous blast shook the basement. He covered his family with his body and whispered reassuring words. "We must stay hidden until the fighting stops," he told Jade, his hand cupped against her ear so the girls could not hear.

"What then?" she asked, eyes wide with concern.

He shifted until his back leaned against a crate. "With our diplomatic status and Kenji's transit papers, they should let us pass, we'll be fine."

"Jade took a deep breath and let it out slowly, as if relieved to know that Yen had a plan. She turned to Su Lin and stroked the child's hair. The girl had such a sweet face and she carried her innocence with pride. If only she could hold on to that innocence through this difficult time.

Yen touched Jade's hand and leaned closer. "I need to go up for a few minutes and look around." When he saw her concern, he added, "To check for any fires... and to get the pistol from the parlor." He turned to his daughters and suggested they try to get some sleep.

As he stepped onto the first stair, Mei Ling grabbed his hand. "Are you sure it's safe to go above, Father? You're staying in the house, aren't you?"

Yen looked at Jade, their eyes communicating the same thought. Without a word, they helped the girls up and into the hiding space and closed the secret panel. Jade put her face close to the hiding area and in a low voice warned "Whispers girls, whispers." And then she followed Yen up the stairs.

Yen inched the trapdoor open and peered out. When he saw that it was clear, he ascended, Jade behind him and moving so quietly he was hardly aware of her presence. When they reached the hallway, they looked around, Yen toward the disintegrated front door and Jade toward the back door and kitchen. "Well, come on, let's go!" she urged.

Yen took her by the arm. "Please be careful," he told her.

She gently pulled her arm away. "It's quiet now and I won't take long, I promise."

His eyes revealed deep concern. "Meet back here in one minute, no more," he told her, then crept down the hall toward the parlor, careful to step across broken panes of glass that had once been his front windows. When he looked out, his face revealed shock. The sky was shimmering in reds and oranges. In every direction, his beloved city was engulfed in flames. He opened the desk, grabbed the remaining bullets and shoved them into his pocket. The sound of faraway explosions gave him pause: he fished out several more bullets and loaded his pistol. He turned to leave and was stopped by a photograph of his family that had been blown to the floor. He picked up the frame and touched the faces of his children. The sound of tanks rolling nearby caused him to rush from the room, just as machine gun bullets ricocheted across his front yard.

A few hundred yards from Yen Hsu's home, one lone tank stood in the middle of the boulevard, taking shots at the last few Chinese soldiers giving their heartfelt best to defend their city. The stalwarts were perched atop the roof of a two-story home nearby, trying to hold off a tank with a single machine gun. The tank's 50-caliber cannon slowly turned toward the top of beautiful house and fired. The machine gunner and his comrades were decimated and a corner of the lovely home gone in a flash. The house caught fire and began to burn.

Yen watched helplessly as his neighbor's house became a conflagration. He turned to rejoin his wife and his elbow nudged a ceramic figurine, which fell to the floor and shattered, a noise that reverberated into the night. His heart beating frantically and he crouched down and looked through the broken window, its tattered curtains fluttering in the cold wind. Several soldiers were standing near his front gate and looking his way. One of them trained his eye on the fragmented front door and then checked the windows, one by one. He made a comment to his comrades and they walked away. Yen mumbled a silent prayer and scurried back toward the trapdoor.

As Jade was emerging from the kitchen, laden with food and drink, she, too, heard the blast from the tank and froze there, unmoving, until Yen appeared and led her to the trap door. He crouched, preparing to shift the rug, and motioned for Jade to come closer. When she did not move, he tried again, but she remained as still as a deer in the forest. Suddenly, he heard a sound and followed her frozen gaze. A Japanese soldier was standing just outside the splintered door, rifle and bayonet at the ready. Everything in Jade's grasp fell crashing to the floor. Yen quickly pushed the small rug over the trap door and backed up, shielding his wife. They stood together, unmoving, as the soldier walked toward them, bayonet extended.

Yen Hsu tried to hand off the pistol surreptitiously to Jade, but she was unable to respond. He saw a second soldier enter, and then two more.

Under the floorboards, Mei Ling gripped her sister's hand, the harsh voices of Japanese soldiers overhead. The girls were motionless, frightened eyes staring straight up.

Within minutes, Yen and Jade had their hands tied behind them and were forced to their knees. With a bayonet pointed at them, the invaders began to rip apart the house. Furniture, china, artwork, everything was taken to a waiting truck. One soldier picked up Yen's gun and waved it at Jade, who squeezed her eyes shut. The same man kicked

Yen with full force in the stomach, causing him to collapse to the floor. The contents of his stomach rushed into his throat and pain shot through his body. "Get up!" demanded the soldier. Yen struggled to his knees, wincing when a knife was placed against his throat. He turned and saw that another soldier had forced Jade's head to the ground with a well-placed boot. For the first time in their marriage, he regretted his wife's beautiful body and elegant clothing.

"Where is your money!" demanded a soldier in bad Chinese.

Yen tried to turn toward the voice, pain gripping his ribs. "I'm a diplomat," he insisted, speaking Japanese, which seemed to surprise and anger the soldiers. "I am a friend of your government. I have official papers, let me—"

One of the soldiers struck Yen across the face with his pistol. As if to exert his authority, he swung around and fired at a large vase, its shattered pieces falling onto Jade's head.

In the hiding place, Su Lin whimpered meekly and Mei Ling covered her mouth. "Say nothing!" she whispered. When the girl nodded, she removed her hand. There was another series of footsteps overhead and Mei Ling felt her sister's body tremble. Before she could respond, a mewing sound came from the girl's throat.

"Did you hear that?" asked one of the soldiers.

Mei Ling looked at her sister, whose eyes were wide with terror. The younger girl opened her mouth, but made no sound. There were more footsteps overhead and then somebody was standing on the trap door. Mei Ling stopped breathing; every second stretched out to an endless, agonizing count.

Sergeant Ushino, a heavy-set brute of a soldier, looked at Jade repeatedly, as if unsure what to do. The insignia on his uniform indicated that he was no ordinary soldier, but part of the diplomatic corp. Jade had only seen this on Kenji's uniform. Her face radiated beauty and strength, her skin luminescent in the dim and foreboding light, but her glare was an affront to the man. No Chinese woman was permitted to look at a Japanese man with such contempt.

"What is wrong with your woman?" demanded Ushino, prodding Yen with his boot.

"She is frightened, that's all, but I assure you—" Before he could go on, a rifle butt was driven into his side.

Ushino grunted and said, "I know who you are, I know all about you." He took a step closer to Jade and touched her hair. "But I never heard about such a nice wife." He ran his hand across her face and down her shoulders, grinning hideously when she tried to turn away. "So tell me, lovely lady, where are your sweet young daughters?"

Jade gasped and Ushino laughed hoarsely. He looked Jade up and down, as if sizing up a racehorse. "I think I know what she wants," he muttered. Grabbing Jade by the arm, he dragged her down the hall and toward the parlor.

"Leave her alone, please!" Yen begged, struggling to gain his footing. When he was kicked again, he fell whimpering to the floor. "I have many things of value, please take them," he pleaded. "Take it all."

Ushino paused for just a moment, as if weighing this offer, and then shoved Jade into the parlor. With Yen yelling behind him, he pinned his captive against the wall. Excited by her beauty, he tore off her jacket and threw her onto the fainting couch. As she twisted and screamed, he ripped away her blouse, revealing the smooth white skin of her breasts. This was the couch on which Yen and Jade had made love, on which their daughters nestled, books in their laps and their parents sitting nearby. Now, this was where Jade was living her worst nightmare.

Ushino continued to rip away her clothing, his breathing rapid and sweat pouring from his pudgy face. Mei Ling and Su Lin heard their mother's screams and could do nothing but remain in the dark, crouched together in terror. Dust kicked up from the tramping soldiers fell through the floorboards and into their eyes. They were only a few feet from the parlor and felt the vibrations from the couch, heard the floorboards creaking. "Yen! Yen!" cried Jade, but Ushino silenced her with a blow to the face. How could a woman fight off such a large man, especially when rage and passion fed his strength?

Yen called out for his wife, but was again struck into silence.

"Where is the money!" demanded the soldier who stood over Yen.

"Tell him to stop and I'll tell you," begged Yen.

"Hey, Ushino!" the soldier cracked from the hallway.

Ushino stopped his attack. Using Jade's blouse, he tied her hands to a knob on the couch and then gagged her with her camisole. He stood and Jade immediately relaxed, as if relieved that the worst was over. Ushino joined his comrade in the hallway and saw him remove a large wad of cash from Yen's sock. The soldier thumbed through it, stuffed it into his pocket, and used his boot to land several swift blows to Yen's midsection. When Yen collapsed and appeared to lose consciousness, he smiled. "We'll divide it later," he told Ushino, who grinned and walked back into the parlor. Behind him, his friend called out, "We've got the money. How about we take these two and leave?"

By then, Ushino was standing over Jade. Tied and gagged, her shoulders and breasts glistening with sweat, she roused his animal passions. As she turned her face away, he pulled at the waistband of her skirt. Jade planted one foot on the floor and pushed so hard that the couch budged. Ushino grinned at her efforts to escape. As he fumbled with his belt, Jade kicked out, her foot digging into his thigh. She spit the gag out of her mouth when Ushino fell back a few feet, stunned. Jade managed to free one hand and then stood, trying to strike out. The much larger Ushino took a fistful of her hair and shoved her, her head striking the couch's frame with a sickening thud. In the hallway, Yen struggled to remain conscious and tried to crawl to his wife. "I am a diplomat!" he kept insisting. "I have friends at your embassy and papers from Kenji Nezumi. For the love of God—"

The soldier reached down and pulled a photograph from his captive's pocket. "Where are these girls!" he screamed, spittle landing on Yen's face.

When Yen said nothing, he suffered another boot to the stomach. "Gone," he gasped, barely raise his head to look the soldier in the eye. "They left yesterday."

"Really?" the soldier questioned, swinging his boot yet again into this uncooperative dignitary. The other soldiers, watching the brutal entertainment, laughed.

"Leave us alone, please!" beseeched Yen, the sound of Jade's cries and Ushino's grunting striking him with more force than any boot.

The soldier landed one last kick against Yen's back. "He's a traitor, even to his own people, he has no honor" he announced. "Take him away, then finish searching this disgusting house." He glanced around, as if shopping in the local furniture store. "I want this table," he instructed, pointing to an ornate table in the hallway. "And those chairs," he added, indicating the two French chairs flanking the table. "Load them into my truck. And then look for those girls! If you find them, let me know right away."

"You bastards!" blurted Yen, trying to muster the energy to fight. A blow to the back of his head knocked him unconscious and he was immediately dragged out of the house and down the stairs, his head bumping against each wooden riser. Black soot rose from the step with each contact.

Inside, the group's commander pointed out assorted rugs, including the small one that covered the trapdoor behind him.

Jade struggled against the pain and tried to rise. Being raped by this animal was one thing; leaving her daughters to the whim of these beasts was quite another. With all her might, she dug her foot into Ushino's groin, causing him to scream so dramatically that several of his comrades raced to his defense. Driven by rage and humiliation, he pushed away his friends and prepared to finish the job. "You bitch," he growled, pants now pulled down. "Nagoya," he barked, calling one of the underlings to his side. "Hold her down for me." Nagoya gripped Jade by both wrists and pulled them above her head, his eyes shining as he watched her writhe under his grasp. She opened her mouth and released a piercing cry, but Ushino struck her and she almost blacked out.

Mei Ling and Su Lin, directly beneath the parlor, looked up, light rays from lanterns and flashlights finding their way through the floorboards and onto the girls' faces. Overhead, someone was causing great harm to their mother. Su Lin shook uncontrollably and clung to her sister, who in turn tried to calm the girl. But Mei Ling, older and more aware, knew what was happening and was helpless to act.

Ushino grabbed Jade by the shoulders, flipped her over and tried to penetrate her from behind. Jade, barely conscious now, struggled, but to no avail. "Anyway you want it, Chinese bitch!" mumbled Ushino. He turned Jade onto her back and penetrated her with a force that tore her flesh.

"Do you see how easily we take China?" he told her, ramming against her with increased frenzy. The commanding officer called out for his men from the front of the house. "Where's Ushino?" he demanded. Nagoya released Jade's wrists and sauntered into the hallway. "He'll be here in a minute; he's poking around for something else." Laughing, he walked down the stairs, past the blown out windows and the crater where a car and a man had once stood. In the yard were all the possessions of the Hsu family that this group thought their superiors would want. Everything that could be salvaged or sold was being piled into the back of the supply truck.

"Come on Ushino, time to go!" yelled Nagoya from the front yard.

Jade cried out for Yen, but his seemingly lifeless body was already dumped into the back of the truck. An old man lying nearby, his own blood pooled around the knife wound in his shoulder, stared toward the house, toward the heart-wrenching sound of a woman's screams. Before she could call yet again, Ushino drew his knife and stabbed her repeatedly in the chest and neck.

Life faded quickly from Yen Hsu's beautiful wife, her blood pumping from the deepest wounds. As she died, she continued to stare defiantly and accusingly at her rapist and murderer. When she took her last shallow breath, her hand reached out and then fell limply over the side of the couch. Her blood dripped rhythmically onto the floor, and then into the floorboards and through the cracks, where it dripped onto the faces of her daughters. Clutched in Jade's hand was Kenji's necklace. Ushino pried open her fingers and removed it, slipping it into his top pocket as his victim stared at him with unseeing eyes.

Below, Jade's daughters remained frozen in agony, as still as a painting, with tears, perspiration, and their mother's blood visible on their faces. Mei Ling closed her eyes and prayed in silent desperation. Su Lin was catatonic, staring straight up at nothing: shock had set in.

Ushino walked rapidly from the house, buckling his belt and straightening his uniform. The truck pulled away, Yen Hsu lying in a fetal position in the back, one hand stretched in desperation toward his disappearing house, his vanishing family.

SIXTEEN

Every street in Nanking was in chaos. The city was a burning ember of what it had been the day before. Everywhere, that is, except for a small zone near the middle, inside the old city walls near the Japanese consulate. The International Safety Zone was still marginally safe, but it had no electricity, little food, and no defense. At the same time, the people within those walls put a lot of faith in their leaders, a handful of missionaries, businessmen and doctors. The safety zone was one of the few areas of the city that had not been attacked. Nevertheless, there was frantic activity, what with thousands of Chinese lining the streets, covering every square inch of usable space. They poured around the corners the way sand rushes in to fill a crevice on the shore.

The Ginling Girls' College was fortunate to be inside this International Safety Zone. Also inside this zone were the Japanese and German embassies, the American University hospital, the American Red Cross office, and a handful of humanitarian facilities. The zone was inside the old city walls, which had managed to keep its inhabitants safe from invaders for a thousand years. Now, however, those old walls seemed fragile and small, when help up to the force of the invading Japanese and their desire to decimate Nanking. In fact, the soldiers were ordered to reduce Nanking to such rubble that all of China would mourn her loss and the defeat of their government. The Japanese believed that China would see their might and surrender to a superior Japanese army and culture. That was the Tanaka Plan. So far, it had worked.

There was no doubt now: the capital was under siege. Troops were there to exact revenge and to finally show the Chinese that resistance to the Japanese army was futile. There was no escape. The army had been ordered to round up all those dishonorable, despicable Chinese deserters and deliver their most noble sentence of death.

Twelve hours after the battle began in earnest, and from nearly every angle, the city appeared destroyed. Dead bodies lay everywhere. If a building was not ablaze, it was being looted. The order of the day was simple: plunder, loot, set fire. Sporadic gunfire rang through streets and cries of pain and hopelessness punctuated the acrid air whenever an individual attempted to defend his world.

Thousands of women and girls took refuge on the Ginling campus. More refugees pressed at the gates, but the gardeners who had been put in charge followed their headmistress's orders and allowed only women and children to enter. Minnie, Wong and Mary stood behind the gates and surveyed this seemingly endless mass of refugees, more than two hundred thousand souls amassed in a kindred pool of fear. Many had managed to get their hands on a lean-to, a tent, or some makeshift structure that they were able to attach to a wall or building for shelter. Minnie noticed that these peasants slept anywhere, everywhere, spread out in front of her gate. As far as her eye could see, there were shattered remains of families dotting the landscape.

A serpentine line of women and children wove outside the science building, each one waiting for a bowl of rice. A teenaged girl walked up to Minnie and offered her bowl to Minnie. "Miss Minnie, are you hungry?"

"Thank you, but no, my child. Please offer it to someone more needy first."

"Are you sure?" she asked, her voice pleading as she held out the food to her beloved headmistress. Minnie looked directly into the eyes of the frail little girl. "I think you should have it, my child. You need to keep warm, too. Go on, I insist."

The girl smiled briefly. "But there must be someone..." She looked into Minnie's face, smiled, then hungrily pushed the rice into her mouth and scurried away.

Minnie kept her eyes on the girl for a moment and then turned to Mary. "Two days ago we were three hundred, now there are thousands."

"We must not let Christian generosity be confused with our need to survive," observed Mary. "We're no help to these people if we fall ill. Besides, what if it takes weeks to get the next supplies?"

Wong sighed loudly. "There are thousands of innocent girls and women outside our gates. Who decides which ones will get the protection of the Ginling?"

Mary seemed to be sifting through responses as she looked first at Wong and then toward the growing crowd at the gates. "There are perhaps a hundred thousand in the safety zone, and those numbers are growing by the hour. Ginling is a girls' college...a college! How can we be expected to take in anymore. I mean—can we, Minnie?"

Minnie's attention had been drawn to a soldier who was dragging a man from his family. The man's wife was crying and pleading for his release. A second soldier hit the woman in the face with the butt of his rifle. "Soldier!" he called. "Your husband is a Chinese soldier, a coward, a traitor!" Having blurted out an excuse for a death sentence, he dragged the man away. The woman insisted that her husband was nothing more than a simple gardener, but his fate was now sealed. For him, there would be no spring, no summer ever again.

Minnie knew that this judge and jury mentality was being repeated throughout Nanking, that it would probably happen time and time again on this day alone. Bodies would be dumped into ditches, ponds and rivers; mass graves would be dug and the bodies unceremoniously buried.

Wong spoke, jarring Minnie back to her friends. "Did you send all of our cash reserves on the Panay?" he asked.

"It's best to be safe during a time of war," she replied, turning slowly to look at him. "It's faith we need, Mr. Wong, not folly, and God will provide." Her voice was calm, yet held a trace of confusion.

While life outside the college was untenable, there were difficulties inside as well. For one thing, refugees were sleeping in the hallways, basements, and attics. Many of the teenage girls, especially the more recent arrivals, knew about the brutality of the Japanese soldiers and were desperate to hide in the far reaches of an attic or storage area. Also, the food supply was dwindling. Minnie and her staff were concerned about this, but also about hygiene. It had not been an easy decision to use the duck pond for human waste.

Minnie surveyed her campus as she walked past her rose bushes, which now grew only thorns. No leaves, certainly no roses, not at a time like this.

Wong watched Minnie, noted how she touched one of the thorny stems and sighed. "Don't worry, Miss Minnie. Next year should be a banner year for the garden; it is the year of the rabbit."

"And this year, Mr. Wong?"

"Year of the ox, meaning we all have an unusual burden to bear. Next year will be better. You'll see: the roses will be special, the flowering shrubs, too."

Minnie studied the man's sincerity and smiled. "Next year, you must give the hedges special attention. For now, however, let's tear out the roses. It's protected from the wind here, so we can set up some more tents for the refugees. Another kitchen can be assembled over there," she added, pointing to an alcove that was once used as a quiet space on campus.

Wong appeared confused and then incredulous. "Miss Minnie, are you saying that you want me to tear out your—"

"Yes," she interrupted. "And next year, when this madness is over, we can take joy in our shrubs again."

Wong thought about this for a moment. "Fine," he said with a firm nod. "Tents it is." Mary stood very quietly. She held a tissue and was pulling at its edges, causing little pieces to break away and float to the ground. Minnie watched her friend for a long moment and then asked, "Mary, what is it?" When the woman said nothing, Minnie stepped directly in front of her and grasped her friend's hands.

"I didn't know how best to tell you," said Mary, the muscles around her mouth quivering. "I just heard that the *Panay* was attacked and sunk."

Minnie waved a hand in the air, as if pushing away this news. "It's an American ship, my dear. There's no reason for the Japanese to bomb an American ship, it must be just a rumor."

"I think so, too, Minnie," agreed Wong.

The three stood together, each one grappling with a feeling that this was no rumor; they were in a state of war. Sadness threatened to overwhelm them. Minnie looked at Wong and pushed away the idea that such a terrible thing could have happened. If she accepted this, then she would have to accept that Yen Hsu's sons and Jade's mother were dead. She allowed her gaze to sweep across her campus, this place that was her child, her life's greatest accomplishment. She loved God so much and felt so blessed to be here. She loved China and, in turn, it loved her back. Times were difficult, but things would improve, the barbarians would be defeated. For the time, her faith was unshakeable.

SEVENTEEN

A large number of refugees were gathered near the river. Over five thousand were already there, with tens of thousands more who had heard that it could be their way out and were on their way. The city was already lost; getting into the safety zone was beyond problematic. Many hoped that they could still escape from the Japanese by crossing the Yangtze River.

The plan made sense, but it was not feasible. They result was a mass of desperate souls trapped on the east bank of this river, with no transportation available. Some of the stronger men had tried to swim, while parents had tied themselves and their children to whatever wood they could find and had paddled into the frigid water. There was no way to know who made it to the other side.

Meanwhile, the Japanese were arriving. There were soldiers everywhere and they stood on the banks and watched refugees throw themselves into the water. They waited until these frantic people were a good distance from shore and then, without waiting for an order, the first sergeant cocked his machine gun and fired. As bullets hit the water, pools of red appeared and bodies disappeared below the surface. The other refugees were horror stricken, many dropping to their knees in shock. Within seconds, the sergeant turned his rifle on these poor souls and opened fire. Row after row of Chinese men and women fell into the river. Soon, as if in sport, the other Japanese soldiers aimed their rifles and began firing at the fleeing civilians. By the end of the day, thousands of bodies lined the banks of the mighty Yangtze.

Who could have anticipated the impudent glee in the eyes of those Japanese victors? These men had been on the knife's edge of the most aggressive fighting force in the twentieth century and they were bred for war, reared for the conquest. At day's end, a few of them looked around and then at each other, as if to ask, "Is this it?" Wanting more, they headed into the heart of the city. Perhaps this was where they could find the civilian mongrels who needed to experience the unparalleled force of the mighty Imperialist army. They, too, would be made an example. There were shopkeepers who needed to be robbed and spoils to be amassed from the homes of the rich. And there were the women and nubile girls, perfect for the taking and to do with as they pleased. These men had tasted blood and hardship, but no victory. What would be sweeter than Nanking falling into their hands?

By morning, the Chinese soldiers who remained had, as their last stand, fortified the two main entrances to the old walled city. At the same time, the Japanese military leaders met and decided to use this Zhonghua Gate as the prototype for the next wave of destruction. The ancient gate had three arches, plus a large open area where civilians continued to amass, pleading to be allowed to pass through the city walls. Using heavy explosives, the Japanese rimmed the supports that buttressed the gate, making certain there was more than enough to get the job done. Standing on top of the wall of the large gate were Chinese soldiers. They took shots at the brazen invaders.

When the explosives were detonated and the gate blew open, nearly fifty Chinese soldiers died instantly. Even Japanese soldiers standing too close to the detonation were killed at once. Of those who stood too close, many felt a twinge and perhaps had just enough time to glance down and see their innards blown away before they died. Most of them were dead before their knees hit the pavement. Debris and metal were projected for more than two hundred yards.

The main force of the Japanese troops entered the city and found many of the side streets still clogged with refugees and addicts. In fact, there were more than 100,000 refugees milling about, plus many injured Chinese soldiers. As soldiers and tanks moved through, the hive of humanity shifted from street to street, like a rising tide of human debris. With the invasion in full swing, more and more Japanese soldiers streamed into the city, aware of their orders to fire at anyone not wearing a Japanese uniform. As the long day came to an end, the first tanks rolled in, having finally got caught up with the supply of fuel. Despite the hordes of people in the streets, there was never a pause in the tanks' movements: they simply rolled over the thousands of people and moved on.

As the Chinese were forced to flee into certain areas of the city, special units of artillery soldiers were sent in to kill. Using mortars and hand grenades, their process of annihilation resulted in streets running with blood. By the time the sounds of gunshot fell quiet, bodies choked the two major roads of Nanking. In some places, they were stacked four- and five-deep.

Mitsui Iwane, the invasion commander, was approaching one of the suburban areas of Nanking, where a large group of Chinese soldiers had been captured. This proved to be a dilemma for Iwane, this problem of more captives and too little space to hold them. Another large number of Chinese infantry and civilians were caught and marched outside the city, not far from Iwane's camp. As it happened, this group of a few hundred were to become the first in a massive parade that would include thousands of Chinese. As for the others, they were felled by machine guns and then pushed into trenches or ponds.

"We are running out of ammunition," complained one of the soldiers.

Iwane looked over the situation and then smiled. "Pour gasoline over them and burn them alive."

In the city itself, the Japanese army swept through, supported by soldiers arriving from all parts. The random killing continued, its victims primarily civilians. Japanese soldiers seemed to enjoy inventing new and inhumane methods of killing. They would shoot, stab, lop off a head, slice open the abdomen, even use live bodies for bayonet practice. This was war; the enemy must be brought to its knees and humiliated.

As the hours passed, the stench of decaying bodies increased. Because these bodies were not removed, the smell only worsened as the bodies' gases expanded. In a short time, even the eyes of the ravagers became numb to this vision of hell on earth. Soldiers found it difficult to eat, their mouths filled with the metallic taste of death.

The gutters of Nanking ran with the blood, decay and the loss of dignity of every Chinese in the world.

EIGHTEEN

The American Red Cross building in Nanking had changed noticeably since the stock market crash of 1929, the year of the snake. Eight years later, the formerly robust enterprise was now quite a bit rougher around the edges and the organization considered itself fortunate to have the dedicated and industrious John Magee at the helm. When Magee and his friend, Ernest Forster, elbowed and plowed through the crushing mass of people and entered the Red Cross office, they looked like men who had survived the very worst. Refugees had pulled at them, torn their clothing, done everything imaginable to gain access to this building. Inside, the two men discovered that they were the only ones there, with the exception of one Chinese worker who was checking the doors every few minutes.

Magee, disheveled, frenzied and ruddy-faced from exertion, fell into his guest chair—a large, well-worn leather wingback—and closed his eyes. From his expression, one might have guessed that he wanted nothing more than to erase all those grisly images he had absorbed over these past few days.

Forster was in front of Magee's desk, hands on knees and panting. His skin was pale, almost green, tinted by exertion and the macabre scenes he had witnessed. "You are insane," Forster gasped. "You told me you—"

"That was close," interrupted Magee. "I couldn't have done it without you. You know that, right?"

Forster stood upright and took a deep breath. After a long pause, he released it with a whooshing sound. "Good Lord, man, when you said you wanted to film some of the battle, I didn't realize you meant we'd actually be in the battle...in the middle of it all. I'm counting my blessings, thank you Lord!" He ran a hand through his hair, then nervously massaged his temple, as if he could will what he had seen out of his mind. Forster studied the perspiration on his hand and then ran his palm across the bottom of his pant leg, wanting to be cleansed.

Unlike Forster, Magee was energized, as if intoxicated by their accomplishment. "No one would've believed it, if we hadn't got it on film," he declared. "Besides," he added, a tinge of bravado in his voice. "That wasn't even a big battle that we shot. God rest their souls, each and every one." As he spoke, he carefully removed the spent film and slipped it into a tin. This film needed to be sent out of Nanking for processing, but he had no idea where. Perhaps Shanghai, if the roads opened anytime soon. Magee had never lived in an occupied territory and found it both terrifying and exhilarating. He took another reel and loaded it into the movie camera.

"I have a lot of faith, but it doesn't negate common sense," declared Forster. "I am not going out there again!"

Magee snapped the film magazine cover closed and, out of habit, checked the lens settings. "Forster, old man, they're not going to shoot us, we're Americans!" He reached into his drawer and pulled out several Red Cross armbands. "Here, put one on each arm," he instructed, tossing them onto the desk. He slipped the armbands onto his arms and then, measuring one to see if it would fit on his fedora, decided against it.

Forster stared at the armbands, but made no move to pick them up. "What in the hell is wrong with you? Didn't you see what was on the other side of that lens, or does standing behind it somehow blur your perception?"

The men stared at one another for ten icy seconds and then Magee leaned forward, elbows on his desk. "I saw the atrocities, the inhumanity of it all. Untold acts of violence on human beings. I'm frightened too, but don't you understand? Those people could die in vain if their story remains untold. If we don't do this, then who? There's no government left, unless you county Tanaka and Kenji's world. The army's gone and no press, unless you count Truman, and he's spending every waking hour trying to get out of here. He wants to tell the story from several days ago, not today, not tomorrow. Only a few in the west will ever know about this if we don't go out and shoot it."

"If we're killed, will it matter?" A split second later, and before Magee could respond, a large shell exploded just outside the safety zone, but close enough to cause plaster to shake loose on the wall of this building. The two men dropped to the floor and tried to take cover, but there was immediately another whistle and then another explosion, shaking the building so violently that Magee's only window shattered, sending large shards of glass across the room, some of it landing inches from the two men.

Forster maneuvered closer to Magee and huddled against his desk. "John, this is unbelievable. Do you think they're going to bomb the safety zone?"

Magee peered over the desk. It was quiet outside; even the foot soldiers were silenced by their proximity to the aerial bombs. He started to rise. "Come on, I don't want to be late for the meeting. Let's see how much leverage Rabe's got with his power plant."

"Germany's a damn ally of the Japs," groused Forster, brushing off his slacks. "You'd think he could pull some strings!"

The men found their way out of the building and managed to get to the library at Nanking University, a facility paid for and supported by American donations, primarily from Yale alumni. It was an impressive building inside and out. Large and western in design, it showed a touch of the

Orient on the corners of the roof. As for the great library, it was more than a depository of books and research. It had become the meeting place for the members of the first International Safety Zone Committee.

At this meeting were Magee and Forster, the other American missionaries, Bates and Smitty, Germans Rabe and Rosen, plus the British representatives, Mackay and Munro-Favre. John Rabe, the dedicated little German and Nazi Party member who was the head of the Siemens Electric plant, stood to take charge of the meeting. "Please, gentlemen, let's have order, we have a lot to cover."

Magee made it clear that order was far from his mind. "We need assurances from the Japanese now!" he blurted out. "We cannot allow them to send their soldiers into the safety zone."

"I think we all understand this," Rabe responded.

Rosen, the other German, jumped to his feet. "Unfortunately, many Chinese soldiers are attempting to find safe haven in the zone, which means that Japanese soldiers are coming in to track them down. What can we do?"

"Either the zone is for safety, or what the hell good is it?" Forster retorted.

The Englishman Mackay turned to the others and, in a voice made even more demeaning by the Oxford accent, questioned, "I say, Rabe, do tell us: what about the power, the electricity? Are we to assume that the Siemens plant is getting protection? After all, you're an ally of these butchers, right-o mate?"

Forster gasped, eyes moving quickly between Mackay and Rabe. "Mackay, everyone is here to help, especially the good man, John Rabe."

The attempt to negotiate a quick détente was not lost on Rabe. He nodded at Forster, then turned abruptly toward Mackay and spat out "Scheitze! My power plant cannot be restarted without trained staff, is this not true? And where is my staff? The so-called allies shot them dead yesterday! Now I must train new workers and that will take time, but I am sending no one to their deaths. The army seems to have no chain of command."

Magee held up both hands. "I'm sure we're all trying to do our best, but this issue is too serious. Rabe, is there a plan for the training? And if so, let's hear it." He tried not to look at the Nazi armband worn by the German.

Rabe stared at Magee for a long beat and then declared, "I said that I am not sending anyone else out there just to get shot. I must have assurances from the Japanese Commander. I think in another day or so they will be demanding electricity to be back on for their occupation, then they will listen to me. All in good time, I must have assurances and guards."

"Speaking of assurances," said Forster, pausing until all eyes were directed to him. "Another major concern should be the Ginling. Minnie's got thousands of women and children there now, all of them unprotected, except for a few rakes and shovels beyond their gates."

Rabe thought about this for a moment. "We will propose a plan for securing the gates with guards. Again, we must get assurances."

The debates continued, interrupted by an occasional raised voice and a few nearby explosions. One of the latter shook the room so violently that several of the committee members moved as if to duck under the table. Nevertheless, the discussions went on unabated.

Minnie walked into her room, her only safe haven from the horrors outside. The little retreat felt more serene with each passing hour, its Spartan décor a stark contrast to the endless wash of people moving about on the campus and in the safety zone. She pulled her Bible off the bookshelf, held it, slipped it back into its place and removed a tome about the fall of the Roman Empire. With a free hand, she searched behind some books and pulled out a pistol. The little gun was so old that it maintained a patina of rust in its surface. A sudden knocking on her door caused her to start.

She tucked the bible inside her jacket and slipped the pistol into her coat pocket. Straightening her clothes, she turned toward the door and said, "Come in."

Mary entered, creases of concern evident on her face. "Minnie, are you alright?"

Minnie smiled sweetly. "I'm fine, dear. I was just taking a moment to think of my girls and all the others who have come here." The two women had been friends for so long that there was no need to explain her need to be alone. "I also needed a few minutes to pray," she said. She waited a moment and then added, "And to get my pistol." She slipped it out of her pocket just long enough for Mary to get a look. "My father gave it to me nearly twenty years ago." She pursed her lips and then turned toward the bookcase. "There's a box of bullets around here somewhere. I had them sent over when we had problems with those wild dogs outside the gates. I don't want to startle the girls, but I do think I should have it handy, just in case."

Mary crossed the room. Since she was several inches taller than Minnie, she reached high up on the shelf and, in seconds, found the box. She handed them to Minnie with an impish smile. "Minnie Vautrin, I swear, if someone had told me that you kept a gun, I would've told them it was impossible."

Minnie shrugged and shook her head. "It seems far-fetched, doesn't it? But it was my father's idea. You know, a young girl in a foreign country. To be honest, I'm surprised I've kept it all this time." She removed the pistol from her pocket and held it, her face suddenly dark with concern. "Last night, Japanese soldiers came over the walls and took two girls from our science building. Neither girl returned. The next time those bastards try it, I'll be ready."

Mary's expression mirrored both disbelief at the language and a shared concern. "Those soldiers carry real weapons, loaded and ready to shoot. My God, Minnie, they'd think nothing about killing you." She gestured toward the old pistol "How do you know that it even works?

And are there bullets in the chamber? Do you know what you're doing?"

Minnie lifted her chin, as if offended by Mary's questions. "I grew up on a farm and I've shot a gun. Besides, I have God in my chamber!"

Mary reached out and took hold of her friend's arm. "Your faith is not in question, my dear. But perhaps a little common sense is needed. Can a little pistol that may not even fire stop a soldier's bayonet? Look at this thing, Minnie, it's rusted out!"

Minnie returned the little weapon to her pocket. "They won't know that, will they?" Before Mary could argue the point, she added, "Let's go find Mr. Wong. I asked him to check on news of the *Panay*. Also, Truman was supposed to be at Rabe's last night, so there's sure to be something from the newspaperman."

The two women walked out together and headed toward the rice lines, near what had been Minnie's lovely gardens. Now, it was only a mass of bodies, each one waiting for the rice being prepared at a makeshift kitchen erected on the back of what was a laundry cart. Minnie looked on with pride as her young students helped an old women and served without complaint. There were hundreds of little girls in this courtyard alone, scattered about, some listening to an elderly grandma tell stories. Everyone seemed to be waiting for something; everyone was hungry.

Wong appeared from around the corner. He was searching the crowd, his face grim.

"Wong, over here!" called Mary, waving her arm.

"Oh good," said Minnie. "Now we can put an end to these rumors."

Wong reached the women and could barely speak. Despite the cold weather, his face was deeply flushed. "Minnie, I have such sorry news."

Minnie placed a hand on his arm and waited.

Wong was close to tears. "The *Panay* was attacked by the bombers," he told her. "About ten miles down the

Yangtze. The ship went down, Minnie. They are looking for survivors, but the Japanese boats make it almost impossible. The word is that everyone died, everyone." His voice cracked and he took a moment to regain his composure. "Yen Hsu's boys and Jade's mother, they were all on the *Panay*, weren't they?"

Minnie stared at Wong for a long moment and then pressed a hand over her mouth. The boys, the old woman, they were her family, people who had welcomed her into their home. What could she do to comfort poor Yen, Jade, Mei Ling and Su Lin when she saw them next? Tears sprang from her eyes. She took Mary and Wong's hands and gestured for them to kneel in prayer. They knelt on the cold cement and, heads bowed, began to pray. Minnie's words were interrupted by her sobs. In the middle of the prayer, she felt Mary tugging on her hand. Looking around, she saw how upset the children were. A firm believer in leading by example, she pulled her emotions together, stood up and, with Mary's help, began to pass out rice bowls, water, and blankets. Smiling at the assembly of eager faces, she muttered to Mary to keep an ear out for any news about Yen's family arriving safely in Hangkow.

NINETEEN

Mei Ling stirred as more soldiers tramped through the house. She heard them declare their delight at discovering the beautiful cabinet where her family had kept its heirlooms, most of which were now in piles of debris in the front yard. She heard the cabinet being moved to the truck and then a soldier call out for help with the long table on which her father had placed the wonderful gifts given to his friends the night before. She heard cupboard doors being slammed open and closed in the pantry and assumed the soldiers were looking for alcohol, money, or valuable jewels. There was stomping on the upper floors and the sound of more doors being kicked open. Her entire home was being violated, but nothing mattered if her parents were dead. Her only task was to keep Sun Lin silent. Only then did they have a chance of surviving this onslaught.

Mei Ling studied her sister's face, rivulets of dried blood giving it an eerie and yet menacing look. She put her lips close to Su Lin's ear. "We must stay very quiet," she whispered. "Do you understand?" Su Lin stared mutely at the floorboards above, not reacting when conversations renewed overhead.

"There must be more," growled a voice. "Go outside and walk around the house. Look for low windows. If you find any, there's a basement."

Mei Ling heard something crash to the floor and caught the odor of rice wine. Within seconds, she creaking noises caused her to recoil and press a hand over Su Lin's mouth.

Tiny slivers of light appeared above; the trap door was revealed.

A corporal peered in, his head leaning over precariously. One of the drunken soldiers tried to see and fell against the corporal, who toppled into the gaping space. The soldier stumbled down the steps behind him.

"What the hell is wrong with you?" cried the officer, pushing the man away. Next to him were shelves covered with rice wine containers. "Here, catch!" he said, tossing a small jug toward his bumbling sidekick. The moment he threw the bottle in the air, he heard the shaking of boards. Head cocked for more sounds, he walked closer to the noise.

A rat dropped scurried around Mei Ling. She held still, paralyzed, as the rodent ran a tongue across her bloodstained arm. Her sense of revulsion was overcome by her sense of survival.

The officer peered toward the hiding place, but just as his face got close, the rat jumped past him and he nearly fell back. The other solider, quite drunk, laughed and announced, "Corporal, you are scared of rats! Maybe you need a drink."

"C'mon, let's go!" demanded the officer. "I'll send the others to bring this wine to the captain."

"But what about your rat?" ribbed his sidekick.

The officer took his pistol and aimed it directly at the rat, which was only inches from where Mei Ling and Su Lin were hiding. He took aim, positioned his finger perfectly on the trigger, and squeezed. The hammer fell and the chamber advanced, but nothing happened.

"Oh, you're killing me!" taunted the soldier. "Do you love this little Chinese rat?"

The man loaded his weapon and aimed. Before the rat could move two feet, the gun exploded and the animal lay dead. The soldiers hefted a case of rice wine over the broken stair and out of the basement. "Mark this one down for the captain's crew," said the officer. "There's a lot more stuff in there."

Mei Ling followed the sound of the soldiers' footsteps as they left the house. In the distance, near the front gates, she heard other soldiers cheer when they caught sight of the wine. When she was sure that all the soldiers were outside, she took a slow, deep breath. Su Lin was still staring blankly at the floorboards overhead. Mei Ling tried to slide the board that hid them, but it would not budge. "Su Lin, you must help me," she urged. When her sister didn't respond, she said "What's wrong with you? Wake up and help me!"

Su Lin could neither move nor speak. Instead, she stared above her, at the floorboards caked with her mother's blood.

Mei Ling was finally able to push and cajole until the board splintered. She rolled toward the opening and pulled herself out of the hiding spot. Able to stand, she stretched hard, loosening the kinks in her back and legs. The remains of the rat made her shudder: they had come so close to being discovered. Mei Ling tugged on her sister's arm and finally succeeded in dragging her from the space. Su Lin nearly toppled to the floor, knocking over a box filled with dishes.

Mei Ling removed some flat bricks in the corner and removed the earthen cooler where her mother stored food. She handed a piece of fish cake to Su Lin, who nibbled on it as she stared. The dead rat stared, too. She wanted more than anything to go upstairs and find her parents.

Mei Ling tiptoed up the broken stairs and opened the trap door just enough to look around. The front door was opened and a soldier stood near the gate. She quickly retreated, pulling the rug over the door and slipping back down into the cellar. "When it's dark," she whispered, "we'll make a run to the Ginling. Minnie will know what to do." When Su Lin did not respond, she kissed her forehead and brushed hair away from her face. Mei Ling tried to re-move the dried blood, too, but it was too dark.

As final light faded into evening and the temperature dropped, Mei Ling felt a penetrating and unsettling cold. She lifted box after box of memorabilia and then searched through some old trunks for warm clothing. When she dis-covered two of her father's old coats, she slipped one over Su Lin's shoulders and the other over herself. Dressed like this, they looked like anything but wealthy children.

Mei Ling did not know how to handle her sister. The girl was obviously traumatized, but they would have to make their way to the college. Mei Ling pulled the coat around her and wondered if she had ever been so afraid. She was afraid of the soldiers outside; afraid of the horror up-stairs; afraid of never seeing her parents again and the state of her sister. If they were going to make it all the way to the Ginling, she needed her sister's help.

"It'll be fine," she murmured, as if soothing Su Lin's concerns. "First we'll get to Minnie's, then Kenji will come and get me and take care of all of us." As she spoke, she cradled her sister in her arms, stroked her head and rocked her gently back and forth.

TWENTY

Minnie, Wong and Mary took turns supervising the main gate. Everyone was trying to be conscientious about who could enter and who could not. "No men" was the mandate handed down by Minnie. However, with so many poor souls seeking refuge, it was an arduous job and they worried about accomplishing their task. The problem was that there was no training for something like this, yet it was perhaps the most important job at the college. Above all, they needed to protect their girls and all those women they were harboring.

Minnie's shift was over and Wong had just arrived. Together, they stared in disbelief at the hordes of humanity pressing to enter the school's grounds. A girl of perhaps thirteen pushed her way through the crowd and arrived at the gate. She held a little boy in her arms. Both of them were filthy, their eyes reflecting the horrors witnessed.

"Miss Minnie!" called out the girl, a supplicating hand shoved through the gate. "I'm a first year student, I am Sang Zee!" She began to weep, clutching the boy closer to her chest. "I went home, but my parents are dead and we have no place to go."

Before Minnie could speak, Wong stepped forward and opened the gate. "Please, right this way," he said, helping the girl and her brother squeeze through the opening. Wong immediately closed and locked the gate.

Minnie placed a comforting hand on the girl's shoulder and offered a gentle smile. "Let's get you some tea and rice cakes. We will find a warm spot for you and your brother in the dorms."

The girl searched her headmistress' face. "But my family is dead, Miss Minnie. My family is lost, I have nothing."

"You have your little brother," Minnie responded, holding the girl to her.

The girl nearly bristled. "He's not my brother. My brother was eleven and he died in my arms last night. He said he was trying to protect my mother when I was hiding. Do you know what they did?" Her voice suddenly became demanding and angry. "They shot him! They shot him and cast him off like trash. He was only eleven!" She broke down, inconsolable, and said, "I had to bury them all and then I found this little boy hiding nearby. Minnie, why would they do this to us?"

Minnie felt a wave of emotion rise in her throat. She guided Sang and the little boy across the garden and into the dormitory. The room was filled with children just like them: no family, no home; all hopes resting on the shoulders of Minnie Vautrin, relying on the kindness of Minnie Vautrin.

Mary approached Minnie outside, her expression almost frantic. "I think we are near capacity. There are so many and we're out of space." She gestured around them, at the mass of homeless and traumatized women and children. "Men are trying to get in by telling us that they're the husbands and fathers of some of these girls. What should we do? I mean, how can we be sure?"

"It doesn't matter, even if they can prove it," said Minnie, with no equivocation. "I will not allow men in the school. The Japanese will assume they are soldiers and will use that as an excuse to enter my campus. And I promise you that no soldiers, Chinese or Japanese, will set foot on my campus, not one! Go remind Wong that the only men allowed through that gate are my fellow missionaries or the men who work for me."

"But if you send the fathers away—"

Minnie held up a hand to stop her friend. "They can stay in the safety zone until it's safe to leave, but they cannot enter the college. These girls and their mothers must be protected, that is our priority. In fact," she added, her expression suddenly changing from determination to that of decision maker, "Where is the list of everyone we've admitted? Someone needs to be held accountable for these people." Minnie looked around, biting down anger and grief. "What have they done to our heaven on earth?" She squared her shoulders and turned to Mary. "As soon as you have that list updated, I want to go to the Japanese embassy and speak with Mr. Tanaka. You can be sure I'll have words for him!"

Minnie returned to the gates and saw how tired Wong was. As much as she wanted to give him a rest, there was much work to be done. "You and I shall go to the Japanese Consulate," she told him.

"It's almost dark," he replied.

"We must secure the gate at night. Perhaps it's best that, at night, no one should be allowed in or out, no exceptions."

"That's exactly my point," said Wong. "It's much too dangerous to be out. Why don't we go to the embassy in the morning?"

Determination took over Minnie's face. "Because this won't wait! I must deliver the roster of the missing or murdered." She leaned closer and said, "Wong, they must put a stop to this now! Our roster shows over five thousand here already, and the abductions and rapes just outside—" Her voice trailed off, the horror of everything happening around her too unspeakable. Hands clenched as she regained composure, she added, "It's high time someone answered to this. Who better than Tanaka?"

Mary showed up holding a teacher's notebook with page after page of names, ages and home addresses. "Minnie, it's being added to hourly, so you can show it to Tanaka, but you must bring it back."

Minnie and Wong left the relative safety of the school and walked toward the embassy. They didn't have far to go—around a few bushes, past some large trees in a clearing about 100 yards long, and then across the embassy's circular drive. They were well into the clearing when a woman suddenly appeared, screaming for help. A Japanese soldier was close behind. He caught her, clapped a hand over her mouth and dragged her into the bushes. Minnie wanted to go to her aid, but Wong gripped her by the elbow and led her toward the embassy.

"But that poor woman—"

With defeat in his voice, he whispered harshly. "If we step in, we'll die too."

They arrived at the building and looked up at the flagpole rising like a tower in the middle of the embassy driveway. From it waved the image known world-wide: the rising sun.

Minnie stopped at the base of wide steps and gazed up at the building.

"Expect nothing to avoid disappointment," counseled Wong.

"Confucius?"

"No," he replied. "Wong!"

They ascended to the top step and faced the Japanese guards. They recognized Minnie and peered closely at Wong. Very soon, they were allowed to pass. A soldier marched in behind them, his bayonet directed toward Wong. They were led to a large door and Minnie knocked firmly. Without awaiting a response, she barged in to a large reception area and headed toward a private office.

"Excuse me, you can't go in there!" insisted Tanaka's personal secretary, jumping to his feet. Before he could come around his desk, Minnie had already opened the door to Tanaka's office and stepped inside. Tanaka looked up from his work, his expression one of surprise. "Mr. Tanaka, I must see you at once!"

The man, overweight yet meticulously dressed, rose from his desk and pulled on his jacket to remove the creases from his belly. "Miss Vautrin, what can I do—?"

"Your men carry on in the safety zone as if there were no command or authority at all. They have no respect for life or the sanctity of a woman's body."

"Miss Vautrin, we—"

"I have thousands of women and children at the Ginling, with many more waiting at the gate. They come to my college to hide from your murderous soldiers."

Tanaka tried again. "Miss Vautrin, please—"

"If the women of Japan knew how their soldiers were conducting themselves, it would bring shame on everyone. And shame on you, Mr. Tanaka!"

Tanaka approached Minnie, took her arm and guided her to a chair. When she continued to rant, he stood over her and demanded "If you want my help, sit down, shut up, and listen!"

"Don't you dare—"

"You walk in here with accusations? Fine, now here is my official response. Chinese soldiers abandoned their posts and fled into the city of Nanking and behind the old city walls. Many more have made it into your safety zone and perhaps into the college. Our loyal soldiers are pursuing them. Deserters or not, Miss Vautrin, they are still the enemy and my men are doing their jobs."

Minnie exploded. "Their jobs? You call raping women and girls part of their job? The murdering of women and children! That's a *job* in your army?"

The man hardly flinched at her accusations. Instead, he tipped his head, as if acknowledging everything as true. "This is war, Miss Vautrin. And, if I recall correctly, you were told to leave long ago. But you stayed, didn't you? What would you like me to say? That you were a fool for staying?"

Minnie fought to contain her anger, her eyes never leaving Tanaka's face. She knew his game and refused to play it. "Yes, it is war, *your* war, and I want assurances that *your* soldiers will not enter *my* college...under any circumstances."

Tanaka studied her face. There were a tenuous ten seconds of silence as his narrowed eyes looked down at her. "Perhaps I could draft a letter," he suggested. "One that bears my seal. You could show this to any officer of the Imperialist Army and they will honor my message."

Minnie thought about this and then nodded. "Thank you, I will wait. But it's getting dark, so please hurry."

Tanaka dismissed her with a wave of his hand. "I will have it delivered tomorrow. Now please, I have pressing issues."

Minnie smiled politely. "Thank you, that is very kind Mr. Tanaka, but I'll wait here." When Tanaka did not respond, she opened her eyes wider and asked, "Shall I make you a cup of tea while we wait?" Her expression was pure innocence. "Mr. Wong makes a very good cup of green tea." She turned to her companion, asking over her shoulder, "Mr. Tanaka, would you like sugar in your tea?"

Wong walked over to the table holding tea and all those accoutrements required for a proper cup. This was the perfunctory preparation area: Tanaka would never have allowed a Chinese to touch his family's ceremonial tea service. Those were on a special table, at the other end of his office.

Tanaka looked at Minnie, at Wong, and back at Minnie, as if deciding if he should strike back for her insolence or express frustration at being trapped in his own office. After a moment, he said "Green, please, there is hot water in the large red pot. No sugar. Please touch nothing else."

Having one-upped Tanaka, Minnie moved quickly. "Mr. Wong, allow me." She crossed to the table and poured the hot water into a small teapot. She felt Wong's eyes on her as she took over and trusted him to stand aside. When the tea was ready, she poured a cup for herself, then carried one to Tanaka and another to Wong, bowing to each like a subservient little Geisha. The expression on her face was controlled victory over this all-powerful invader. In her mind, Tanaka's cooperation was a large step forward toward normalizing the situation. She also realized that Tanaka understood this very well.

"Now I will write the letter," announced Tanaka. There were two pens on the desk: a lacquered fountain pen with gold filigree scrolling and a plain pen that was tossed on his stack of papers. He picked up the plain one and began to write. Meanwhile, Minnie sipped her tea and walked around the office, looking at photos of Emperor Hirohito and exterior shots of the embassy and Nanking before the war. She stopped at a large photograph of old Nanking. Wong stood just behind her.

"Nanking had such dignity," Wong said, his voice defiant.

Tanaka looked up from his writing. "It will be restored in the Emperor's eyes," he stated, glaring at the very proud Mr. Wong.

Wong glanced at Tanaka and then back at the photograph. "And do the Emperor's eyes bear witness to the atrocities perpetrated by his people?"

Tanaka folded the letter and dripped wax on its edge. Taking a carved seal, he pressed it into the wax. "My seal will keep soldiers from your gate," he said, head titled as he forced a smile. "Now really, I have much work to do and you must go."

Minnie stepped forward and took the letter. "Thank you very much, sir. You are a gentleman amongst the savages, I assure you." She turned, as if to leave, and then turned back. "There is one more thing." She opened her purse and removed a small book.

"What is this?" demanded Tanaka, all pretenses of good manners quickly fading.

"It's a list of missing men and families provided by some of the women at the Ginling. I want to know where are their husbands, fathers, and brothers and where will they be taken. My staff accounted for more than ten thousand missing. Where are they, Mr. Tanaka?"

"I can't do this," he scoffed, brushing away the offensive book.

"But you can! These are fathers, brothers, sons of innocent families! Shopkeepers and farmers, not soldiers. I demand to know where you are taking these men!"

Tanaka stood, hands clenched into fists. With a jerk of his head, he motioned for Wong to escort this nuisance out. His face was flushed, shoulders hunched around his neck. Minnie was in no hurry to leave. She turned to a family photo on the wall and said, "You have five daughters, Mr. Tanaka. How blessed you are."

Tanaka sneered. "*Blessed* would have been five sons, Miss Vautrin. Now please, enough about my family."

Minnie put the book under his nose. "Imagine if they were gone, disappeared or even worse, dragged off by your soldiers." Before he could respond, she raised the book and shook it. "I want to know where these families are!"

Kenji Nezumi appeared at the office door, knocked and entered. Tanaka visibly relaxed. "Kenji, please escort Miss Vautrin back to the Ginling."

Minnie tucked the notebook under her arm and bowed to Tanaka. "Thank you for your kindness and understanding, Mr. Tanaka, truly."

The man stared at this brash little woman for a moment and then said, "Your heart is like the dragon in my worst dreams, Minnie Vautrin. Good night to you." Turning to his undersecretary, he said, "Kenji, see that she gets safely to her gates."

"Yes, sir, of course. Is there anything else?" He bowed as he exited.

"Not for now, just show her out."

Kenji, Minnie, and Wong descended the steps and Minnie was struck by how tidy everything seemed. Nanking was in shambles, but this place looked clean, everything in place. They continued past the mass of confusion congregated near the embassy and through the cluster of well-dressed Japanese soldiers, young men smoking cigarettes and laughing, showing each other the jewelry and trinkets stolen from the people they had killed. Minnie walked between Wong and the dapper Kenji, whose presence guaranteed them safe passage.

Kenji was a friend of the Ginling and the only Japanese man Minnie thought she could trust. The Japanese Consul in Tokyo had sent him to Nanking at the age of eighteen. Upon his arrival, he had marched into the college to apply for English lessons. She remembered telling him that the school was only for young women, but he would not be deterred. It was during his early studies of English that he first fell for Mei Ling. At first, Minnie thought he was just struck by her alluring beauty, like so many young men, and she set him straight early on, explaining that Mei Ling was untouchable. During those first two years, he did nothing more than smile at Mei Ling, shake her hand and thank her. Minnie had no idea that they had been infatuated for nearly four years and romantic for the last two. Every time she thought she knew this man, he surprised her. But she would never be more shocked than on this day.

"Do you think they are in Hangkow by now," she asked. "Have they wired you?" If anyone knew the truth about the *Panay*, it would be Kenji.

Kenji whispered, "I saw the house, Minnie."

"What house?"

"And the car was gone too, the house was–."

"What are you saying?"

"I was waiting for Mei Ling in my car, and Xiang's car was hit in front of the house. Bombs were raining down. It could have been a Chinese bomb, but…" His voice trailed off and then he added hopefully, "Were they—"

Minnie stopped him cold with a hard stare. "You were there and you did nothing."

"Don't you see, I couldn't. I don't know, I couldn't…"

"You couldn't what! For the love of God, this is Mei Ling and her family we're talking about! Why didn't you make the effort to see if they were hurt?"

Wong looked around, eyebrows raised in concern as he felt the gaze of Japanese soldiers.

"I tried to," said Kenji. "But the explosions were everywhere and the Chinese soldiers were coming."

"Soldiers…at the house? You left them there to–?"

"I couldn't have done much—could I? I mean, it was just me, my driver was going to leave me, Minnie."

"You left them? But were they hurt? You could have brought them back here, where it's safe. This is your army doing this?" She looked in all directions, as if unsure where to turn. "We must go for them now, you and I."

They approached the school's gates and Kenji blurted out, "I'll get the Consulate vehicle, they will let us pass. We'll go to them. Give me five minutes and I will return with the car."

"Five minutes?" Wong asked, leering at Kenji.

Kenji stood boldly. "I may have left her, but I had to leave, my driver would have left me. We must save my darling Mei Ling."

"She is far from yours," huffed Minnie. "And if she finds out how you abandoned her and her family—what kind of man—"

"You must promise never to tell her I was there, or I will not take you now. I will go by myself."

Minnie thought about this for a moment. Kenji was in a predicament, no doubt about it, but she needed to get to that house. "Fine, you have my word."

"I must go with you to protect you," murmured Wong. "I do not trust Kenji-san."

Minnie shook her head. "No, you stay in case something happens to me. The Ginling needs you." She saw deep concern in her loyal friend's face. "The Japanese occupy the city, and we'll be in their embassy's car."

Minnie and Wong stood just inside the college gates, waiting for Kenji to return. While there, they witnessed an intense argument between Mary and four Japanese soldiers. The men were demanding entrance, which Mary was steadfastly refusing.

"What's going on?" demanded Minnie, facing down the soldiers.

"They insist on coming in," said Mary. "I told them no, but they won't listen."

The conversation continued until interrupted by the arrival of Kenji. He climbed out of the official car and flashed his diplomatic identification. The sergeant saluted him. "This is a girl's college in the safety zone," Kenji said. "What are you doing, sergeant?"

"I was ordered to remove Chinese soldiers from the premises, sir." The sergeant took Kenji by the arm and pulled him aside. "That's not all, sir." The man leaned closer to Kenji and whispered, "My commander wants comfort for his officers."

Kenji's expression turned to amazement and then anger. Minnie walked over, took the letter from her purse and pushed it toward the soldier. "See this?" she taunted. "It means get away from the Ginling now. Get out, you and your animals!"

"Minnie, please," Kenji whispered. "I'm taking care of it." He murmured some words to the soldiers and they left.

Within minutes, Kenji returned in the black sedan, bedecked as usual with rising sun flags. "I think they're going to be fine when we get there," he told Minnie, helping her into the car. "I saw red and the explosion and the fire, but it was all outside the house, nothing inside." Kenji started the engine. Before he could pull away, Wong opened Minnie's door.

"Are you sure I can't go with you?" asked Wong.

Kenji turned on the lights, revved the engine and called out "Close the door, man, we must go now." The door slammed shut and the car drove off.

The official vehicle moved down Sikang Street, in front of the Ginling and past the Japanese consulate, where it turned onto the broad Shung Shan Street and finally out the smaller Y Chang Men Gate. Kenji explained to Minnie that this route would be fastest and she nodded. The lovely Yangtzekiang Hotel by the river was in shambles, soldiers having looted the place from top to bottom.

Some of Nanking's streets were as wide as the boulevards of Paris, although this was not so evident now. On this day, the city was burning, littered with refugees and the dead, covered with thousands of toppled carts, piles of rags and remnants of discarded Chinese army uniforms.

"I thought there was a surrender," said Minnie. "Why so much destruction?"

Kenji was preoccupied with other thoughts. "She should have stayed with you, that was our plan."

"Your plan?"

"Yes, we were planning for her to stay. I could have—"

"You could have what? Saved her from your own people?"

"I am not them!"

"Prove it!"

"You could have hired her for the next semester and she would have stayed to support you."

"Me? But, I'm not her family. How could I ask her to not leave with her family?"

"She would have stayed!"

"Kenji, I am not her mother. She has a family, and family is first."

He turned onto another street and swerved to avoid an old couple pushing an overloaded cart. "You could have done more."

Minnie's face reddened and she stared out the window. "You knew the plan before anyone, I know you did." Her voice was hard, accusing. "You could have warned us, but you didn't."

"No one can be trusted in war."

Minnie turned toward Kenji and studied his determined face. "Obviously, you're at the top of that list."

His hands gripped the steering wheel as the car continued past the merchant area. Every store was in the process of being looted or had already been burned to the ground. Japanese soldiers ignored the official Consulate vehicle and carried their spoils through the streets. Kenji turned onto a street just a block away from Yen Hsu's neighborhood and slammed on the brakes. Ahead, there was a crowd of civilian men being prodded by Japanese soldiers, machine guns at the ready.

"You see?" said Kenji, as if vindicated. "Captured soldiers!"

"Those aren't soldiers," argued Minnie. "Those are young boys, shopkeepers and farmers. Where are they being taken? Your people must account for this, I'll see to that."

Kenji took the back way down another street. No matter which route he chose, he could not avoid the atrocities. The father shot in the back and the mother's clothes ripped away; men and women and children being shot and burned, like unspent coal. There were three men raping two girls on the side of a street. Kenji tried to cover Minnie's eyes. "I am so sorry," he said. "There is barbarism I admit."

She shook herself free from his touch. "Mark my word, Kenji, whenever I teach, I will describe Hell to be what I have witnessed tonight, at the hands of your people."

They reached a cross street and were stopped by troops on the move. Kenji flashed his consulate badge and the car was quickly searched. The inspection over, they had to wait for trucks and soldiers to pass. As they waited, Minnie prayed.

TWENTY-ONE

Night had fallen before Mei Ling dared to inch open the trap door and look around above her basement hideaway. What she saw was her lovely home in ruin, devastation. She peered down at Su Lin, who was still unresponsive. "I'll be right back," she whispered, but there was no indication that the girl had heard.

Mei Ling crept up the last stairs and immediately crouched in the corner. The house was quiet, but echoes of gunplay surrounded her neighborhood. Soldiers could be anywhere and assuming safety could prove fatal. She looked toward the kitchen, then turned and saw the blown out windows in front. Rising, she made her way gingerly to the back door. Outside, the yard was in shambles with broken glass and discarded items, including pieces of furniture she did not recognize.

She returned her attention to the kitchen, where evidence of looting and pillaging was obvious. Everything that could possibly break lay in fragments and shards on the floor. Had anything survived this onslaught?

Mei Ling walked through the rest of the house, her senses almost numb to the horror before her. Every photograph, every fragment reminded her of her mother, the woman she might never again see or hold; the mother who was her nurturer, mentor and friend.

In the alcove, she found the family shrine in pieces. Framed Chinese calligraphy, Tao, and Christian writings were askew on the wall and smashed on the floor. Under the little table, she found a small Buddha and cross. She picked them up and put them in her pocket.

Suddenly, the rumble of footsteps running in step and orders being barked urged Mei Ling into the shadows near the parlor entrance. She peered through the dark, toward the front gate, and saw a soldier looking in her direction. He seemed to pause, as if unsure of something; as if sensing that something awaited him inside. Slipping to the floor, she scuttled backward, away from any possible visibility and found herself at the threshold to the parlor. With apprehension, she turned away, pressing her hand over her mouth and stifling a heart wrenching sob. There, sprawled out before her, lay her beloved mother.

She couldn't bear to look, yet she could not turn away. With eyes downcast, she knew that her mother was dead. Dead, and most certainly raped. She had heard the brutal attack; now, she had no choice but to see the result. Nothing in her life had prepared her for such evil.

The only light came from a waning moon and the distant glow of a burning city. Dried blood was everywhere, on the sofa and pooled on the floor. There was a large, bloody handprint on the wall where her mother had taken her last grasp at life.

Mei Ling stood very still, the pain of so much loss flooding over her. She had to put her mother to rest in some way and her mother's soul needed her. She would be the good, dutiful and loving daughter. She shifted until she was facing her mother's nearly naked body. A gash on the woman's abdomen still oozed blood, but most of her life force had already spilled onto the couch and the floor. Mei Ling found her mother's garments and took the next few minutes working the panties over Jade's feet and legs, pulling them up until her mother was covered. The outer garments were also difficult because the extremities were becoming stiff and unyielding. With the tenacity that she approached every challenge, Mei Long persevered. Her mother had been dignified in life; she would be no less dignified in death.

With her mother now clothed, Mei Ling took a blanket and spread it on the floor. Very carefully, she lowered her mother onto the blanket and wrapped it over her. She picked up one end of the blanket and began to pull it along the hardwood floor. "I'm going to rest you by your plum tree in the back," she whispered, glancing behind her. Suddenly, through what had once been the parlor window, Mei Ling saw a flickering light. She froze and waited. When nothing happened, she exhaled and continued her journey toward the back garden. As she pulled the heavy weight around a corner, she bumped into Su Lin. The girl stared at her older sister and then, stepping around her, looked down at the bundle wrapped at her feet. There was no gasping, no crying, just a girl remaining rigid, her expression empty.

Mei Ling realized that they were standing in clear view of a soldier less than fifty yards away. She pulled Su Lin down with her and, crouching, pulled her mother further toward the back of the house. The blanket slipped and Jade's hand was exposed. Before Mei Ling could cover it, Su Lin reached for it and held it tightly, her movement causing the blanket to fall open, revealing a glimpse of her mother's body. Mei Ling reached out to cover her sister's mouth and then realized that the girl was incapable of a verbal response. "Ma would want us to bury her in the yard," she whispered. "But I need you to help me, can you do that?" Without awaiting a response, she took a firm grasp of the bundle and dragged it toward the back of the house. Su Lin followed, bending low and still gripping her mother's torso to help move it. They made their way down the dark hallway, out the back door and down the steps to the yard. Within minutes, they were in the yard and looking out to the very English landscape. Jade had always liked the English gardens she had seen in Shanghai and Hong Kong, so Yen had created one for her. It had become her favorite place to rest. Now, she would rest there forever.

"I'll be right back, stay here!" Mei Ling whispered. She rushed into the greenhouse for a shovel. Crossing the garden toward Su Lin, she stepped on shattered glass and froze, listening for any signs that the soldier had heard them. For a long moment, all was silent and her heart slowed to a more normal beat. As quickly as relief arrived, it was broken by music coming from the house. It was too dark to see anyone inside, but someone was there, playing Gershwin, Jade's favorite.

Mei Ling soon heard footsteps moving through the room, boots landing on broken cups and shattered dreams. She slipped into the shadows behind a bush, just as the soldier walked down the steps and entered the garden. Su Lin was seated on the little bench under the plum tree holding her mother's hand. The red glow of night silhouetted the girl's shoulders and head. The soldier moved toward her. "Hey, little chicken," he crooned. "Come over here so I can see you." Su Lin remained motionless, gripping her mother's hand. "I say come here, girl!" he repeated in his best Chinese. When there was no response, he moved closer. "What have you got there, little girl?" He stopped in front of the catatonic child and kicked her mother's feet. "Not talking, heh?" He laughed, as if understanding that this was war and a sweet young girl could be considered the spoils. He ran a hand across her shiny black hair and then along her slender throat. "You're a lovely little—" His face froze, mouth opened and eyes wide. The impact of the shovel against the back of his head drove him forward, the momentum causing him to fall on Su Lin and carry her with him onto the cold, damp ground.

Mei Ling tossed the shovel aside and jumped onto him, realizing he was unconscious. She rolled his unconscious body away from her sister and mother and helped Su Lin to her feet. "We have to hurry," she urged, picking up one end of the blanket. As if understanding, Su Lin grabbed the other end and helped Mei Ling drag their mother several feet away from the soldier.

In less than ten minutes, Mei Ling had dug a fairly deep hole in the moist soil. Stepping back, she nearly cried, aware of how much more work lay ahead. With every thrust of the shovel's blade, she looked back to check on their attacker. "I don't think he's dead, so watch him."

From far away in the parlor came the faint and repetitive sound of *An American in Paris* skipping at its end. Mei Ling continued to dig, while Su Lin sat motionless on the bench. "Ma loved the plum blossoms," said Mei Ling, ignoring the Victrola's repetitions. "Now she can sleep under them forever." The hole finally deep enough, Mei Ling threw the shovel onto the ground and started to crawl out of the shallow grave. Just as her feet cleared the hole, a boot stepped hard on her back.

The solider stood over her, hands positioned on his rifle, ready to fire. Mei Ling attempted to scuttle away, but he used the butt of his rifle to knock her back into the impromptu grave. As she cowered, he spit words at her in rapid Japanese, his face contorted with rage. A thread of blood ran through his scalp and onto his jacket.

Su Lin watched silently, but made no move to help or run.

The soldier unbuckled his pants, eyes never leaving Mei Ling. Behind him, Su Lin was reaching down very slowly, her hand inching toward the shovel, as if she were a mime in a slow-motion skit.

"What will you do to me?" asked Mei Ling, more a question of curiosity than one of fear. Su Lin gripped the shovel's handle and pulled it slowly toward her.

Oh, I will have you," laughed the soldier. "And then I will take her." He gestured toward Su Lin and then turned to gloat. It was the last expression his face would ever reveal. Su Lin hit him with full force, broadside against his temple. There was a loud crack of fractured skull, followed by a sudden exhalation of breath. As he fell, Su Lin took another swing and made contact with the base of his skull. Standing there, bloody shovel in hand, she appeared stunned. After releasing a little cry, she raised the tool one last time and split his head open, killing him instantly. Then she sat on the bench and waited for Mei Ling to finish burying their mother.

When the task was completed, Mei Ling took the cross and Buddha from her pocket and placed them at the head of the mound of fresh-dug earth.

The sisters stood together, holding hands in their shared grief, faces smudged with the dirt of their mother's grave. There were no tears, no sounds of weeping, only a hollow silence that filled the garden. Within minutes, they dragged the dead soldier to the fence and pushed him into the neighbor's yard.

"Listen!" whispered Mei Ling. From nearby came the sound of boots running through the alley behind the house. Without a word, she took Sun Lin's hand and ran to the front yard. There, huddled under the cherry tree, Mei Ling took one deep breath after another, as if summoning the courage to make this escape. Su Lin still had blood on her face. Mei Ling tried to wash it off with saliva, but to no avail. When it seemed safe to proceed, she led her sister to the fountain, now full of debris, and sloshed a handful of murky liquid onto her face. The water had been clean only a day ago, but now it was murky and foul. Looking closely, she realized that an arm was floating among the debris. It had to be Xiang's. She gasped, vomited into the fountain, and then wiped her face repeatedly, moaning "Oh God, oh God!"

Before Su Lin could see this grotesque symbol of war, Mei Ling grabbed her hand and pulled her from the yard, moving a full speed across the broad street in front of their house, and into a small shop on the other side of the road. It was where she had bought ice cream with her father only a week earlier. They heard gunfire erupt in the alley behind them and crept into a storage cabinet at the end of a hallway. Beyond her field of vision, a tank was heading down the road from one direction and Kenji's car was coming from the other.

Kenji turned into the driveway of the Hsu home and drove through the opening that had once been blocked by a majestic gate. That gate now hung by one broken hinge and banged into the passenger side as the car passed. Minnie's eyes grew wide when she saw the devastation in the what had once been the front of the house. There was a large crater of blackened earth, with car parts and remnants of the lovely tree strewn across the yard. Her tree, her beautiful winter-blooming cherry tree that was her gift to Yen and Jade when they were married, was splintered in half like a used matchstick.

Kenji was able to brake just before the car fell into the crater. He maneuvered to the edge of the yard, where he had spoken to Mei Ling the night before. Minnie jumped from the car and Kenji, taking a moment to gather his courage, soon followed. They stood together and stared at the broken windows, at a house blackened by fire and riddled with metal from the car. Remnants of the Hsu household were partially burnt and strewn across the yard. Other items that had exploded out of the luggage when the car was hit were plastered onto the front of the house. Minnie moved cautiously, while calling out "Yen Hsu, Jade, Mei Ling, Su Lin!"

Kenji made a shushing sound and warned "Not so loud, we don't want soldiers coming."

Minnie's mouth twisted with disdain. "They've been here already, don't you think?" After a moment, anger was replaced by concern. "I hope to God everyone got out. It looks that way, right? I think they got out last night, don't you?" She was hoping and praying at the same time, yet the evidence before her was foreboding.

Kenji went first, climbing the stairs to the front of the house. Minnie followed, instinctively reaching for his hand. The stairs were littered with glass and debris, but the stairs themselves had withstood the blast. There was a layer of sooty film everywhere and they could see footprints coming and going up and down the stairs.

They entered the house. Kenji walked into the hall, stopping to look down into the opening that led to the basement. At the same time, Minnie peered into the parlor and nearly cried out. There was so much blood! She saw the Hsu's Victrola with the speaker cone askew and noted that almost everything in the room was broken. But mostly, she saw the blood. There was blood on the couch, the floor, so much of it still moist, still with that sickly smell, that pungent scent that sticks to the back of the throat. She became ill and had to turn her head. When this did not work, she left the room and leaned against the wall in the hallway, the same hallway that had been used as a little dance floor the night before; the same hallway that had been filled with gifts, history, pride, love and friendship.

Minnie regained her strength and looked frantically through the house, searching for any sign of her friends. She heard Kenji climb down into the basement while she resumed her search, looking in the ransacked kitchen and dining area. She was about to go upstairs when Kenji approached her, his face pasty white. "I went into basement," he told her, "but no one is there." Kenji walked solemnly past Minnie and into the parlor. He saw the blood and tried to glance away, but could not. Clutching his chest, he asked, "What do you think happened?" His voice was hoarse, as if he could not absorb this reality.

Minnie walked to the back yard and called out "Mei Ling! Su Lin! Jade!"

Su Lin and Mei Ling heard nothing from their hiding spot across the street. They were still inside the cabinet, listening intently to boots running past, occasional gunfire, and the grumblings of soldiers behind in the alley. They heard the sound of a tank turret turning, its motor grinding to a halt, and then one round of canons. Suddenly, the noise stopped and Su Lin's head cocked toward the silence. Like a lost duckling that had just heard her mother, she strained toward her home. Mei Ling held her sister back while concentrating to come up with a solution to their dilemma. She finally whispered into Su Lin's ear, "I think we can make it to the school if we take the back streets. We'll have to run the whole way." She had no sooner finished her words than the cannon atop the tank blasted the corner of the building behind them, where the lone machine gunner was perched. The blast rattled the floor, the cabinet in which they were hiding, and their nerves.

Su Lin's head was cocked in another direction but she was nodding. Mei Ling watched her for a moment and there was fear in her eyes. Is this what Su Lin was to be for the rest of her life?

Only five hundred feet away, Minnie discovered the fresh grave in the backyard. Her knees buckled and she reached out for support, but none was to be found. "Kenji," she called. "Kenji, I need you!"

"What is it?" he asked, stepping down from the house. When he saw the grave, a cry escaped from his throat. Minnie knelt and picked up the little cross and Buddha. How could this be happening? Her hands closed around the objects and she turned slowly and deliberately to face him. "She is dead," intoned Minnie, her voice flat and accusing. "You let her die; you could have warned them. You knew something, didn't you? That's why you were here last night. So why didn't you tell them? Why?" She struck out at him, her fists landing harmlessly against his chest. "Look at what you've done!" she said, opening her hands to reveal the icons.

Kenji stared at the Buddha and cross, his face ashen. "It is Mei Ling," he said, emotion choking each word. When Minnie said nothing, he looked beseechingly at her. "Only Mei Ling would be buried with a Buddha and a cross; she was the only true Christian in the family."

Tears appeared in Minnie's eyes and streamed down her face. "No, it cannot be, not our Mei Ling."

All of the conflict of Kenji's love rose up and exploded in anger. "Your Christian school did this!" he accused. "Her father should have let her stay with me, I would have protected her. You have killed her, all of you weak missionaries, with your preaching of love and peace!"

Minnie turned on him, her face twisted in anger. "You love only Kenji. If you had loved her, she was there to be saved, but you did nothing. When she trusted you, you deceived her and left her when she needed you most. What kind of man are you? Look at what your people have done." She advanced closer, pointing an accusing finger in his face. "This was the most perfect family I have ever known. Two boys, a grandmother, a beautiful daughter, are all gone in a matter of days. Who knows where the rest are? Take me to your camps, Kenji. Take me so that I can save Jade, Yen Hsu and Su Lin... and all those others who need me. Minnie Vautrin dropped to her knees and recited a prayer for Mei Ling, the light of her life.

"I cannot take you," he finally said. "And I will not." His hands pushed through the air, his gestures short and determined. "I must go back now; I have a duty to perform for my country and the Emperor."

Minnie stared at him for a long moment. "You knew all about this, didn't you?"

A vein pulsed across Kenji's brow. "I will not be a traitor and face a firing squad."

"You are already a traitor, Kenji-san, a traitor to humanity. Minnie drew the pistol from her pocket and pointed it at his head. "You will drive me to the camps!" she demanded. "And then you will help me find the people I love. For once, you must do what is right and honorable. If you do not, I will shoot you!"

Minnie never saw the lightning-fast movement that knocked her to the ground. By the time she regained her balance, Kenji was gone. Minnie picked up the rusty pistol and limped toward the house, clutching the gun with one hand and a bruised rib with the other. Beaten physically, mentally, and emotionally, she collapsed onto the porch. Sitting there, unable to accept the reality of Mei Ling's death, she saw a figure across the street. She squinted, pushed her face forward for a closer look. The girl was staring at Minnie and then pointing at her. Suddenly, she smiled and tried to jump to feet, only to wince as she took off across the yard and the dangerous street. It was twilight, the air was filled with smoke and defeat, but she would recognize that face anywhere. With joy beating in her chest, she watched the girl run toward her, toward her house and the only home she ever had ever known.

As Su Lin ran, she pointed, laughed and called out "M—mm—Ma!"

"Come here!" shouted a voice from inside the building. Moments later, Mei Ling appeared, turning in every direction as she searched for her sister. She finally spotted her running across the street and darted after her. She was nearly even with Su Lin when she stopped and cried out "Minnie! Minnie!"

Minnie Vautrin ran out the gate and there, in front of what had once been the home of the Hsu family, she threw her arms around the two girls she thought of as her own. The three fell to the ground and embraced each other tearfully. "Mei Ling," sobbed Minnie, "I thought you were dead."

"It's Ma," wept Mei Ling, the hours of fear and tragedy pouring out of her. She clung to Minnie, as if she would never let go.

"Jade?" Minnie whispered. "Oh, God, no." Her tears resumed and she held the girls close to her, rocking them as if they were infants. Finally aware of how exposed they were, she separated herself from the girls and said, "We must return to the Ginling at once."

"I know all the side streets," said Mei Ling. "Father never let us go that way, but I know how."

They made their way toward the school, along the way getting a macabre glimpse of what was happening to their beautiful Nanking. Piles of bodies lay crumpled on the ground, most of them having been shot execution style or gutted by bayonets. The streets were littered with the remnants of life. A random mortar shell went off nearby and they were careful to move only under the cover of shadows and darkness. Gunfire erupted and they stopped, pressed against a deserted building, then proceeded. The gunfire echoed through the city streets, then dissolved into screams and, finally, silence. Rapid shots rang out and troops marched nearby. Minnie and the girls held their breath in collective fear as the tramping soldiers' steps receded.

"Mei Ling," Minnie whispered. "Where is your father?"

"He was beaten and taken away and—"

"But where?" she pressed, her voice urgent, insistent.

Mei Ling clenched her fists, agitation written in her eyes. "We were hiding in the basement and I heard him calling out. Then I heard Mother screaming and then— nothing—and then blood—on my face." She pressed her cheek against Minnie's chest and sobbed yet again.

Su Lin slowly leaned into Minnie as well, saying nothing.

Minnie held the girls and waited for her miracle, for her faith to be revealed. God might let her suffer, but why these innocent girls? Why would her benevolent God not heed the suffering?

TWENTY-TWO

Yen Hsu was able to lift his head. The vision in his right eye was cloudy, but he could make out a small procession of vehicles arriving at the camp. A throbbing pain shot through his cheek and he winced at the touch. His fingers probed carefully and he found the tissue swollen and tender. He remembered heavy boots landing on him, causing him to buckle and cry out. His hands were badly cut, no doubt from trying to defend himself. He was in a makeshift prison surrounded by barbed wire. When he had arrived the day before, this area was adjacent to a duck pond. Now, that pond was filled with floating corpses.

Yen followed the sound of marching and saw soldiers with machine guns. Nearby was a line of prisoners, perhaps twenty. With a nod from the commander, weapons were raised and fired, bodies dropped to the ground. Another group of soldiers ran in, dragged the bodies to the pond and heaved them in. Within minutes, another group of twenty was lined up. This routine continued, precise and effective, while at the same time trucks came and went, off-loading more prisoners and ill-gotten gains, and then turning around and heading back toward Nanking.

In the background, the city burned, its red-orange reflections flickering across the pond and lighting whatever spaces remained between the bodies. Yen turned his head slowly and his eyes fell upon a cluster of large mounds and deep ditches. As he watched, a group of peasants was marched to the top of one of the mounds. Suddenly a Japanese officer arrived in a jeep, jumped out, and approached the commander. "Stop!" he demanded. "Something must be done!"

"Yes, sir," responded the commander. "About what, sir?"

"We're running low on ammunition!"

Yen saw that a peasant standing nearby was observing the heated conversation. He had spoken to the man earlier and knew that the invaders had ransacked his farm that morning. He had been forced to watch four soldiers rape his thirteen year-old daughter. When his wife tried to stop them, she was shot in the face. Another daughter was dragged away and his little boy was hiding or dead, he had no way of knowing. Yen turned away from the peasant and saw a deep trench that ran for nearly a hundred yards and was filled with the dead. Who were they? Perhaps farmers or shopkeepers, bankers, husbands and fathers, men of all ages.

A soldier walked up behind the peasant. "Looking for someone?" he demanded in broken Chinese.

The man stared at the soldier, terror in his eyes.

"I'll help you look for them," growled the soldier. Before the prisoner could respond, the soldier raised his sword and, with one swing of the blade, severed the man's head. Its mouth gaping open, it dropped with a sickening thud and rolled toward the trench. The man's body fell to the ground, extremities twitching for several seconds.

The commander approached the soldier and clapped him on the back. "Excellent idea!" he declared, smiling broadly. "No more wasted bullets!"

As if having received a direct command, other soldiers removed their swords and charged. There were twice as many peasants as soldiers, yet the peasants froze. One by one, their heads were severed. When the act was completed, the officer walked among the corpses to survey his work. Satisfied, he gestured for his men to proceed and the next batch of peasants was lined up and beheaded. And the next. Within a short time, headless torsos covered every mound of soil.

Yen Hsu was marched out of his holding area and stood with the others, lips moving silently as he said his good-byes to his family, his country, his life. The men around him stared in horror at their impending slaughter, barely responding when bellies were prodded with bayonets.

"I need to move property from the Chung Yang area," announced the commander. "Who will volunteer?"

Yen Hsu immediately took one step forward and saluted. "I know this area very well," he said in Japanese. "I can help."

A soldier standing behind Yen struck him in the side with the butt of his rifle. "Shut up! You do not speak to the commander!"

Yen clutched his midsection and fought mightily to hold back the vomit rising in his throat. To show pain or weakness would be his death sentence.

The commander approached Yen and looked him over. This prisoner was not dressed like the peasants, nor the shopkeepers. He waved Yen to step forward. "You're from Chung Yang?"

"Yes, sir, and I can show you the richest houses."

"Why do you speak Japanese?"

"It is a superior language," responded Yen. "I am a banker."

"Good answer!" The commander gestured to his aide. "Bring him and four strong ones."

The aide turned to Yen. "You, banker, pick four to work."

Panic rushed through Yen. To have this power to choose who would live and who would die was something he never wanted: the fate of those he did not pick would weigh heavily upon him. "We may need more than four, sir, for particularly heavy items."

The soldier studied Yen Hsu's expression, as if looking for deceit, and walked to him, pistol drawn. "By chance, are you trying to save this man?" he asked, pointing to a peasant standing nearby.

Before Yen could speak, the soldier raised his pistol and shot the man between the eyes. He turned back to Yen. "Or perhaps you think that this man will help you escape." He walked up to another man standing near Yen and shot him as well. Turning to Yen, he smiled and then shouted "Four!"

Every man within earshot looked at Yen for even a touch of hope, if only for a few hours. Their eyes were pleading, fiery with desire to live another few minutes. Yen could not bear to look these men in the eyes. Instead, he randomly gestured toward the four strongest looking men and then lined up with them near a truck. All the while, a soldier stood in front of Yen and aimed his pistol at his head.

"Go as soon as possible," demanded the commander.

His sergeant saluted smartly and responded, "At first light, sir?"

"General Matsui arrives in the morning," said the commander. "We must leave now!"

The soldiers directed Yen Hsu and the four others into the back of a large military truck. Yen sat close to the tailgate. A fat soldier was directly opposite him, his machine gun pointed at the prisoners. A second soldier, this one with terrible acne, was seated nearer the cab. As the truck moved toward Nanking, Yen closed his eyes and thought of his daughters, then muttered a silent prayer for their safety. If only they were able to stay in hiding until the soldiers left the house.

The truck passed another row of bodies shoved into a mass grave. Yen noted how sparks flew from a makeshift grinding wheel and that soldiers were lined up to have their swords and bayonets sharpened. Further away, two men were methodically beheading peasants and kicking their bodies into a ditch. Yen thought it ironic that the murderers were rubbing their shoulders, made sore from this taxing work.

The truck rolled forward and Yen saw children digging through the endless piles of corpses. Were they looking for clothing...or their parents? Japanese soldiers dragged a Chinese couple from their doorway, one of the soldiers stopping long enough to rip the dress off the woman. The husband broke free and tried to throw himself between his wife and the attacker, but he was immediately shot in the back. He fell against his wife and they both toppled to the ground. The corpulent soldier seated across from Yen laughed.

"What's so funny?" asked the one with bad skin, leaning against the cab as if enjoying an outing.

"These stupid Chinese, come look." When his friend remained seated, the fat one grabbed the side of the truck and stood up, twisting for a better view.

Yen Hsu glanced at the pock-marked soldier nearest the cab and saw that he was looking away. Without pause, Yen leapt to his feet and kicked the fat man with all his might, causing the soldier to double over. In one motion, Yen placed his foot against the man's back and shoved him out of the truck. When he landed, there was a snapping sound, an indication that he was dead. Yen quickly resumed his place, his expression the epitome of innocence. As the truck completed the turn, the second guard realized that his comrade was gone. As he made his way to the back of the truck, one of the other Chinese extended a foot and the soldier stumbled forward. Before he could regain his balance, Yen sent him out the back as well.

There was a long, stunned pause, followed by sudden activity. Yen leapt from the back of the truck, instinctively tucking his head so he would roll on impact and minimize injury. One by one, the prisoners followed, each man quickly disappearing into the cold, damp night. The vehicle had traveled several hundred yards before anyone in cab noted their absence. The driver jammed on the brakes and a screeching sound pierced the night.

Yen Hsu sprinted into an alley, hurdling over bodies and debris. When he came across a dead woman and child, he turned toward the wall and retched. Before he could move on, a pair of patrolling soldiers suddenly appeared. Yen threw himself onto the pile of bodies and held his breath. The soldiers were closer, one of them firing into a pile of bodies several feet away. The other man began to scavenge through the pile where Yen lay, but his comrade made a joke about a house down the street that looked untouched and they rushed off.

Yen wiped vomit from his mouth and rushed in the opposite direction, holding to the shadows as he moved toward Chung Lo Street. As he neared his house, he became more daring, leaping over fences and into back yards, no longer creeping cautiously for fear of his life.

Suddenly, he was standing before his neighbor's home, the one that had received a direct blast from cannon fire. It still smoldered, although most of the house was reduced to ash. He was nearly atop the wall separating this house from his own when he espied soldiers coming down his steps. One of them was carrying his Victrola. The pillagers stood together, chatting with excitement about the quality of goods they had acquired. Still talking, one of the soldiers looked toward the fence and then began to walk in that direction.

Yen Hsu darted across the street and hid behind a large mound of debris. Fearful of being discovered, he rushed into the building and dove under an old carpet, glass breaking beneath him. His heart raced when he heard footsteps. He knew that one of the soldiers was walking nearby, the other probably circling the building. Yen had no way of knowing that, only a few feet away, Minnie and his daughters were also hiding.

Minnie and the girls cowered in their hideout and listened to the movements outside. Boxes were being kicked, footsteps were audible, glass was splintering under heavy boots. She had no idea how many soldiers there were, but they were perilously close, perhaps only a few feet away. She pressed a hand over her mouth to muffle the deep intake of breath, heart racing with a fear greater than any she had never known. Su Lin stared confidently at Minnie, remaining silent as the soldier walked past.

The man approached the rugs where Yen Hsu was hiding and saw part of Yen's shoe. As he readied his rifle, Yen heard the noise and said a silent prayer.

Minnie and the girls bolted from behind the closet, knocking it over and sending it crashing to the floor. As they fled out the back door, the soldier spun on his heels, raised his rifle, and fired. One bullet grazed Minnie's jacket, but struck no flesh.

The three women continued to run, clutching each other's hands and moving at full speed past debris and dumpsters, down an alley and along dank passageways. They ducked into another abandoned building, rushed upstairs and into a room. Mei Ling shoved the door closed and Minnie jammed anything she could find against it. They crept to a window, its pane long since destroyed, and peeked into a dismal and desolate night. There were bombers overhead, gunfire and explosions in the distance. The sky was red, orange, black and gray, the wind whipping across Minnie's face so cold that it bit into her bones. Everywhere she looked, Nanking was being destroyed. She pressed a hand against Su Lin's cheek. "We'll be in the safety of my home soon," she promised.

Su Lin stared outside and said nothing.

Mei Ling took her sister's hand and squeezed it. "She's been like this since—"

"She'll be fine," interjected Minnie. "It's shock, but it will pass. Our only goal is to get to the Ginling."

Yen Hsu peeked out from under the filthy rug, still not sure what had just happened. His body shook like a rabbit on the run from a large predator. When it was evident that he was alone, he sidled to a nearby window, saw that the street was clear, then rushed outside and back to his house. He bolted past the fountain, up the once-welcoming stairs and into the parlor. Jade was gone, but the sofa was soaked in blood. There was more blood trailing across the wooden floor toward the back of the house. He ran to the trap door, which stood open. "Mei Ling, Su Lin," he called out. "It is Father." Lighting a match, he searched the hiding space repeatedly, hoping that his eyes were deceiving him. When he accepted that they were gone, he fell to his knees and sobbed. After a time, he willed himself to stop and evaluate the possibilities. That they were gone did not mean they were dead. "My girls are smart," he told himself. "If possible, they'll go directly to the Ginling and to Minnie." He tried to stand, but his legs gave out from under him and slumped to the floor in a faint.

Minnie and the girls remained motionless as soldiers jogged past their hiding place. When the echo of footsteps retreated, she peered out and whispered, "We must leave now. They'll be back, and we'll freeze if we stay here much longer." She led the way and they crept around the corner and darted from building to building, holding hands when possible, moving like crabs sidling from rock to rock during low tide. They passed a storefront and Su Lin broke away for a closer look. Suddenly, a Japanese supply truck appeared from a side street. From behind a fallen rickshaw, Minnie and Mei Ling looked on in horror as one of the soldiers pointed to Su Lin.

The truck slowed and the soldier made as if to climb down. Before that was possible, the driver called out "Is there only one?"

"Yeah," replied the first. "Let's go to the Ginling, where there are thousands!"

The moment the truck was out of sight, Minnie and Mei Ling grabbed Su Lin by the arms and ran deeper into the al-

ley. They came to a corner and stopped. Mei Ling shook her
sister gently and looked her in the eye. Nothing. She shook
her again, this time harder, and then slapped her. Mei Ling
immediately cried out "I'm sorry, I'm so sorry," and pulled
the girl to her and stroked her hair, oblivious to the sudden,
biting rain.

"We must get to the school," insisted Minnie.

Mei Ling used the rainwater to wipe blood and grime
from her sister's face. As she washed, she murmured words
of comfort.

"Mei Ling, it's imperative," urged Minnie, her face
white with fear.

To the surprise of both women, Su Lin looked directly
at Minnie and nodded. Mei Ling took the girl's hand and
lead her stealthily across the street, Minnie close behind.
After traveling for only a few minutes, they found a lean-to
with fire smoldering under its makeshift roof. Inside were
two Chinese men seated around a small fire and smoking an
opium pipe. The men argued over some found object, as if
the women were not standing just outside in the rain. One of
the men finally beckoned the three inside and, as if orches-
trated for effect, the sky opened to a deluge.

Minnie placed herself between the girls and the drugged
men. Mei Ling sat and tucked her sister onto her lap, under
her arms. They nestled among the debris, as close to the fire
as they could sit, until Su Lin nodded off, opium smoke
wafting past her. Mei Ling soon fell asleep as well, but
Minnie stayed alert. She watched one of the men open a
package of opium, its seal bearing the rising sun emblem.
He put the drug into his pipe and lit it, inhaling deeply as
rain pounded against the sheet metal, a cacophonous reminder of the echoes of war all around. When he offered his
pipe to Minnie, she asked, "Would Buddha poison his
mind?"

"Are you Buddha?" the man responded quickly.

Minnie lifted her chin. "What you're doing is unclean
for the mind and the soul."

"I have not seen many clean souls, have you?" he asked, lighting another match and putting it to the drug.

"You need to find God."

"God? Lady, I can't find my wife or my children. Please, tell me when your God shows up, I have many questions." With that, he took another deep draw and closed his eyes.

Minnie was at a rare loss for words. As much as she abhorred what he was doing, she found no more words to chastise him. How could she, with all of them sitting in the middle of hell on earth. She continued to keep an eye on the men, while fatigue washed over her. Slipping into sleep, she thought how the rain might wash the blood from their faces, but never from their hearts.

TWENTY-THREE

Gentle rain fell on Mei Ling's face as she gazed at the burnished sky. It was full of puffy white clouds spinning in high-speed motion. As they spun, they turned darker and darker. She and Su Lin were standing near the Yangtze, holding hands and laughing among the billowing plum blossoms. The sky was suddenly saturated with storm clouds and Mother and Father were urging the girls to pose with their two younger brothers. They all danced and laughed as the skies opened and rain fell upon them. They ran across a lovely Nanking business street down by the riverfront and took cover inside a little shop. Father bought them candy and he smiled and stroked Mei Ling's long hair; they stood together under the alcove, safe from the rain.

One of the opium smokers moved closer to the beautiful, sleeping Mei Ling. In his stupor, he ran a filthy hand across her hair. The girl, fast asleep, nuzzled toward his hand and he thought she was beautiful, so lovely in the amber glow of the fire. Mei Ling continued to dream about being with her family on a bustling Nanking street.

Minnie and Kenji were on opposite sides of the street, taking photos of a passing marriage procession that consisted of two peasants in a rickshaw and the family following behind, dancing and prancing. They passed from view and the streets became busy, rickshaws and pedestrians running noisily in every direction. Mei Ling tried to cross the street between the rickshaws, toward Minnie and Kenji, but she could not make it. She called to them, but there was too much noise. The sky clouded over and lightning and thunder began.

Mei Ling awoke to the sound of Japanese soldiers standing next to the shelter, kicking at the metal sheets and causing a roaring noise to penetrate the little space. The opium smoker's hand was on her and she pulled back in disgust. At the same time, she grabbed hold of Su Lin, who stirred next to her. Minnie awoke with a start and shook off the dulled sense of sleep. She looked around, as if trying to get her bearings.

"Addicts, whores, get out!" called a voice from the exterior. A soldier appeared, bending over so that his face was visible.

Minnie sat rod-straight and glared at the soldier. "I beg your pardon," she retorted, as if speaking to someone of lowly rank. "I am Minnie Vautrin, an American citizen, and headmistress of the Ginling College. You must take me there at once."

"We need a head mistress!" laughed one of the soldiers, and the other joined in, reaching down and slipping both hands against Su Lin's backside.

Mei Ling struck at him wildly, spitting curses in his face until she was kicked to the ground. Minnie pushed herself in front of Mei Ling and announced, "You must take us to the Ginling at once. This young woman is the fiancée of the secretary to the Japanese Consul."

The soldiers laughed even harder and leered at the girls. "No matter," scoffed one of them. "I'm her fiancé now."

The soldiers shoved the opium users out of the lean-to, causing them to fall against the can containing the fire. Within seconds, the space was ablaze, its former inhabitants safely outside, and the rain had doused the fire.

"These men have nothing for you," begged Minnie, a cry escaping from her throat. "Leave them alone, for God's sake."

One of the soldiers leaned over and sniffed at Su Lin like a hungry dog. Another grabbed Mei Ling and pulled her arms back, exposing the contours of her body for the others to see. The soldiers grabbed her and tied her hands before she could reach the gun hidden in her coat. Mei Ling, along with Minnie and Su Lin, were marched off in the cold rain, down the middle of the street and between another group of soldiers.

Magee and Forster finished filming the bodies of two women tied to a post, their legs spread-eagle from their assault. Forster, pale and shaken, stood near the Red Cross car and vomited. When he was done, he wiped his mouth politely with his handkerchief and asked, "May we go now?"

Magee turned and caught sight of Minnie, Mei Ling, and Su Lin, in the company of soldiers. Magee ran up to them and flashed his armband. "There must be a mistake," he said, keeping his voice official. "May I ask what you are doing with these women?"

Forster whipped out his official papers and shoved them toward the soldiers. "Look at these," he demanded. "Look!" When one soldier took the documents, he began to fumble with the ropes binding Mei Ling's wrists.

"Thank God you're here," said Minnie, the words coming out as a grateful moan.

A soldier stepped forward and grabbed Forster's arm. "Stop now, or we will shoot!"

"At whom?" asked Forster, extricating his arm with a tug. "These women cannot be taken as prisoners. They are with us, at the mission. And Miss Vautrin here is headmistress at the college."

As if undaunted by the raised bayonets, Forster resumed his work on the knots and freed Mei Ling's wrists. Minnie handed over the letter written by Tanaka. "Read this!" she demanded, glaring triumphantly. A few of the soldiers scanned the document and backed away at once. The others seemed reluctant to move along, but changed their minds and joined their friends.

"Ladies," said Forster, doing his very best nobleman's impression. "I suggest we get the hell out of hell!" He urged everyone into the car and muttered a prayer of thanks as the engine fired up. They drove off toward the Ginling, as if they were five friends on an outing.

Forster picked up speed, turning the wheel to avoid pockets of people, carts, trash, and the dead. He made a sharp turn and arrived in front of a large gate. The sidewalk was teeming with refugees. A sign above the gate read *International Safety Zone*. Forster drove confidently toward the gate and hardly slowed as the gatekeepers cleared a path for the car flying Red Cross flags. When they entered the zone, a collective sigh rushed through the car.

"Minnie, what were you doing out there?" asked Magee.

"I went to save them," she said, her voice barely a whisper. "I had to!"

Mei Ling reached over and grasped Minnie's hand. "We would not have made it back without you."

Su Lin looked over at Minnie and something in her eyes suddenly changed. It was if a light had been ignited.

Magee, in the passenger seat, twisted around to face his friend. "Minnie, you should have told us," he scolded. "We would have driven you to the house and back. Just look at this mess," he demanded, gesturing outside the vehicle. "You should have never left without us."

Minnie listened and remained silent for several moments. Finally, she said, "The truth is, I thought I'd be safe with Kenji." Her face shifted to anger. "But he abandoned me when he thought he had caused Mei Ling's death."

"My—?"

"He thinks you're dead," explained Minnie.

"If he was able to abandon you," declared Forster, "perhaps his thinking that Mei Ling died is for the best."

Mei Ling buried her face in both hands. "My God, Ma's dead and Father—we don't even know."

"I'm so sorry," said Magee. "We'll do everything we can to find him, I promise."

Forster steered the car through the crowded streets. "Minnie, straight to your residence?"

"Yes, please. We all need to get settled in a bit. And Su Lin's still in a dreadful shock, I fear."

The car weaved between rows of huddling peasants and refugees, most of them women and children, with an occasional elderly man. Mei Ling covered her mouth and nose with the fabric from her skirt, the stench of rotting corpses permeating the air inside the car. The fires around which the displaced huddled for warmth increased the stink.

The car drove through the gated entrance to the Ginling. Minnie looked out and saw Mary running toward them, lantern in hand. "What on earth are you doing out now?" she asked, but it came out as a demand. Bending, she peered into the back and saw the three women. Her face broke into a smile and then she began to cry. "By the good graces of the Lord, look what we have here!"

Magee nearly laughed. "We plucked 'em from the hands of the enemy."

Mary rushed through an explanation of how fearful she had been when Kenji had returned to the consulate without Minnie. "I was beside myself with fear," she said. "I went to the Consul, but Kenji refused to see me. Then I–" Her voice trailed off as she realized how exhausted her friends were. "What can I do?" she asked, helping Minnie out of the car.

"Give Su Lin a hand," she replied.

"But be very gentle," said Mei Ling. "She hasn't said a word since—"

Minnie held up a hand and Mei Ling fell silent. "Let's just get her inside and warmed up, with some tea and biscuits."

Mei Ling suddenly began to cry, her body shaking from fear and grief. She clung to her little sister as they walked from the car. Forster and Magee followed, eyes filled with tears.

Minnie leaned closer to Mary. "Please, do not tell the others that Mei Ling is here. And no matter what, Kenji is NOT to enter the Ginling again."

Mary nodded and followed Minnie, who walked with both arms draped over the girls' shoulders, like ducklings being protected under their mother's wings. They passed groups of women and children huddled in the hallways and continued until they reached Minnie's little house.

Sometime later, a dazed, but clean Su Lin was tucked into a makeshift bed in the sitting room, her favorite quilt—the one Minnie had carried from Illinois more than twenty years earlier—keeping her warm.

While Minnie tended to Su Lin, Mei Ling washed her face in a bowl of water. Straightening up, she caught sight of her reflection and felt a shock, as if there was something in her appearance that she did not recognize.

There were several rapid knocks at the door. Minnie brushed a hand against Su Lin's face and then went to open it. She smiled at Wong, ushered him inside and filled him in on what had occurred. When he asked how the girls were doing, Minnie told him "Fine, physically, but spiritually—I'm sick in my heart. This violence festers like a disease all over the city." Her mouth began to quiver and she looked away. "The things I've seen," she said, her voice low. "If this keeps up, I'm afraid civilization will be lost."   Wong stood quietly, one hand kneading the fingers of the other. "You need to rest, all of you."

As if he had never spoken, Minnie took a step closer and grabbed his wrist. "Listen to me: it is imperative that no one knows the girls are here. No one, especially Kenji."

Wong seemed confused and then alarmed. "Kenji?"

Minnie waved the name away with an angry gesture. "He struck me, that spineless man, and then he left me for dead."

"Miss Minnie, I'm sure he didn't know that—" He was caught open-mouthed when Mei Ling appeared, disheveled but in tune with the conversation.

Mei Ling turned to Minnie. "You do know that I must see him."

Minnie's eyes flashed in anger. "I forbid it."

"His people might be—but he's—"

"Mei Ling, he struck me, abandoned me and left me for dead. Do you understand? He cares for no one but himself. A man like that is not capable of loving. He left you, me, your whole family out there to die."

Tears came to Mei Ling's eyes. "But you would never have found us if he hadn't tried to help."

"I told you, I forbid it," demanded Minnie. "And that is all I will say."

"But—"

Wong interrupted with an upheld hand and a firm voice. "You will listen to Miss Minnie, she has wisdom and faith. And she loves you."

"And what of me," cried Mei Ling. "What faith should I have now? At least Kenji went looking for me, that gives me faith!"

Minnie shook her head, as if dismissing everything Mei Ling said. "He could be the death of us all," she insisted. "He knew what was coming to Nanking and he did nothing to warn us. No," she added with conviction, "you will not see him." Minnie gestured Wong toward the door, signaling for him to leave them alone. When he was near the door, she placed an arm around Mei Ling's stiff shoulders. "We must not discuss this anymore tonight. I cannot, please."

"Minnie, I love you, but he promised—"

"Promises that cannot be kept should never be made, my dear. Do you really think that a Japanese Consulate member can be seen with a Chinese girlfriend, let alone a wife? He has been lying to you, I'm sure of it."

Minnie blew out the candles and saw that Wong remained at the door. After the girls were settled, he whispered to Minnie, "The Ginling is now home to perhaps ten thousand refugees. We need you more than ever so please, never leave without me again." After a long pause, he added, "I would die without your spirit. I must tell you now that I—"

Minnie placed a hand on his arm. "I know, Wong, I know."

Words that did not need to be said were conveyed through their eyes. Finally, after Minnie extinguished the last candle, Wong kissed her on the forehead and left, closing the door quietly behind him.

Mei Ling tried to stay awake, staring up at the strands of smoke that danced across the ceiling in the moon's dull glow. How was it possible that Kenji had left poor Minnie? And was it true that he had struck her? Only when she convinced herself that Minnie exaggerated—most likely because Kenji was Japanese—was she able to fall asleep.

TWENTY-FOUR

The Commander in Chief of the Japanese Army, General Matsui Iwane, sat atop his military steed just outside the city gates. He was positioned at the head of the long processional of armaments, tanks, cannons, and troops that stretched far behind him. Raising his arm straight overhead, the general waved the procession forward. With great pageantry, they entered the city gates through the old city wall, Iwane looking very much the conquering Roman Emperor. Even his horse had the gait of a noble conqueror. A seemingly endless parade of soldiers followed behind, occasionally firing their weapons overhead, the blasts heard above the reverberating thud of thousands of marching feet. Chinese citizens cowered by the sides of the road. Despite having been assured that the arrival of this general would herald the end of brutality, that the presence of such an important figure would encourage captains and lieutenants to calm their violent troops, they watched the arrival of this force with defeat and fear etched into their faces. There was no one left to defend them, to hold the Japanese invaders accountable for anything, except for that handful of missionaries and those few members of the International Safety Zone Committee. All government personnel had abandoned the city, followed closely by city officials and workers. The last to leave was Chinese army.

Occasional echoes of shelling and gunplay came down from the mountains, where insurgents did their best to aggravate and spy on the Japanese, but the citizenry was not comforted. Those shopkeepers, farmers, peasants, and other unfortunates unable to leave were about to lose everything, if they had not already. And if all material possessions were to be lost, why had they remained? What had they hoped to salvage? The answers were apparent in their sagging shoulders and their heavily creased brows.

The grand entrance of General Iwane and his troops was caught on film by John Magee, who was always at the ready these days. His camera rolled as the spectacle unfolded, his eyes growing wider as the pageantry passed before him. The same could not be said of his reluctant advocate, Ernest Forster, who now accompanied Magee on every outing. He watched his friend, the fearless Magee, who was so intent on documenting this, and most every other event of the occupation, that his zeal bordered on obsession. Forster was certain that, without realizing it, Magee's fixation on documenting this war would secure his place in history.

Forster stood to the side and watched Magee shoot and wind, shoot and wind, as if nothing mattered but the action unfolding before them. After lots of thought, he decided that Magee used his camera not only to record history, but to help him deal with the barbarity around him. Shooting film, worrying about light and shadows, staying alive, these forced him into a certain state of detachment that allowed him to do his work.

Forster had seen cameras used by the Japanese. Often, the shooter was a military attaché lurking in the shadows, trying to capture soldiers taking target practice on live bodies, or bayonet training on bodies tied to posts. If the first soldier, running at full speed, failed to penetrate the heart and cause instant death, the photographer knew that the next attempt could be the one. There were those Japanese who photographed only to prove the beauty of their victory. These were the men who took pictures of children being fed, of girls being marched to internment camps; the images that would look good in the Tokyo papers.

Forster and Magee moved with the flow of the procession, which was adjacent to the safety zone. Japanese soldiers attempted to clean the streets before their general arrived, but they were heavily littered with bodies and the detritus of war. "This is what we need the world to see," said Magee, capturing the carnage through his lens. He saw the general approach and raised the camera. "Just look at that pretentious bastard," he mumbled, the camera whirring away.

Forster watched the display for a few minutes. "Who would've expected the capital city of China to fall so fast? Certainly not Chiang Kai-shek."

Magee shifted the rolling camera from the army's entrance to a street just behind him, where several women were tied to chairs. They were dead, stabbed in the belly, heads sagging in a final and grotesque pose.

"That's bloody morbid," protested Forster. "Leave it, Magee, I feel ill again." He rubbed his eyes. "We can't bury everyone, but I—"

Magee stopped shooting and lowered the camera. "God rest their souls, Ernest. We'll have to send for help to bury these women. No one should have to see this."

"Then why must you film it?" Just as Forster spoke, a platoon of Japanese soldiers moved toward them. He tugged on Magee's sleeve and the men rushed away and darted down an alley. There they found a group of Chinese men being forced to load Japanese supply trucks. From what Magee and Forster could discern, these prisoners were expected to help soldiers loot their own stores. One of the shopkeepers bowed near his door each time he entered. Magee pointed the camera and zoomed in as much as he could, the lens partially revealing the corpse of a woman lying on the floor just inside the man's shop. Magee scanned the scene closely, following the man as he loaded the last crate from his store onto the back of the overloaded truck. Magee shot the contents—bolts of silk, crates of fine china, silverware, many casks of rice wine—and then turned the camera on the shopkeeper's face. Before he could pull away, one of the soldiers put a bullet in the man's head. With that, the soldiers climbed into their truck and drove off.

Forster grabbed Magee's arm and pulled him close. "John, we absolutely must get this footage out of here, so the world will understand what's happening."

Magee nodded numbly, the image of one man's death causing his eyes to burn. "The next American boat is scheduled for January, if it's still coming. But with the *Panay* getting sunk, who knows?"

The two men watched the final parade of soldiers pass by before they made their way back to the entrance of the safety zone. Both of them were lost in private thoughts about war, death and life. They arrived at the Red Cross building, entered Magee's office and collapsed into the chairs. Magee sat in his oversized chair and closed his eyes. For the time being, he was safe, but his mind ached from having witnessed a savageness he had once hoped would disappear. Rising with a heavy sigh, he began to prepare tea. One quick glance toward Forster told him that his friend was even more rattled than he. Was he growing numb to it all? A good Episcopalian his whole life, it was unlikely that could happen.

Forster walked over and picked up his friend's old putter. He began to hit golf balls between the two books on the floor—*The Last Puritan*, which was a best seller from the year before, and *The Classic Age of Chinese Thought* by Confucius. For the moment, he found it less painful to pretend he was on his favorite golf course than to acknowledge the horrors just witnessed. He tapped a ball and watched it roll toward the door. When the door opened, the ball was putted back to his feet.

George Fitch pushed open the door and leaned against the jamb. A quick glance at his disheveled friends and it was clear that their day had not been easy. "Not a lot of golf to be played these days, eh?"

Magee attempted a smile. "Too many people to care for, too much war. Is it that simple?"

"I'm glad to see both of you back in one piece. I was told that you were driving around the city, which doesn't sound like a pleasant outing." As he spoke, all levity disappeared from his voice.

"We're flying our American flags so high and mighty and from head to toe," said Forster, showing off his armbands. Along with the stars and stripes was an armband emblazoned with the rising sun. "Magee called it insurance," he said. "And it seems to be working."

"Now that you boys are back, I guess I'll be on my way to the Ginling to drop off more provisions." Fitch seemed anxious to leave.

"What's the hurry?" asked Magee.

Forster smiled. "I think he's afraid you'll enlist his services for your off-site moving picture production."

"Better I leave that to Forster," nodded Fitch. When Forster grunted, the men smiled and Fitch walked out.

Magee gave a little wave to his friend's disappearing back, then said, "We've only got a few reels of film left, y'know."

Forster thought about this for a moment. "I can take the used film on the *Oahu* in January, or we can see if the Kodak office in Shanghai had reopened."

"If the building's still there," said Magee. "Besides, it'll be treason if they catch you with this sort of footage in occupied territory. Maybe we should try to ship it all back to the States."

Forster smiled and winked. "I guess that depends on who catches me."

Magee picked up a broadsheet distributed by some of Chiang Kai-shek's people. "It says here that the Americans are supporting Chiang and—listen to this—at the same time, they're supplying the Japanese with raw materials. Politics," he groused, tossing the paper onto the desk."

"Kind of like betting on win, place, and show," suggested Forster.

Magee thought about this for a moment. "I'm almost certain that Truman would agree to carry the reels out."

"Truman's a newspaperman," laughed Forster. "He'll probably try to sell them!"

Magee was not easily amused. "If anything happens to me, the only proof of this carnage would be lost."

Forster saw his friend's concern. "Morbid thought," he declared. "And for the record, I'm coming out of this in one piece. And why shouldn't I? I'm not at war with them damn Japs, am I? And you're not at war with them. And America's sure as hell not at war with anyone, either."

Magee stepped over to the window and looked out toward the Ginling. There was no way to know what fate awaited his friends.

On the streets in the safety zone, thousands of peasants stood in food or clothing lines. It was eerily quiet, with no pushing or demanding, just defeated souls trying to remain alive. It was getting colder, so the line for blankets and coats was nearly as long as the rice line. There was resigned acceptance on everyone's faces, as if they were saying, "This is what life has delivered: the need to take another few steps forward for a little cup of rice." No one seemed concerned that they did not have a cup in which to put it. Despite the fact that dysentery was settling into the camp, this stopped no one from licking bits of rice from their fingers. At the front of the line, in the serving area, toddlers were on their knees, picking up every dropped grain of rice and stuffing it into their pockets. One child, a bloodied bandage taped over one eye, chased off a scavenging crow with the fervor of a religious man going after Satan himself.

At the entrance to the college, George Fitch pulled up in the Red Cross truck and waved to Minnie. His arrival was cause for relief because the thousands of refugees under her wing had again exhausted all of the medical supplies. Minnie had no idea that the Red Cross was nearly out of gauze, morphine and surgical thread.

Fitch jumped from the car, opened the back door and began to remove boxes. "This might be the last load for a while," he said. "So you'll have to stretch it out as best you can."

Minnie's mouth opened, although it was a moment before she could speak. "But what about the reserves?"

"Minnie, I'm sorry, but these are the reserves. The Chinese made promises before they left, but we can't find a thing in the storage sheds. We think the Japanese army took it all before we got there."

Minnie picked up one of the boxes. "I guess anything's a blessing these days. I'm deeply grateful, but I'm still going to have to pay Tanaka another visit."

Fitch leaned in close and whispered, "Don't tell anybody, but I'm going into the film distribution business."

Minnie shook her head. "You be careful, George Fitch. If you're caught, it won't be a church social in Charleston, with a round of golf to follow."

"Ah, come on, Miss Minnie, you know I can always rely on my Southern charm." With that, he put an arm around her and winked.

"You are a flirtatious man, Fitch, but you can't sweet-talk this old bird."

It took several trips before the boxes could be carried from the car into the main office. When the last of them were in place, Fitch leaned against the wall and crossed his arms. "How're the girls doing?"

"Better this morning," replied Minnie. "Like them, we've all witnessed too much. It's hard to give them hope when my own faith has been shaken to the core. These poor girls have lost everyone." She waved away the thought with a flip of her hand. "I don't want to talk about it, George, I'm sorry. At the moment, I'm looking for solutions, not tribulations. Maybe if we could just get them out, on a safe ship to the States—"

Fitch and Minnie remained there in silence, each lost in his own thoughts, until Minnie finally said, "George, this war in Nanking frightens me and challenges our faith. Would you pray with me?"

With the world outside the college continuing to disintegrate, Minnie and George held hands and bowed their heads, hoping they might find, now more than ever before, a more direct alliance with God.

It was the first official meeting of the International Safety Zone Committee. The meeting was called to order in a large office at the American Red Cross building. The electricity was out again and the room was lit by lanterns, yet nearly a dozen men sat around the conference table. John Rabe, a bespectacled German in his mid-fifties, opened with "The numbers are staggering." As if this were a stock tally, he added, "We have a crisis of massive proportions on our hands."

Mackay, in his roguish accent, chimed in like a reporter. "In a matter of days, we have gone from ten thousand to two hundred and fifty thousand refugees."

Magee scanned the faces around him, noting that most of the members were in attendance. "From the Red Cross perspective, there's a dangerous lack of fresh water and medical supplies. We face the threat of starvation and disease. So where are the supplies we were counting on?"

Another member, Bates, nodded slowly and gazed around the table. "We were promised twenty thousand bags of rice, but less than half has made it here. And there's no flour," he added.

Forster, the man known for his concerns about the weather, added "People are freezing and frostbite could get ugly. It's cold and dreary out there, so where are the Red Cross blankets?" He turned to the Red Cross representative and asked, "Magee?"

John Magee was exhausted, as were they all. The siege had left them scrambling for supplies, where none could be found. "The blankets? Well, most were stolen by soldiers when they entered my buildings for inspection. I guess they wanted to make sure we had room for the rice they were going to give us." The irony was not lost on his colleagues. Despite the gloomy mood, some actually smiled. "Of course, they never delivered the rice, and along with the blankets they also carried off most our medical supplies."

Dr. Trimmer, the representative from University Hospital, asked "How about gauze and plasma, Magee? I need them above everything else in the surgical room."

"We already gave you all we had," Magee answered with an apologetic shrug.

Rabe nodded as he listened and then announced, "Gentlemen, I will talk to Tanaka myself. Japan is an ally of Germany and, since I'm German and a standing member of the Nazi party, I will convey the message that my government would rightly never allow such atrocities. Let me meet with Tanaka at the embassy, then I suggest we invite the conquering general for dinner. We need his support."

Magee leaned forward, mouth opened, the expression on his face one of incredulity. "Are you saying that we should invite him because…it's good business?"

"No," replied Rabe, cocking his head toward the reverend. "I'm saying we should invite him because it is what a gentleman would do."

Rosen watched this exchange and then jumped in, addressing his comments to John Magee. "You must remember that we Germans have a relationship with the Japanese. I think Mr. Rabe is suggesting that perhaps we can use this to our advantage, in order to help the peasants." Looking about the room, he added, "It's really quite simple, gentlemen."

"Have you seen what's out there?" interjected Forster. "I've witnessed far more than I care to admit. I can't just sit here and wait for you to *say* something. I want to know if you'll apply real diplomatic pressure on them. For heaven's sake," he added, shaking his head forcefully. "Somebody has to do something."

Rabe was known to go about his business as the perfunctory executive and negotiator. At the same time, the others in the room did not forget that on two separate occasions he had saved the lives of Chinese families. They also knew that Rabe took good care of his own. Nevertheless, it was also Rabe who had tried to escape early on. There was a general consensus that he would be given their full support because, at the end of the day, he was a good man. Most of the members around this table were relieved to know that the Japanese desperately needed Rabe. Only with his leadership would they get the power back on in Nanking. And power was one thing that the Japanese always wanted.

TWENTY-FIVE

Daylight peeked in through the broken basement windows of the once-regal Hsu home. Yen Hsu groaned and rolled, awake on the floor. He opened his eyes to see the dead rat lying across the room, entrails hanging out. The alarming sight caused him to scramble to his feet, head spinning and cheekbone throbbing from the wounds suffered two days earlier. He looked around the basement one last time and then climbed the stairs. Peering out of the trap door, sadness gripped his heart. Where were his children?

Yen crawled out quietly and walked toward the parlor. It was a wreck and the blood on the sofa brought him first to his knees and then to tears.   Broken glass from picture frames lay everywhere. Shattered glass, dreams, and hope lay in the remnants of his once graceful parlor. He saw that a pool of blood remained, where it had pumped through the wound in Jade's heart and down her arm to an outstretched hand. The floor was soaked, still wet and tacky. He knew that this was above where his girls had been hiding, but he could not concentrate on such an image. This could not be his home; he had to get out of this room, this building that had once been his home.

Yen leaned down and plucked a photo from its broken frame. It was a shot of his family taken in the back yard, by the giant winter-blossoming cherry tree. He dreamed for just a moment that everything might be all right after all, but then he heard more soldiers and the sound of trucks rolling down the street. He slipped the photo into his pocket and followed the drops of blood to the back door. Standing there, as he stared at a mound of dirt near the beloved cherry tree, a cold wind slammed the door shut behind him.

Yen walked past his shattered green house, past the shovel, and beyond scores of footprints, both large and small, pressed into the moist ground near the newly dug grave. He fell to his knees and saw the small cross and Buddha. He kneeled low and faced the misty morning sun. After a moment, he picked up the little porcelain Buddha that his wife had so admired and slipped it into his pocket. Mei Ling would have been the one to leave these icons at her mother's grave; she was the devout Christian, the daughter always upset by how much her mother continued to live as a Taoist. Jade loved her Buddha and the learned aphorisms of Confucius. Yen could not help but cry when he thought of how she loved the optimism of the Chosen One. He could hear her saying "It is better to light one candle than to curse the darkness." Darkness had befallen Nanking.

"Jade, my love," Yen murmured. "I will find and protect our daughters; I will reunite with our sons and I will keep this family intact. This, I swear."

Yen saw where the dirt was etched, as if boots had been dragged. He crossed to the fence, looked over and saw the soldier's body crumpled in a heap. He turned back toward his war-torn house. A shadow was moving through one of the rooms and Yen jumped over the back fence, into the alleyway. He scoured the passage behind the brick wall for signs of soldiers and then entered his neighbor's back yard.

Soldiers were everywhere, ransacking houses and searching for valuables. One of them suddenly walked toward Yen, who managed to crouch unseen behind his neighbor's tool shed. The rotund soldier stopped within ten feet, removed his jacket and placed it neatly over a tree branch. He wiped sweat from his face, unzipped his pants and urinated on a rose bush. Yen grabbed a length of wire, wrapped the ends around his fists and lunged, twisting the wire around the soldier's neck and pulling back with all his strength. The soldier's knees buckled and he collapsed into the rose bush. Yen dragged the soldier into the shed and stripped him of his weapons, belt and hat. He took the jacket from the tree and did his best to make it fit over his taller frame.

"Hey, Mako!" a voice called out.

Yen snatched the dagger from the dead man's his pant leg, tucked it into his waist-band and then took the stance of a man urinating.

"Times up, Mako! Hey, did it fall off? Come, we've gotta go!" When there was no response, the soldier moved closer. "I'm talking to you!"

Before the soldier could register the deception, Yen Hsu turned and, in one swift motion, removed the knife from his waistband and slashed the man's throat. He grabbed the soldier's cap, pistol and keys, as well as two hand grenades, which he tucked into his belt.

Resembling the worst-dressed, most ill-fitted Japanese soldier, Yen crept up behind a Japanese supply truck, where two other soldiers were waiting. He took one of the grenades, pulled the pin, and lobbed it as far from the truck as possible. It landed in the middle of a neighbor's greenhouse and exploded, glass and wood frames splintering in the cold air. The soldiers ran toward the explosion, guns drawn, while Yen rushed to the driver's side and jumped in. He put the key in the ignition and exhaled loudly when the engine rumbled to a start. Within seconds, he was roaring away and the soldiers were frantic to stop him.

Yen continued down the alley and onto a side street, where he turned directly into a parade of soldiers marching down the middle of the street. A platoon of perhaps twenty scrambled to avoid disaster, waving their fists at the driver. Moments later, the men who had been chasing the truck came out of the alley yelling "Stolen truck!   Stop him!" Several soldiers took aim and fired, but Yen was safely away.

The little Buddha now sitting on the dashboard, Yen headed across Nanking and toward the commercial district that housed the safety zone and the Ginling College. In his mind, that was the logical place for his daughters to be. He was a good distance before arriving at the gates leading into the safety zone when he maneuvered the truck onto a smaller street. A large group of soldiers were marching toward him. Adrenalin shot through Yen and he instinctively swerved into a building ripped apart by shrapnel. He checked that the pistol was loaded and then jumped into the back of the truck, where he discovered rice and assorted supplies. Well hidden from the street, he opened a tin of military-issue fish and had a quick meal, hand gun and grenade at the ready.

Su Lin sat in the rocking chair, a blanket enfolding her like a cocoon. She stared vacantly at Minnie, who was still in woolen gloves and an overcoat. No matter what the headmistress did, this chill would not go away. She took another blanket and wrapped it around the girl. "This has got to be the coldest day of the year, don't you think?"

Su Lin rocked while Minnie continued to speak as if everything were fine. "Are you warm enough?" She walked to the Victrola. "Here, I'll put some music on for you. Sorry that I don't have any dance or jazzy numbers, but Bach seems to settle my soul. Shall we listen to some Bach?"

Minnie chose one of her favorites, the *Bach Inventions*. When the old recording echoed its scratches, she did not notice. Instead, she listened to the counterpoint weave its first voice into the other. How Minnie could start a counterpoint with Su Lin was beyond her. She had no experience dealing with such severe psychological ailments. "Time heals," said a voice in the back of her mind. But how does one heal a mind that has seen so much? Was faith the answer? Su Lin was surrounded by love, so perhaps she had lost her faith. Minnie prayed for an answer from God

A plane suddenly roared overhead and dropped its payload somewhere around Nanking. The bombs, now relentless, may have landed in the hills far from the Ginling, but Minnie was nevertheless aware that someone, somewhere, had lost a life, a home, a business. That hope she had held—that the fighting might be over, that the killing would stop—was again shattered by the sound of one single bomb. Peace would not come soon.

Yen was also startled by the low-flying plane and the distant explosion, his reminder that it was time to get inside the safety zone. He traveled only a few blocks before nearing a Japanese checkpoint. Yen approached slowly and then moved with speed around the waiting Chinese carts and refugees, while at the same time waving to the guards. To them, it was simply another one of those Japanese convoy trucks that they were instructed to admit. When Yen was nodded through without pause, he smiled.

Further on, he waved at another group of soldiers who, in turn, saluted. "I'm audacious at best," he thought, approaching the school.

A truck suddenly passed roared past him, coming from the opposite direction. It was loaded with Chinese girls crying out. "Jo-ming! Jo-ming!" to anyone who dared to look in their direction. "Save our lives! Save our lives!" He saw that some of them were silent, cowering, heads lowered in shame. Before he could react, the truck was gone.

Yen Hsu pulled up to the crowded checkpoint at the Hanchung Men Gate. It was the southernmost entrance and the one closest to the Ginling and the Red Cross building. He honked the horn loudly and tried to pull right, hoping that this would be as easy as the first checkpoint. When he saw that it was manned by members of the International Safety Zone, he nearly smiled. Moving to the second checkpoint, he recognized his old friend, George Fitch.

Fitch watched a Japanese truck edging into his zone and he was alarmed. The rule was very clear: no soldiers. He confidently waved his Red Cross credentials, as if trying to bring the truck to a complete stop. When Yen rolled down the window and called out "George!" it fell on nearly deaf ears. Fitch's ears were still ringing from a close call with a mortar. Nevertheless, he looked around for the source of the voice and then approached the truck. When he saw the driver, his eyes grew wide. Before he could speak his friend's name, Yen motioned him into silence, pointing to the Japanese checkpoint only yards behind them.

Fitch jumped on the running board, called for the gate to be opened, and Yen drove toward the Red Cross building. "What the hell happened to you?" asked Fitch. "And do I dare ask what you're doing in a Japanese uniform and driving a Japanese truck?" Before Yen could reply, he added, "Good God, man, if the Japs discovered a Chinese diplomat behind the wheel of one of their supply trucks, you'd be shot on sight."

Yen had more pressing issues than his own safety. "Where are my girls?" he begged. "They're here, right? Please, tell me they're all right!"

Fitch clapped a hand on Yen's shoulder. "They're fine, I promise, and they'll be overjoyed to see you. We've all been so worried about you." He glanced toward the back of the truck. "Go straight to the Ginling. They need this rice as much as anyone." He smiled and added, "Looks like dinner's on Hirohito tonight."

Yen slowed the truck until it was nearly stopped. He looked at his friend and said, "Jade's gone, George."

Fitch lowered his head and nodded. "I know, and I don't know what to say." What was there to say, when a dear friend has been so brutally murdered?

They stopped in front of the college and Fitch told Yen to leave the truck and go check on his daughters. "I'll pull the truck in," he added. After a moment, he said, "Yen, there's something you need to know."

The two friends stood face to face. What is it, man?" urged Yen, the words nearly catching in his throat. "Fitch?"

Fitch pressed his lips together, as if attempting to hold back a terrible truth. "I'm so sorry," he said, his voice barely above a whisper. "But there's a rumor that the *Panay* was sunk. We've tried to confirm it, but we haven't been able to get any information about who—"

"No!" cried Yen. "Please, God, no! Not my little boys." Yen grabbed Fitch by the shoulders. "Please, it can't be so. My boys? Jade's poor Ma? My God, George," he implored. "Can three generations be lost just like that?"

Fitch tried to console Yen, did his best to comfort and reassure this man he considered his dearest friend, but the task was beyond his ken. "Everyone said that was the safest way out," insisted Yen. "It's an American ship, for the love of God. To what purpose…"

Fitch looked around, as if hoping for someone to appear and comfort Yen. "No one's sure," he said. "Everyone's praying that your family is fine." As he spoke, Yen removed the soldier's jacket. Fitch took it and rolled it into a ball. "I'll burn this at once," he promised. When Yen said nothing, Fitch said, "Yen, I promise you, I'll do what I can. For now, you must go to your girls. They need you, perhaps more than ever."

Yen stood there in the harsh winter cold, no jacket to warm him, and felt nothing. Gathering himself, he nodded his thanks and rushed toward the college. His wife, sons, and mother-in-law were dead. Perhaps there was still a part of his family he could save.

TWENTY-SIX

Mei Ling handed out rice bowls to the poor by the tens, hundreds, and then thousands. Her delicate hands ached and her body shook as she spooned rice. The line seemed to go on forever, one little face after another, huddled in the cold, some with rice bags wrapped over their heads. She tried to concentrate on everyone's needs, but she had so much on her mind. At the same time, she felt somewhat ashamed. Was it selfish to ponder her future, while handing out rice to those who had no future? She was certain that she must see Kenji, that he would know what to do, as her father always did. He was so close, just across that field, and he loved her, he had told her so.

Mei Ling thought about what Minnie had said and tried to convince herself that her friend had been confused. Kenji was probably frantic, wondering what had happened to her. But then she thought, "How would he know? He must think I'm dead, Oh, poor Kenji, thinking I'm dead!" The thought of Kenji dying brought tears to her eyes.

She looked in the direction of the embassy. It was so close, certainly no one would notice her missing for a short time. She could go to him. He loved her, he would help. Wouldn't he do anything within his power to make her feel safe again?

Mei Ling put aside her serving spoon and enlisted another volunteer to take her spot. It was time that she helped herself and Kenji, no matter what the others believed. As soon as she built up the courage to walk toward the gate, she slipped into the background. It was darker near the fence, so she stopped under an illuminated corner of the wall and removed a letter from her pocket. She read it and then pressed it against her. If she couldn't see Kenji, at least she could leave this for him. Then he would know how she felt and he would come to her. They could be together; he would make her life safe once again. As a consulate member, he might even be able to find medication for Su Lin. "Kenji will make it right," she thought. Before moving on, Mei Ling read the letter again.

Dear Kenji, you know with all my heart that I love you. You must now act like the   man I know and love and come to me. I have been hurt. A horrible thing has   happened to my family, I need you. I will explain when I see you. I need your   protection now as a man...as my husband. We must enact a plan at once.

> *With all my love,*
> *Mei Ling*

As Mei Ling distanced herself from the Ginling, she also distanced herself from her promise to Minnie. She had to see Kenji, one way or another, or how else would he know to protect her?"

Mei Ling reached the back gate and saw no one of interest. Using her key, she opened the lock and slipped out. She started across the field, passing a large banyan tree. It was over 100 feet tall and its bulky leaves should have all fallen by now, but winter was slow in coming. When the freeze arrived, it did awful things to the large trees. This tree looked like it was draped in a quilt of large black and brown leaves that helplessly dangled in the evenings damp air. She spotted Minnie and Mr. Wong walking toward her and crouched behind the tree. As they came closer, she climbed up into its branches. The bark felt ice-cold and Mei Ling held tightly to avoid losing her grip. Minnie and Wong were walking briskly toward the embassy. As they passed below her, she heard Minnie say, "Yen Hsu would never allow them to be together. Mei Ling hasn't a clue about—"

As they moved away, their words were lost in the cold night. Mei Ling had no need to hear the rest; it all sounded bad, as if Minnie were in total agreement with her father. What did Minnie care about love? She cared more about what people thought. What could she know about Kenji, about his heart? He had only taken a few courses from Minnie! "I must see him now!" she uttered, climbing down from the tree.

As soon as she cleared the fence, she rushed toward the first group of tall bushes. Hiding, trying to catch her breath, she thought back to how she had met Kenji and the memory made her smile. She had waited two years for him to kiss her and now this damn war was ruining her life! Mei Ling inhaled sharply. How could she be so callous? Her mother was dead and her sister was in a terrible state. And where was her father? All of these thoughts brought her back to Kenji. He would help her make some sense of it all; she had to see him now.

Mei Ling began to run across the divide between the campus and the embassy. When soldiers suddenly walked out of the building, she scrambled up another tree. She could wait. Once inside with Kenji, she would be safe. She dangled high above the ground, her body spread across a large branch. The smell of the banyan tree permeated her clothing and she kept warm by imagining that it was Kenji enveloping her.

Minnie and Wong neared the embassy and were stopped by two soldiers marching in step. Frustrated, Minnie waved her arms and one of the soldiers pushed her aside. The other soldier grabbed Wong and threw him to the ground. Minnie rushed to his aid, glancing at the soldiers and calling out "Tanaka-san, Tanaka-san" over and over. A looming figure appeared at the top of the embassy stairs. A command was shouted and the soldiers immediately released Wong and allowed Minnie to pass. Minnie saw that the electricity was still out and lanterns lit the rooms inside the building. She and Wong arrived at the steps and were greeted by an official holding a lantern. Two other soldiers stood nearby, bodies relaxed. When they saw the official, they stomped out their cigarettes and jumped to attention. One of the armed guards stepped in front of Minnie and blocked her way. The official did nothing to stop him.

Minnie raised her head and called out "Kenji-san!"

The armed guard tried to cover her mouth, but Minnie pushed his hand away. "Tanaka!" she screamed, even louder. Kenji came running from the building. When he saw Minnie, he seemed nervous and unsettled. "Minnie, what can I do for you?"

"You? You can do nothing for me. I demand to see Tanaka."

Unblinking, Kenji stared at her for a few moments. "I'll get Mr. Tanaka," he finally said, and entered the building.

Minnie pushed past the guard, rushed up the stairs and into the darkened building. "Your family must be filled with shame!" she blurted, but Kenji was too far ahead to hear. Fearlessly, she followed him and found herself in an office. Everyone was working by candlelight and lanterns; the place was abuzz with activity. She watched people coming and going, carrying stacks of papers. Most of the documents were being put into delivery parcels; new crates were arriving, filled with supplies.

Kenji saw that Minnie had followed him and his posture became suddenly rigid. "Miss Minnie, I am sorry," he said, his voice anything but sorrowful. "I was afraid the soldiers would—"

"You were afraid of your own soldiers? Let's be honest, Kenji. You were afraid of what they might have done to Mei Ling, what they probably did do. And what about the rapes and murders? Are you sorry for those, too?" She stared at the man she had once considered her friend. Now, what she felt for him was only contempt. "I insist on seeing Tanaka now. Unlike you, perhaps he has some honor left."

Like a dark cloud settling on the sunset, the imposing Tanaka stepped in front of Kenji. "Miss Vautrin, all missionaries were ordered to leave over a month ago. Your government advised you as well, yet you chose to stay."

Minnie pulled herself to full height. "You must stop this madness, Tanaka-san! There must be accountability by your government for these godless renegades." She pulled a small booklet from her pocket and held it out. "This is an updated list of missing men. What are you going to do?"

He took the booklet and calmly asked, "Anything else?"

"Yes, keep your soldiers away from my campus. And him, too," she added, pointing at Kenji.

"Our soldiers have been instructed to find Chinese nationalists in the safety zone. Those are the orders. These desperate Chinese soldiers present a serious danger to you and your girls. So you see," he added, a little smirk crossing his mouth. "We are doing our best to protect all of you."

Minnie stared at the man for a long moment. "Your soldiers are not protection, they are danger. God is watching, Mr. Tanaka. God is watching what you do, so tell your army to stay out!" Before he could respond, she turned and called back, "Good night, Tanaka-san."

There was a flickering and then the electricity came on, filling the room with light. "So you see, Miss Vautrin," announced Tanaka. "Things are already improving."

"God will be the judge of that," she snapped, and walked away.

From her perch, Mei Ling saw Minnie and Wong leave the building and walk toward the campus. There was also an old Chinese father passing with a teenage girl. They were quite a distance from Mei Ling when a soldier from the embassy approached them. The diminutive Chinese man showed his Red Cross armband and pointed to the girl. Suddenly, the father was hit with the butt of a rifle and lay unconscious. A second soldier came up behind the girl and clamped a hand over her mouth. The two dragged her into the bushes.

Mei Ling was stunned and expected someone from the consulate to rush to this girl's aid. Instead, she heard the soldiers laughter and the girl's terrible cries as she begged for her life. Mei Ling heard clothing being torn away and brutal sounds. She covered her ears and silently begged for it to stop.

A short time later, Mei Ling heard nothing and nearly dropped to the ground. Before she could move, one of the soldiers emerged, pulling up his pants and walking toward Mei Ling. His accomplice came out from the darkness and accepted a cigarette from his friend. Together, they sat below the tree, blowing smoke rings and chatting about their good fortune.

TWENTY-SEVEN

Japanese soldiers crouched in readiness atop the old city wall above the college. They had found the perfect spot, at one of the lowest points in the wall, and then jumped onto a patch of garden when given the signal. It had started to rain and the men held close to the wall for shelter. One soldier whispered to the others that a truck would be waiting at the gate behind the embassy. There was nodding and then another soldier smiled and announced, "Remember, only the best girls—get the young ones!"

They checked that their bayonets were fixed to their rifles and then they ran toward the closest building, the science building, just inside the college. At the top of the steps, they discovered that the doors were locked. Two soldiers shouldered their way in, bursting the doors from their locks. They knocked a woman out of the way and rushed into the room. "Nothing but old women," complained one of the soldiers. "Let's try the next floor."

The invaders thundered up the stairs, boots echoing along the hallways. Again, they burst through a locked door, causing women to awaken with terror and scurry to the back of the room. Some were in their nightclothes and barefoot; the younger girls clung to their mothers or to each other.

Minnie walked back into her office, exhausted and in tears. She sat at her desk and looked over at Su Lin. The girl was still in a catatonic state and Minnie was feeling herself wanting to slip away as well. Perhaps it was better to feel no pain, have no perception, no reality. Minnie leaned forward and began to speak to Su Lin, as if she were there and able to communicate. "Su Lin, when you start talking to me, do begin slowly." She stood and walked over to the girl, looking directly into her eyes. "To talk slowly, but to think quickly, is a gift. Would you like to try that?" Su Lin turned her head toward Minnie and smiled slightly. "Well, hello, my dear!" Minnie offered.

A loud knock interrupted the exchange. Minnie squeezed Su Lin's hand before moving slowly toward the door. One of the teachers stood there, concern and fear etched in every feature of her face. "They are coming from all sides, Miss Minnie."

"Who is? Where?"

"Please, come at once, we need you! Soldiers are attacking the women!"

Minnie looked back and Su Lin, grabbed her pistol, and followed the frightened woman out the door. She was exhausted and hungry; her ankles ached from the chill. Wind whipped between the buildings as they raced past the library and entered the science building. She rushed upstairs in time to hear a man announce, "We need women to work for us. We can pay. You are starving here. You will be fed and paid."

Minnie entered the large room and found two soldiers holding at least fifty women and girls at bay. She placed herself in front of the women and faced the soldiers. "These women cannot be bought and sold," she announced. "Now get out! Leave my campus, you have no right to be here."

One of the soldiers stepped forward, his posture menacing as he faced the diminutive headmistress. "We have orders to hire some women. We can put them to work."

"These are innocent girls," insisted Minnie. "And I doubt that you have *work* in mind. Go find what you need elsewhere."

The soldier leaned close, his face inches from hers. "We have found what we want right here." He moved toward two adolescent girls. When Minnie blocked his way, he slapped her with the back of his hand.

She barely flinched, but her eyes turned steely hard. "I will contact the authorities at the embassy," she told him. "As well as the International Safety Zone Committee, which was authorized by—"

The larger soldier struck Minnie with his elbow and she dropped to the floor. Barely conscious, she lay there, unable to move. Many of the girls screamed, while others cried out and begged for their lives. A girl close to Minnie saw her headmistress attempt to stand and helped her up.

The soldier turned on Minnie, screaming, "How stupid are you? Do you want to die?" At the same time, his cohorts began to grab several of the girls.

Minnie stood there, legs wobbling, face mirroring defiance, but no fear.

The soldier shook his head and slowly removed his pistol. He pointed the gun directly at Minnie's head. "I will kill you if you don't move away from me."

Minnie remained there, unyielding, clutching her profound faith, even as he cocked the gun. When he pulled the trigger, the sound was deafening and then there was absolute silence. When it was clear that no one had been shot, the girls glanced fearfully at one another. Suddenly, one of the older girls stepped forward. "I will work for you," she said, "but only if you leave Miss Minnie alone." Five other girls stepped forward as well and the soldiers smiled with the knowledge that they would have their way.

An elderly refugee stepped forward. "I will go with them and see to their safety and survival. Do not worry, Miss Minnie, these girls know what is expected."

One of the girls, with tightly braided hair that flopped around her shoulders, asked, "We get paid and we get good food, right?"

One of the soldiers smiled. "We keep our word, we are honorable men."

Minnie turned to the girls, eyes wide with fear. "This is insane! These men are monsters."

Two more young women came forward. They gathered around the soldiers and, with the other girls, walked out the door, submissive and ready for their fate.

"You can't go!" cried Minnie. As the door closed, she fell to her knees and wept. Her very faith had been called to test, and she had failed. As she cried, she thought of Su Lin, sitting alone in the room and rocking in the chair. The girl had not said a word since returning to the college and Minnie now understood the silence. Amidst the murmuring of suffering, there was always a layer of silence.

TWENTY-EIGHT

Yen Hsu arrived at the gate to the college. "Let me in," he called out. "I am a friend of Miss Vautrin."

A man unknown to Yen approached the gate. "I'm sorry sir, but my orders are to let no men enter the college after dark."

Yen Hsu gripped the bars of the gate until his hands nearly bled. "Those soldiers will kill me if you do not let me in. Mei Ling is my daughter, she teaches here. Open the gate, for God's sake!"

The guard reluctantly unlocked the gate just as a group of Japanese soldiers closed in. Yen moved closer and the man's face registered recognition. "You're the photo man, right? Go on, run and hide."

Yen Hsu ran past him, calling over his shoulder "Thank you! Now lock it!"

The guard turned the key just as the soldiers arrived.

Yen Hsu ran into the middle of the crowded quad, turned and saw the soldiers at the gate. Within seconds he was mixed into the fray of nearly ten thousand people, most of them huddled in a state of semi-existence. He charged through the building, driven by a need to see his children.

Minnie heard the commotion and crept from the room; Mei Ling and Su Lin were finally asleep in the corner. Following the noise, she rounded the corner and collided with Yen Hsu. With no thought toward propriety, she threw her arms around the man she dearly loved and held him tight.

Tears fell from Yen Hsu's eye as he clung desperately to his old friend. "My girls, Minnie, are they—?"

As she opened her mouth to speak, a shot echoed through the halls. Wong rushed up to them and Minnie silenced him with an upheld hand. "Take Yen to my quarters," she told him. Yen's face suddenly changed to hope. Was it possible that his daughters might still be alive? Minnie smiled and touched his hand. "They're fine," she reassured. "Go to them." Before he could move, she added, "Su Lin is very fragile. She's not able to speak, at least not yet."

Yen bent down and kissed Minnie on the forehead. "Thank you, my dear friend Minnie Vautrin. You are indeed a godsend." With that, he turned and rushed off.

Wong hung back just long enough to whisper to Minnie that he had suspicions that Mei Ling had left for the embassy.

"She wouldn't," sputtered Minnie. "I forbade it!" With that, she rushed outside to find her gatekeeper holding off soldiers of the Japanese army.

A Japanese corporal stood at the entrance, his revolver pointing upward and the acrid scent of saltpeter drifting across the quad. "You open this gate at once," he screamed, "or you will die!"

Another shot rang out and nearly everyone close to the gate fell to the ground. Minnie arrived in time to see the man aim his weapon between the eyes of a very nervous guard. "One—two—three—"

"Stop this! Stop this now!" shouted Minnie, placing herself between the guard and his assailant. The corporal ignored Minnie's presence and barked "Open this gate at once! You are hiding dangerous Chinese traitors. Open it now!"

Minnie had been through so much, she would not be cowed by this bully. "Your men were here before and found no soldiers," she told him. "Are you listening? We have no soldiers here! Furthermore, we do not permit men, other than our staff, into the college." She waited for his response, but there was only silence. As if taking that for agreement, she rushed ahead. "We don't want more trouble from you, so please, just go. Can't you understand that we are at our wits' end here and–"

The colonel moved closer to the gate and signaled for his men to move in. "No more excuses! You will open the gates now! I have my orders!"

On cue, the truck's driver revved the engine. Mounted on the truck was a battering device, one certainly large enough to do significant damage to the gates. The truck's headlights came on, illuminating Minnie's face. She threw up an arm to protect her eyes from the powerful glare.

Mary came through the crowd and joined Minnie. Leaning close, she said, "Maybe if they had an escort?"

Minnie shook her head violently. "Do you see those machine guns?" she asked, pointing to several buildings near the gates. "And that?" she added, indicating a nearby jeep that was ready to fire on the crowd She turned her attention back to the colonel. "There are less than ten men inside, and they've all been with us for years. You have my word, none is a soldier."

The colonel responding by cocking his gun and pointing it at Minnie, "Your word means nothing to me. I have orders to search this campus!"

Minnie looked around her, as if weighing her options. Finally, she turned to Mary and said, "Find all the men and bring them here." With Mary on her way, Minnie turned back to the obstinate soldier and stared coldly at him. "You will see that our men are not soldiers." The corporal maintained his threatening stance, lest anyone under his command doubt who was in charge. As if to assert that leadership, he commanded his soldiers to ready their bayonets for attack and the machine gunners to prepare to fire.

Time passed and the corporal instructed the ramming truck to pull closer. "Your men have abandoned you," he sneered. "They dishonor you. Open the gates."

"I will not!" insisted Minnie.

Just as the colonel was giving the order to attack, a commotion ran through the crowd. Like the Red Sea, bodies parted and made room for the men of the Ginling. Nine of them, all out of breath, some having been awakened from sleep, others with cooking utensils or tools still in hand, rushed to Minnie's side. "Miss Minnie, are you all right?" implored her favorite cook.

The corporal narrowed his eyes and then ordered, "All of you, out here now!"

Minnie thrust out her arm to stop her men from moving forward. "They will not go through these gates," she said. "Just look at them. Anyone can see that these are not soldiers!" She pulled the cook into the light and gestured toward his apron stained with food and wear, the result of his unflagging dedication to feeding the nearly ten thousand who now considered the school their last refuge.

"These men need to be inspected! Open the gate!"

Minnie sighed loudly, as if put upon by this man's absurd demands. "You said you wanted to inspect the men at the Ginling and here they are. As for entering my campus— I will not allow it." The colonel clutched his pistol, knuckles white from the pressure being caused by this determined and very difficult schoolmarm. "Do you see that truck?" he stated, pointing to the ramming device. "On my command, we will destroy this gate and everyone in front of it. "

"You sir, are in the International Safety Zone!" declared Minnie, pointing to the flag that flew in front of her college.

Out of nowhere, Kenji Nezumi appeared and approached the tense standoff. "Corporal," he stated, a message of authority in his voice. "This is a girls' college."

Minnie glared at Kenji, trying not to show how surprised she was to see him.

The colonel faced Kenji. "We know that," he replied. "We've followed an enemy soldier here and we believe there are spies inside."

"Corporal, you're inside the safety zone," insisted Kenji. "Our government has made it clear that we are not at war with the Americans." He looked at the rumpled collection of men from the college and nearly laughed. "Do you really think these men are a threat? Trust me, I've seen these men around the college for years and they are not soldiers."

The colonel was not impressed with this young man. No matter that he could argue in Japanese, Mandarin Chinese, Cantonese, French, English, or German, he was still a diplomat, not a fighter. It was the fighter who would win this war. "It has been reported that Chinese soldiers are hiding—"

"Listen," interrupted Kenji. "I understand that you're doing your job, but you are not helping our cause by harassing supporters like Miss Vautrin. I wrote a report which your commander read. Please, sir."

Minnie wanted to slap him for calling her a supporter, but she was too exhausted and, for the moment, allowed Kenji to fight this battle for her. As for his comments—had he planned any of this? How could she trust him? As for his sense of honor, she nearly chortled at the thought. When the impasse continued, Kenji finally asked what could be done to resolve it. The corporal was quick to respond. "Bring the men outside the gate for our inspection. We will take four of our men and search the campus." He ordered four men forward, speaking quietly to one of them.

Minnie frowned at this arrangement. "When you see that they are cooks and gardeners, do you guarantee that they will not be dragged away? I need these men to help me operate this college and feed everyone displaced by you."

"We must inspect for the markings of soldiers."

"With God as my witness!" Minnie declared, throwing up her hands.

Kenji stepped forward. "I will enter with these soldiers and supervise their walk-through. Trust me, please." Lowering his voice, he added, "I know that I have erred, but this will soon be over."

Minnie was a firm believer in the redemption of the evil soul. "Fine, but only four men. And when my men are cleared, they will return with me, agreed?"

Kenji turned to the colonel, who nodded. "Then it's settled."

"Excellent," declared the colonel, his face suddenly alive with excitement. "Now open the gate!"

Minnie took her time opening the lock. The gate opened, her men made their way out, each one exchanging glances with Minnie as they passed. As much as she tried to look encouraging, an ominous feeling besieged her.

The Japanese troops quickly shoved the men against the gates, forcing them to their knees. They remained there, hands outstretched, palms up, with one soldier standing above them, his rifle at the ready.

The four soldiers entered, with Kenji following. He looked at Minnie and mustered an embarrassed smile, but she ignored him and shut the gates. Minnie watched the invaders push through the horde of people milling about the quad and then run up the stairs to the north dorms. Women and small children scurried away at the sight of the enemy, while others cowered under whatever clothing or blankets were near at hand. There was a sudden flurry of activity and a Japanese soldier announced, "Sir, the hands of a soldier!"

The corporal immediately answered, "Arrest him!"

Minnie cried out, "No! He is not a soldier! This man has worked for me for more than ten years." The soldier grabbed the gardener's hands and displayed them. "These are a soldier's hands, look!"

"He is a gardener!" argued Minnie. "Of course his hands are rough." Despite her feverish protests, two more gardeners were brought to the truck, their hands tied behind their backs. They looked at Minnie for hope, but she was helpless to intercede.

One of the soldiers strode up to the gardener, Chang, and kicked him. With this hands tied, the gardener could only take the blow. After a second kick, he fell forward, his head pressed into the ground.

Minnie, still inside the gates, she stood helplessly by.

Minutes passed before one of the soldiers assigned to search the school ran up to his leader and whispered in his ear. At the same time, Minnie clung to the hope that the Japanese would soon leave them in peace.

The colonel turned to Minnie. "The inspection is now completed," he told her.

Minnie eyed him suspiciously. "And you now see that these men are innocent."

Kenji jointed them near the gate. "You can trust the word of Miss Vautrin. She is an honorable and respected woman in Nanking."

The colonel shrugged and responded, "If you say so, fine. Release them all."

Minnie watched in astonishment as the soldiers untied the two gardeners and backed away toward the truck. As delighted as she was to unlock the gate and get these men inside, something was niggling away in her brain. It had all been too easy, over too quickly. Nevertheless, she forced a smile and, bowing, said, "Thank you and God bless you. You are an honorable man, thank you so much."

Just then, a truck flew by the gates. Inside were at least a dozen of her girls. Two of them looked up from the blanket that covered them, their eyes filled with terror. A smiling soldier pushed their heads down and replaced the blanket.

"You godless bastards!" Minnie screamed, sobs choking her voice. "You will go to hell for this!"

As the truck disappeared down the road, cries of "Minnie, save us! Minnie, help me, please!" filled the night. Minnie fell to her knees, put her head in her hands and prayed. As she prayed, she wept, her supplications to God mixed with soulful and mournful crying.

The soldiers drove off through the safety zone, honking for the helpless to get out of their way, laughing at their conquest. It was as if they were saying, We got what we wanted, and we always do.

While the altercation was going on at the gate, Yen Hsu was reuniting with his daughters. After rushing with Wong through the crowded hallways and passageways, moving through the thousands of displaced and frightened women and children, the men arrived at Minnie's room. Before they entered, Yen turned to Wong.

"Thank you for taking care of them," he said.

Wong shrugged and then replied quietly "About Su Lin—"

"How is she...really? The mere thought of her spirit helped me keep my faith."

Wong opened the door. Su Lin was rocking in a chair, staring out the window.

Yen rushed forward and tried to gather her in his arms. "Su Lin, my precious child!"

Su Lin continued to rock, alone in her own world.

Yen bent low and touched her hand. "My daughter, can't you hear me?"

"We think it is shock," said Wong.

Yen straightened and looked at Wong. "What have those bastards done?" Turning back to Su Lin, he hugged her rigid little body. Tears filled his eyes, and then hers, as he clung to her. Overwhelmed by grief and fear, Yen lifted his daughter and held her for a moment. Settling into the rocking chair, he held her as he had when she was a baby. He felt her move closer, as if aware that she was now safe. Yen looked into her blank eyes and, as he gently pushed the long hair away from her perfect face, he cried openly.

TWENTY-NINE

Mei Ling waited high in the banyan tree. The two Japanese soldiers had settled in and had fallen asleep. At one point, so had she. Now that they were awake and strolling back toward the embassy, she was anxious to reunite with Kenji. In the distance, she heard his voice and then saw him enter the building. She looked around in the cold, heavy air and, catlike, slipped down the tree and raced across the darkened pathway. She wanted only to join with Kenji, feel the safety of his protection. If she had to enter the embassy to achieve this, she would. Mei Ling rubbed her hands together, hoping to introduce some warmth into the freezing skin. A light shone brightly on the flag that hung over the embassy and she hurried her steps.

As she neared the top of the steps, two guards jumped in front of her. "Where do you think you're going?" asked one of the military policeman, his uniform so tight that it gaped at the buttons.

His partner assumed a cunning stance, the look on his face reflecting desire for this beautiful young woman.

"I have an important document for Kenji-san and he told me to bring it–" she said, as she continued to walk up the last two steps.

"A Chinese girl cannot enter the Embassy," said the guard.

"Perhaps if we let her in, Ushino, she'd show her appreciation," laughed the other guard.

Mei Ling stood very tall, chin high. "I was told by Miss Vautrin that I must deliver it myself. I am a teacher at the Ginling and Kenji-san knows who I am. I have been in your embassy before." She took a step forward, intending to enter the building.

"Kenji-san is busy," barked the soldier. "Give it to me."

Mei Ling looked toward the entrance and yelled "Kenji!"

The man slapped her hard across the cheek and her eyes grew wide. Two other soldiers burst into laughter when she tried to hit the soldier back. He grabbed her by the wrist and bent it back until she had to kneel before him. When the pain became too great, she lost her grip on the letter.

Ushino grabbed the letter and opened it. The other soldier was still bending her wrist, and at such an awkward angle that Mei Ling had to thrust her chest upward to alleviate the pain. Ushino watched her writhe and smiled. "Now go on," he said, waving her away. "Get out of here, you stupid girl."

"Kenji! Kenji-san!" Mei Ling called out as she moved reluctantly down the stairs.

This time, the guard knocked against her and she tumbled down the five stairs to the ground. Ushino descended and stood over Mei Ling. "Kenji-san is much too important to be bothered by a Chinese girl. Besides, he can have any girl he wants; he's an important man in Nanking. So leave, before I arrest you and send you to the camps." The other guard appeared embarrassed and offered Mei Ling his hand.

Mei Ling wiped blood from her mouth and turned away. Rising from the ground, she smoothed down her dress and started to leave.

Ushino watched her attentively and then called out, "Hey, come here, little chicken." He lit a cigarette and waited for her to approach him.

Mei Ling ignored Ushino and continued toward the college. Her heart raced, knowing she would have to pass the big tree and the open area where the girl had been dragged away.

As his partner walked up the stairs to deliver the letter, Ushino sped off after Mei Ling. He saw that she had reached the halfway mark and had turned back, determination on her face. Ushino's cigarette glowed in the dark and he inhaled one last time before tossing it onto the damp ground.

Mei Ling saw him coming and turned back toward the school, picking up her pace as he began to jog toward her.

Kenji sat inside the embassy and worked the short wave radio. He scanned the radio waves, dialing back and forth in order to pick up the broadcasts. His had become a mindless job and he felt nothing in his heart. And now that he had lost Mei Ling, the only woman he had truly loved, his life felt empty and without purpose.

At first, there was nothing but scratchy interference, then an English accent cut in from either Shanghai or Hong Kong. "Nanking has fallen. The once proud capital has been cut off from the outside world; thousands are reported dead. The Japanese leadership says all is calm. The city fell quickly after Chinese Nationalist soldiers deserted in droves. As soon as we hear more, we will—"

Kenji tuned the radio and caught a French broadcast. "Le *U.S.S. Panay* a étéit coulé par des avions japonais—" Scanning again, he found a German broadcast, and then glanced out the window next to his desk and jumped to his feet. Outside, a girl resembling Mei Ling was running across the grounds towards the Ginling. One of his guards, Ushino, was pursuing her. He rushed toward the door and was stopped by the arrival of Tanaka.

"You are not done with those translations Kenji-san?"

"Outside, sir, there is a disturbance," Kenji snapped.

"I need this transmission sent now. The Emperor's secretary is waiting."

Kenji looked out the window, saw the soldier closing in on Mei Ling, and said, "But, Mr. Tanaka—"

"Kenji-san!" Tanaka barked, furrowing his brow and pointing to the radio.

Kenji sat down at the telegraph, across from the short wave radio, and took one last glance out the window. Ushino was tugging on Mei Ling's arm and pushing her past the row of hedges. Mei Ling kept turning back, as if looking for help.

Kenji could not see across the field. He quickly pounded on the teletype, frantic and fast. He had to save Mei Ling.

Tanaka, behind him, blurted, "Too fast, Kenji-san, they will never understand it."

"They are the best, they hear very well, sir. Fine, I'm done, please excuse me now, sir. I must—"

Two guards suddenly charged into the room. "Consul Tanaka, sir."

"What are you thinking, storming into my private office?"

"Sir, you should see this at once, it is treasonous."

The guard handed Mei Ling's letter to Tanaka as a distant, piercing, scream erupted somewhere outside. Everyone ignored it but Kenji. He turned to the window but saw nothing. Whatever was happening in those bushes beyond the embassy was out of his view. Kenji tried to move to another window, but Tanaka's gesture caused his way to be blocked.

"Let me see this," demanded Tanaka, grabbing the letter. He read it, nodded a few times, and then handed it to Kenji.

Kenji began to read and his eyes grew wide as he discovered that Mei Ling was still alive. His mind raced as he told himself that he must not show excitement in front of Tanaka. Mei Ling was not dead…but she was outside and in danger. He had to save her. So many questions raced through his head: How did she survive the blast? What about the rest of the family? Did she know of the USS *Panay* being sunk and the loss of her grandmother and brothers? He blinked fast and hoped that Tanaka did not understand.

But Tanaka understood very well. He had only to read two lines to know that his aide had betrayed him. He looked at Kenji with steely eyes. Kenji, who was like a son to him, yet had conspired with the daughter of his nemesis, Yen Hsu. Tanaka's throat grew dry and scratchy and he coughed several times.

Kenji tried to recover his poise, but Tanaka's silence ran through him like a knife. When the guard released his revolver, Kenji fought to remain composed. At the same time, sweat glistened on his forehead. Tanaka coughed loudly and Kenji said, "Sir, let me get you some tea. I can explain."

Tanaka held his hand up for silence. He lit a cigarette and breathed in the smoke; oddly, it stopped his cough. He smiled at Kenji and the guards, exhaling the foul smoke, and then draped an arm over Kenji's shoulder. Turning, the man looked directly into the younger man's eyes. "Kenji, if you want to have one of these stupid Chinese girls, you don't have to tell her that you love her. It's unfortunate that you desire a Ginling girl. You know that we mean no harm to the Ginling."

The guard stared at Tanaka and Kenji, waiting for something bigger. When nothing happened, he said, "Sir, she wrote about running away to Hangkow with Kenji-san. That's treason, to run away with a Chinese national, isn't it? And she's the daughter of that diplomat with Chiang Kai-shek. That should be high treason!"

Tanaka frowned, leaned closer, his stared drilling into Kenji. "No, it's just a girl's fantasy, right Kenji-san? You would never abandon your post during wartime, would you?"

"Absolutely not, sir. And yes, it's all a fantasy. She is very naïve and was in my English class. I've done no harm to anyone, sir. As you know, I am an honorable solider for the Emperor."

"Excellent!" declared Tanaka. He turned to the guards. "You men go back to your posts. Next time you enter an office of the Consular General at this Embassy, I expect you to knock first and then announce yourself, as is the doctrine of our office. Thank you, good night." With his arm still gripped around Kenji's shoulder, Tanaka brushed the two soldiers away.

Mei Ling was pushed by Ushino into the same thicket where the other assault had taken place. She licked her bloody lip and felt that it was already quite swollen.

"So you like it rough?" said Ushino. He placed his hands against her chest and shoved her hard to the ground.

Mei Ling fell back, crying out when her head landed against the spiked twigs and rough rocks that littered the ground. She tried to rise, but Ushino drove his boot into her stomach, holding it there until she gasped for air. He slipped off the rifle and pointed the bayonet at her throat. "Now," he instructed, cocking his rifle, "take off your clothes."

Mei Ling shook her head, eyes reflecting terror. "I have never—no, you will not!" She saw that his face was nearly purple with rage, and there was something in his voice that she recognized. She pushed these thoughts away and tried to think of ways to escape. The man leered at her, his crooked teeth stained from smoking.

Ushino pressed down even harder and then, reaching down, tore at the front of her blouse. It ripped, but did not come off.

Mei Ling clawed at his boot it, calling out in Japanese, "No, you cannot. Kenji-san is my... Kenji!"

Ushino stood over her and viewed his prize. When she tried to rise, he struck her with the butt of his rifle.

Mei Ling doubled over. As she groped for balance, her hand struck something fleshy. Looking down, she saw a foot and knew at once that it belonged to the girl who had been dragged away. Barely conscious, she swore to herself that she would not suffer the same fate. She was her mother's daughter and she knew how to fight.

Ushino laughed. "There will be no Kenji-san for you, only Ushino." He unbuckled his military belt and let it fall to the ground.

Mei Ling stared, mouth dry, watching him prepare for the attack. When he placed his rifle against the woodpile, her heart began to race.

Inside the embassy, Tanaka ordered the anxious Kenji into his large office at the back of the building. It had a view toward the Ginling and its own little tearoom, where pictures of Tanaka with many military leaders and his family adorned the walls. The biggest picture was that of the Emperor. Kenji did not know what to expect when Tanaka motioned him to sit at a small couch in front of an ornate Japanese table. The heavily inlaid antique was like a puzzle of drawers on every side. Tanaka, still standing and towering over Kenji, began to talk as he poured hot water into a teapot. "Great love and great achievements, they involve great risks. Our ancestors knew this. Our Emperor knows this now."

Tanaka sat down on the low couch and Kenji wondered where this story was heading. And why now? He took a deep breath and tried to relax before he said, "Mr. Tanaka-san, I am sorry if I have let you down in any way."

"When you say that you are sorry to an honorable man, you must look him in the eye, or you will remain suspicious in the heart of that honorable man."

Kenji immediately looked at Tanaka, but his eyes began to well up, his emotions and fear triggering restlessness in his fingers and blinking of his eyelids. He tried to hide his tears, acting as if his eyes were irritated.

"Are those tears for you or for the girl, Kenji?"

Fear rose in his throat. "She was a dream sir, only a dream."

Tanaka slowly opened a hidden drawer at the base of the ornate table and removed a pair of Japanese knives. "Seppuku knives are for honorable men, when it is needed to keep the respect of one's family and country." He fingered the knives. "These are my ancestors' seppuku; they are over five hundred years old." Tanaka took another knife from the drawer and held it toward Kenji, who grasped it and eyed it suspiciously. "These knives have never been used, Kenji-san. Our family honor is intact; my ancestors hold their heads high."

Mei Ling was flat on her back in a clearing in the bushes and she tried to keep her eyes closed, but Ushino loomed above her like a dark thunderhead. She felt his eyes riveted to the frilly undergarments peeking out from under her skirt and she sensed his perverse excitement. She knew that he was readying himself for her and, if she intended to defend herself, she needed to clear the grogginess from her head and push away the terror.

"So beautiful," he murmured in Japanese, looking at her lovely face. "The most beautiful Chinese girl I have ever seen. And you are so young, like an untouchable geisha."

Mei Ling remained motionless, every nerve in her body electrified by the rifle propped nearby. There was no one to save her, no one to stop this beastly man. The only solution to her problem lay within inches of her reach. Her body ached and her head pounded, but she was the daughter of Jade and Yen Hsu and she would not be defiled without a fight.

Ushino looked her over again and then roared "I take you now! You will like Ushino!" His breath steamed in the cold air.

In that brief moment between opening his pants and coming down on top of her, Mei Ling was able to stretch her leg toward the rifle and kick at it. Ushino realized what she had done and tried to grab the weapon, but he stumbled on his own lowered trousers. Mei Ling kicked the rifle again and the bayonet fell toward her. She grabbed the shaft and swung the rifle around, until the bayonet pointed at her attacker's heart. Ushino lunged to grab the rifle and Mei Ling put every ounce of strength she had into driving that bayonet through his shirt, into his flesh, and then into that space between his ribs, where the sharp point tore open the wall of his heart. The gurgling sound was barely audible. Within seconds, life pumped from his heart and he lay dead.

Mei Ling was firmly wedged between the cold, unyielding earth and the warm, bleeding body of her would-be rapist. She struggled to free herself and something slid from the man's pocket. It was the necklace that Kenji had given her, the one confiscated by her mother. How was it that this soldier was in possession of her necklace? A feeling of dread engulfed Mei Ling when she realized that it could only mean one thing: this man had been in her house. And then she remembered the voice overhead, its taunting and hideous sound making its way through the floorboards. She had just killed her mother's rapist and murderer. Mei Ling pushed the fat body to the ground. Standing, she filled her mouth with sputum and spat in his face. She gripped the necklace and straightened her clothing, now covered with this man's blood. With a quick glance around her, Mei Ling emerged from the density of shrubs and trees. A soldier was moving toward her and ducked back into the foliage. As she cowered even further into the dark, a twig snapped underfoot. The soldier paused, looking around, squinting as he gazed into the heavy brush.

Tanaka brought out the family sake and poured another shot of the potent rice wine into the ceremonial porcelain cups. Kenji picked up the tiny cup but, before bringing it to his lips, he set it down with a clink. There was so much to be gained in this war, but he was losing something very precious. How could a young man get it all? With a shake of his head, Kenji picked up the little cup.

Tanaka ignored Kenji's hesitancy. "Let's celebrate our families, kanpai!"

They drank another shot. Kenji eyed the knives. "Perhaps we should we put the knives away?"

Tanaka studied his aide's face. "Why? I thought you might need one after that letter." He poured another round of sake, then paused and stared again into Kenji's eyes. He waited for several seconds and then exploded in laughter. " Kanpai!" he exclaimed again, saluting Kenji with his sake before downing it all.

"I believe that you mock me, sir," observed Kenji, taking a little sip.

"Kenji, forget the girl, do not dishonor your family, our embassy, and our esteemed Emperor." At the mention of their ultimate leader, both men both bowed their heads.

"I understand, sir." Kenji rubbed a slender finger over the blade of the seppuku.

"It is honorable to believe in love, Kenji-san, but you cannot go home with a Chinese girl and be an honorable man."

"Yes, sir, but—"

Tanaka cut him off with a wave of his hand. "Enough!"

Tanaka pushed the knives closer to Kenji's body, so close that Kenji saw the reflection of his worn face in the polished blades. Tanaka stared at Kenji for a long time and then replaced the seppuku knives in the secret drawer. "Kenji, I have no sons, only daughters; you are like a son to me. You must remember that we have the trust of our ancestors, centuries-old. My great-grandfather died as a samurai; we have blood in our veins of honor and strength. You must not let the weakness of the flesh sway your birthright. You are Japanese." He raised the sake cup and declared "Kanpai!"

They took one last drink before Tanaka put his fleshy arm around Kenji's shoulder and rested his head on the young man's. Kenji froze, unsure of what to do.

Mei Ling tugged on the rifle, trying to free it from her assailant's grip. Mustering strength, she jerked on it so hard that her hands broke loose and the necklace flew from her hand, landing on the boots of the soldier. He looked at the necklace, at the blood-covered Mei Ling, and then the body of Ushino, a bayonet impaled in his chest. The soldier raised his gun. "You murdering bitch," he seethed, reaching for his whistle. Before he could blow, a startled look took over his face.

Mei Ling contracted into herself, prepared for the end. This soldier's expression confused her. And then she saw Minnie, standing behind the soldier, the muzzle of a pistol pressed into the base of his skull. She cocked the trigger and he lowered his weapon. "Drop it," she said, her voice hard and insistent. He did as ordered and Minnie increased the pressure of contact. "Run, Mei Ling," she said, urgency in her voice. "Get out of here now!"

Mei Ling stared up at Minnie for only a moment, but it seemed like an hour, as if the world were in a slow-motion turn. Getting to her feet, she turned and ran from the thicket, heading toward the school. Half way across the field, she stopped, turned and went back to help Minnie.

The soldier slowly turned until he was facing his aggressor. To stare into her eyes meant looking down. Without shifting his gaze, he reached behind him for his gutting knife, which was tucked into a sheath on the back of his belt. His movement was silent, by increments, and all the while he held Minnie's stare. With deadly precision, his fingers wrapped around the weapon.

"You are an evil man," Minnie hissed. "God will have words with you!"

"I know you," he sneered. "You're the religious woman from that girl's school, the missionary. You can't shoot me. Besides, you're an American, we have no problem with you."

Minnie backed up one step, and then another. To the side, she saw that Mei Ling was waiting for her just outside the thicket. It was then that she recognized how the soldier's hand was positioned to strike from his back. A shot rang out from the rusty old pistol, a weapon that Minnie had never fired and that had been collecting dust in her room for almost twenty years. Why was it that the same gun that failed her yesterday went off today? These thoughts crossed Minnie Vautrin's mind as the bullet pierced the soldier's forehead and then shattered the rear of his skull. Blood and brain matter splattered onto the barren branches behind him and steam began to emanate from the wound. He dropped to the ground, as if his legs had been cut off, and fell on top of Ushino.

Minnie stared, muscles frozen. She inhaled the acrid smell of gunpowder, singed blood and flesh and then began to weep. What had this war done to everyone? She had killed a man; another lay dead under him, killed by Mei Ling. A young girl, maybe one of hers, lay raped and dead a few feet away.

Mei Ling rushed into the bushes and grabbed Minnie by the arm. She looked at the gun and then at the soldier, as if, even with his brains strewn around, he might come back to life. "We must go," she urged, and they bolted from the bushes, Kenji's mother's necklace resting near the boot of a dead Japanese sentry.

The two women, bound by a fierce sense of survival, ran as best they could to the Ginling gate. Minnie smiled in an odd way, through her panting in the cold air, and it was an expression of mingled fear, surprise, wonder and curiosity. "It was a miracle the thing fired," she murmured. "He was going to kill me, but my little old gun went off when I squeezed the trigger…and now that evil man is on his way to hell."

"Come on, Minnie," said Mei Ling. "We must get to the Ginling and hide." It had become her mantra, *get to the Ginling*, the only place left where she felt safe.

Night sirens from the embassy interrupted the quiet as the women neared the college. A squad of soldiers poured from behind the embassy, flashlights illuminating the air and bayonets drawn. The flag of the rising sun lay still as they passed.

Minnie and Mei Ling made it through the gates, the same gates Mei Ling had passed through the day before, a naïve and adoring young woman in search of her heart and lover. Now, disheartened in every way, it had been Minnie who had come for her. Come for her and rescued her Minnie, there for her as she had always been, no one else.

They walked toward the infirmary, clothes covered in blood, Minnie still shaking from fear, yet oddly euphoric. It was as if her very soul had struck back at evil, had stared death in the face, and had survived, and she had saved her Mei Ling. Minnie, Mei Ling, the rusty weapon, all of them were part of a miracle. It must have been God's will.

The first guard to arrive at the scene of the murders stood over Ushino's body and blew on a whistle. Two akita guard dogs barked and sniffed at the scene. How could two Japanese soldiers be dead, and so close to the embassy, right inside the safety zone? Was the killer a Chinese soldier or a spy? The dogs panted and growled; there was blood everywhere. The corporal pulled back on the leashes, trying to calm the animals excited by the smell of blood. Lanterns and flashlights moved through the air in all directions.

Kenji saw the action from the top of the stairs and feared the worst. He bounded down the steps and encountered a medical truck as it entered the scene. Stepping into the fray, he craned to get a clear view of the crime scene, but all he could see were two dead soldiers and the body of a girl with the long black hair, legs twisted under her.

Ushino's body was still partially propped up on his own bayonet, like a fish on a hook at the bottom of a bloody boat. A few feet away was the dead young girl. From Kenji's vantage, it looked like Mei Ling's hair, hand, and arm. The whiteness of skin near her exposed breast shocked him and the contrast of blood fresh and dried against her pale skin made her appear even whiter, even more ghost-like. Kenji felt nausea rise in his stomach and had to step aside. He looked down and saw the necklace, his mother's necklace, the one he had given to Mei Ling. He snatched it up and stuffed it in his pocket. "Why Mei Ling?" he whispered, desperation rising within him.

Mei Ling and Minnie burst into the busy infirmary. Standing in the light, they recognized for the first time how much blood was on their clothing. In Mei Ling's case, it was her own blood oozing from a wound in her head, as well as her attacker's blood smeared across her mid-section. The helpers and patients in the room stared at both women in stunned silence. Mary, who had been there for hours, walked through the door and gasped. "God in heaven, Minnie, what has happened? And Mei Ling!" she declared, rushing up to the young woman. "Have you been stabbed?"

She guided them into a small room at the back of the infirmary where she instructed Mei Ling to lie on the last remaining bed. Minnie removed her own clothing and changed into a patient's garb. "I killed a soldier," she said. "He was going to—Mei Ling was—I decided—you know the gun? I used it. It worked. I killed him." She forced a smile, but her hands began to shake uncontrollably.

Mary took a damp swab and cleaned Mei Lin's bloody eye and lip. She took a closer look. "If Minnie shot him," she said, "then how on God's earth did you end up looking like this?" She leaned closer and removed dirt and blood from the area around Mei Ling's wounded lip. Finally, she said "Let's get you into a hot shower and wash off this blood. It's the best way to see if you're wounded elsewhere." Mary helped Mei Ling off the table and grabbed a few more hospital gowns.

The two women followed her obediently, both of them relieved to have someone looking after them. Mary's matter-of-fact attitude and her unshakeable Irish demeanor were what Minnie admired about her. "Thank God for Mary Twynam," Minnie thought.

Mary turned on the water and adjusted the heat. Very soon, steam was drifting from the stall. Mei Ling walked fully clothed into the shower and began to strip off each garment. The water poured over her, blood turning the white tiles a gruesome shade of red. The letter she had tried to deliver to Kenji fell to the floor, but no one bothered to retrieve it. Mary handed her a washcloth and soap and Mei Ling set to scrubbing her hands, arms, belly, every inch of her perfect body. She worked to get the blood out of her fingernails and appeared grateful when Mary handed her a nailbrush.

"Isn't that better now?" Mary cooed.

Mei Ling scowled, continuing to attack the blood under her nails. It was not coming out and she began to shake. "What's better?" she demanded, emotions flooding over her. "Nothing's better! Kenji left me for dead, to be raped or killed. He said he loved me, that he would do anything for me." She turned her back to Mary and continued to run the course brush over her nails.

Minnie removed her shoes and pulled down on her dress, trying not to get more blood on her hands. Nearly naked, she stepped into the shower and groaned from the pleasure of having clean, hot water running over her body. She removed the rest of her clothes and put her head under the hot water, as if she wanted to disappear in the warmth of the shower.

Mary held out a towel to Mei Ling. Before taking it, she threw the nailbrush. It bounced off the wall and landed next to the letter, which was now soaked in blood and soapy water. Mei Ling accepted the towel and quickly dried herself, then slipped on a clean hospital gown. "Do you think that scrubbing a little blood off my nails will clean me up?

Where's my mother? Dead! Where are my brothers? I have no family! I have no love. These bastards are going to kill us all. They can kill us and rape us and we have no way to protect ourselves. We are all going to die!" Mei Ling burst into tears. Leaning against the tiled wall, she rocked back and forth, both hands covering her face.

Mary draped an arm around the distraught young woman and led her away from the shower. "Let's get some tea and biscuits," said Mary. "No one's going to harm you, not while you're here with Minnie and Mary Twynam, and that's a promise. And I'll tell you something else: no one gets into my infirmary without my say-so, and no one gets into the Ginling without Minnie's. Honestly, Mei Ling, you're safe now."

"We're all going to die," sobbed Ming Lei. "Just like Ma. Poor Ma, I miss her so, she loved me no matter what I said or did. I miss my Ma."

Mary made hushing sounds and held Mei Ling tighter. "No, no, we're going to be fine, aren't we Minnie?"

Minnie was scrubbing her skin, while trying to avoid stepping into the rivulets of blood still flowing from Mei Ling's clothing. With her face tilted up and hot water cleansing her, she said, "Yes, with God's help, we're going to get through this." In the drama of the moment, Minnie had forgotten that Mei Ling was unaware that her father was alive and tending to of Su Lin nearby.

Mary poured tea, while Mei Ling sat in silence. Still dressed in hospital garb, the white fabric gave her pale skin an eerie look. She was broken, grief-stricken, with none of her former spirit evident in her face. She accepted the tea from Mary and took a sip.

"Here," said Mary, picking up a clean towel. "Let me." She began to dry Mei Ling's hair, her touch gentle and maternal.

Mei Ling appeared numb. "When I was a little girl," she said, her voice low and flat. "My mother used to dry my hair and then brush it. One hundred strokes, she told me."

Mary picked up a brush and began to comb Mei Ling's hair. "How do you know your mother is gone? Maybe she—"

"I buried her," said Mei Ling, her voice flat.

Mary dropped her arms, the brush falling to the floor. "Oh, my darling girl, you are too young for all this." She placed her hands on Mei Ling's shoulders, but they were shaken off.

"Are you saying there is a right age for a girl to see her mother raped and bludgeoned?"

Tears sprang to Mary's eyes. "I'm so sorry, I didn't—" She pressed her fingers against her mouth, as if unable to hold back the words.

At that moment, Minnie came into the room. "I found this in a drawer," she told Mary, indicating the traditional Chinese clothing she was wearing. "It's clean, isn't it?"

"It belonged to a woman in the infirmary," said Mary. "Yes, it's clean." When she looked at Minnie, her eyes were pleading.

"You mean she's dead," said Mei Ling.

The three women stood together in silence, each one lost in her own frightened and confused thoughts. Finally, it was Mei Ling who spoke. "Minnie, what are you going to do?"

"Do?" Minnie looked confused. At this point, however, everything confused her. Here she was, a missionary and a generous giver of God's word. Not only was she was wearing the clothes of a dead woman, she had just killed someone. What *was* she to do? The answer came swiftly: she could protect and serve her girls with all the love and might she could muster. That is, unless God had another plan.

The air in the room changed noticeably and the three women turned toward the door. There stood Yen Hsu. When he saw Mei Ling, he let out a cry and rushed to his child. He pulled her from the chair and held her so tightly it seemed he would never let go. "Thank God," he said, "Thank God." He repeated the phrase over and over, tears running from his cheeks and into his daughter's hair. At that moment, no one cared about Kenji or invasions, violence or despair. One man had been reunited with his child and now they could weep together, and Mei Ling's face glowed with real hope for the first time in days.

Minnie stood back and saw how Yen Hsu's eyes had taken on the look of a man who knew too much, who had seen things no man should have to see. She could not resist to joining them, putting her arms around Yen Hsu and Mei Ling and hugging the two most important people in her life. When they finally separated, emotions spent, Minnie said to her old friend, "Yen, I have taken a life."

"But you saved my life when you killed that bastard!" declared Mei Ling, her voice ringing through the room. She had never used a word like that in front of her father. From the look on his face, he thought it righteous. Mei stepped back into her father's embrace. She felt so small in his arms, so protected. For the moment, she wanted him all to herself, so that he could hold her and keep her safe from the hell her life had become.

Yen pulled her even closer. "I love you, my daughter, more than you will ever know."

"Father, I have–"

"You have saved yourself and you have saved Su Lin. Is there more that you could have done?"

Minnie stood as close to them as possible, as if she were being drawn to them, like a moth to the flame; like one heart seeking the warmth of a love shared by two others. These were the two people she loved without question; she had killed a man to save one of them. As much as she suffered that act, she knew in her heart that she would give her life, everything she was, to save Yen Hsu and his family.

The four soldiers and special service officer with the two large Akitas marched toward the Ginling gates. The snarling dogs, searching for two women, were pulling tautly on their leashes as they followed the scent.

"Murderous Chinese bitch!" the officer mumbled. "She killed Ushino."

"We'll find her and shoot her between the eyes!" another blurted.

"That bitch deserves a slow death," said another soldier. "When we catch her, I will shoot her up her ass."

Following them slowly was a truck carrying more soldiers. There was a machinegun mounted on the roof of the cab; attached to the front was a large bumper that was used as a battering ram. The truck rolled up to the back gate of the college and was forced to stop. Had the gate been wider, it could have been rammed open. Instead, one of the soldiers was forced to fire his weapon into the air, in order to attract attention.

Everyone in the room heard the shot. "We should move any of those girls who are near the back gate," said Mary.

"And no one can know that Mei Ling or Yen Hsu are here," insisted Minnie. "I mean no one at all. If someone asks, she's dead!"

Mei Ling appeared surprised by the force of Minnie's words, but Yen nodded, understanding very well the urgency of keeping Mei Ling hidden.

Mary rushed to collect the clothing and Mei Ling reached out for Minnie. "He did nothing." Her voice was low with anger and pain.

Minnie looked at Mei Ling, searched her lovely face for meaning. Finally, she touched the girl's cheek and said "I know that, my dear. You killed him before he could."

"Not him."

Minnie shook her head. "Then who?"

"Kenji!" Mei Ling's eyes filled with tears, yet her jaw was tight, angry. "He saw that soldier chasing me and he did nothing. Nothing!" She clenched her fists, her face twisted with pain. "How could he do nothing?"

"He has lost his soul to his Emperor's bidding," said Yen, sadness washing across his face.

Mei Ling looked at her father, eyes flashing in anger. "He heard me screaming his name, I know it!"

Mary had grabbed her coat and was standing at the door. Before closing it, she got Minnie's attention. "Lock it behind me," she instructed. "And open it for no one!"

With Mary's footsteps still audible in the hallway, Minnie turned to Yen. "Stay with her," she instructed, and rushed out of the room.

Minnie made her way out and to the side of the building. There were dogs and soldiers running around, everyone taking positions for what she was certain would be a second assault on her beloved school. Mary had joined Wong at the gate and the soldiers were firing their weapons in their direction. One of these soldiers rushed up to Mary and pushed the point of his bayonet against her jaw. "We want the girl!" he demanded. "Where is she? She's a murderer, we have witnesses."

More weapons were fired, startling the dogs into incessant barking. Minnie saw that Mary was unsure about what to do and was afraid the soldiers would shoot them. Unable to watch her friend being subjected to this, she rushed forward screaming, "She's dead, dead! Your bloody rapist killed her! She's dead, so get away from my gates!"

"I want to see the dead bitch," said the leader. "She's a spy, too, and we know who she is. She worked here, so maybe that makes you a spy too. Are you ready to die?"

"What difference does it make!" Minnie screamed. "She's dead, raped and murdered by your bloody army!"

Kenji suddenly arrived, looking frantic and panting for breath. His overcoat was draped over his shoulders, like a little Napoleon, and he grabbed the gates, shaking them. "I must see Mei Ling!"

"The bitch is dead," one of the soldiers announced.

Kenji's eyes fell on Minnie and he pressed his face hard against the bars. "Minnie, thank God! What can I do?"

Minnie walked closer to the gate, hatred in her eyes. "You've done quite enough. Certainly enough for one day, for one war, one life. There is nothing for you to do except go to hell."

"But I—" he whined.

"You're as pathetic as the rest," she sneered. "Leave us, I have too many to care for, without your sorry self."

"Minnie, please, you know I would—"

"I know you've destroyed the most precious heart in China," she said, cutting him off with her angry words. "I know you let these monsters have their way. As of today, you are nothing to me or this college. We never want see your face again, so go, leave with the rest of your rapists."

Kenji threw himself against the gate. "Minnie, please take this," he begged. "Bury it with her, that's all I ask."

He held out an open palm. Resting on it was the blood-stained necklace. Minnie looked at it, then into his eyes with an emotion so powerful even she was caught by surprise. Without a word, she turned and walked away, leaving them all—the dogs, the soldiers, her old friend Kenji—to stare at her disappearing back.

Kenji pulled himself together and ordered the soldiers to leave. "The murderer is dead," he told them. He would take full responsibility with Tanaka later.

Minnie walked to the chapel, opened the big doors, and tried to retreat into her soul, if even for a minute.

Kenji crept into Tanaka's office. It still smelled of tea, sake, and the sweat of an old man. He lit a candle on the antique Chinese table, the one that told the story of Nanking, and then he cried, his head resting in his blood-stained hands.

It seemed like such a long time since he was last here with Tanaka, being given a lesson about knives and the honor of seppuku. Kenji reached into the hidden drawer and removed the two ceremonial knives. He walked to the center of the finest Chinese rug in the room, the one that had been woven in a province that had fallen far easier and faster than Nanking. No matter, because soon all of China would be among the Japanese colonies, and then they would take the Pacific. The Tanaka plan would have made Kenji a wealthy and powerful man.

With his legs tucked under him, Kenji sat on the floor, both knives pressed against his abdomen. He looked out the window, toward the flagpole and the small shaft of light illuminating the flag of the rising sun. He questioned whether he had the courage do to this. The flag flapped in a gust of wind and the shutter on a nearby window slapped against the outside wall once, twice. On the third strike, Kenji lunged his body onto the razor-sharp blades. He fell forward, driving them even deeper, gasping for air but finding none, and then he collapsed onto the floor, his blood creating a slow-growing stain on the magnificent rug. With his face turned toward the window—toward the park-like clearing and the buildings of the Ginling—Kenji's life drained from him. As consciousness slipped away, he saw first his mother's face and then Mei Ling's, her eyes soft and then angry. With his last breath, Kenji saw for the last time his beloved flag of the rising sun.

THIRTY

Almost one month to the day later, an unusually warm January morning surprised Nanking. The bright sunshine was a blessing on a ravaged city and all those unfortunate souls who had lost their homes, their businesses and their love ones. At the Ginling, rice was being served and the mass of refugees was grateful for the quiet and the shelter. As they ate, a car drove in through the gates carrying three elderly Japanese women, all of them representatives of the Women's National Defense Organization. They made few comments and seemed interested primarily in looking around. Everything appeared very orderly. Crowded, yes, but definitely under control.

Minnie wished she could speak a better Japanese so she could explain what these people had experienced. That job had always fallen on Kenji, her trusted friend and translator. She abruptly pushed his name from her mind and smiled politely at her unwelcome guests.

The visitors walked purposefully, viewing the refugees under the full escort of the military. They took a few photographs of an officer feeding a refugee and Minnie said nothing. In her mind, however, she knew that these were token shots, attempts to show the Japanese in a glowing light. Perhaps she should mention that this refugee had lost her husband and two teenage boys; that her daughter had been dragged away by soldiers to be raped and had not been seen since. How could this mother respond? She spoke no Japanese and her proper upbringing dictated that she sit quietly and graciously accept a bowl of rice from the man who had given the order to kill her husband and sons.

Minnie checked the area to be sure Mei Ling was nowhere around. She was still kept hidden, trying to disguise her appearance those few times she left her quarters. As far as anyone knew, Mei Ling was dead.

It had been a month—and what seemed like a lifetime—since the invasion began and Nanking's plight was clear. The Japanese had sealed the river port to everyone and everything, except for their own supply ships, meaning that no one had been able to leave. The last American ship on the river, the *U.S.S. Panay,* had been sunk in broad daylight, taking with it half of Yen's family. The Japanese were still claiming that, because of the weather, it had been a case of mistaken identity. Photographs taken when the ship set sail revealed a clear and sunny day.

When news came that another American ship was scheduled to re-supply the missionaries and the Red Cross, there was cause for joy. It was the *U.S.S. Oahu* and its comings and goings were being carefully monitored, although Minnie was aware that plans to protect this ship were being made throughout the safety zone. The real question was not Who will protect the *Oahu*, but Who would be able to leave. Even more, what was needed to secure their safety? Minnie had heard from Magee and Forster that the American Embassy was nearly frantic, as were the German, Japanese, British, and Russian governments, trying to decide what and who could get out.

When Minnie heard about the *Oahu* coming up the Yangtze, she decided to host a dinner. She knew that she could muster up some sort of a meal, but hated the idea of taking food from the refugees. When Magee offered to bring tins of fish he had stashed somewhere and Forster said he could contribute a piece of cheese that had been sealed in wax, plans for a feast picked up speed. Everyone knew that this meal would be nothing like those banquets created by the great chef, Jade Hsu, but it might lift everyone's spirits, if only for an evening. There would no colorful lanterns, but Minnie thought she could find some candles, perhaps borrow a few alcohol burners from the science building.

More important than planning the meal was deciding what next to do. The safety zone was abuzz with activity about the ship and the possibility of getting out of Nanking. Would they need visas from the Japanese? Would this be considered an international passage? Would the little ship be stopped downriver and searched? Would they stop in Shanghai? No one knew the answers, but they were certain that precaution was still the mode of the day.

Minnie was told that another meeting of the International Safety Zone Committee was going to be held and she made Magee promise to bring back notes about everything that was discussed. When he arrived at the school, he had several pages of notes. One of his reports had to do with John Rabe. "He's so proud that his men at the plant have had the electricity running for over a week," said Magee. "I gather that the water pipes are still making strange sounds when the water's turned on and we have to boil it before we use it, but at least there's water."

Minnie was impressed that the tenacious little Nazi had demanded guarantees from the Japanese and had actually received them. She knew that Rabe was a tough negotiator and, in his own way, was making their lives a little easier every day. On a few occasions, he had even managed to get rice from the invaders. She later heard from Magee that the rice came from a storage area reserved for the Chinese army, which made the stable all the more delicious. "I don't care where it's from," Magee confided to Minnie, "as long as it makes it into the safety zone and the Red Cross can distribute it."

There was another reason why Minnie was looking forward to the arrival of the ship. Magee had long since run out of film and she knew he was going to be irritating until those first reels got developed and fresh film arrived. The plan for the used film was to hide it well and have it smuggled out by the chosen carrier, George Fitch. With security so tight at the port, he wasn't as excited about smuggling the film out as he had been a month earlier.

As for the college, it had become a patchwork of living conditions. The number of residents that had once ranged three hundred to three thousand had swelled to nearly ten thousand. Under Minnie's guidance, everyone was fed something each day. The spirit of her staff remained high, except for those days when rice went missing or the sanitation systems broke down. These were cause for depression, short tempers and often tears.

If there was one truth, it was that the Ginling was no longer the happy, well-managed school Minnie knew and loved. Instead, it was a very large and bustling refugee camp, a recovery center for girls and women who had been raped, an infirmary for those who were sick or wounded. It was a counseling center for the distraught who might not otherwise survive in war: victims who had lost their husbands, fathers, and brothers; parents who had lost their children; children who had lost their families. There was no one living inside that fence who was not suffering, not a living soul who had not been trampled, either physically or spiritually. Despite the size of the campus, there was no place for a moment's respite from the cold, nor from the gloom of occupation. Minnie and Mei Ling looked forward to quiet time in the little church, but it was usually filled with people who needed to pray and then found comfort and decided to stay for a while. Whatever this place had become, it was no longer the Ginling.

Mei Ling and Su Lin spent most of their time in Minnie's quarters. They were both pale in the cheeks and much thinner than they had ever been. According to Mary, however, they were surprisingly healthy. Mei Ling's head was still partially bandaged, but this was more for disguise than medical necessity. As usual, she wore hospital clothing and sported a nametag that said *Chang*.

After Mei Ling heard of Kenji's suicide, she chose to spend her time with the patients. Soon, she found that she was especially effective with the young rape victims, many of them girls of only twelve or thirteen who had little understanding of what was happening to their bodies or to their country. Some were so traumatized that they sat unmoving for hours, and then experienced sudden outbursts, lashing out at anyone who came near. Mei Ling learned from the girls that many soldiers were either ashamed after they had committed the rape or were trying to eliminate the witness by killing the girl, leaving no one to report the incident. Therefore, many of the girls had also been stabbed and left for dead. The day before, two girls had stumbled into the infirmary, holding their bellies as they bled. The younger girl died several hours later.

While the sun was still setting, friends began to converge on Minnie's residence. Word was out that there was to be a decent meal, at least by current Nanking standards. There would also be fine china laid out for the meager food and, hopefully, a few tasty sauces. Minnie had no problem forgoing their normal feast, but she was painfully aware that this would be the first time everyone had gathered since that fateful evening in Yen's. It seemed like a lifetime ago, but it had only been one month. In that time, Christmas had come and gone without much fanfare, the missionaries recited some prayers and thanked God, but there was little that they could find for which to be thankful. Except, perhaps, that they were still alive.

Mei Ling brought Su Lin into Minnie's little kitchen and sat her down. On the table were some lemons and a sack of rice. Su Lin began to pick up the rice kernels, one by one, and place them in her other hand. She was engaged in what seemed to be a mindless task when her father entered. He watched Su Lin, who was now staring into her palm, and sadness marked his face. She had not spoken since her mother's death. Yen leaned down and hugged her gently, stroking her hair and kissing the top of her head.

Minnie noticed how Mei Ling bit back her tears and turned away. The young woman was still fragile, yet able to pull it together when necessary. Minnie had seen her do this many times at the infirmary and whenever her sister needed her. As much as she tried, Minnie could not forgive the man who had deceived this beautiful girl.

There was a sense among this close-knit group that they had been through the worst and that somehow, even in the smallest ways, life would get better.

There were now seven grains of rice on Su Lin's palm. Mei Ling counted them: seven. Perhaps they represented Mei Ling, Sun Lin, Mother, Father, Grandmother and two brothers. Seven pieces of a family. Su Lin stared at her hand and moved the little pieces around till they were separated into two little lots of three and four grains.

Mei Ling leaned close to her sister, their father standing behind. She cupped the girl's face in her hands and waited, as if expecting the girl to look her way. "Su Lin," she murmured. "Please, I need to hear your voice."

Su Lin's hand formed around the grains of rice, until her hand was a fist.

Yen Hsu studied his younger child, eyes imploring, and then he shifted his gaze to Mei Ling. "Sometimes," he told her, "you remind me so much of your mother, with your loving heart."

There was a quick knock at the door and Magee and Forster entered. Both men were carrying food and held their little trays out for Minnie to see.

"Go ahead and put everything in those bowls," she told them, gesturing toward a collection of little bowls stacked near the stove. "Does anything need to be heated?" Before anyone could respond, she added, "If not, then put the bowls in the dining room, would you?" An observer might have thought she was cooking a Christmas dinner.

There were many big bowls, both Chinese and American, each one containing modest amounts of food. The table setting was sparse, yet perfect in its own way.

"Oh, gentlemen, I have wine, too!" declared Minnie, faced flushed with the excitement of the moment.

Forster suddenly showed an interest. "Where did you get wine?"

Minnie smiled mischievously and then said, "Mary regrets not being here, but she wanted to contribute. I asked her what could possibly be so important that such a fine Irish woman wouldn't be joining us." She saw Forster dip a finger into one of the sauces. He would have gone for another taste, had she not brushed his hand away. "She said she has ten thousand mouths to feed and that someone has to keep an eye on that kitchen of hers. She also mentioned that Mr. Wong is becoming quite the rascal." Minnie shook her head, unsure of what Wong could possibly do to earn that reputation. "Oh, and then made some course remark about my cooking and the potato famine. To soften the insult, she gave me a bottle of Australian wine. She's had it stashed for ages, waiting for the right occasion."

Chatter continued as Minnie rearranged the food in the bowls, spreading it so that there seemed to be more food than there actually was. Magee appeared and said, "You never know when a good Catholic girl might need some redemption!" Everyone laughed at their Episcopalian friend's little dig at the Catholic savior of the Ginling.

Minnie laughed, told Magee to remove his silly hat, and handed the wine bottle to Magee. As he began to open it, the festive spirit grew.

In the dining area, Mei Ling walked around the room and lit all the little candles taken from her room. The glows of oranges and yellows gave the space the appearance of a Rembrandt. With everyone congregated, she led Su Lin to a chair next to hers, then directed her father to the head of the table. Magee and Forster sat across from the girls and Minnie's place was where Jade had once sat, next to Yen. When

Minnie entered the room, she recognized at once that Mei Ling had seated everyone in the same order as they had been during their last meal at the Hsu's.

Mei Ling lit four more candles and the glow in the room became even more remarkable. The guests around the table were briefly silenced by the effect and then they joined hands. The prayer was said, yet they continued to hold hands, each one content to be there, sensing how special this was, perhaps amazed that all of them but one had survived.

When the meager feast was completed and the bottle of wine emptied, Yen pulled Fitch aside, reached into his pocket and handed a packet of papers to his friend. "These are from the Japanese Embassy; Kenji brought them the day Nanking fell."

Fitch inspected them closely. "They're made out for Mei Ling Nezumi and Su Lin Nezumi, signed by Kenji. Are you sure they'll work?"

"Tanaka thinks Minnie killed that soldier and that Mei Ling is dead," explained Yen. "This may be hard to believe, but she dropped that gun after shooting the bastard!" He shook his head and smiled. "Over the last twenty years, at one time or another, she's shown that silly weapon to just about everyone. Anyway, Tanaka's busy repairing all the damage he's caused. Blaming that murder on an American shows politically savvy."

"But what about you," demanded Fisk. "You're a wanted man, a Nationalist Party member. Hell, you're the one taking the biggest risk by staying. You've got to get out, too."

"I'll be fine," he responded. "I can pose as a gardener or chef and I can stay until Minnie leaves in the spring." He took Fitch by the arm and led him back toward the group, whispering "Besides—and this is between us—Tanaka's no fool. He knows I might be good for something, at some point: hostage, negotiator, who knows? Maybe someday I'll be the token Chinese mayor of Nanking."

Fitch pocketed the official papers and the men rejoined the others.

As they settled into their places, Mei Ling stared hard at her father. Without missing a beat, she asked "Father, more tea?" He held up a hand and she placed the little teapot on the table. In a voice both accusatory and fearful, she announced, "You're not coming with us, are you?"

"I can't explain it all, my daughter, but I must stay." Yen had no definitive argument, but a strong feeling in his gut. "Our dear friend here has promised to chaperone you and stay with you, all the way to America. He'll help you get a job at an American university and Su Lin will receive the help she needs." He turned to Fitch and added, "Isn't that right, George?"

"Agreed, and you will be safe, and—"

"Do my sister and I not have a say?" Mei Ling demanded, placing a hand on Su Lin's arm.

"Of course you do," said Yen, although the expression on his face said otherwise.

"But you must come with us, Father!" insisted Mei Ling, eyes darting from her father to Fitch and then to Minnie.

Minnie looked at her softly. "Mei Ling, your father's presence might even jeopardize your safety. Is that what you are thinking Yen?"

Mei Ling held out a hand and Fitch handed her the documents. She opened them and read the names. "Su Lin Nezumi, Mei Ling Nezumi—these are the passes from Kenji?"

Yen fidgeted in his chair. "I thought they would be useful some day. The problem is that mine says I'm an official of the Nationalist Government of Chiang Kai-shek. Do you understand what this means? If I try to leave the country, I could be shot."

"That's not what you said ten minutes ago, when you talked about leaving," protested Mei Ling.

"I will stay and help Minnie," explained Yen. "I'll make sure to keep her safe. And then when she leaves, I will go to America with her. That gives me time to get new travel papers." His daughter opened her mouth to speak, but Yen rushed ahead. "Meanwhile, Fitch and his wife will take good care of both of you. Remember, he is like my brother."

Minnie saw a look of concern on Su Lin's face. The child was so delicate and showing only marginal signs of improvement. "Su Lin, do you understand all of this?" When Su Lin turned away and cast her eyes to the floor, Minnie sighed.

"I was not able to protect you, your mother, or your brothers," continued Yen, his voice filled with growing emotions. "I fear for you every minute of every day, my daughter. In America, there is hope for you. They are not at war with anyone; there is only peace."

Mei Ling seemed pensive as she nibbled on a dry cracker. When she suddenly straightened her back and lifted her chin, it seemed that she had accepted the inevitability of her father's decision. "Perhaps this is best," she told Su Lin, as if they were alone. "There will be nothing in America to make you afraid. Isn't that right, Minnie?" she added, glancing toward her mentor. "We will come back after the war, isn't that right?"

Minnie reached over and patted Mei Ling's hand. "Of course, my child, just as I promised. I'll take a leave in May and come to see you and, if it's not safe here, I'll stay. By then, you will already be enrolled and comfortable at a university." She flashed a bright smile and added, "America needs strong women like you."

"But so does China," Mei Ling snapped.

Yen Hsu chewed his meal and his words carefully. "You girls carry the blood of five thousand years of Chinese history. You must honor your ancestry. Of course China will need you. When peace returns to China, you, too, shall return."

Minnie nodded. "And your father will be safe here, until we leave. I need his help because we have thousands to care for. We so appreciate his help and his friendship." She looked into Yen's eyes and smiled.

"So you see," announced Yen. "You'll know how and where to find me: I'll be gardening carrots and turnips for Minnie Vautrin at the Ginling Girls' College!"

Mei Ling smiled. "I suggest the infirmary, Father. You have gentle hands and a kind spirit."

Magee laughed in agreement and joined in. "Okay, so it's settled: Fitch and Forster will see to it that the girls arrive safely in America. Once they're settled, I can promise that we'll provide a good Christian home and education."

That's right," said Forster. "And Mei Ling will be teaching college in no time. When this war is over, she'll come back and teach for Minnie!"

Minnie laughed and nodded enthusiastically. "*Take my place* is more like it; I'm an old bird now. She can run the place!"

Magee raised his glass, looked from face to face, and smiled. "Ladies and gentlemen, a toast: To Mei Ling and Su Lin, to their new home in America, and to Minnie Vautrin, headmistress of a college of ten thousand and heroine to us all."

"Here, here!" they toasted, followed by a loud "Cheers!"

The chatting ceased and this extended family resumed eating their last meal together. Occasionally, one person would look around, as of to make sure that everyone was still there. After seeing so much tragedy and violence, it was impossible not to remain guarded and on guard.

A sound reached the ears of the diners, almost imperceptible at first, and then more pronounced. They looked at Su Lin and found that the girl was weeping.

"Are you okay, my little sister?" asked Mei Ling. She took her sister's chin in her hand and gently tried to turn it toward her. Mei Ling's face—and the faces of every person at that table—glowed with the possibility that Su Lin might be returning to them.

THIRTY-ONE

Two weeks later, on January 28, 1938, the *U.S.S Oahu* arrived in Nanking and emptied its supplies and restocking for the Red Cross. Rice, flour, medical equipment and provisions were delivered onto the docks. Mailbags from all over the safety zone were collected and at the docks, successfully inspected and loaded. Everything leaving the occupied city was carefully scrutinized, most especially the people.

John Magee's Red Cross sedan exited the Ginling gates. In front sat Fitch, Magee and Forster; in the back were Minnie, Yen Hsu and the two girls. Because of the limited space, Yen Hsu was perched on the hump of the floorboard. He had insisted on going, even if it meant that everyone would be forced to squeeze together. There was a blanket on Minnie's lap, under which Yen could hide at a moment's notice. The chances of his being recognized were lessened by his disguise: a long goatee and thick eyebrows. Mei Ling had warned everyone that he looked ridiculous, but everyone quickly reminded her that, ridiculous or not, he resembled no one they had ever seen.

The sedan sped along the streets of Nanking, making its way toward the river. Many of the streets were still unclean with the refuse of war, including rotting bodies of dead soldiers. As the car neared the port, everyone saw that only two ships were docked among the smaller Chinese fishing boats. One was the *U.S.S. Oahu,* and the other a Japanese freighter unloading military supplies and weapons onto the dock. The freighter seemed foreboding.

In preparation for the arrival of its passengers, the *Oahu*'s gangplanks were down. There was no guard, captain, or purser in sight, but there was activity in the bridge. The Japanese had built an inspection station that included several tables on which passenger luggage was inspected.

This was the first time an American boat had docked in Nanking since the sinking of the *Panay*. The day was clear and there was no problem spotting the ever-present Tanaka, standing on a hillside that overlooked the little river port. The man stood tall, arms folded, a figure in charge and resolute in his power. He took the binoculars from his driver and trained them on the ship. Tanaka had been told to be especially attentive of the *Oahu*'s comings and goings. Positioned on this hill, he could see for himself who was escaping and who remained. That morning, before leaving his office, he had told his aide that he wished that all those meddlesome Americans would leave and that he would be happy to see them go. "What's the point of staying?" he asked rhetorically. "Nanking is now a Japanese territory and these interlopers are not wanted!" At the same time, Tanaka derived great pleasure from the fact that the hundreds of thousands of people the Japanese had turned into refugees were being cared for by foreigners, not by him.

The *Oahu*'s flags waved high. According to its manifest, it was scheduled to take out of Nanking a group of Americans and about twenty refugees. It was not a large ship, but big enough, and her presence offered hope to the people of Nanking, a community more than overdue for hope.

The U.S. soldiers and personnel on the ship knew little, if anything, about the massacre. They had heard rumors, but the Japanese had little to say, except that some of their men might have become overanxious or overzealous in the heat of battle. The ship's crew was also assured that it was the

Japanese army's intention to make Nanking their last battle in the war against the Nationalists. The general message was: When we show the Chinese what we can do in Nanking, it will crush the morale of the resistance, of Chiang Kai-shek and, hopefully, of that escape artist, Mao Tse-Tung.

Whatever rumors, innuendo, or denials floated around regarding the invasion and rape of Nanking, they no longer mattered. Now, there was irrefutable evidence and it was stored in a bag that was about to be carried onto the *Oahu* and revealed to the Western world. The film shot by Magee and Forster would undoubtedly alter world opinion, but only if they could get it out of Nanking.

Mei Ling, Su Lin, and Yen Hsu gathered before the inspection area with Minnie, Wong, Magee, and other passengers. Oddly, Mei Ling and Su Lin were dressed in western clothing, while Minnie was dressed in the Chinese fashion of the day. Yen, wearing a traditional robe, Fu Manchu goatee, mustache, bushy eyebrows and a little beanie hat, resembled a character from a Chinese opera, not an important member of a consulate. Magee and Forster had been ribbing him since they left the Ginling, and continued their jibes while waiting on the docks. "A truly stunning man, I've always said that about him," admired Forster, eyes sparkling with humor. "And the beanie is definitely a lovely touch."

"I can't tell if he's a mad diplomat," added Magee, "or a character from a Marx Brothers movie!"

The laughter had been honest, while at the same time everyone was becoming more focused on getting the girls safely aboard and those reels of undeveloped film out of Nanking and into the right hands. Fitch knew this was to be his most challenging acting role since preparatory school and he was up to the task. He knew what Magee and Forster had been through just to shoot those reels of film and he was determined to get them delivered safely, and to the people who would use them best.

Several hundred yards away and draped in the flag of the rising sun sat a Japanese ceremonial casket. Nearby were many crates, each one ready to be shipped back to Japan; each one holding the spoils of war.

Yen Hsu smiled at the kidding, but his hands were clenched into fists under his robe. A muscle in his jaw twitched as he struggled to hold back his emotions. The man was seldom so quiet, but the magnitude of pain he was feeling each time he thought of his daughters about to float far away, out of his reach and to a foreign land, left him bereft. When that ship sailed, he would have no family left in Nanking.

Magee, ever the archivist, could not resist that one last photograph. "Come on, everyone," he announced, making a gathering motion with his arms. "One more for the history books." His friends came together, taking their places in two shorts rows, all of them looking straight ahead, stoic, but posed. Briefly, their expressions resembled Su Lin's blank stare. "Okay now," directed Magee, "move in closer...that's it...now smile." He gave a thumbs-up, pressed the shutter release button, and the group relaxed.

After just a few minutes, everyone huddled together, as if painfully aware that, in only minutes, their little group would be no more.

"Fitch," asked Magee. "Is everything in order?"

Magee patted the duffle bag. "Got everything right here," he replied. Inside were special pockets for the film canisters.

Yen Hsu clutched the hands of his daughters. "You are the bright lights of China," he told them. "And now, those lights will illuminate America. Be kind, be loving."

Minnie stepped up to Mei Ling and wrapped the girl in her arms. At the same time, Yen pressed Su Lin close to him, eyes spilling with tears. Su Lin responded by squeezing her father very tightly. Suddenly, she was crying, too, and then her eyes became intense and her fists clenched like her father's had been and she blurted out, "Father, no! No! I cannot leave you!"

There was a stunned silence on the dock, as if something strange, but wonderful, had flown on the breeze and landed at their feet.

"Su Lin?" said Mei Ling and Minnie in one voice.

The girl shook her head again, eyes flashing with anger. "I will not, I will not!"

"You will not what, my dear?" asked Minnie, voice gentle as the breeze that stirred along the dock.

Yen Hsu bent down, nearly to his knees, and held both of Su Lin's hands in his own. "What is it, Su Lin, tell me."

"I am staying with you, Father!" she announced boldly, and then she looked at the others, determination evident in every part of her little body. "I must take care of Father, it is my job now. We will be needed in China. With Mei Ling in America, someone must care for Father and that will be Su Lin Hsu. I shall not leave father alone without any family, I cannot do that."

Yen shook his head. "My child, to escape now might very well save your life."

"No, Father, I will save your life. I am Chinese and I am staying in China."

Just then, the ship's horn blew loudly, signaling its imminent departure. The loudspeakers called for all passengers to come aboard, the message delivered in Chinese, Japanese, German, and English.

Yen Hsu put his hand on Su Lin's shoulder. "My daughters, both of you please, it is time to go. Please, Su Lin, go with your sister." He tried to give her a gentle push in Mei Ling's direction, but she refused to budge. Mei Ling was adventurous and willing, but Su Lin had been ill for so long and he questioned if she could make the voyage. He wanted her to stay with him, but perhaps she needed the American hospitals. On the other hand, she had recovered the ability to speak. In fact, her voice was stronger than ever.

"Father, I am staying. If Mei Ling wants to go to America, this is good, but Mother would want me with you."

Yen Hsu did not know what to do with his daughter's assertion. He reached into his pocket and removed the little Buddha from Jade's grave and placed it lovingly in Mei Ling's hand. He hugged her and then kissed her on the forehead. She slipped into his arms and held on to him with a force he never knew she possessed. At the same time, she slipped a letter into his pocket.

Yen and Mei Ling continued to embrace, neither really prepared to let go. Minnie and the others stood by, each one working to remain stoic and hide the heartache. Minnie hugged her compatriots. "I will say a prayer."

Yen Hsu turned to the man who would be his daughter's chaperone. "It seems that only one bird takes flight today," he said.

Another car arrived, stirring up dust as it sped toward them. It stopped with a screech, the doors opened, and Grace Bauer appeared with Dr. Trimmer. He carried her luggage to the inspection station and Grace joined her friends. The back door of the car opened and Truman, the writer from the Tribune, climbed from the backseat. With a notepad clutched in one hand, he looked over the group, his eyes soon fixed on the odd-looking monk, or whatever he was, standing close to Mei Ling and holding hands with Su Lin. His brow creased and then he nodded, recognizing the man wanted by the Japanese.

The America-bound survivors—Fitch, Forster, Grace Bauer, Mei Ling and Truman—lined up before two Japanese customs agents. It was their job to inspect everyone's papers and bags before allowing them to ascend the gangplank, step on to the little ship, and sail away from Nanking. The larger man pulled Fitch aside, demanding that he open his suitcase. When this was done, he tore open another bag, finding a large round tin, the type that stored film.

Minnie gasped slightly, but Fitch did not hesitate. "Please, it's sealed with wax to preserve it. Don't open—"

The inspector looked him over carefully and then ignored him and broke the seal. Several sprigs of a cherry blossom tree tumbled out of the package and onto the inspection table.

"Oh, now look what you've done," complained Fitch, speaking as loudly as possible, as if the inspector were a naughty boy who needed to be sent to the back of the class.

The inspector picked up one of the twigs and smelled it.

"Fitch," declared Grace. "You're taking cherry trees home?"

"What, there are no cherry trees in Iowa?" teased Magee.

"Of course there are," he responded. "But Nanking cherries bloom in the winter!" Having spoken, he exchanged conspiratorial glances with Forster and Magee.

Grace laughed and helped reassemble his baggage, avoiding his undergarments in a prim and proper way. The inspector looked at them suspiciously, but let them pass this phase of the inspection.

The second inspector had worked at this job for a long time, perhaps too long. He mistrusted Americans and often found that things were never straight with them, that one thing always led to another. In his opinion, they were not to be trusted. He yelled to Forster, "You, over there, let me see that bag." Forster walked over and handed the inspector the bag. The man immediately pulled out a square tin canister. Prying it open, he revealed a bundle of photographs. "What are these?" he demanded. "Are you an American government spy?" He looked over the culprit as if he were not only a spy, but a spy carrying a bomb.

"I am a missionary," explained Forster. "And these are my personal photographs. Please," he added, "your fingers are filthy be careful, please!"

The inspector scanned through the many photographs, as if searching for anything to hold back and use against this man. But the only pictures he saw were old photographs taken before the invasion, as well as a few artistic ones taken by Yen Hsu. He glared at Forster and then at Fitch. "Go on," he grumbled. "You need never return to Nanking, we don't want you or your god here anymore."

Fitch and Forster clambered up the rickety ramp, jostling one another a bit. They were eager to get on the ship and away from this hell they had lived for the past six weeks. As they ascended, a strong gust of wind blew across the ramp and yet, despite its force, Fitch's cloth hat remained firmly in place. The two friends exchanged expressions of relief and continued up the gangplank.

The smaller inspector turned his attention to Mei Ling, who was behind Grace. Both were dressed in the fashion of the States, and both wore a Red Cross badge on their arm. "Aren't you Chinese?" he asked.

"Yes," Mei Ling answered, smiling politely.

Grace, a little too eager, interjected, "She's a Christian refugee traveling with Reverend Forster and me."

"Your papers," he commanded.

Mei Ling handed him the documents prepared by Kenji. There was a large wax seal stamped in the middle, representative of the Japanese Consul. As she stood there, she closed her eyes, trying to ignore the pain that worked its way through her heart.

The man took the documents and noted that they were open-ended, the best kind. He held one up to the sun and nodded. Then he referred to the names on his roster, as well as several sketches of Chinese women, all of them wanted by the authorities. As he glanced at the list of names again, he saw "Hsu" and passed over it. He was looking for a Mei Ling Nezumi, but it was not there. His brow pulled together in confusion. The ship blasted yet another warning for its passengers to board.

Grace leaned forward. "Sir, please, we must go now. Thank you."

The man stared hard at Mei Ling. "I thought you were Chinese. These papers have a Japanese name. Who are you?"

Without a pause, Mei Ling responded in perfect Japanese, "My husband died in the war; he would have wanted me to leave Nanking. I plan to visit his mother in Japan."

The inspector quickly spoke Japanese to her. "Where is his mother in Japan?"

Mei Ling paused to grasp it all, in perfect Japanese said, "I will meet her in Kofu. She is the wife of a famous war hero."

The inspector was beyond satisfied and even bowed to her. "Thank you, you may go." Because she was an important person, he served him to be especially helpful. "It will be best to get off this boat in Shanghai. You will find much faster boats to Japan from there."

"Domo arigato" said Mei Ling with a smile. She turned and started up the gangplank, knees weak and her nerves close to breaking.

The warning horn blasted again and Grace's plea became more urgent. "Please sir, I really must go, or I'll miss the boat."

"Fine," he stated, and stamped her documents.

The women made their way toward the gangplank, relief evident in their faces. They had survived the first challenge. Now, all they had to do was deal with the dread of leaving for parts, and a life, unknown. Mei Ling turned back several times to look at her father and sister. Each time, they were staring up, waving and trying to smile.

The ship pulled away from the pier. Forster, Fitch, Truman, Mei Ling and Grace stood at the rails, waving their arms in one large wave. On the pier stood Magee, Yen Hsu and Su Lin, Dr. Trimmer and Minnie. Magee raised his camera and began to film the departing group. This was his last reel of film. At the same time, Truman was on the boat and taking still shots of his friends on the pier.

In the little Japanese ship behind the *Oahu*, the casket landed gently onto the deck. Mei Ling held her slender fingers over her eyes and watched the casket disappear into the hold. She shifted her gaze away from the boat and up the hill, to where Tanaka stood, binoculars in hand, staring directly at her.

At her elbow, Forster asked, "Are you all right?"

"I will be," she replied.

"Tears will come later," said Grace, placing a hand on Mei Ling's back. As always, her touch had a calming effect.

Mei Ling looked into the Grace's eyes. "I cry for my sister," she said. "For my mother and my brothers, my grandmother and China. I cry for love that is lost forever."

"That is the very definition of war," sighed Grace. "Speed the day when it is no more, my dear, speed the day."

Yen Hsu remained on the pier, one arm around Su Lin's shoulder as he watched the ship pull away from the pier and begin its journey down the Yangtze. He slipped his hand into his pocket and found the letter from Mei Ling. It was addressed to Minnie.

"I guess this is for you," he said, handing it over to his old friend.

The *Oahu* began to move slowly, regally, and Mei Ling stood its deck, waving to the people she loved and wiping away tears. She saw her father take the letter from his pocket and hand it to Minnie. She saw Minnie remove the letter and begin. As Minnie read, Mei Ling silently recited, "China will never know another Minnie Vautrin. I do not know how you keep such a big heart. You shall one day walk amongst the saints and Buddha will be there, too! You have given me such faith, such strength, and I will always love you, Minnie Vautrin. Signed, Mei Ling Hsu. P.S.: Sometimes, Father needs a hug."

Minnie's face slowly rose from the page and she watched the ship make its way further out, into the mighty Yangtze. Her tears blurred the water, everything running together as the boat released a blast of steam and was carried away with the wind. A tear fell and ran the ink on the little letter.

As the ship moved away, Minnie and Yen Hsu stood silently together. After a time, she reached for Yen's hand and, at the same time, he reached for Su Lin's.

The ship became smaller as it churned the muddy waters. Just as it disappeared from view, Minnie turned toward Yen, leaned her head against his broad shoulder and let her tears flow. He draped an arm around her and shared her grief. Seconds later, Su Lin pulled on her father's arm. "To the Ginling, Father? Minnie, to the Ginling?"

"Yes, my dear," said Minnie, "to the Ginling."

Minnie, Yen Hsu and Su Lin returned to the car. They sat in silence as they rode back to Nanking, inside the safety zone and through the gates of the Ginling Girls' College. Whatever they had, whatever they lost, they knew that Nanking would never be the same.

THIRTY-TWO

SECOR, ILLINOIS, May 14, 1941.

It was one year and a day since Minnie left Nanking, since she departed from the same docks that Mei Ling had left from in January of 1938. As her ship left the docks, Yen Hsu and Su Lin stood there and waved good-bye, just as they had with Mei Ling.

Minnie sat alone at her dining table and stared at a photograph. She was tired now and wanted nothing more than a good night's rest, but sleep had been illusive since the invasion three and a half years ago. It seemed that she could never catch up: nights were sleepless; days were restless; and when depression set in, it never left.

Minnie decided that would not write anything in her journal today and placed the pen on the table. Sitting there in the quiet and loneliness of her house, she pressed both hands over her face, like a child hiding from the dark.

The New York Times was opened to an article about how Minnie Vautrin had saved 10,000 innocents, how she had helped to save two hundred and fifty thousand others. She was called a *Goddess of Mercy*, a *Living Empress* and *One of the Greatest American Heroes of All Time*. All well and good, but what about the two or three hundred thousand she could not save? Most had died in those first six weeks! Nanking had suffered one of the greatest atrocities the world had seen and she was there to witness it. She had done what she could, but to call her a *hero* was nonsense.

There was a familiar knock at her door. She knew that rhythm instantly, recognized it as the pattern used by Mei Ling since she was a little girl. Was it possible? Or was it that, at age fifty-three, fatigue and depression had finally carried her into the world of delusion?

There it was again, that familiar knock, but how could it be Mei Ling? Minnie moved quickly toward the door and her speed surprised her: she had been lethargic for months. But that rhythm, it was unmistakable. Mei Ling always timed her knocks as if telegraphing a cadence from Bach himself.

Minnie worked the deadbolt, which turned noisily, her spindly fingers fumbling with the device. All those times she had expected her, hoped for her arrival, and she now she was here. Mei Ling was here, finally coming to take her home! Her prayers had finally been answered.

Minnie threw open the door and a dusky light filled her darkened hallway. Standing there not three feet in front of her was a shapely and well-groomed Asian woman in her mid-twenties. It was Mei Ling, dressed in an exquisite black suit with a matching pillbox hat. The young woman's eyes were filled with emotion. Mei Ling reached out and pulled the diminutive Minnie toward her, holding her as if every moment of her life had been planned for this occasion.

Minnie held on as well, her heart filling with love and hope. If Mei Ling came, it must be to keep her promise and see her safely back to her girls, her college, her Nanking. After several moments, the women separated and Minnie waited for Mei Ling to speak.

Out on the road, a taxi was parked just beyond the rickety picket fence. The cabbie leaned out the window and called, "Not much time, lady. It's gonna start rainin' soon, too. Just look at them thunderheads!" Mei Ling turned and waved a dismissive hand and the man opened the car door, got out and lit a cigarette.

Minnie took Mei Ling's hand and led her inside. "Come in, come in, there's so much to plan."

"I'm so happy to see you," said Mei Ling. "And I'm so glad that you're, well, that you're...fine".

"I am," responded Minnie. "And I have my things packed!" When she saw Mei Ling's eyebrows rise, she smiled. "It's true, I packed a week after I got out of the hospital. I knew that if I didn't get back to Nanking, it was going to kill me. I've been waiting for over six months for you and I can be ready to go in ten minutes!"

When Mei Ling had departed on the *U.S.S Oahu* three years earlier, the thought crossed Minnie's mind that she might never see her again. She got the occasional letter from Mei Ling or George Fitch and learned that she had earned her degree in English and was teaching Chinese at the University, but there was never anything personal. Now here she was, standing stately and tall in front of her. Minnie stared at Mei Ling and realized that she looked strikingly like her mother. "I thought about you every day," said Minnie.

"What's that smell?" Mei Ling suddenly asked, her brow creased as she sought out the source.

"I'm making some tea. Would you like a cup before we—"

"I smell gas!" declared Mei Ling. She rushed past Minnie toward the kitchen, sniffing for the source, with Minnie following close behind. The odor of gas permeated the kitchen. Mei Ling hurriedly turned off the burners and then, with a quick look around, crossed to the back door and opened it wide. She took Minnie's hand and pulled her out the door.

When they were safely away from the house, standing in the back yard, Mei Ling turned to face her old friend. "Why weren't those burners lit?" she asked.

"I guess the pilot went out." Minnie felt Mei Ling's gaze burn into her own and had to look away, toward the dark thunderheads forming in the south. "Could be tornado weather, you sure its safe for us to fly?"

Mei Ling fidgeted, hands nervously picking at imagined lint on her suit, eyes studying Minnie's face, as if looking for signs of danger.

Minnie recognized the concern and sighed. "The doctors insist I'm well now. Yes, I had some bouts with my nerves and all, but that was before. I'm perfectly well now and ready to go with you back to Nanking." She glanced in the direction of the hospital and smiled. "Funny, but our little infirmary at the Ginling was so much better than...where I was sent. It was barbaric, Mei Ling. Truly, I need to get home."

"But Minnie, how can you think–"

"We are going home now, aren't we?" The response in Mei Ling's expression drove a pain through Minnie's heart. She allowed the young woman to lead her to an old set of Adirondack chairs, where they sat together looking at the clouds rising thousands of feet in the southern horizon. To the west were incredible beacons of light, like shards of glass emanating from the setting sun that lit the nether portion of the great Midwest sky. Mei Ling was the first to speak. "The war is worse than ever. Did you know that the Japanese are all the way to Burma and Indonesia?" She looked at Minnie as if they were colleagues in a coffee shop. "I don't understand why America is still sitting by. I keep hearing about the politics of war, but it's very difficult to accept."

As Mei Ling spoke, Minnie felt her heart become heavy. Mei Ling was not going to discuss taking with her. Was there nothing she could do to convince her otherwise?

Mei Ling leaned closer to Minnie and put a hand on her arm. "I know a Chinese doctor in Chicago, an acupuncturist and a specialist. If I call him, he'll make the drive to see you. I met him at the university and he really can do miracles." Still waiting for Minnie to respond, she quickly added, "He's an old friend of Father's, you may have met him in Nanking." Her voice dropped and she added, "Minnie, he's one of the people who listened to Father's advice and got out early. I wish to God that father had listened to himself."

Minnie shifted in her seat, her head pushed forward by an urgency that ran through her. "You must understand, Mei Ling: I need to get back to the Ginling. I need to help your father and I must get back to work. He's still there, you know, holding down the place for me, I'm sure he needs my help."

Mei Ling took a deep breath and let it out slowly. "Minnie, I'm returning with an international group that's helping refugees. There are more than twenty thousand European Jews needing help in Shanghai."

"So we're going to Shanghai first!" Minnie's head perked up.

"It would not be safe. I'm working with the U.S. government; Madame Chiang Kai-shek has put up the money."

"But Mei Ling, you told me that—"

"This is a very dangerous time, Minnie, you must understand that I cannot put you at risk. As it is, my friends and professors tell me that I'm crazy to go back."

"But I'd happy to go, and I don't think you're crazy at all—it's what we women must do during war."

The sound of a horn reached the back yard and Mei Ling rose slowly from the chair. "There's a plane I must catch, Minnie. It breaks my heart, but I cannot take you with me. I'll arrange it so that, by tomorrow, there will be people here to help you. Do you need money?"

Minnie felt frustration and humiliation rising from a pit in her stomach. "You should have planned better, Mei Ling. I taught you the value of planning."

"You taught me well," said Mei Ling, her eyes combative like they were when she was defending Kenji's honor, in what seemed a lifetime ago. "I was told by the State Department that I had no time to visit you, but I told them that the good Madame Chiang Kai-shek would just have to wait one more day. That's what I said, Minnie. That is how well I planned."

"But you've been here ten minutes, not an hour, not a day, not even time for a cup of tea!" Minnie was frustrated; she knew she needed a friend right now. Perhaps for the first time in her life, she needed someone special to be with.

"Please, don't make this harder than it is," pleaded Mei Ling.

Minnie studied the woman's face as she rose from her chair. Without thinking, she blurted out, "I saved your life!"

Mei Ling took a step back, as if having been slapped in the face. Yes, Minnie had saved her life, and had kept her from the terrorizing rape. And she had been right about the tragedy that was Kenji Nezumi. Still, to be reminded like this... "Minnie, you were there for me, but I—"

"You are just like your father, aren't you?" insisted Minnie. "You can set your emotions on a shelf, where they remain safe and untouched. I have always loved you and your father and I expected that you would take me with you. Or, at the least, stay for a day and catch me up on your life and education. I hardly know you now, and look at you, you're a woman."

Mei Ling crossed the shabby little garden to the back door leading to the kitchen. The smell of gas was gone. Minnie followed closely. When they reached the dining room, Mei Ling slowed her pace, having noticed for the first time the collection of photographs and newspaper clippings on the table. Minnie watched Mei Ling's face as she studied the shocking imagery. It was what Minnie looked at day after day. Mei Ling bent closer to photographs of mass graves, women tied up, bayonet victims. It was horrible by any account, but to be left on the dining room table was something she could not understand. After a moment, she straightened up and faced her mentor. "Minnie, you cannot dwell on this. What are you trying to do? Looking at this will drive you crazy."

Minnie brushed away the comment with a sweep of her hand. "Don't be silly, it doesn't work like that. I don't want to forget—what happened there cannot be forgotten, swept away. No one talks about it. Sure, John Magee's out trying to show his footage, but no wants to know. How can that be?"

The taxi's horn sounded again. Mei Ling looked at Minnie with intensity. "I am sending a doctor, an acupuncturist and a nutritionist...and a maid to get this place cleaned up. You don't have to live like this, you deserve better."

"I did what I had to do and neither you nor God owe anything to me." Minnie gazed out the window, her eyes hooded and her mouth turned down. "Nanking is my home, don't you understand? I just want to go home. You want me to get better, but I will never get better here." Her voice began to rise as composure slipped away. "China is where I belong and you more than anyone should be able to understand. China—is—my—home! And I must go back. That's all I want to do before I—go."

"Don't think like that!" insisted Mei Ling. "The Nanking we once knew is gone. I don't even know if I can get back myself. Have you forgotten all that happened?"

Minnie couldn't let it go. "I remember every moment of every day, don't you see?" She gestured dramatically toward the table and her attention was drawn to Magee's invitation. "Did you see that they're calling me a hero? A hero of what?"

"Of course I know this," declared Mei Ling. "Everyone knows, and it's true. In China, you're a national hero. How many people save ten thousand innocent lives—ever! Trust me, people will know your name one hundred years from now."

Minnie's face changed suddenly and there was ridicule around her mouth. "I failed miserably in the end, don't you see? I can only think of how many died, how many hundreds of thousands."

Mei Ling gestured as if to shake off what she was hearing. "Do you honestly believe you could have saved everyone? You're the reason I'm standing here. Ten thousand others like me would be dead, if not for you!"

"I must go back and help those souls one way or another," whispered Minnie. "I've never lost focus on my one earthly desire: to return to Nanking."

Mei Ling's brow furled in concern and confusion. "I watched everyone I love fade away when you put me on that ship. But I did it because you believed it was the right thing to do. What I learned from you, no woman in China was ready to teach me. Now I am going to go to back to China, and not as a Chinese woman, but as a Ginling woman, a woman prepared with all the tools of life, including the most important ones of all: love and faith in myself, faith in God. Don't you see? I am going back as the embodiment of your teaching. Yes, I am of the Yen Hsu family, but I am of the Ginling family, too!" Mei Ling stared into Minnie's eyes, waiting for her to fully grasp the intensity of her proclamation.

Minnie remained silent for some time, the only sound being yet another honk from the cabby's horn. "You are the embodiment of your father," she said. "Your words are so like a speech he gave in 1927, before the rebuilding of the new Nanking. You are his bright light. I did so little." Tears came to Minnie's eyes and she brushed them quickly away. "I thought that I was the one to save him and have been plagued by that thought for far too long. In fact, it has weighed me down since last year, when I was forced to leave Nanking. You do know that I left because my nerves couldn't take it anymore." She looked at the images spread out before her. "Perhaps you are right and I've done all I can for this world." Her focus remained on the table. "I have productive things I can do here. In fact, everything I need is right here." She turned slowly away from the photos and faced Mei Ling. "I understand now what I must do."

Mei Ling looked tired, defeated. "Minnie, what can I do for you, if I can't stay and I can't take you with me?"

There was only one thing Minnie wanted to know, before she was left alone. "Just tell me, is there news from your father?"

Mei Ling smiled, acknowledging that this was a subject they could discuss. "I received a letter last month. Did you know that he married a woman who lost her husband in thirty-seven? She's a nurse. And Su Lin is married, to a young inventor of some sort who's been stranded in Nanking since the fighting started. I heard he had a company in Shanghai and lost everything when they tried to escape to Nanking. The poor man is stuck at the American Hospital, making medical devices for Dr. Trimmer. Su Lin is expecting a child soon. God Bless her, Minnie. If it's a girl, she will be called Jade."

Minnie forced a broad smile onto her face. "Well, isn't that good news." So Yen was married again and little Su Lin was with child. It certainly was not the world she had left just one year and one day ago.

A long, loud blast of a horn brought the women back to the present. Minnie sighed deeply and said, "So now you are leaving me." How could she, Minnie Vautrin the heroine to thousands, admit that she desperately needed someone she loved to be nearby this day? Mei Ling was like her child, yet she knew that it was time to accept the inevitable: that children leave home and, in so doing, often leave behind an emptiness that parents are loath to admit.

"Oh, Minnie!" Mei Ling blurted out, as she hugged Minnie tightly, a cry coming from her that sounded more like the whimpering of the little girl Minnie knew so long ago.

Minnie felt stronger being able to comfort, being one of those rare people who were strongest when helping, comforting, teaching and loving. None of these could she do here, living on the plains of America, so far from her Nanking. "I expect to hear from you the moment you arrive in China," she said, separating Mei Ling from herself. She looked straight into the woman's eyes. "Now go, Mei Ling.

Go and make this a better world. It is your calling, it is why you are here." Her own words caused passion to rise from her heart. "This is what your father would ask and what your mother would expect. And when the war is over, you must promise to come for me and take me home."

There was a tentative knock on the door. Mei Ling helped Minnie walk to the front door and onto the porch. The driver stood there, hat in hand, as he faced these contrasting women. "Excuse me, Ma'am," he said to Mei Ling, "but if we don't leave soon, you're not gonna make your flight. And look," he added, gesturing outside. "Dad burn'it if it hasn't started to rain." He stared at Minnie, as if this were her fault.

"Give me a second," said Mei Ling.

The driver shrugged and turned away, mumbling "It's your nickel lady, not mine."

Mei Ling looked deeply into Minnie's eyes and took hold of her war-worn hands. "And you, Minnie Vautrin, your heart is bigger than all of this. Many horrible things did happen, unjustified, but there were great things as well. In the depths of human despair rose a spirit in you that gave everyone hope. You taught me that there is so much to life, that I had to look for the lesson within the lesson. Life's real purpose is never obvious. If it were, what would be the point? I remember you saying that to me when I was perhaps ten." She took a step back and added, "Even if you don't want to be a hero to those ten thousand girls, you will be my hero forever."

Minnie reflected on Mei Ling's words, but dread crept into her veins. No matter how respected and honored she was, she was still going to be left alone on these dreary plains, in a country with big dark clouds looming down on her. And she would never again see her real home, her Nanking. She released was sounded like a sigh of acceptance. "Go, Mei Ling, go and accomplish what life holds for you. I'll be fine. And never forget: I'll always be waiting for you to take me home."

Mei Ling hesitated for a moment, gazing into Minnie's face as if trying to look all the way into her soul. "I'll write to you, and you keep your journal going, too." She gave Minnie one last hug, a short kiss on the cheek, and then ran toward the taxi. Spinning around, she called out "I love you, Minnie Vautrin!" and then rushed into the taxi, never turning back, tears streaming down her cheeks.

Minnie watched Mei Ling lower the window and remove a red silk handkerchief from her bag. As the cab pulled away, she used the handkerchief to wave good-bye, the elegant silk trailing in the wind as the car picked up speed. Minnie stood there for a very long time, the rain starting to batter its rhythm against her old roof. "Don't be a hero, Mei Ling," she whispered, as the tail lights disappeared into the dusty darkness.

She closed the door, the latch clicking into place, and walked into the kitchen, where she firmly shut and locked the back door. Reaching high into the cupboard, she took down the Chinese teapot that Jade had given her more than twenty years earlier. She placed it carefully next to the stove, turned the knob for the burner and walked out to the living room.

In the living room, Minnie stood at the window and, with drapes parted, cupped both hands around her face and leaned close to the window, watching the little red tail lights fade into the rain far down the desolate country road. When she yanked the curtains together, dust rose from the old fabric and she coughed. Turning, she walked to dining room and the table that drew her in.

Seated at what had been her family's dining room table, Minnie picked up Magee's invitation for the screening of his movie *Nanking Atrocities*, an event she knew she would not attend. She slowly set the invite down and picked up her favorite photo by Magee, the class picture of 1937. Minnie looked carefully at all the little faces, at her Ginling girls on the day before the invasion of December 10, 1937. She thought about walking across the quad with Mei

Ling, before spotting Magee in his fedora behind his camera for that one last photograph. She thought of Yen and how he offered his advice and his talented eye.

A fraction of a smile played on her lips when she saw the little face of Su Lin standing next to her. And there was Mary, Mr. Wong, Fitch and Forster, everyone she adored and respected, except Jade. She thought about her friends both living and gone, and then she drifted off, the hissing of the stove whispered in her ears.

AUTHORS' NOTES

China lost an estimated forty million lives during the Japanese invasion. The Nanking invasion was the single worst massacre of unarmed troops and civilians in the twentieth century. No one knows exactly how many lives were lost in Nanking during the invasion. The monument states three hundred thousand. Magee's film footage and a few photographs are the only irrefutable witness to the brutality of the invasion.

It has been claimed that Magee's film footage was forwarded to the Japanese government and their ally, Nazi Germany. It was also sent to the American Government. The reverend John Magee himself showed the film at many American universities before he became ill. His son carried on.

Those twenty odd missionaries, doctors, and businessmen who stayed in Nanking as part of the International Safety Zone Committee, have been credited with saving over two hundred and fifty thousand lives, innocent lives. By any generation's account, they would be called great. By the account of the "greatest generation", they were saints.

Oddly enough, Minnie Vautrin never thought of herself as a hero. She believed she had failed somehow, that she should have done more. Yet, little Minnie Vautrin was personally responsible for saving about ten thousand innocent girls during the rape of Nanking in 1937. In my world, Minnie Vautrin goes down in history as one of the greatest heroes of all time.

Kevin A. Kent

HISTORICAL COMMENTARY

Ideological and military developments in Japan in the 1920's and 1930's set the stage for war, not just for China, but also for the entire Pacific region. The Japanese were encroaching on China from the north, initially from Korea. While Mao Tse Tung and Chiang Kai-Shek battled internally, they failed to foresee that China was more vulnerable to the bigger threat from Japanese Imperialists.

Japan's seizure of Korea and Manchuria in northern China was merely a preamble to its expression of the entire Tanaka Plan. This Japanese war doctrine was founded on the belief that the Japanese were a superior race, and that their country's long-term economic survival depended on colonizing China, its rich natural resources, and if need be, enslaving its people. Asia, Australia, the entire Pacific, and even the West Coast of America were also in Japan's sights.

In 1937, from their established strongholds in northern China, the Japanese launched a southward invasion. They took Peking, and, in the summer of 1937, attacked Shanghai with a large force from land, sea, and air. The bustling commercial center near the mouth of the Yangtze was, and is today, China's largest city, and its most critical port. It was a supremely important strategic target. Further up the Yangtze River was Nanking, the new capital of Nationalist China.

After their success in Peking, the Japanese were quite astonished by the heavy resistance they encountered by Chiang Kai-Shek's army outside of Shanghai. The battle raged for months, killing tens of thousands. Japanese General Matsui Iwane quickly ran out of excuses to give his impatient superiors for his failure to seize this important port city. Angered, frustrated, and determined to break the city's resistance, the general resorted to unscrupulous tactics: He violated the rules of the Geneva Convention by ordering air attacks on city streets filled with civilians. The pilots shot down anyone in their sights: men, women, and children.

They intentionally bombed civilian homes and businesses. The Japanese had rewritten the rules of engagement. This was only the beginning.

Within the city of Shanghai was a small, increasingly overcrowded, yet reasonably secure Shanghai International Safety Zone. This area was filled with British, Americans, and Australians, whom the Japanese saw no point in antagonizing, at least not yet. Furthermore, the Safety Zone was the home of a particularly valuable piece of real estate as far as the Japanese were concerned: the Japanese Embassy.

By November 1937, Shanghai fell. A bloody moat of death surrounded the besieged city. Only the Safety Zone remained relatively untouched. Chiang Kai-Shek ordered his exhausted army to retreat 250 miles inland along the Yangtze River to Nanking, his capital city. It was his last chance to escape the Japanese onslaught as they turned the army south. On November 11, the Japanese army began closing in on Nanking.

The beautiful city of Nanking rested gracefully by the Yangtze River. The capital was a robust, modern city. During the 1930s, Nanking's population had grown from a few hundred thousand to over one million. This growth was due largely to the Japanese occupation of Manchuria and other areas of China.

Broad, tree-lined streets, beautiful parks, and enchanting ponds and lakes characterized Nanking. It was known as "the Paris of Asia". Within the new city was nestled a smaller, ancient, walled city. This three-square-mile precinct was home to colleges, universities, and a few embassies including the Japanese. It was a welcoming environment for educators, and a place where an eager missionary could make her mark. This ancient city was to become Nanking's own International Safety Zone.

General Matsui's humiliation at Shanghai hardened his resolve to cut through any sign of Chinese resistance. He wanted to maintain the military's honor in victory. He issued orders forbidding mistreatment of the Chinese people, but these orders unfortunately, fell on deaf ears. Matsui's men were bitter over their experience in Shanghai. They were fatigued, ill supplied, and hungry for food and victory. The Japanese advancement had been ordered to go so swiftly that the supply lines had not been able to keep up.

Officers began ordering the execution of surrendering Chinese soldiers. They had nothing to feed them. Furthermore, according to orders, any Chinese man between the ages of thirteen and seventy was to be considered a possible spy. Unofficially, it became common practice to split twenty-five Chinese men off from a group (or fifty, or a hundred) and shoot them. During the advancement towards Nanking, if the army ran into refugee families, all men of draft age were routinely shot.

As conditions in the battlefield deteriorated, the fate of Nanking looked more and more bleak. Tokyo's continued failure to establish supply lines caused soldiers to resort to stealing food wherever they could find it. Every farmhouse was fair game, and the angry, battle-hardened soldiers took more than food. On their way to Nanking, they descended deeper and deeper into depravity, raping and murdering innocent civilians, leaving a devastated countryside in their wake. These atrocities became the first documented war crimes of World War II.

With the Japanese army pressing on towards Nanking, Chiang Kai-Shek was reluctant to abandon his capital completely. He ordered 100,000 soldiers to stay and defend the city. In early December 1937, the Japanese began bombarding the beautiful city of Nanking with air and ground artillery.

The Japanese demanded the city's surrender, announcing that, in response to any resistance by the Chinese, "all the horrors of war would be let loose." Chiang Kai-Shek at first refused to permit the surrender of the capital, but eventually ordered his defenders to evacuate. Panic overtook the city. Chinese soldiers and civilians desperately tried to flee

Nanking before the Japanese made their entry. The soldiers ripped off their army uniforms and donned whatever civilian clothing they could muster.

Before the Japanese army entered the city, they relentlessly bombed Nanking. Historically, a conquering general would preserve the most valuable real estate of his conquest as booty, but the Japanese specifically bombed the wealthier and more populated areas of the city to demoralize the population. Even hospitals marked with a red cross were targeted along with refugee camps. Power plants, water works, and radio stations were all fair game.

A small group of American and European business people, doctors, nurses, college professors, and Christian missionaries had remained in Nanking against the advice of their governments, friends, and families. As the chaos mounted, these brave people created the International Committee. They established a safety zone inside the city's ancient walls. They gave refuge to many, dispensed food, and maintained a semblance of order. They did what they could to mitigate the hell that had befallen Nanking. They saved many lives. They saved the lives of the people they loved -- the Chinese. By the end of the siege, they had saved an estimated 250,000 lives.

The committee elected John Rabe, a German businessman from the Siemens Company, as their representative. Rabe headed the Nazi Party in Nanking. He was a slight man who had a big heart. Because his power plant provided electricity to the city, he later carried out many negotiations with the Japanese occupiers. After the war, he was given "The Order of the Jade" award by the Nationalist government.

An American missionary named Minnie Vautrin received the "The Order of the Jade" award, as well. No one in her hometown in Illinois could have ever believed it. Little Wilhelmina (Minnie) Vautrin, raised by an impoverished Illinois family near Bloomington-Normal in the late 1800s, would become a heroine to thousands of Chinese people in

December 1937, when Nanking fell to the Japanese army. Minnie had come to China during a wave of missionary zeal after World War I. Minnie was a young and innocent college-educated woman, sent by the United Christian Missionary Association to teach English and Christianity in China. Once she got to Nanking, she knew this was her destiny. Minnie began as a teacher, but rose through the ranks with her dedication and loyalty to eventually run the girls' school. The school housed the daughters of wealthy landowners and merchants, as well as the daughters of diplomats and other government officials. It was the best school in Nanking for girls and young women.

The Ginling Girls' College was located inside the old city walls, in what would become the International Safety Zone, quite near the Japanese and German embassies, and not far from the American Hospital and the Red Cross building.

The Ginling's grounds were like a park. Minnie had spent years cultivating her shrubs and flowers. She loved her garden and the birds that made their homes on her campus. Minnie loved China and the Chinese people. She first arrived in China in 1912, twenty-five years earlier. She devoted her life to China, but her soul she had given to her Lord. She was a woman of uncommon faith; but during the Japanese occupation of Nanking, that faith would be tried over and over.

Besides the photos and films taken by Magee and Forster, a 190-page official document was sent to Berlin from the Nazi Embassy in Nanking. It proved to be most revealing. The manuscript was released by the Potsdam Archives in the early nineties, and it confirms the duration and magnitude of the massacre.

The verdict of the *International Military Tribunal for the Far East* reads in part:

Approximately 20,000 cases occurred within the city during the first month of the occupation. The total number of civilians and prisoners of war murdered in Nanking during the six weeks was over 200,000... These figures do not take into account those persons whose bodies were destroyed by burning or by being thrown into the Yangtze River or otherwise disposed.

Memorial Hall of the Victims in the Nanking Massacre
(1937-1938)

*Chinese must seek justice for themselves, but rest of the
civilized world needs to understand and give them support. It is the sense of justice that makes us human.*
– Dongxiao Yue

南京市各慈善团体（个人）掩埋尸体统计（部分）			
掩埋尸体组织	掩埋队人数（人）	收埋尸体日期	收埋尸体数（具）
世界红卍字会南京分会	最多达600名	1937.12.22～1938年10月	43,071
崇 善 堂	4个队固定工役48人	1937.12.28～1938.4	112,267
中国红十字会南京分会	2个队	1937.12～1938.5	22,671
刘连详 等人	最多达104人	1937.12.16～1938.1.30	3,240
芮芳缘 等人	难民30余人	1938.1.4～1938.2	7,000
同 善 堂	不 详	1937.12～1938.2	7,000以上
总 计			195,249

The 200,000+ accounted for in this Japanese document
did not include victims whose bodies were disposed by
Japanese (as common in the early stages of the massacre) or
by individuals Chinese other than the charities, other
groups, nor did it include those who were massacred after
the first six weeks.

DEDICATED TO THE MEMORY OF IRIS CHANG & MINNIE VAUTRIN

The souls of the people of Nanking hopefully speak from these pages. But another spoke loudly for them long before this fictionalized account was ever conceived, Iris Chang. She wrote outside of academia during the 1990's and, as a result, wrote the bestselling book on the subject; *The Rape of Nanking: The Forgotten Holocaust of World War II.*

Iris Chang committed suicide on November 9th, 2004. Iris left behind a two-year-old son and a husband. She was only thirty-six, a brave and heroic soul. She should have been in the prime of her life, but she had been clinically depressed for some time. Like Minnie, the miracles of modern science could not heal her. At the time, I was in the middle of writing this book.

Her family made a statement about a note Iris left before she committed suicide. She asked, *"to be remembered as the person she was before she became ill, engaged with life, committed to her causes, her writing and her family."*

I dedicate this book to Iris, Minnie, and to the innocents of Nanking who lost their lives before their time.

Kevin A. Kent

ABOUT THE AUTHOR – THANKS

I am a first generation American. With a family tree dating back almost 1,000 years in Europe, history is in my blood, quite literally. On my immigrant father's side, the family tree goes back to the 1100's in Great Britain. On my dear mother's side, it goes back to John Alden arriving on the Mayflower. The love of history is in my DNA, so writing about it only seemed natural. I just never expected my first novel to be about an American hero in China, yet alone, a woman missionary.

Primarily a screenwriter, I originally created a historical drama screenplay that took place in 1937, off the coast of California, called Catalina. An old friend, Todd Seligman, handed it off to a Chinese funded start-up company. During the first meetings with Stanley Tong and Nina, we discussed adapting a book about John Rabe. I tried for almost a year to get the rights to that book, but finally gave up. A German company was set on making a mini-series. I wanted to do a movie. Sitting at lunch at the end of the year, I said to Stanley Tong that I should quit. I had stacks of correspondence in my brief case, I was going to throw in the towel. But, at this point I knew the subject quite well, and from a unique American POV...but without a book to option, I thought I was done. I remember as clear as can be that Stanley looked across his Caesar salad and asked the obvious, "Why don't you write your own story about what happened in Nanking? Do it from your point of view."

I would like to thank Janet Yang (producer of "The Joy Luck Club") for her early comments on the story so very long ago, and her more recent remark..."Kevin, are you still obsessed with Nanking?"

Nina and Bob, thank you for your kind support. I would to thank my old friend John Sutton-Smith for his early contributions on the screenplay and my friend Curtis Wong, who has been there from the start.

A special thanks also to those early readers of the rough drafts -- especially Bea Wong and Susan Serpa who both encouraged me when it was in rough shape and of course Gail O'Hea and the Newport Beach women's book club!

I would like to thank my two favorite readers; my wife, Price and my son, Max, and of course little Alex who sat by and watched the long winded discussions about it all. I'd like to thank my extended family for their endurance and patience throughout my mission during my extra long weekends in Big Bear; reading, researching, writing, and endlessly editing.

Lastly, my new pal and legal eagle Allan Kassirer, who asked some of those questions about the story that just had to be asked, and no one else did. It is a better story for it, thanks so much Allan.

I want to thank Victoria Zackheim, author, editor, writing guru and the woman who dared to tackle the hardest job of all, editing the writings of the man who writes one hundred miles an hour, with or without the aid of commas! Thank you for your wit and love of the English language. The story soars higher than ever because of you.

Finally, I thank God for heroes like Minnie Vautrin. Where would the world be without the Minnie's of the world?

Kevin A. Kent

READERS GROUP QUESTIONS

1. The massacre at Nanking was the single most atrocious and brutal assault on unarmed civilians in the 20th century. Why do you think so few people have heard of it?

2. Has this novel changed your understanding of Chinese American history?

3. Would you have had the fortitude and faith of Minnie?

4. Reverend Magee was driven to capture the historical significance of the events on film. If you were in his position, would you have done the same?

5. America was supporting Chiang Kai Chek with advisors and military aid while doing the same for Mao Tse Tung. What was America doing to aid Japan's in 1937?

6. Why do you think America did so little on the Panay incident?

7. Has your faith ever been challenged like Minnies?

8. What do you think might have been said by Hitler, Roosevelt or the Imperial leaders of Japan after viewing Magee's footage?

If you would like to know more about NANKING and the answers and opinions of the author, please go to the website about the book. www.NankingTheBook.com